Acknowledgements.
I am very grateful to Colin Weyer for documentation on the Supreme
Silent Sunbeam; and to Caroline and Stephen Egerton for inside infor-
mation about details of the diplomatic life.

The original text of telegrams and despatches can be found in:

British Documents on the Origin of the War 1898-1914, edited by G.P. Gooch and H. Temperley, Volume XI; H.M. Stationery Office, 1926

The Outbreak of the War of 1914-18, C. Oman; H.M. Stationery Office, 1919

The History of Twelve Days, July 24 to August 4, 1914, J.W. Headlam, Historical Adviser to the Foreign Office; 1915.

I have modified a few messages and invented two or three, for narrative purposes but not for any historical adjustment.

PART ONE

I

When gunfire ceased, foraging crows returned in the November sky, black on grey, circling the ruined earth for spoil. Those left alive in the field heard this sudden silence as a final, deafening knock at the eardrum. Armistice, indifferent as the shell with your number on it, had struck; and all those farewells, strung along years like barbs on wire — rolled up, to be pitched on unmarked graves.

But no shell had carried Colonel Proby's number. He waited for the recall to duty and after six months of peace was greatly relieved to have his offer of services taken up by the King's Foreign Messenger Corps; he laid the Messengers' silver greyhound medallion in a drawer alongside his other decorations, and felt that life was really on the march again when in June 1919 the Foreign Office ordered him to Washington.

'We would like you to carry on as far as the Central American Republics where we have a new Minister, Mr Theodore Harris,' he was told by the Chief Clerk, a junior diplomat impatient for a livelier posting.

'Very glad to go there,' said Proby, 'I have an interest in the ancient Mayan civilisation.'

The Chief Clerk smiled. 'Not human sacrifice and all that, Colonel Proby? Haven't we rather had our fill? Drained the cup so to speak?' He shot a glance at the new Messenger's right cheek, ripped by shrapnel in 1917.

'I quite believe the architectural remains are worth crossing the world to see, moreover that the Maya discovered for themselves the mathematical principle of the zero,' Proby said stiffly.

The young Chief Clerk smiled again. 'You are an explorer?'

'Say an inquisitive survivor.'

'May I offer you lunch at the Travellers', Colonel Proby? I have a slightly sensitive question . . .'

Usually this meant a demand to carry something personal through customs in the diplomatic bag. But it wasn't that, and Proby had to wait until the coffee to find out what it was.

'The British Legation in Guatemala City, where there was a devastating earthquake only last year, is a very isolated one,' said the chief clerk, crossing and uncrossing his legs restlessly.

'Excellent. I will reach it on horseback.'

'I meant isolated in the sense that the Minister has little to report and the Foreign Office almost nothing to send him.'

'I go on some other mission, then?'

'Not a mission, Colonel, no. We would like to hear from you how Theodore Harris is settling in.'

'His wife is with him?'

'They are separated and she lives on the French Riviera. Divorce has even been mentioned.'

'Ah,' said Proby, and waited.

'The Central American Republics are Catholic countries, that's the trouble.'

'Ah,' said Proby again. 'So the Minister is isolated and lonely too, eh?'

'We felt that with your experience in the field you would probably understand.'

'I'll keep my eyes open.'

'Oh I say,' said the man from the Foreign Office, laughing, 'not too wide open. Stick to the essential.' He carefully placed the lunch bill in his notecase for reimbursement later.

THE STEAMER ANCHORED offshore, Guatemala having no natural harbour on the Pacific, and Colonel Proby was carried to dry land at Puerto San José on a leaking, listing, rusting pinnace. He could see that indiscipline ruled here but he was used to dealing with that, and within an hour or so had bought a good horse for himself and a nag for the Indian he hired to lead him across country to Guatemala City. He was enjoying himself so much that he laughed aloud, often for no apparent cause, during the two day ride in the rain through palm and banana forests of the United Fruit Company of America and towards the range of volcanoes on the skyline.

But evidence of last year's earthquake in the capital city silenced laughter. Orphaned children, hunting rats for food, haunted the rubble, and the odour of unburied dead saturated the ruined masonry and hung on the air as it had for weeks and months in fields and villages to the rear of the trenches. The British Legation seemed to be one of the few buildings still standing, four square and confident, on the long avenue running through the centre; earthquake hadn't uprooted trees, or disturbed birds or dispersed wandering dogs, only brought low the constructions of man. Proby handed the reins of his mount to the Indian and climbed the flight of steps from the street to the high entrance door of His Majesty's Legation.

'His Excellency the Minister expects me. I am the King's Messenger.' Colonel Proby stood to attention while delivering this message; until you were acquainted with the head of mission you didn't know just how much formality was required. Some Ministers were greater sticklers for it than Generals in the field.

'Come in, do,' said the disheveled individual who opened the door, supporting himself on a stick, and as he spoke a light alcoholic breeze blew from him. 'Where's the bag?' Proby looked hard to see if he was drunk or just a reasonable, steady drinker. He decided that this man, whose voice had a slight softness about the consonants as sometimes heard in the Mess of Irish regiments, came into the second category.

'Strapped to my saddle.'

'Let's get it in before the earth moves again.'

'Actually,' said Proby, 'the bag's practically empty.'

'Surely there must be something for me?'

'Are you Mr Dillon?'

'Oliver Dillon.'

'A couple of brown envelopes, that's all.'

'Women are never prolific writers until the day they sit down on their lovely posteriors to become the authors of novels,' Dillon said. As the chief clerk at the Foreign Office had warned the Colonel, this was an isolated Legation. Leading the way, Dillon leaned still more heavily on the stick and Proby judged from experience that his left leg was amputated at the knee.

'The war, Mr Dillon?'

'In a manner of speaking.'

'THIS IS A skeleton mission, Oliver and I hold the fort,' said the Minister with a faint hesitation in his speech, like a trip of the hoof caught in a photograph by Muybridge, not interrupting the horse's pace. Good tactics, Proby thought, it made you attend more carefully to what he had to say. 'Oliver is our archivist.' Perhaps seeing the Colonel's blank response to this information, the Minister elaborated. 'He has followed me faithfully since our time in Belgrade. In '14, you know.'

Proby began to see his way more clearly here — these were civilian casualties of war, armchair casualties. 'That must have been an interesting time sir, professionally,' he said. Harris was about his own age but a 'sir' here and there costs a soldier little or nothing.

'It was. Sun going down on the old world and all that.' After thinking about this for a moment the Minister added, 'Not a paradise lost, if you want my opinion.' Proby, not having asked for it, let this pass. 'The King's Messenger who came to us there was called Cripps,' Harris continued; 'never quite sure of him.'

'Cripps was gassed on the Somme.' There was a silence.

'Oliver Dillon was an able man, once,' Harris went on, 'but he has a weakness, you know.'

The Minister, whose white linen suit was almost creaseless even in this humid heat, glanced over the few papers Colonel Proby had brought with him all the way from Whitehall. 'Not much here,' he said after a moment. 'Hardly worth your journey, Colonel?'

'There was some private correspondence.'

'So I see. Something from my wife's solicitors.' Harris laughed in a way that made Proby wonder about his mental state; during four years so many men had been marched up before him with their nerves in ruins that nothing could surprise him.

'What other staff have you here sir?'

'Oh,' the Minister waved a hand vaguely in the direction of the interior of the building, away from the view out of his office windows over the wreckage of the capital. 'My stenographer who has been with me since Belgrade too, and a young relation of hers wounded in the early days of fighting.'

'Invalided out?'

'You might say that, yes.' To the Colonel's sharp eye Mr Harris didn't look at ease about this. 'This is a god-forsaken Legation, Colonel Proby, not Madrid or Vienna.'

What was he saying? That a man whose only post in the bag was a letter from his wife's solicitor must learn to make do with the stenographer? If true, how apparently sad, yet for some reason Proby didn't find it so. He cast his mind back; at the word stenographer, so it seemed to him, a little flame had flared in the Minister's dark eye.

'If I may, sir, I will take my luggage to my quarters and smarten up after a two day ride through the rain, under the banana leaves.'

'For God's sake, Colonel, stop calling me sir, and I won't address you as Colonel any more. We're at one of the world's backwaters, let's make the most of the freedom.'

THE PICTURE in Proby's head of a stenographer — distant, mechanical, contained — was wiped out for good the moment he met Miss Ciganović at dinner. For one thing, she looked too restless for dictation; she was made for movement, you could sense it in her features and eyes like the surface of a lake reflecting every shift in the atmosphere. For another, she was young and let her shoulder brush against his when she turned away to greet the other guest. He felt arousal and tried to concentrate on this fellow guest, the French Minister, Monsieur Boppe. Proby's range of French was primitive, and Monsieur Boppe made it plain at once that French was the language of diplomacy and as a matter of principle he would speak no other. So their communication was halting and Boppe soon turned his attention elsewhere.

'Monsieur Boppe was already Minister in Belgrade when I was merely first secretary and Chargé d'affaires there,' said Harris. 'It seems to me you will never be an Ambassador, Boppe,' he called out unkindly. 'You're becoming one of the forgotten, on the shelf, left to go slowly mad in an outpost.'

'We'll see about all that, Harris, I'll have an Embassy before you,' Boppe said but the tone of his voice didn't match the challenge.

Miss Ciganović couldn't be more than about twenty-seven. Though not contained in the way usual for a stenographer, in another way she was, like a grenade. What could keep her here, five thousand feet above sea-level on an isolated table land with ruins stinking of mortality all about? One look told you she was not a woman to live celibate for long, with her narrow eyes. 'I hope you avoided the earthquake?' Proby asked.

'No, we were here. We worked for days digging up the poor people.' She spoke a strongly accented English, musical and easy.

'How terrible,' said Proby who had seen so much civilian tragedy in Flanders it no longer moved him, except as a formality. This girl's presence still moved him, though, and the picture of her digging in the fallen masonry. 'How brave of you.'

'The danger was past.'

'Did His Excellency dig beside you? I presume not.'

'But of course he did. What do you think? Theo is naturally a very feeling sort of man.' Proby felt himself rebuked and emptied his glass of white wine; but at least he could guess a little more now about the relations of this Minister and his stenographer. 'Milan will bring you more.' She turned to Monsieur Boppe, leaning towards him as if to nurse his self-esteem with tempting proximity. The door from the kitchen quarters swung open and a young man charged in like an injured animal. Miss Ciganović spoke to him in German, in her harsh voice under which was a tone profoundly tender. The young man looked hard at her without answering, then came to Proby's side and filled his glass from the bottle he was carrying.

'Thank you.'

'Nothings,' the young man answered in a surly voice.

'How well did the water supply survive the earthquake?' Proby asked, leaning towards Mr Harris and speaking loudly.

'Every drop has to be boiled. It has a filthy taste and you're far safer with wine.'

'But you drink nothing,' Miss Ciganović said.

Harris smiled at her. 'A little. By the way, where's Oliver?'

'I think coming. And you must be nice to him, please.'

'I am always nice to him.'

'You think so?'

'We're very old friends.'

'Aux questions sérieuses!' said Monsieur Boppe sharply. 'I am invited to dinner!' Miss Ciganović put a hand on his arm.

The door from the main reception room where the evening had started out in some formality with a glass of dry sherry now opened, and Dillon hobbled in. He hadn't been present for the sherry but seemed to have taken his own aperitif and plenty of it. The young man with the wine bottle guided him to a chair and sat next to him.

'So there you are at last, Oliver.'

'Mr Dillon has been very busy at his work in the archive,' Miss Ciganović explained to the French Minister.

'I know about archive work,' Boppe said and grinned, showing a couple of eye-teeth ground down to a sharp point by a lifetime of diplomatic scavenging. 'Archives are where inconvenient truth remains hidden, for a time.'

'Old Boppe,' said Dillon, leaning across the table toward Proby and speaking loudly but thickly, 'went to pieces in Belgrade, you know. Ever since then he follows us about and hangs on to us like a life belt. It must be because he needs a scapegoat,' Dillon continued in a more fuddled voice, 'to change the metaphor.' His head sank slowly forward till his long chin rested on his collar.

'Not sleep now, Oliver,' said Milan beside him, putting an arm round his shoulders and shaking him gently like a child.

Proby decided that never mind his instructions to keep an eye open and report, the situation here was beyond him. 'I have a great ambition to go one day into the forest of Petén, Minister, as an amateur archaeologist,' he said, addressing himself to Monsieur Boppe. 'Have you penetrated there?'

The French Minister stroked the silver wings of his hair into place. 'But naturally Colonel. I have penetrated naturally everywhere.'

The meal consisted of a gamey soup, then guinea-fowl and potatoes in their skins; every now and then a native girl darted out of the kitchen with a dish or bowl, then darted back again followed by the stern eye of Milan from under his thick eyebrows. Perhaps the kitchen quarters were Milan's disciplinary domain.

'The air of Guatemala City is unhealthy,' Boppe announced. 'It has redoubtable consequences for the digestion — the liver is a delicate organ.' He turned to Miss Ciganović. 'You don't find this?'

'We are quite high up in our Legation,' she said. 'Yours is more among the ruins where there are still many bodies.'

'Precisely. The Spanish and Italian Ministers have already gone to Antigua Guatemala and are installed there in charming counter-Reformation buildings. We should follow them, Harris.'

'You go, Boppe. Let me hear how you get on.'

'You remain because the American Legation is still here?'

'No, I remain because the people need help.'

'What help can we bring to the people?' Boppe asked with a shrug and there was no answer to that.

Milan ate with a fierce appetite, performed well with the wine bottles but drank nothing himself and said nothing. Yet some strong feeling issued from him like the breath he exhaled; so what was it that his silence hid and the fierceness of his appetite expressed? One of His Majesty's Legations is not the place for powerful feelings, especially in remote quarters of the world where an example should be set. Every now and then, without raising his head, the young man seemed to shoot a lethal glance towards Mr Harris and seeing it, Proby felt shocked. A British Minister is by definition a good man, a handler of sensibilities, a smoother of rough edges; how was it then that the rough edges of Miss Ciganović's young relation remained so raw? The Colonel decided it was time to talk to her again, even though her leg occasionally brushing against his under the table meant that the safest thing would have been to talk to anyone else.

Safety, however, is not very interesting.

'You left Serbia after our eventual victory?' he asked her. 'Or before?'

'We all left together,' she said.

'Mr Harris was recalled in 1914, I believe?'

'Theo was given the Serbian Eagle by King Peter for nearly stopping the war.'

'Nearly stopping it?'

'I mean he knew what should be done. But it wasn't done.'

'No, Miss Ciganović, whatever it was, it wasn't done.'

The plates for the guinea fowl had been taken away and new ones brought for the fruit which lay in a vast pyramid in the centre of the table. Miss Ciganović took from it a ripe guava which she split open and spread apart, then passed to Milan on her plate. Mr Harris, seeing Proby watch this operation in wonder, leaned forward and said in a low conciliating voice, 'Close-knit families, you know. Looked after him always.'

Proby, an orderly man, pencilled a note in his diary before he went to bed: *Legation like remote country house inhabited by family with secret. French Minister the suspicious neighbour.*

PERHAPS IT WAS that white wine; new wine in strange land should be cautiously approached even by a survivor with a military head, but Proby's this morning was hell; all the same there was duty to be done, protocol respected. His Indian with the two mounts was waiting for him outside the Legation in his black breeches to the knee, bare legs below, propped against a surviving pillar; the horse and the nag, heads hanging, seeming to lean also into each other and against the fatality of their labour. Colonel Proby was fond of horses, trusted them, and the remains of his heart bled quietly for the animal which had brought him up the mountain, would take him back, and then be delivered to the mercies of that Indian. He shook himself and his head felt as if Flanders shells still thudded there.

There was the Minister to pay his parting respects to. Proby liked the Minister for his easy-going side while remaining wary of him because of the ironical light he caught behind the eye-glass and the quick little trip of a stammer challenging you to keep up with him. There was no one about; Dillon hadn't shown up at breakfast time and Milan, after a few words with the Colonel on the subject of horses, had disappeared.

'I have a horse too,' he'd said.

'Here?' Milan didn't answer this obtuse question. Where else but here could he have a horse? 'You ride out?'

'The people say this is the most beautiful country in the world. In the forest you can ride for ever. Many who go into the forest never come back.' Decidedly, he was a gloomy fellow; but gloom didn't explain his apparent hatred of the Minister nor why, hating him so, Milan remained — unless for love of someone else.

Proby climbed the long staircase leading to the Minister's study at the top of the house, taking it easy and appreciating the generous depth of stone tread and the shallowness of risers. From the Minister's windows, he remembered, there was a tremendous view beyond the town and over coffee plantations towards the ring of volcanoes. He would be glad when he got up there and could rest his throbbing eyes on it. From the foot of the stairs he seemed to hear faint rhythms of music; he dismissed the impression but it grew more the higher he went. There was no doubt — from the direction of the Ministerial study where you would expect serious matters to be under way, dance strains emanated. A tango, perhaps. On the landing at the head of the stairs the colonel stopped and gazed through the open door. A gramophone stood on the Minister's desk and Mr Harris and Miss Ciganović were engaged in that passionate yet detached formal step, moving expertly to the rhythm on a cleared space between the windows and the desk. When the Minister leaned over the ample form of Miss Ciganović, their arms encircling one another, the volcanoes in the distance became visible through the glass. Colonel Proby cleared his throat.

'Ah, my dear Proby,' said Harris, righting himself and letting go of his stenographer. 'I have a despatch or two for you to take back. Sit down.' He was as well turned out as ever, in a different suit perfectly pressed. His canvas shoes had certainly been blancoed that very morning. By whom? Surely not one of those Indian girls who scuttled in and out of the dining room, scared as the guinea fowl they served up. Could it be that Milan did the valeting? 'I know what you need. Xenia, the aspirin, please.'

She had no need to leave the study; the aspirin was in the drawer of her own desk at one side of the room and she brought it to Colonel Proby with a glass of water and a smile of such indulgence that his head quite soon cleared. It looked as if Theo Harris must be lucky with the sex, though God knew just why. Yes, he was well made, well dressed, his moustache well trimmed, but so were thousands of others. Yet the word round the Foreign Office corridors was that Harris had a beautiful wife abandoned on the Riviera; and here he rejoiced in apparent possession of this alluring young woman who could make an impression in any of the world's capitals, the colonel thought. 'Thank you so much,' he said.

'Your horses are ready? I'll walk with you a bit of the way along the Avenida. You know we have a motor-car and could have driven you down to the coast?'

'I like the journey without maps.'

'Yes, I thought so.'

'I would have liked to say goodbye to Mr Dillon but I didn't see him this morning.'

The Minister looked at him with that black look from under heavy lids and his eyes and mouth stirred with silent laughter. 'Don't worry, he'll turn out. I'll leave you with him a minute or two, Oliver may have something for the bag.' He was right; Dillon, with a parcel tucked under his arm, was in the street standing close up to the tethered horses, and Proby could guess what was in his head. The Minister had Miss Ciganović — Xenia, apparently, her name; Milan had his silent anger which as any old soldier knows can fill the heart; Monsieur Boppe had the universal republican mission; Dillon had nothing. Strangely, he looked no worse for last night's wear. The sun was fierce but due to altitude the air keen and clear.

'You had a good night?' Dillon asked.

'So so.'

'It'll be much hotter than this as you go down into the coastal plain.'

'I believe you.'

Harris had reentered the cool of the Legation. 'I hope you'll be visiting us again even if only to bring an empty bag,' Dillon said.

'If they send me.'

'I dare say that depends on what they want to know, don't you, Colonel?' said Dillon, and Proby remembered that you must never underestimate the acumen of an Irishman.

'I'm sure I'll be making another visit to the Central American Republics,' Proby said with a movement of the eyelid, 'and when I do, I look forward to more talk with you, Mr Dillon.'

'Oliver.'

'Yes of course, Oliver. And have you something there to pop back to London in the bag?'

Oliver's expression became serious. 'Personal archive,' he said.

'Not for the Under-Secretary?'

Dillon opened the package from under his arm and produced a cardboard folder containing what seemed a lengthy manuscript. 'It's that.'

Had he written a novel which he hoped Proby would place with pub-

— 16 —

lishers in London? Was it an autobiography, or a history of the Dillon family — sardonic and fierce — from the time of the Norman inroad into Ireland to the present day?

'This is a highly secret text,' Oliver said in a half whisper.

'What am I to do with it?'

'Take it.'

'I would rather know more of its nature, if it's an unofficial document.'

'I'm glad you say that. Read it, then do what you think you should.'

'What duty dictates?'

'That's right.'

'Very well, I will. And by the way, what is Milan's surname?' Proby asked, liking to tie up loose ends.

'Igman,' Dillon answered promptly, just as Harris reappeared on the steps.

THE FORMER CITY was paved with slabs three foot by two rooted in the ground, but the earthquake had loosened the stones like old teeth and now they lay uneven, shed onto the streets. Through gaps in walls you saw abandoned gardens, abandoned animals tethered. The calm of the interior of the Legation, cool vaults, rooms with views to the mountains, was here replaced by chaos and accidental cruelty.

'The population crawls back by degrees,' Harris said. 'Mortality was appalling. But surviving children and old people come in from the hills to tend those animals because animals are working capital.' He put a hand to Proby's shoulder. 'Life returns,' he said comfortingly as if he felt distress for the colonel's distress at unexpectedly meeting in Central America disastrous scenes, recently so European.

Along the downward slope of the Avenida files of scurrying small figures ran between the ruins on both sides, carrying buckets of rubble out and material for new walls in, a stone at a time. A foreman carried a long black baton at his wrist.

'Voluntary labour?'

'Prisoners.'

'I dare say one or two manage to escape,' said the colonel.

'Not many, not far and not for long,' the Minister said. 'They crucify the ones they catch.' He looked round him as though he too needed emotional support; female perhaps, a breast for his head. But there was no sign of Miss Ciganović anywhere.

LOADED TO THE gunwales with bananas, the colonel's ship chugged out into the Pacific. From the bridge the colonel viewed the swampy shore, the sloping plain, and the horizon on which the highest of the cones was faintly visible. He had enjoyed his visit. He would like to come back. Dillon's bulky manuscript was safe in the bag and he intended to have a look at it tonight. He might even get through it, as the banana ship ploughed its slow way through the waves to the Panama Canal.

And he did get through it, with mounting consternation. What on earth was this text that subverted official histories while feeding on them? Was it the realistic notebook of a man who spent his life like a worm in the archives? A fiction, a revenge? A dictated diary? Colonel Proby reached Southampton and the London train still undecided, even after reading the manuscript twice over and becoming himself part of the story.

II

Vienna, June 19, 1914
The visit last week of the German Emperor to the Archduke Franz Ferdinand at Konopischt has occupied a large space in the Vienna press. When the peace of Europe is again threatened by conditions in the Balkan peninsula, it is consoling to the Austrian mind to have the alliance with Germany confirmed — much is made of the cordiality displayed by His Majesty during a visit devoted mainly to the Archducal rose gardens, but possibly not excluding conversations on other than horticultural matters.
Sir Maurice de Bunsen, Ambassador, Vienna, to Sir Edward Grey, Foreign Secretary.

'VIENNA! Vienna express!'

A whistle blasts from the locomotive at the front of the train, and another from the the rear as a handbell is rung on the platform. Our departing Minister Ramsay's reserved seat is well away from soot and noise, in the coach next to the dining-car where Hermann has seen to it that his place is ready and his morning half bottle of champagne in the ice bucket, just as it would be in the Legation.

'A good journey, Minister, and good sport in the Highlands! I read that grouse are excellent this year,' I say as he settles down.

'The king will be happy about that.'

'We should shake in our shoes otherwise.'

Ramsay, known for lack of all humour, inclines his head gravely. 'Normally, Harris, I would hate to go and leave you in charge alone for two whole months, and with your wife away as well. But at least we know

— 19 —

nothing is going to happen here in Belgrade before September. God knows how you will employ your time.'

'I look forward to your return.'

'Oh did I forget to mention? I won't be coming back. I have been recalled at the last moment.' The locomotive gives a final peremptory blast. 'You are practically *plénipotentiaire*. But *nothing* will happen. The summer of this year 1914 will go down in history as a perfect oasis in the . . . ' Ramsay, one of the least capable diplomatists I have ever met and supported only by a hierarchy instilled with the values of the last century, runs out of images to complete the picture; then waves cheerily from the window of his compartment as the train moves off. I remain on the platform, waving back, until the guard's van disappears round the curve in the line that takes it to the Danube bridge. H.M.'s ex-Minister to Serbia is practically in Hungary already and will reach Vienna by nightfall, not to stay in the Embassy but at a discreet hotel in Prinz Eugen Strasse where a bachelor finds appropriate company, at the right price.

WELL, SO MUCH for him, now for Belgrade, summer, latitude; Ramsay is certainly right that nothing much will happen here to eat into my time which can be given over to the real business of living.

Harmless old Hermann with his waxed moustaches is waiting for me in the square beside the Sunbeam, dusting a speck from the bonnet. 'Do you wish me to return to the legation on foot, *Exzellenz?*' Is there any point in reminding him that I'm still only a first secretary, not yet an excellency? I don't think so. Butlers like to work for men of rank.

'No no, Hermann, get in beside me.' I mount the Sunbeam by its one door on the passenger side and Hermann stoops and winds the starting handle. The 16 H.P. engine purrs sweetly as we float along the rue du Prince-Miloche towards the Royal Palace.

'Has Mrs Harris reached Dubrovnik safely?' Hermann asks.

'I believe she's already on the sea to Marseille.'

Hermann says no more about this but glares with hatred at the population of Belgrade as we make our way among them. He was devoted to Kitty and followed her about like a slave as most men do, fascinated by the beauty for ever out of reach, beauty in love only with the mirror.

I leave the Sunbeam in the Legation stable yard, wave Hermann away and walk back in the direction of the Palace; it is one o'clock, the air is warm but light, the cafés are busy and all along the street the skirts sway and swing. Our stenographer may be somewhere, she may be anywhere. I buy a a small red rose for my button-hole. The buildings around the palace are in the grandiose Viennese style of the 80's and 90's, over-blown and all that my mother's friends Mackmurdo and Mackintosh of *The Century Guild Hobby Horse* would have held anathema, and worst of all not matched to the Serbian character which abhors pretension. It's imposing enough, though, on the street rising toward the sky above the plain of the Danube. The sun is strong but it's still a dry heat, crystalline. Peace is in the air, Belgrade is at rest, the government is scattered about the country, the British Chargé d'affaires (myself) can think about things.

The immediate future, for example. I have an idea for a story and even if the *Savoy* days are behind us, *Blackwood's* might take it. I believe I should write a story about the stenographer; no brutal realism, no naturalist dissection, an exploration of her strangely direct though withdrawn personality, that mixture of open and occult and its origins in her peasant background — at least as I imagine it, and her. Because when she's with me I still live her presence as imaginary.

They are laying the tables for lunch on the terrace of the Hôtel Impérial. In a silver-plated funnel in the middle of each table is a single red rose like the one in my button-hole, and I'm not sure whether to take that for a good omen or bad. Xenia, with her back to the street, is at one of the tables nearest to the hotel. My heart gives a jolt at the sight, and I saunter over to the table with a smile.

'Good morning Xenia.'

'*Guten Morgen,* Mr Harris.'

'You're meeting someone?'

'I am meeting you.'

She has told me she makes her own clothes, and that is why they owe so little to fashion. Today she has on a cotton dress so loose and easy to wear it makes you see how simple it must be to take off. A button here, a fastener there. It has a pattern of red paeonies, the flower of the field of Kosovo. Kosovo Day is in three weeks' time, she must have made the dress specially for that day when she will go dancing.

'I expect some gentlemen from the Chamber of Commerce at the Legation. Important business men.'

'There was no appointment in your appointment book.'

'They telephoned.'

'Hermann will tell them you are delayed.'

'They are expecting lunch.'

'Hermann will give it to them.'

'You have something to tell me?'

'I work for you, Mr Harris, I don't tell you things.'

I sit down opposite her and the waiter hurries forward, I wave him away but he doesn't go far, knowing from the sight of her what outcome to expect. Under the small round table our legs touch. 'Then you know I have official duties.'

'You are the *Exzellenz* now.'

'I am a mere Chargé d'affaires, not a Minister.'

Xenia shrugs a bit impatiently. 'It is the same.' She leans forward across the table, picks the rose out of the silvered funnel and pins it to the front of her dress by means of a little silver brooch she wears there, which I gave her a week ago. Then she smiles, looking at the rose in my buttonhole. 'We are like brother and sister today.'

I laugh at her. 'You say that because you're an only child.'

'You think so?'

'You told me you were an only child.'

'I will think about it,' Xenia says.

'Would you like some champagne?'

'I am hungry,' Xenia answers. She is always hungry. Her appetite and the speed at which she burns up calories would amaze any young girl in those western capitals where slenderness is back in vogue. 'Very very hungry.'

I signal for the waiter who arrives almost before my hand has left the table. If she doesn't need any champagne I feel I do, today being the first of a season of latitude. She can have all she wants to eat in a minute or two.

IT IS AGREED that we return separately to duty at the Legation, myself first, Xenia following an hour later. My meeting with the men from the Chamber of Commerce won't require the help of a stenographer and in any case Xenia's skills are still at the formative stage. You might say she is a nominal stenographer who threatens, when crossed, to return to her métier of dancer. She was not, frankly, a very good one. A dancer must exteriorise imagined emotions; Xenia's emotions are too real and too close to her so she lacks detachment.

Hermann bows as I run up the few steps to the Legation door. Hierarchy is everything in the German-speaking world — rank, and submission, because there is always someone above you ready to strike. Many people in England, even in the Liberal government, regret that this is an attitude no longer widespread at home. My father, the most liberal of Liberals, had his own special version; with his friend Francis Galton he helped found the science of eugenics whereby *elimination of the ill-adapted* will be speeded up by disincentives to breeding.

'I served the gentlemen and expressed your regrets, *Exzellenz,* and showed them out.'

'Well done, Hermann, they will make an appointment for another day.'

'They are only Serb nobodies, *Exzellenz,* who have no right to be annoyed.'

'I will write a note and explain. Is *Fräulein* Ciganović in her little office?'

Hermann doesn't flinch. His eyes above the ends of his waxed moustache express a perfect discipline. 'She has been delayed, *Exzellenz.* '

'Send her to me for dictation when she comes in, will you?'

Actually, Hermann knows all about Xenia and with his hatred of Serbs he disapproves, but now that doesn't matter. He can be counted on to hold the fort should I be away for a day or two, and to keep an eye out for Oliver Dillon, archivist and now the only other inhabitant of the Legation, and not let anyone near him when he's the worse for wear.

The terrace of the Legation is the best part of it. The house itself is like a London club on a modest scale — muted pomp — but the terrace, dominating the junction of Danube and Save and the Hungarian plain reaching beyond as far as the eye can see, is grand in the best sense. Geraniums and orange trees in pots and some roses to remind you of home; and then a prospect of mile upon mile of corn and dried-up grassland with white villages strewn about it like dice on a carpet. Oliver is sitting there on a wicker-work deck chair, his legs stretched out, a glass on the tiles beside him.

'Hallo Oliver. No pressing duties, I see.' It's unfair to tease him when he's not at his best, I know, but I have a long history of unfairness with Oliver. His habits diminish him, which annoys me, and as Kitty and Xenia have both separately pointed out, annoyance makes me unkind.

'You missed those business men, Theo. I won't ask what you were up to.'

'I want you to go down to the office of the Electric Telegraph Company Oliver, and see if the F.O. has anything to say about a replacement for Ramsay. If not, you can expect to answer to me for the rest of the summer at least.'

'Oh I see,' Oliver says, 'you're hoping to be appointed Minister.' He picks up his glass and glares at the empty space within it. 'I expect you will be.' He turns towards me in his deck chair and smiles. 'You should be, and even when you're an Ambassador you'll need a discreet man in the archive.'

Our professional relations have become infected with all the indulgence that goes with too much mutual knowledge. He knows I will never complain in higher quarters of his drinking, and I know he will always view my private life with a kind of unhappy envy.

'Well, are you going?'

Oliver lowers his feet to the tiles and stands up bit by bit. He's a tall, thin man and though he is only a couple of years older than I am you have the sense that his joints are seizing up like ungreased springs.

'You know as well as I do that the F.O. is fast asleep for the season and there'll be nothing.' He leans on the balustrade overlooking central Europe. 'You've seen the papers? The Kaiser is shortly sailing away to the Norwegian fjords. Poincaré is on his way to Saint Petersbourg with Madame Poincaré, bless her, who everyone says is *bouleversée* to be included in the invitation. Even the Serbian government has slunk off somewhere.' He has found the wine bottle his eyes have been searching for as he spoke and leaning creakily down, he fills his glass.

I notice that his suit is sadly crumpled. Ramsay was too busy thinking about his holiday to pay attention to matters like turnout. 'You should speak to Hermann about getting your clothes pressed,' I tell Oliver. 'You look like a member of an American Legation.' He strides away in silence on stilt-like legs, then turns back.

'I suppose Prince George, like Kitty, is on his way to the south of France?' he says.

'I believe not.'

'You mean not yet.'

I TAKE MY PLACE on Oliver's deck chair beside the orange tree. I should be looking over the scribbled instructions left by Ramsay on his writing table to get myself ready for presentation to Grujić the Foreign Minister and Pašić the Prime Minister himself; but they both know me already and they're both away, and in any case the long-running drama of the Balkans has reached the interval. Nothing is happening, and here on the terrace no one will disturb me for a good half hour. I close my eyes.

When I awake, I feel the pressure of a hand on my shoulder, growing heavier as the mist of afternoon sleep recedes. It is Hermann.

'His Highness Prince George is here, *Exzellenz,*' Hermann says, his voice a little hushed despite his contempt for all Serbs.

— 24 —

I leap to my feet and hurry inside. Not from undue reverence for Prince George but because he has promised to lease me the lodge in the woods of his estate at Topčider. I need him to give me the keys and I suppose he needs me to hand over the rent. Since he was cut out of the succession he is chronically short of money but has done nothing to retrench. Such is the way of princes. As I hurry along to the Minister's study, my study, I wonder which one among his uniforms the prince will be wearing today. '*Mon cher Théo,*' the prince shouts from the leather armchair he occupies before the empty fireplace, his feet on the fender. 'Do sit down. You may do so.' This is mere defiance. He feels inferior because he is disinherited.

'Highness, I trust you haven't been long waiting.'

George bangs the side of the leather armchair with his scabbard as if it was his horse. He's a handsome young man like almost any peasant you see in the fields and forests of Serbia, and in his unhappy expression you can see all the loss of the dispossessed. 'Ages,' he says, laughing. 'I suppose you were very busy, Theo, in the way we know ?'

'I was awaiting our Foreign Office telegrams for the day,' I say, and seat myself for the first time behind the broad ministerial desk. Across the room the windows give on to the Danube landscape, all Belgrade is below and behind you, climbing gently up the slope to Kalemegdan, the gardens, and the rock where the British Legation broods, benevolent, over the swarming town. 'And I have been to the Bank.'

'Ah,' says George. 'Good. To be frank, I have to pay for my ticket and sleeper to Trieste.' He sounds unhappy. Having come down in the world, though by no means to the level of his great grandfather who really was a peasant, he is easily saddened by necessities and his difficulties in meeting them.

'You're going on holiday, Highness?' I know where he's going. He's going where he thinks Kitty is to be found and that secretly amuses me, knowing the chill he is in for if he catches up with her. Perhaps I should feel jealousy, still groundless as hers once was, but I'm too elated at the moment to be jealous of anything.

Prince George, to do him justice, looks uncomfortable. 'I have a maiden aunt in Rome. I must visit her, she may leave me her money,' he says.

'A *maiden* aunt? Never pursued by pleasure loving princelings?'

'Theo, you must speak with respect.'

'I was tempted by alliteration.'

'I remember about alliteration from Eton,' George says. ' — "meandering with a mazy motion" — that's alliteration. That's what alliteration is.' He bangs the point home with another thump to the side of the chair with his scabbard.

'Where does your aunt reside, in Rome? I know the city quite well.'

Prince George rises to his feet, bracing his knees backward to give prominence to the front of his yellow Royal Lancer's pantaloons. 'You mentioned you'd passed by the Bank, Theo? I have to pack my things, you know, and catch a train.'

'Surely your manservant will see to your luggage?' I am playing with him. The reason for the Crown Prince's disinheritance was that in 1913 he punished his then manservant too vigorously and the man died of it. King Peter, a loving father, was displeased, but Pašić, dependent on votes to be reelected, was furious. The prince joined the ranks of the dispossessed, the haunted princelings of Europe.

'The money, please, Theo.' His hand is outstretched.

He has asked politely so he must have it. I reach into my pocket and bring out an envelope containing six months' rent for the hunting lodge in Topčider woods, aware, as I hand it over, that without it the prince would probably not be able to run after my wife to the Riviera where she loves to be. And where, reclining as usual in the shade of the lemon trees and oleanders in her aerial Paris summer dresses, she will look too good to resist.

'Thank you, Theo, you're a friend. You may collect the keys of the lodge from my offices at the Palace.'

'I hoped you might bring them with you.'

'A set of keys is a bulky thing,' the prince points out. 'I have no trouser pockets, unlike a civilian.'

'Very well.'

He doesn't even think to count the money. If I were a prince I would do so, to show that I wasn't patronising my friend. But of course this prince is really a peasant. 'And now,' George says with relief, 'I want a drink. Some of your whisky to toast in your traditional English way our Balkan bargain.'

I ring for Hermann who is probably asleep and is a long time coming. I suppose it's lucky for him he isn't employed by the prince or the delay could well cost him his life.

XENIA AND OLIVER Dillon reappear at the Legation together. By that time I am watching from the window which overlooks the steps, anxious for her return. They are laughing. With me, Xenia never laughs, she simmers with amusement but no more; now her teeth and her tongue are all visible, there on the steps of the Legation. I bang on the window pane. She doesn't come in with Oliver, she must have gone straight to her office, due to what she believes is the convention — a stenographer has no place in a Legation reception room. This is one of the reasons I am impatient to get to Topčider, the woods, the open air. Oliver looks at me quite sympathetically as if he understands this well enough.

'Article from Vienna by your friend Wickham Steed in yesterday's *Times*,' he says, taking it out from under his arm, folded and crumpled. 'He says the odour of the charnel-house hangs over the place.'

'He's an acquaintance, not a friend. What does he mean?'

'The miasma of death and moral stench,' Oliver says with relish. 'Read it for yourself.'

'Steed likes to be sensational when there's no news. Pay no attention.'

'I think you ought to report it to London all the same.'

'Don't you think, Oliver, that the Foreign Office gets its own copy of *The Times* on the day of publication?'

'I mean the Serb reaction, Theo.'

'And what do you know about that?'

'Outside the Telegraph offices there was a gathering in the street, the Narodna Odbrana, very excited about something. Our stenographer seemed to know some of them.'

'Well?'

'One of them was waving a copy of *The Times* and shouting about the charnel-house of Vienna.'

'And what do you mean, Xenia knew these people?'

'She had a bit of a talk with one of them. She put her hand to his face like this — ' Oliver with a lonely man's gesture lays his palm against his own cheek ' — then she kissed him.'

'They're affectionate and demonstrative people you know. I expect he was an uncle or something.'

'He was a boy and she kissed him on the mouth.'

'Yes?'

'I'm not suggesting you report that detail to London.'

The worst effect of alcohol is that it releases the brakes. Oliver is one of my oldest friends, he may be trying to warn me of something he doesn't understand, but he drives headlong into the wall. I leave the room with my mind almost made up to have him seconded to some vice-consulate in a God-forsaken spot — Sarajevo, for example.

Berlin, June 1914

The recent visit of the British squadron to Kiel has passed off successfully.

The utmost good fellowship prevailed between Officers and men of both nations — In this connection, I venture to report the following: the correspondent of the 'Daily Mail' asked one of the British warrant officers what was the state of the feeling between the sailors of the two nations. The officer, not knowing who his interlocutor was, replied: "There is nothing the matter with the feeling if the f...... press would only leave it alone."

Sir Horace Rumbold , Counsellor of Embassy, Berlin, to Grey.

We have no resident foreign press corps in Belgrade because too little happens to warrant it. There's no aristocracy leading scandalous lives, very few actresses or opera singers, and among a people whose attitude to the relation of the sexes is healthy and sane the *crime passionel* is almost unknown. Plenty of ordinary murders, yes, but as a part of everyday life; so the journalists only swarm down here from Vienna on the train when there's a revolution or a war.

'Xenia, I have dictation for you.' I have put my head round the door of her little office where she sits, waiting for orders in her bucket shaped chair.

She smiles. 'I am ready, Mr Harris.'

'Come with me.' This game follows the same course and ends the same way; later, I tell her that I have the keys to Topčider and that we will be driving out there this very evening in the Sunbeam, to settle in. 'We will come down to the Legation every morning for a couple of hours and then while away the rest of the summer months in the cool shade of the oak trees.'

'How lovely that will be,' Xenia says.

'You must pack whatever you need. I will come round to your lodging in my motor car at five o'clock.'

'Your Sunbeam motor car.' Her eyes shine but behind them I seem to detect a doubt. 'When we come to the Legation I must also go to my room. There may be a message or something for me, you know?' Her head turns on my arm so she is gazing straight at me with that little signal of doubt at the back of her eyes. I hope things will be different at Topčider.

WELL-WISHERS in the Foreign Office warned me before I came to Belgrade about the lack of social diversion, and every diplomat gets the same advance notice from those in the know. We depend for pleasure in European capitals on the social circle, the court ball, the merry-go round. None of these expectations survives a year's burial in Belgrade. I shout up the stairs and then through the study window which gives onto the terrace, for Oliver.

'The *Herr* archivist is working in the archives,' Hermann says, lumbering sleepily out of nowhere like Fafner from the underworld. 'In the cellar.'

'You locked the wine cellar, Hermann?'

'The *Herr* archivist has all the keys. It is his duty to have the keys. The *Herr* archivist is my ... '

'I know. He's your superior. But you must put an extra padlock on the wine cellar.'

'Very well, *Exzellenz.* '

He won't do it because he hates anything to break the chain of hierarchy, the ordained system, and he may be right. The ordained system rules us, I was born into it, my father supported me there, yet I secretly hope all the time for its replacement by something lighter, cooler, easier to wear. But Hermann's chain holds our civilised world and what could take its place? The new, the feared, the shambles? I go down the stone stairs to the archives in the cellar.

'Oliver?'

'Yes?'

'What are you doing down here?'

'When all else fails, I work.' He's there, on a hard wooden chair at a table, with a lot of useless old papers spread out before him.

'What has failed?'

'You know as well as I do.'

He means Kitty, and I must go gently with him. I need to go gently with myself too but Oliver's passion is an illness, a consumption, it burns in him day and night and I suppose it always will. I've never experienced such a thing but with Oliver I witness it; you look into him and watch the destroying flame. If he'd ever had her, he'd know more; not knowing is what destroys.

'You shouldn't sit here in the dark,' I look around for signs of a glass and find them. 'Drinking, Oliver, all on your own.'

'It's very well for you, you have satisfactions denied me.' Self-pity is one of the most difficult behaviours to manage diplomatically so for the moment I say no more. 'Don't you ever think how you hurt your own wife?' he asks.

'My dear Oliver, what are you saying? You know she and I can't hurt each other any more.'

'You mean you can't be hurt.'

'I hoped she would stay in Belgrade,' I lie. 'She chose not to.'

'She could see what's happening.'

'She saw what wasn't there.'

'But now it is.'

I don't have to answer Oliver's charge; I could take offence but there's the affection on my side and the weakness on his. 'Take some leave, Oliver. Go to the Riviera and see her. Find her out in front of the mirror.'

'Sometimes you talk like a cad, Theo,' Oliver says. He unfolds his length from the hard wood chair with glass in one hand and bottle in the other, and makes, I admit, a dignified exit from the underworld of the archive and up the stairs to disappear finally in the direction of his bedroom, where he will remain until Hermann wakes him for dinner. Poor old Oliver.

He will eat alone in the Legation dining-room before the portraits of Edward VII and Queen Alexandra staring deafly, uncomprehendingly at each other from opposite ends of the table. Now there *was* a cad, and a serious interferer in diplomatic business as well. But it's getting on for five and I am about to drive over to Xenia's street and wait under her window at the wheel of my car.

III

*Families which are likely to produce valuable citizens deserve at
the very least the care that a gardener takes of plants of promise. They
should be helped when help is needed to procure a larger measure of
sanitation, of food, and of all else that falls under the comprehensive title
of 'Nurture' than would otherwise have been within their power. I do not,
of course, propose to neglect the sick, the feeble, or the unfortunate, but
I would exact an equivalent for the charitable assistance they receive,
namely, that by means of isolation . . . a stop should be put to the produc-
tion of families of children likely to include degenerates.*

*'Hereditary Genius': Francis Galton; from a lecture delivered at the
inauguration of the Eugenics Education Society, June 1908.*

JAMES HARRIS was spent but happy by the end of the meeting. Galton, although no public speaker, had been audible even from the back
of the room; two members of the Cabinet had attended and Constance
appeared to James's eye as shining as ever and as animated. Theo, it
was true, stood about at the reception after the lecture looking sarcastic
and disapproving. Even in old age, James often wished he'd been a little sterner when Theo was a boy but he was an indulgent parent, seeing
in his own son that hereditary promise that should, on eugenic lines, be
comprehensively nurtured. And then the boy had that stammer which any
harshness could only aggravate. At least so Theo always insisted through
his attempts at coherent speech and James, thinking how an impediment
as serious as Theo's in one of the disadvantaged classes might be mis-
taken for a sign of degeneracy, took patient care of him always. And now
here he was, stammer reduced to nothing, treating his father with distant
irony. 'First you wrote a book advocating the voluntary method of population control, Papa, now you recommend isolation. At least you show
a sense of sexual realities.' Haldane stayed on after most of the guests

had left — other than a handful of Constance's protégés, listening to her accounts of Hardy and James and Moore entertained in the very room where these young people now sat sipping champagne — and it was obvious that Haldane required a brandy. His whole over-heated person expressed the need.

'A brandy in the library, Haldane?'

'Well why not, Harris? I have a quarter of an hour.'

'The War Office can spare you?'

'I am the War Office, Harris.' That was true enough. The Secretary for War dominated his department as he dominated the Cabinet. It was said that the new Prime Minister was in awe of him, and of his mind which like the breech of a howitzer opened, loaded, slammed shut and fired, wreaking intellectual havoc at close and distant range. Only very old friends like James Harris were unafraid.

'We'll ask my son Theo to join us for a minute or two.'

'Quite right. I don't care to drink alone.'

James drank no spirits and hadn't meant to offer any to Theo, only thought he might profit by the occasion to please the Secretary for War with his social charm and so hasten his rise in the Service. Theo had already done very well but no opportunity for self-promotion with a powerful member of the government should be missed, as James Harris, who had missed many, knew better than anyone.

'Well, Theodore,' Haldane boomed, once he was sitting with his brandy gently circulating like oil warmed within the glass in his hand. 'Are you still in Vienna?'

'I am indeed, sir,' Theo said, not looking disapproving or sarcastic any more but bowing gracefully towards the ministerial mass in the library armchair.

'And what do you think of your father's Eugenics Education Society?'

'Papa has always been a moving spirit.'

Haldane laughed, his belly thrust out and in and out again by the upheaval. 'A diplomatic answer signifying nothing.'

'Oh no, it signifies emulation.'

'I see.' Haldane turned to James Harris and winked. He turned back to Theo, leaned forward and touched the back of his hand with his own free hand. 'I remember you well when you were a speechless boy,' he said.

'Theodore overcame that long ago, Haldane,' said his father quickly. Haldane with his cigar seemed to retire into a smoky inner world of brandy fumes, and cordite, and rumours of war. Probably he was thinking of his Territorials, and his Expeditionary Force, and his General Staff. For a moment James thought he might drop off to sleep which would be annoying, he would have to be woken and the glass prevented from falling onto the carpet and the cigar from tipping onto his waistcoat.

'Your science of eugenics, Harris, puts me in mind of Nietzsche.'

'I defer to you on German philosophy, Haldane.' James Harris felt indignant. He had always believed in nurture, guidance, planning; not in ruthless theory. Hadn't he suffered political disapproval ever since the publication of the book Theo mentioned? And why was Theo sitting there in silence and not leaping to his defence? 'But beyond good and evil — what can there be beyond them?'

'Nonsense, Harris,' said Haldane, 'you confuse doctrines. I am saying that your programme does little more than echo that of Nietzsche when he spoke of modelling the man of the future. You want to circumvent the arrival of degenerates in the world, he speaks of the energy needed to wipe them out.'

Theo cleared his throat gently at this point and put down his unfinished glass. 'By annihilation, Mr Haldane, must we understand war, do you think?'

'It's the quickest way,' Haldane answered.

'And the more we defend ourselves, the more salutary the annihilation?'

Haldane looked hard at Theo. 'You have certainly lost your hesitation of speech. Enemies believe I've built up the Territorial Army and created the Expeditionary Force for the reason you mention and that reason alone. But enemies are blind, I ignore them. Another drop, Harris, and I must return to Whitehall and duty.'

'So should we react violently to the first provocation, and hasten the process? Or diplomatically and hope to save a few lives, even botched?'

'You are a servant of the Foreign Office, your question should be put to your Under Secretary, not to the Minister for War.' Haldane swallowed off the remains of his brandy in a gulp and rose majestically to his feet. James felt secret pleasure at seeing his son annoy so powerful a Minister, even though impertinence might tell against him in the long run, Ministers being full of pride.

Just as Haldane reached the door it opened, and Constance appeared in it so they found themselves face to face. Too close for Haldane's comfort, apparently, as he stepped abruptly backward, knocking over a small table. 'I have something to say to you, Richard,' Constance announced in her carrying, theatrical voice which was music to the ears of James Harris but sometimes grated on those of others who had never been in love with her. Haldane was one of these.

'What can it be, dear Constance?' The question was followed by a groan, Haldane knowing quite well what it was likely to be. 'How fine you look tonight.' He caught himself up. 'Every night. I mean whenever I see you, your star never pales.'

Constance laughed as she came into the room, carrying Mr James's latest volume and trailing the aura of all those giants who around the turn of the century haunted her evenings at home. 'Thank you. You've put on weight, you must take more care of yourself.' She showed no sign of sitting down so they all stood waiting for her to tell the Minister what it was she required of him.

'I know you won't have any brandy, my love,' James said, 'and Haldane is leaving.'

'I will have a drop.'

'I have no glass here for you, Constance,' James said firmly. 'Do you want me to ring? You know Haldane must return to Whitehall.'

Constance always gave way at once to any manifestation of James's will, and then took it out on someone else. She turned on Haldane, who gave a grim smile. 'What is the government going to do about the suffragist demands, Richard? That's what I want to know.'

'We will listen with courtesy.'

'But not yield because only women are making them.'

'It's soon for decisions, my dear Constance. You better than anyone know how long it was before Ibsen, for example, was seriously heard.'

'The women will come to your door, I foresee it. They will chain themselves to your railings, you will have to whip them off. They will, the poor women will have the vote.' Her hand loaded with rings waved in the air in front of his nose. 'I am not a suffragist, I need no vote — but gentlemen of the government, prepare yourselves.'

Theo stepped forward and took his mother's arm. 'We mustn't make Papa's heart beat too fast, Mother,' he said. 'And Mr Haldane's hansom will be waiting at the steps by now.' Constance seemed to yield at the touch, but no one who knew her would make the mistake of imagining that she softened.

THE OAKS OF Topčider grow like columns and Prince George's hunting lodge, a nineteenth century rococo folly, lies in a clearing among them approached by a sandy track and surrounded by sleeping, patient woodland. The arrival of a British diplomatist and his stenographer in search of seclusion in this glade seems as nothing, a wing-beat on the air and then gone.

The car, hood down, rolls to a gentle halt and I pat it affectionately as I would a horse. It is all its makers claim for it: 'unapproachable for its quietness on the level, power on hills and restful comfort on any roads, at whatever speed.' I couldn't have put it better.

'There are servants here, Mr Harris?' Xenia asks.

'I think there are a couple of women.'

'I will send them away.'

'Oh surely — '

'I will cook our meals how I was taught. If these women are servants of the prince they can return when he does.'

I never argue about domestic arrangements; moreover between Xenia and me there seems to be a process of convergence so that potential disagreement always ends as perfect harmony.

'You agree, Mr Harris?'

'I agree perfectly, Xenia.' It amuses her to go on calling me Mr Harris. It amuses me too, it preserves a fiction of unfamiliarity. 'I'll carry the suitcases, you can take my portfolio.' She shows even teeth in one of her rare wide smiles. 'I expect it will be good not having Hermann always at our elbow.'

'It will be very good. Horrible Austrian Hermann.'

SERBIAN COOKING is an expression of the national character — generous, violent, contemptuous of refinement. Watching Xenia tuck into the result of her own efforts I wonder at the perfection of her waistline.

'You liked it?'

'I loved it, thank you.'

'Tomorrow will be a day of real meals. This was vorspeise.'

'You know, Xenia, I have a quite moderate appetite.'

'Not in everything, in some things you are greedy, really. Now I will fetch the damson pastry.'

IT ISN'T THE damson and the dark sweet wine of last night that give me this feeling of new essence distilled in me. Here in Topčider woods I planned for calm, equanimity through satisfaction of the senses, the serene writing of a story or two. What I'm getting are ferment and forgetfulness and you can't write stories on a diet of those.

Xenia is busy in the kitchen. From the study I can hear that humming she makes when she's happy, like a hive you don't disturb. Another huge meal is on the way. Through the open window the trees send a familiar odour, the smell of sawn oak and moss and acorn. The old house at Orchard Harris — just a big farmhouse really — lay in a more stunted, twisted oak wood than this one, producing nothing of value but logs and the odour of sawing. My mother brought a young maid down one year, the wood was a thicket in places, the moss deep. But of course London was then the place where literary study must be carried on. No young writer would dream of writing about the countryside and raptures under the oaks. It had to be prostitutes and the great devouring city, penury, and despair, or you were dismissed. So I put the experience in the woods behind me and wrote some stories about the sort of girl an attaché working short hours in the Foreign Office was likely to have dealings with, young women with savings and a tidy nest in Chelsea or Pimlico, but my stories found no takers. I tried one or two tales lower down the scale, bordering frankly on the sordid, but with no better results. My mother applauded these efforts, thinking of Zola; my father strongly advised me in the event of any of them being accepted to publish under an assumed name.

'Remember that some of the permanent officials come from narrower backgrounds than ours,' he said, perspicacious as usual, 'and while you're on the lower rungs they have power. The sordid would not appeal to them.' He thought about it and added, 'It might, but they wouldn't thank you for bringing that home to them.'

So in the end it was when I turned back to pastoral that success found me. This new piece was a psychological study of a rustic smallholder in love with a girl abandoned by the local seducer. I forget the details but the thought of the smallholder's great sacrifice for her still brings tears to my eyes, and the story was taken by The Savoy and published just as I sailed for the Madrid embassy as second secretary. After that there was Kitty in whose company nothing as stealthy and patient as writing would be thinkable. At first she was at too close quarters to leave room for reflective study of any kind; and soon she was too offended by the demands close quarters made on her. She judged them excessive and when I read her the passage in Havelock Ellis where he speaks of 'the links that bind the absolutely normal manifestation of sex with the most extreme violations of all human law,' she was outraged.

'Normal! Now I know what you must have been doing before our engagement when I was visiting maman at Biarritz! Oh Theo, that little widow at the Italian Embassy you paid attention to until we we were married! And not even young any more. She is over thirty.' I laughed but the sad thing was that it wasn't a joke and I knew already that Kitty would never come round. Before leaving me to go and sulk before the mirror in the bedroom she snatched the Havelock Ellis from my hands, returning with it five minutes later, white in the face. 'You see what this Mr Havelock says here in your dirty book? He says wives are vastly underpaid for services rendered and marriage is only a more fashionable form of prostitution. And I believed it was a sacrament.' She went out slamming the door so a valuable Dresden dish received as a wedding present fell from the wall and smashed to smithereens on the carpet.

WHAT I SHOULD do in Topčider woods during these torpid weeks of 1914 is to study Xenia and imagine her, not as I see her by the light of day but as she is. Creation and woman will overlap, coincide, and then it will be natural and simple to put us on paper. Woman is an instrument from which man evokes music, Havelock Ellis says; high-flown, over-blown no doubt, but I mean to be happy this summer with music in my ears, and no news of any kind on the international front for His Majesty's head of Legation to disturb himself with.

I am still at grips with the opening words of my story — *It was the fair at Amou. On the ox-market, under the plane-trees, a sea of blue bérets; an incoherent waving of ox-goads* — is incoherent the right word there? no matter — *hundreds of sleek, fawn coloured backs and curved, bristling horns. Etienne Mattou had been found murdered* — when Xenia calls from the dining-room. Just as well perhaps. The fair at Amou and the late Etienne Mattou feel, to be honest, a little out of date as a starting point. I go downstairs for lunch.

But it isn't lunch, it's Oliver who has come up to Topčider on the electric tramway to see me; the prince, or the royal Comptroller, having had the telephone cut off before I moved in. 'What do you want, Oliver? I'm working.'

'Working, Theo? What at? Are you studying Serbo-Croat folk songs?' Xenia's humming is clearly audible from the kitchen regions.

'I am writing a story.'

Oliver laughs unkindly, his pink-rimmed eyes screwed up and his surprisingly white teeth all on view. 'Don't let Sir Eyre Crowe of the Foreign Office hear about it.'

'Eyre Crowe is a liberal who would approve of literary effort. I suppose you want a glass of white wine?'

'It was hot on that tram, and I'm dying of thirst, bless you,' Oliver says, looking more amiable, and I notice that his suit has been pressed.

'Come into the dining-room. If Xenia knows you're here, prepare yourself for a very substantial lunch.'

The dining-room has French windows that give onto what was once a garden but is now an uncertain zone of earth, and dry grass, and dead rose bushes with the great oak trees beyond like an antique audience staring grimly down at neglect and disorder.

'Is this where the prince murdered his manservant?' Oliver asks.

'I have no idea.'

'I read that it was in the dining-room. The man spilled the soup on his Highness's breeches.'

'Nonsense, Oliver. Prince George is a decent fellow, the incident was exaggerated.'

'He's a madman and we both know where he is now.'

Obviously it's better to turn the conversation away and I take a bottle of white wine from the sideboard and a corkscrew from the drawer and hand them to him. 'No telegrams, I presume?'

'The whole world's asleep,' Oliver says as the cork comes out.

'Then you've come for company.'

'The King's Messenger was passing through on his way to Constantinople,' Oliver says with that gleam in his eye which I know is the signal of a lie to come. 'He wasn't stopping so I had a word with him in his sleeper while the train was at the platform.'

'A friend of yours?'

'That fellow Cripps.'

'Yes?'

'Cripps mentioned that a new Minister may soon be on the way.'

So that is Oliver's lie and his reason for coming out on the electric tram. Calm is called for. 'What an excellent piece of news. He can make his own assessment of the efficiency of the Legation staff when he gets here.' The truth is, of course, that the arrival of a new Minister would be a tremendous, inconvenient bore. A new Minister demands that everyone account to him for everything that has happened since the departure of the last one, and is unlikely to approve the Chargé d'affaires settling for the summer with the stenographer in a lodge in the woods some miles from the capital. 'How long was your conversation with Cripps?'

'A minute or two. Don't worry, he didn't ask after you.'

'Did he have a name to put on this new Minister?'

'Yes, as a matter of fact he did. Des Graz.'

So Oliver may not be lying after all. Des Graz is just the sort of man they would send to Belgrade — fat, lazy and officious, a bachelor with a jealous temperament so he'd make it his duty to torment me with complaints as if I were married to him. Des Graz must be kept from Belgrade at all costs, at least for the summer. I shall have to go down and telegraph some sort of news — a rumoured dysentery outbreak, for example — as deterrent. I recall that Des Graz's last post was in the Central American Republics where he'd have had his fill of dysentery, I imagine. 'After lunch I'll drive you back in the motor-car, Oliver. You did well to come up and warn me. Des Graz would do neither of us any good here, not just at the moment.'

'Also, the Russian Minister telephoned and asked for you.'

'Ah.'

'He has invited you to dinner.'

'I see.'

'He expects an answer today.'

'You didn't mention Des Graz?'

'Would I do such a thing when I know how the Russian Minister counts on you?'

'It would depend on your condition when you spoke on the telephone.'

'Well of course I didn't.'

'Quite right. We'll put the wind up Des Graz so he stays safely in London, and we will say nothing to the Russian Minister, and after I've had dinner with him I can come back here.'

'And get on with it.'

'As you uncouthly put it, Oliver.'

'I referred to literary effusion Theo.'

HARTWIG, THE RUSSIAN Minister, is the doyen of the Belgrade Diplomatic Corps, a violent Slavophil, mainstay of the Balkan League and once feared throughout Europe for his mischief-making; but it happens that he and I have built up a relationship closer than the usual links between a Minister and a mere Chargé d'affaires. 'This is the Chargé d'affaires at the British Legation speaking. May I please speak to his Excellency the Minister, Monsieur Hartwig?'

'Moment.'

The moment proves to be a long one. Hartwig is trying me out. 'Harris, *mon cher*. I hear you have been away.'

'Only for a few days, and not far. I have remained in close touch with the Legation at all times,' I say without a trace of stammer.

Hartwig laughs. 'Yes, I spoke to your archivist, Monsieur Dillon.'

'He mentioned it.'

'Is this archivist also a friend, Harris?'

'Dillon has been a friend since Oxford.'

'Ah, since Oxford.' As always when you mention it the name has an oddly quelling effect, even on a man as pugnacious as Hartwig. The cult spreads like a mystery over the Western world. 'I invite you to dinner here at the Legation tomorrow at seven o'clock. Please bring Monsieur Dillon.'

'That is very kind,' I say. 'I accept with pleasure for myself, but I must consult him to see if he has any engagement.'

'An archivist invited to dinner by the doyen can have no engagement.'

'Quite so. We will both come at seven.'

'I have something of importance to discuss with you, Harris. There will be no one else. A quite serious matter I assure you.'

'Very well, Minister.'

'Such formality, Harris! You know perfectly well I prefer to be addressed man to man.'

'Very well, Hartwig.'

'A demain, cher ami.'

Hartwig must have some panSlav scheme up his sleeve to tease the Austrians or Germans and needs my help. He is the exemplar of old diplomacy in which the Minister invented his own policy, paid his own spies, despised his government whom he kept in the dark and tricked into accepting whatever fait accompli he chose to present them with. The advent of the local telephone has made this system less easy to practise, the international lines, when they come, will make it impossible; but meanwhile Hartwig like the last dinosaur rules the earth around him by terror of what he may do next. I am looking forward to tomorrow.

But for tonight I will return to Topčider. 'It would be too much to ask you to leave the Russian Legation sober since almost no one ever has, but do try to arrive not drunk,' I tell Oliver.

'Do you think Des Graz will want to have me recalled?'

'I think it's likely.'

'I'll draft an alarming telegram about the rumoured dysentery for you to approve on your return to Belgrade tomorrow evening.'

'Thank you, Oliver. We will send it en clair.'

'A wise decision. Then we'll be left in peace.'

THERE'S A FULL moon, the nightingales are tuning up after the afternoon's heat and the distant street lamps of Belgrade appear as no more than a scattering beyond the wooded slope in the moonlight. We are lying on the dried grass under the oaks in the garden.

'You thought the dinner was good?' Xenia asks because she is as unsure of her culinary as of her stenographic skills. Actually she's a far better cook than secretary, but why say so?

'It was lovely.'

'I don't think you mean it.'

'I do mean it Xenia, I promise you.'

'It is peasant cooking, I know, like my peasant dancing.' She turns away onto her side. 'You only want me in one sort of peasant work.'

I put out an arm to turn her back but she resists. 'You're quite wrong Xenia, I appreciate you in every way.' I feel an emotion I'm not used to. 'You make me alive. You give me life. You've made me young again.'

'Have I, Mr Harris?' It must have been the right thing to say because she turns back. 'Is it your heart that says this?'

'Yes, it's my heart.'

'But you know so little what I am.'

IV

Foreign Office, June 24, 1914

I told the German Ambassador that I felt some difficulty in talking to him about our relations with France and Russia. It was quite easy for me to say, and quite true, that there was no agreement committing us to action — On the other hand, I did not wish to mislead him by making him think that the relations that we had with France and Russia were less cordial and intimate than they were. But this intimacy was not used for aggression against Germany. France, as he knew, was now most peacefully disposed.

Prince Lichnowsky cordially agreed. He said that our being in the group we were was a good thing, and he regarded our intimacy with France and Russia without any misgiving, because he was sure it was used for peace.

Tomorrow I go to Northumberland for some fishing.

Grey to Sir Edward Goschen, Ambassador, Berlin.

THE RUSSIAN LEGATION, although still the diplomatic hub of Belgrade, is in a ramshackle old house left over from the Ottoman Empire with closed quarters for women and open ones for the ruling half of humanity. Hartwig, a bachelor, has preserved the arrangement except that there is now no one in the women's quarters. For him, diplomatic mischief has probably taken the room of love. The Minister's bureau is a huge, dark cavern furnished in oriental style and smelling of burnt herbs, with a lot of sofas and stacks of papers and letters on a vast table. Hartwig wears a striped dressing gown embroidered with imperial eagles and other symbols of panSlav fealty, open over his dress shirt and white tie. 'So here is Monsieur Dillon.' Hartwig thumps him on the back while shaking his hand. 'I can see already that you are a man to enjoy a vodka with me. Harris drinks like a girl.' Hartwig claps his hands and a young man hurries forward with a tray carrying glasses, a bottle, and a dish of caviar. 'Cheerio!' Hartwig shouts to make us feel at home as his first glass goes down. I have placed myself near a palm and empty mine into it while he watches his own and Oliver's refilled. 'Harris! For once you are drinking correctly! More! Pósha!' I'm quite safe standing next to the palm and I let Pósha pour on.

'I'm surprised you remain in Belgrade among the mosquitoes for the summer, Hartwig. I imagine you more easily at Yalta, or Nice.'

'And what does your imagination tell you I could do, at Yalta or Nice? I am not a parasite Harris, I am a catalyst.'

As I thought, Hartwig is up to something, though what it could be at this season no one in Whitehall or the Quai d'Orsay would waste much time worrying about. Hartwig is frankly viewed in those centres of power as something of a spent force and the Balkan War of 1913 as his hour. All the same, I ought to try and find out and that shouldn't be difficult, he's bursting at the seams with it even before I make my tactful opening move.

'Even the Prime Minister is away — ' I say.

'And mice will play,' Hartwig answers, looking more than ever like a seedy circus tiger in his dressing gown with the transverse stripe motif.

THE RUSSIAN Legation's kitchens are full of cooks from St Petersburg and the dinner is the result. Hartwig eats and drinks enough for two or three Ministers but it would be a mistake ever to suppose him drunk. He is excited, his imagination stirred up, his appetites inflamed, he might be thought a bit mad in London or Paris but here he is still redoubtable. Elbows on the table, he leans forward. 'Prince George, you know this already Harris, has a bad reputation for his rapports with women.'

'I have heard that, yes. But I think he's a gentleman at bottom.'

'A gentleman! How sad! How must this term be degraded to include a man like him!'

'But he is a great admirer of yours, Hartwig.'

'I allow this,' Hartwig concedes grandly. 'It is your wife I am thinking of.'

'I think the prince is not quite adult. Kitty is like a mother figure for him.'

Hartwig pushes his dish of wild boar away from him and splashes red wine into a glass the size of a small tankard. 'You have been reading those Viennese charlatans,' he says. 'But I have more important things to discuss with you.' He looks at Oliver. 'I think Monsieur Dillon is safe?'

'As houses.'

Hartwig lowers his voice almost to a whisper. 'I can see that he is your satellite, Harris, but let me warn you — even a satellite can break loose.'

'I will be vigilant.'

'You laugh at me but what I must say concerns your private affairs. You have enough experience to know that anything a diplomatist does is instantly known to all the intelligence services?'

'None of them have ever taken any interest in me before.'

'That's what you think. But now you are Chargé d'affaires, and your country is the linch-pin of Europe.'

'Well,' I say cautiously, 'I'm sure the intelligence services have only the most innocent of private details to tell of me.'

'That you have a mistress? Naturally. You are an ordinary man, Harris. I am an extraordinary one. I am circumspect, you are lustful, impatient and careless. It is not a matter of age, it's a matter of discretion. You are sating your lusts . . .' he refills his tankard and takes a gulp from it, swallowing noisily like a dog at a trough . . . 'in dangerous company.'

'What can you mean, Hartwig? Xenia Ciganović — '

'I'm told she is a dancer, and you too like dancing. I have seen you at the French Legation with your wife giving a demonstration of that new Latin American step . . . the tango, is it? You created an illusion of passionate harmony.'

Oliver suddenly stirs from somnolence at his end of the table where he has been placed almost out of earshot. 'Kitty does the tango like a dream,' he says quite distinctly, then drifts away again.

'I understand now,' Hartwig says. 'Your satellite circles you both. That is the risk you run when you marry a beautiful woman. A diplomatic wife should never be a star, but you're a vain man Harris, and you chose to adorn yourself with one.'

I let this pass because I'm fond of Hartwig and a little afraid of him and also feel, in a way hard to explain, raised in self-esteem by the pleasure he takes in my company. He is like an approving tutor, though I'm past the age for tutors. 'That passionate harmony was more apparent than real, I'm afraid.'

'Any fool knew that,' Hartwig says. 'You danced with art.'

'I would like another glass of wine Hartwig, if I may.'

'Yes, you should be more free with yourself, without it you will become an official, not an Ambassador.' He rises slowly and goes to a side table where a rank of opened bottles stands ready. 'Pósha will be eating his supper by now, we will send for the poor boy when we need him. You and I, Harris, we can look after ourselves.' Hartwig sits again, filling his chair and the space around him with his presence. His breathing is heavy, difficult.

I wait. He will come to the boil in his own time, or he'll decide there was nothing he wanted to say to me after all, in which case Oliver can be drafted into the front line and he and the Russian Minister drink themselves into a stupor while I make my way back to Topčider and Xenia.

'In Vienna you were presented to the Archduke Francis Ferdinand and his consort, the Duchess of Hohenberg I suppose, Harris?'

'I saw them, I hadn't the honour to be presented,' I say, taken aback.

'You were too junior,' Hartwig admits, 'but now the accidents of history and love are catching you up.' What can he mean? 'Pósha!' he bellows, turning his head toward a curtain in the corner of the cavern. 'My pipe.' I don't know what Hartwig smokes but I pull my chair a bit further from his. 'The Archduke and his duchess are about to descend on Bosnia. Their train stands at the station in Vienna ready to leave for Trieste.'

'Bosnia? Where are they going in Bosnia?'

'They are going to Sarajevo, Harris.'

'Why?'

'Army manoeuvres, inspections, provocations. How should I know? There are a great many Serbian Bosnians in Sarajevo.'

'And a great many Muslims.'

'Exactly. The secret people, one can hide among them.'

Silence falls over the table where at one end Oliver seems asleep while at the other Hartwig sucks away at his tube, shrewd eyes missing nothing. 'Perhaps the population will greet the archducal couple with loyal enthusiasm,' I say.

'That is what I wish to talk to you about,' says Hartwig, and I know that the serious part of the conversation is about to begin.

HARTWIG SAYS that anti-Austrian manifestations, possibly violent, are to be feared. 'It will be St Vitus' Day, Kosovo Day, when the Imperial couple presume to enter Serb territory,' he says.

'Kosovo was nearly six hundred years ago and St Vitus, whoever he was, must have been martyred in the age of eunuchs.'

'You are being trivial, Harris, you are thinking of Gibbon whom I know you read and who was forever harping back to the question of eunuchs. Perhaps his hydrocele weighed on his mind.'

I don't want to argue about this, and in any case a Chargé d'affaires should not argue with a Minister. The most he can do is gently return a discussion to its more favourable aspect. 'You did refer to the accidents of history?'

'Yes.' Hartwig now considers me and I make an effort to distance myself from any personal element. 'So you are installed in Prince George's house at Topčider?'

'For a few weeks of summer. A month perhaps.'

'The little Ciganović is there also?'

'Yes.'

'My services tell me that her friends are unable to reach her.'

'I had no idea she had friends who were trying to do that.'

'You are something of a beginner in such affairs, it seems to me. She is a member of the Narodna Odbrana.'

'I'm sure you would agree, Hartwig, that her relations with me and mine with her — ' I check myself, aware that the implication is of two separate orders of relation — 'our relations . . . are no concern of the Narodna Odbrana.'

'They concern its less innocuous sister organisation however, the Black Hand.'

I look quickly at Oliver to see if he's awake. 'I feel sure she has no connection with them.'

'You feel sure? Feeling sure is not knowledge, Harris.'

'We made the appropriate enquiries — well, Dillon made them — before Xenia was employed at the Legation.'

'Before you fell in love with her.'

'Yes.'

'And now you have no detachment.'

'Little, I admit.'

'You have none. And the Narodna Odbrana knows it. It would be a pity if the Foreign Office came to know it too.'

I smile. Due to Slav love of conspiracy, Hartwig speaks of the Narodna Odbrana and the Black Hand as if they had fingers in every pie but in fact such organisations are seldom nowadays to be taken seriously. They only make trouble at a humble level. All the same — those permanent officials at the Foreign Office — 'Rumours, a pity, yes.'

'A serious pity, should rumour be swollen by report.'

— 46 —

What does he want, I wonder? Oliver dozes away at the far end of the table, the witness whose presence Hartwig required, never quite all there, never altogether unconscious. 'Oliver!' I call.

'Leave him,' Hartwig says. He leans further towards me and lowers his voice. 'Don't be afraid. We have the same interest. I want to protect your Xenia from dangerous company and so do you. Tell her that her brother should make his whereabouts known to his friends.'

'Her brother? I believe she's an only child.'

'Perhaps not, Harris. There is a young man of the same name whom our services desire to contact urgently before damage is done. You must help us do this.'

'I think quite a lot of people are called Ciganović,' I say feebly.

'Our services, believe this Harris, are well able to tell one Ciganović from another.'

'Your services are the friends you refer to?'

'Yes.

'And you want me to give Xenia that message?'

'I have already said so.' Hartwig seems to have grown and spread during the last minutes so the table on which his elbows and forearms are resting is crushed by the weight above them. He has turned himself into the monster that many people, particularly the Austrians and Germans, take him for. 'You have no more time to play, Harris.'

CRIPPS IS PASSING through on his way back to Vienna and I am about to give him a private dispatch for the Foreign Secretary, proving that I am still the eyes and ears and mouth of the Service here in Belgrade:

Belgrade, June 26, 1914
I have the honour to report that the Russian Minister informs me that a train carrying the Archduke Francis Ferdinand and the Duchess of Hohenberg is now on its way to Trieste. The Archduke and the Duchess are expected at Sarajevo in a matter of days.

The Russian Minister expressed some little anxiety about the possibility of public disturbances during the Archduke's visit, but I have reason to think his fears exaggerated. The Russian Minister is known to have more than one iron in the fire!

Archduke Francis Ferdinand is, in fact, favourably viewed in Serbian political circles, due to his support for the project of a Triple Monarchy to include Serbia with Hungary and Austria herself. He is, I believe, detested in Hungary and disapproved in Austria for just that reason.

It therefore seems reasonable to think that if disturbance there is, at Sarajevo or elsewhere in Austrian Bosnia, it is unlikely to come from the quarter of the Bosnian Serbs.

Harris to Grey.

IS THIS WHAT it's reasonable to think, and do I think it? Somewhere within me reality is detaching itself from duty, and I am becoming alien to what I was. Xenia says there are to be races on the downs below the Topčider woods, and she wants to go to them. She is restless. The races, she says, are the Belgrade event of the year when all, rich and poor, young and old are equal as in the French Revolution.

'It will be hot,' I object in the shade of the oaks.

'I have had enough of your objections. We must go to the races.'

When she's like that there is no point in annoying her further. All she wants, after all, is to get into the open air. 'Wait a moment while I put on my suit.'

'Your suit, Mr Harris! You don't need any suit at Topčider races. We will go now, with you in your shirt like that, open at the neck — ' she undoes another button — 'and your smart white trousers ironed by Hermann before you left.'

She wears a loose cotton dress floating about her, vibrant when she is excited, at rest when she's calm. The sun beats furiously on the burned-up grass as we walk down the hill to meet the growing crowd of people coming up from the city toward the open downland space where these races are to be held. There is no grandstand or enclosure, just a popular crowd happy for the afternoon. I think suddenly of Frith's Derby Day, painted when joy was still an English thing, and in the heat of the June sun and the emotion of these days easy tears well up.

'Don't be sad,' Xenia says. 'For today you can be young.'

'Young? I'm only forty-two.' But she has run on ahead in her low-heeled shoes, the green dress flapping and billowing against her calves and I am not going to break into a run to catch her up. The crowd may include people who would recognise the British Chargé d'affaires scampering after his stenographer through a throng without tie or jacket. But I walk as fast as my position allows, not losing sight of her head of hair among so many, dull copper coloured like an old penny but with the beginnings of a burnished stripe due to the Topčider sun. However, by the time I reach the thicker part of the crowd she has disappeared into it and I catch sight of the copper and the stripe no more.

What I do see is that a Serbian race gathering is an exception among crowds of our new century, perhaps because this is a society without barriers. No one in Serbia is shut in a class, no one is too poor, too rich. There are no Serb servants; the business world is rudimentary, vested parasites few. Men and women seem to live together in a condition of desiring trust. The crowd at Topčider today reflects a social pleasure like Frith's on Epsom Down in 1858, free of guilt, free of fear. The sun on this hillside is the same sun. And suddenly I catch sight of Xenia in the shade of some trees far away to the side of the crowd, standing with a young man, her arm about his shoulder. I can see that the embrace is familiar but, I think, not passionate. Her passionate embraces are tight as a noose, this is more like a farewell. But farewell to what? I have been married to Kitty since 1899, and jealousy is a contagion. I find myself hating the meagre, muscular boy whose neck Xenia's brown arm is around, yet I know, if Hartwig's word is anything to go on, that this is probably only her brother. Why, then, does she stay so long under those trees in that embrace with him?

I shout and wave but they don't seem to hear me. They appear to be speaking with their mouths almost touching, words, breath intermingled. It's the intimacy of love where part of your own body is as much part of the other.

THE SUN SETS behind the hill so the sky over dark woods is bathed in red; in the last light the final races are being run, as I can tell from the waves of shouts that drift uphill and die under the oaks where I'm sitting, while cicadas go silent and evening comes on. I thought it better to return without Xenia and let suspicion drain away.

And now with pen and paper in the dusk I try another start.

For he was unfaithful to his wife, I write with decision. *It was inevitable that the temptation, in guise of a craving for change, should come — not from the outside but from within himself . . . as if in his effort to match his personality to hers, he had put a strain upon the better part of himself. He never analysed the matter more exhaustively than this, the treacherous longing had gripped him at certain moments —*

And why on earth should he analyse the matter? I can see I've changed since I last seriously took up the pen in 1896; these days I am concentrated at the surface. Perhaps the diary form would suit me. Perhaps I will never manage another story for publication but I'll try again tomorrow; for now the mosquitoes are coming out, and I can hear a woman's footfall on the gravel. This situation may need careful handling.

'I WAITED for you a long time,' Xenia accuses. 'You leave me to walk home alone.'
'Where did you wait?'
'Not just in one place, I move about.'
'That's how you missed me.'
She gives me a reproving look. 'If you were there I would find you, I think.'
'I waited, too.'
'How long?'
'Long enough for anyone to finish an ordinary conversation.'
This answer silences her for a time. No accusations have been made — oh yes, she accused me of abandoning her — but nothing serious. She has thrown her straw hat onto a chair in the entrance hall and now she straightens her skirt, smooths her bodice. 'I must prepare your supper,' she says, 'even if I am tired.'
'You should have let me keep the prince's servants so that you could have a proper holiday.'
'They were Bulgarians who would have poisoned you.'
'Why do you think so?'
'It is their nature.'
'Perhaps I can help you?'
Xenia laughs as if no joke was ever half so good. 'You, help in the kitchen in your white trousers Hermann ironed so carefully? Mr Harris, I never want to see you for as long as I live anywhere near a kitchen.'

Brother, there is in Serbia a society called the Narodna Odbrana; many people must join this society; many have been enrolled in Bosnia and Herzegovina, as well as in the whole Monarchy. Among them are people of intelligence and means, long-headed people; and if they can do it, why should not we do it too?
From the evidence of Jovan Jagličić, Austrian Red Book.

IN THE NIGHT a storm got up. We heard the first rumour from the mountains in the far west, then a wind, and, after a long interval, flashes almost overhead, war in the sky, downpour. Xenia climbed under the sheets and has explained this morning that lightning is the only thing she fears, which I can believe. Now the sky is clear again, brilliantly clear and the oppressive heat of yesterday has become this crystalline dry radiance. The birds are full of song and energy for work. The Eugenics Education Society would applaud the health of their reaction because these birds too suffered the violence of the storm.

Xenia has already forgotten about it; but the Narodna Odbrana is another matter, one that I must take up with her, sooner or later. When I do, will she run away from me? Will duty make me lose her? Do I really have to ask who was the youth she was with yesterday at the races? If she can put her head under the sheets to hide from the storm, can't I keep mine in the sand? I decide to put the whole thing off, and instead propose a drive and a picnic in the forest, somewhere or other, with hours of recreation in the shade of the trees.

'Where, please?' she asks.

'Wherever you like. It's your country. Did you have some favourite place you went when you were children? You and that brother?'

'We were not children together,' she says quickly.

I smile, take her hand and look down at the back of it. 'But you weren't a Belgrade child. So where did you come from?'

'From outside.'

'Outside the city? Or outside the frontier?'

'The roads away from Belgrade are too terrible for your beautiful motor-car. We have this picnic here in the wood, and later go into the city to see if there is any letter for me.'

It seems the easiest way out for both of us.

Sarajevo, June 28, 1914. 12.30 pm
According to news received here heir apparent and his consort assassinated this morning by means of an explosive nature.
Mr Francis Jones, Consul, Sarajevo, to Grey.

Vienna, June 28, 1914
Vice-Consul at Sarajevo telegraphs Archduke Franz Ferdinand and Duchess of Hohenberg assassinated this morning at Sarajevo by means of explosives. From another source I hear that bomb was first thrown at their carriage on their way to town hall, several persons being injured, and later young Serbian student shot them both with a revolver as they were returning to Konak.
de Bunsen to Grey.

ST VITUS'S DAY, Kosovo Day. Xenia explains that since the battle in thirteen hundred and something the field of Kosovo on this day is covered in wild red paeonies which were not in flower yesterday and will be extinct tomorrow. They bloom for the one day of the slain, she says. Her eyes, usually narrowed as if the light's too strong for them, are enlarged and seem ready to brim over. I am touched and put my arms round her.

'You don't believe in anything, you have no faith. I think the English are all like that.'

'Oh no, many of them are as gullible as you like.'

'Gullible?'

'Believing anything.'

'Many of them? The others are nothing to me. One Englishman without faith, I may make him softer, more like a woman.'

When I began to fall in love with Xenia Ciganović I treated the situation rationally, as a man would who woke up to discover himself standing on the edge of a cliff — and I considered then that I knew her well enough. Kitty, I hadn't known at all at the same stage, we had never been alone in each other's company before the day when the Spanish priest united us; but Xenia after all — she and I worked at dictation together, heads leaning over the same page. Now I'm not sure I knew enough, but it's too late; we're over the cliff.

'We will drive into Belgrade to see if I have any telegrams to deal with. Oliver will tell me, then we'll go to your street to see if you have a letter and I will wait for you in the car. But,' I add firmly, 'not like at the races. No nonsense of disappearing. I will wait ten minutes and then come up to your door and be very angry.'

Xenia doesn't look as if this threat surprises her; she may be used to threats and skilled at eluding them. 'I am only your Serbian stenographer, Mr Harris, not your wife. If you come to my door to be angry I don't open to you.'

Belgrade is bathed in festivity for Kosovo Day; peasants have swarmed in to the city on horseback from the outlying lands, soldiers are in dress uniforms, great girls like haystacks covered in flowers parade laughing through the streets. Hermann stands stiffly to attention as I enter the doors of the Legation, and Oliver, who may have seen the car approach and halt at the steps, is in the hall.

'Happy Kosovo Day, Theo,' he says, beaming and sober.

'Thank you, Oliver, the same to you.' Has he met a good woman to influence him? The chances of that in Belgrade are as good as anywhere because the Serbs are sexually healthy people. If Oliver has struck lucky at last he may be successful too in time, and forget all about Kitty.

'A lot of post for you on your desk,' he says, 'to whom will you dictate your replies?' I don't think he has found a good woman at all, I think he is denying himself drink. He follows me into the Minister's study with the uncertain step of the recently converted. 'The Russian Minister requires your presence at lunch today.'

'Did he say, "require"?'

'I didn't pay particular attention to the vocabulary.'

'You should. Are you invited too?'

'Naturally, Theo, I am invited. Hartwig has taken to me and he knows the importance of witnesses.'

'I'm sure nothing will need witnessing on Kosovo Day at the Russian Legation,' I say, and sit at the desk before the pile of post.

'He seems to have an unusual influence over you,' Oliver says, changing tack. 'Practically paternal.'

'We will leave the Legation at twelve-thirty sharp,' I say. I have doubts about the voice I use — is it firm? is it weak? did I stammer on the letter t as I do when things aren't going well? I look hard at Oliver, aware that from a professional point of view he and I should have been separated some time ago; one member of a Mission in love with the wife of another is a familiar situation, soon known and swiftly resolved, as a rule. The junior diplomat is sent to cool himself off in Japan or Central America while the wife, unless her husband is the Ambassador, goes home to put her children to boarding-school. But we have kept the secret. I ring for Hermann.

'*Exzellenz?*'

'A half-bottle of champagne, Hermann.'

'One glass, *Exzellenz?*'

'Two.'

'Uniform, for this luncheon, Theo?'

'Uniform, Oliver. We are celebrating Kosovo Day in the name of King George.'

'The Feast of Saint Vitus,' Oliver says. 'On with the dance.'

THE RUSSIAN LEGATION stands opposite the old palace, now disused, where the last of the Obrenović family, King Alexander and Queen Draga, were assassinated in the night of June 11th 1903 and their naked bodies thrown from the bedroom window into the courtyard below facing the street. Hartwig, who was first secretary at the time, saw them still there on the paving stones in the morning. 'A rather misshapen couple,' was his comment. The Karadjordjević family in the person of King Peter and his sons stepped into the dead king's shoes and installed themselves in a new palace near the British Legation. Hartwig has always feared that this move symbolised a shift in the weight of influence and has been furiously active ever since.

The sun beats down on the street and uniform is hot, tight and heavy in the midday glare. At last the door of the Legation opens and there is Pósha. 'His Excellency is in the grand salon,' he says, pointing in the direction from which comes a sound of shouts and breaking glass and music on fiddles accompanied by a shrill wind instrument like a powerful whistle. 'I will take your tunics if you find it too warm. His Excellency is in his shirt sleeves.'

'No thank you,' I say firmly.

'His Britannic Majesty's Chargé d'affaires,' Pósha shouts in a high voice at the door of the grand salon. 'And Monsieur Dillon.'

Hartwig is conducting the band with his cigar, a tumbler held up in the other hand. 'Harris,' he shouts, 'come here. I must talk to you. Pósha, bring Mr Harris a big glass of vodka. Mr Dillon will look after himself.' Hartwig's colour is unhealthily high.

'I think we should sit, to talk, Hartwig.'

'Sit? I never sit when there is music. Sitting when there is music is for duennas and wallflowers as you call them.' Even in his shirtsleeves, he is sweating profusely and perspiration accumulates in the hollows under his reddened eyes. 'Come, we will talk over here near the window where there's some air.'

The huge room is only half full but all voices are raised to make themselves heard above the din of the band, and the rhythmical shouts of some Serbian officers dancing with their arms about each other's shoulders at the further end, among the potted palms and the hideous giant enamelled vases from Damascus. Everyone who is anyone and still in Belgrade during the heat wave is here. I can see Boppe, the French Minister, leaning against a fireplace and holding forth to a group of polite listeners. What a French Minister has to say anywhere in the world is respectfully listened to by all who know what terrible offence will be taken if it isn't.

Suddenly, there is a hush, the band stops, the shouting dies down. Pósha is at attention beside the doorway, while within it but a little withdrawn as if reluctant to push himself forward is a tall, old, stooping, bearded figure with long white moustaches.

'His Majesty the King,' pipes Pósha and everyone bows deeply except the young officers standing like stone. Hartwig is already half way across the room and miraculously has his coat on. He leads the King to a chair facing the band who play the National Anthem while His Majesty painfully lowers himself into place. Hartwig turns and beckons me forward.

'Where is the English Minister?' the King asks suspiciously as Hartwig presents me.

I explain that I am in charge of the Legation during an interim while a new Minister is appointed, makes his way home from wherever he is, equips himself in London for his new post, awaits word to attend at the Foreign Office and receive his instructions from Sir Edward Grey —

'You need not go on,' the King says. 'And after all that, We will see this gentleman here in Belgrade if before then the whole of Europe is not in flames.'

'Mr Harris and I are about to have a full discussion of the international situation, Sire,' Hartwig says, though this is the first I've heard of it.

'I believe you are a friend of my son George,' the King says, ignoring Hartwig.'

'I have the honour to be acquainted — '

'You are a friend. Where has he gone?'

'I believe his Highness took the train to Trieste, your Majesty.'

'He's a madman, you know that I suppose, Mr Harris? Why did he go to Trieste?'

'I understand he had it in mind to sail to Genoa . . . or Marseille . . .'

'He's after some unfortunate woman. I hope he doesn't murder her as he did that wretched valet of his. Our throne was quite shaken by it.' The King doesn't seem truly concerned enough with the international situation for Hartwig whose expression has turned sullen. This sovereign whose great grandfather was a swineherd in the Macedonian mountains cannot hold the attention of the Russian Minister for long unless he keeps to the point, which King Peter seems past doing.

Having waved away the vodka in a golden cup on a crystal tray offered by Pósha the King creakily rises as the last strains of the National Anthem die away for the third time. 'The King of England will come to Our rescue when the enemy strikes Us,' he intones in the voice of faith tempered by supplication.

'Indeed, Sir.'

'And George is a good boy, though he behaves like a Macedonian peasant.' The King stops to think for a moment before shuffling away towards the guards awaiting him by the doors. 'A mad peasant. Yet We foretell — ' his huge old eyes roll back — 'he will be the one to look after Us in Our senility.'

'Which will soon enough be upon Us,' Hartwig says as the royal party disappears and the heavy outside doors crash shut behind them. 'Now we will have our discussion.'

'KING PETER played a vital role for ten years after the Obrenović assassination, but what we now see in Europe is too great a danger for an old man to bear and he turns his face to the wall,' Hartwig says. 'Our Emperors and Kings are young men. Even Poincaré is only fifty. And we have the solidarity of monarchies.'

'Francis Joseph is in his eighties,' I point out.

'It is Francis Ferdinand who counts.' Hartwig sweeps my petty objection to one side. 'Finesse, my dear Harris, is one thing, quibbling is another.'

'I'm sorry. Please continue.'

'This brings me to the serious matter I wish to discuss with you.' We are standing in the great window that looks out onto the rue du Roi Milan with the Palace opposite and the dome of the Parliament building visible above the roofs. There are still many more horses than motor-cars in the streets of Belgrade and the thud of their hooves on the wooden paving is like distant hammering from a timber yard. The crowds in their Kosovo Day dress move in flux and reflux from one end of the street, low down near the Danube, to the other up on the hill of Kalemegdan and our Legation, bands playing, streamers streaming. I expect Xenia is somewhere in those crowds — who with? exchanging what messages? what confidences?

'It's a happy sight,' I say.

'But Europe is not happy. Our old nations are taut as bows, or if you prefer with every pistol cocked. You must know that in Russia there are many millions of men in reserve. And in Germany the mightiest army ever seen on earth.'

'Yes.'

'While you go on sailing round the oceans and milking the riches of the world from your colonies.'

'I demur at your term "milking" Hartwig.'

'You may demur till the cow comes home — you see how I know your idiom — in London your government thinks of nothing but the Navy, as though the struggle to come will be fought on water. It will be fought on ground — ground soaked in the blood of us all. Mud, and flesh burned to the bone.'

Does he really believe all this? His eyes are half closed, his speech slurred and he sways more dangerously by the minute. If only he would sit down and keep quiet for a minute, breathe deeply, and let Europe sleep.

'When the balloons go up,' he manages to articulate as though this were his last message, 'your stammering Britannia with her trident will be facing the wrong way with her big feet in the water but she will be Europe's only hope of peace.'

The allusion to stammering is one I take personally, however hard I try to remember that what is meant is the hesitation of democratic governments, the dithering of parliamentary majorities, the prevarication of cabinets. All well known characteristics of British policy. But to me, stammering means my own self-mastery. 'I believe Sir Edward Grey scarcely needs a lesson — ' I stop myself. 'But I can only concur with your analysis, Hartwig, and offer thanks for your sharing it with me.' That should do. In a few minutes Hartwig, already only half-conscious, will pass out completely and the conversation will vanish into the limbo of diplomatic mutterings. History teaches besides that Britannia and her trident are always shown to be facing the right way in the end.

'More vodka, Harris, where is your glass?' He takes my arm in a powerful grip like a man steadying himself on a lamp post. 'Remember what I said. Send a dispatch — the Russian Minister, from his deep knowledge of Serbia and the panSlav spirit, warns your masters that here at the pivot peace trembles in the balance.' Isn't he being, after all, a bit rhetorical even for a pan-Slavist? 'London's weight is all that remains to place in that balance. You must declare yourselves to be with us. King George is the cousin of the Czar.'

'And of the Kaiser too, you know. But yes, of course, I will make it my duty to transmit your views.'

'I trust you to do it. And now we must join those good-looking young officers to dance Queen Draga's Kolo. You know the Kolo? I will teach you. I know you are an accomplished dancer, better even than the French Minister who has so high an opinion of himself. You recall how Lev Nikoláevich Tolstóy characterised the archetypal conceited Frenchman? No? "He believes himself both physically and mentally irresistible to both men and women" — perhaps poor Boppe doesn't go quite so far as that.' Hartwig seems almost fully revived.

Although the wretched Queen Draga was accused of being a barren whore and an Austrian spy, and was murdered by the Colonels and Captains of the Guard, the Kolo in her honour is still a favourite with the military. The young officers here are only waiting, with their arms about each others' shoulders, for the Minister to give the signal. Hartwig waves his tumbler at the band, they strike up, he joins the circle with myself still held by the arm. The Kolo is danced to a furious and accelerating rhythm, with intricate footwork like a Highland reel. Hartwig, whose pace I copy as we revolve, is surprisingly nimble and I'm picking it up too, just when a junior secretary of Legation approaches and shouts a message at him. Hartwig stops, the circle halts, the band dies down.

'I am called to speak on the telephone,' he says. 'Mr Dillon will take my place in the circle.'

Oliver's reform has not lasted. Whether he is more drunk than the young officers is doubtful, but he is older, more desperate, less irresponsible and it shows. He lurches into the circle and I find myself next to him. 'Just hang onto me and the fellow on the other side and it'll be all right,' I tell him. The band strikes up again, but the Kolo has lost its sparkle. When Hartwig reappears he signals for silence.

He is on the steps at the end of the reception room, his mass of thick grey hair standing out wildly from his head like mistletoe on an oak, and when he speaks his voice is solemn and incantatory.

'Your Excellencies, General, honoured colleagues,' he drones. I have never seen him like this before — he seems to be taking even himself seriously so I know that something grievous has happened. Perhaps he has been recalled, the news passed by telephone from Vienna where the lines now reach, and we will see no more of the great pantomime that enlivens our diplomatic life. Belgrade will seem sad without it. But suddenly his voice rises and in its expression I hear the note I recognise, the jubilation of mischief present and to come. 'It has been announced to me on the telephone that a great event has taken place at Sarajevo, which will change all our lives, the lives of your children and their children. The Archduke Francis Ferdinand and the Duchess of Hohenberg have been shot dead in their motor-car on the way to the town hall. We must bow our heads in sorrow and compunction with the Imperial family.'

Compunction is not what I read in his bloodshot eyes, I read joy and I'm happy that Hartwig has not been recalled, but I know my duty, the joy I read is like a passage in a book studied after the lights have been put out. I disengage myself from the dancers and make for the doors. A telegram in code must be sent to London and I drag Oliver along after me.

'Wait!' Hartwig shouts. 'Where are you going? The Kolo hasn't reached the end, it's sacrilege to break the dance, it causes the slaughter of heroes. On the eve of the Battle of Kosovo a Kolo was begun and abandoned.' He signals to the musicians. 'We will resume where we left off. You were just getting — what do you say? — the hang of it!'

V

Belgrade, June 29, 1914

I have the honour to report that the news of the assassination of the Archduke and his consort the Duchess produced in Belgrade a sensation rather of stupefaction than of regret. Excited public opinion in Servia and anti-Austrian demonstrations would not fail to lead to serious complications and I fear that the manner and personality of my Russian colleague, who enjoys great popularity here, are unlikely to have the effect of oil poured on troubled waters.

I am informed by my French colleague that an interview of considerable violence took place on the occasion of the Austrian Minister's visit to the Ministry of Foreign Affairs, and for the moment relations between the Austrian Legation and the Servian Ministry for Foreign Affairs are very strained.

Harris to Grey.

WARY RESERVE is the aim in diplomatic correspondence, so I stick to hints and keep insights to myself. Who, after all, would be helped by them? But I think Hartwig has a taste for war; like a circling condor he sees motion and prepares for carnage. As for Boppe, I saw revenge and the blue line of the Vosges at the back of his eyes as he told me about the meeting in the Foreign Ministry. So one way or another, agression is awake, as in certain dreams when though you know catastrophe lies at the end of the road, round the corner of the building, at the foot of the bed, you charge on.

Well, I'll return to Topčider until Oliver calls me back; work with my notebook and pencil under the oaks and await developments since these are on the way and beyond my influence, perhaps beyond all human influence.

'How can we do our work at Topčider where there is no telephone, Mr Harris?' Xenia asks as we leave the stony road and roll under the trees of the park along a sandy track.

'Mr Dillon will come out on the tram whenever it's necessary.'

'Yes?'

'We'll be at peace and away from the heat, at least for the month of July.'

'What happens after July?'

'A new Minister may arrive from London.'

'When?'

'Perhaps not before September. He has to equip.'

'By September,' Xenia says, 'what equipment will he need?' It's a rhetorical question and I let it go. 'I think I will not be so happy now at Topčider,' she says sadly.

'Are you lonely here? I'm not often away, do you miss anything?'

'In the Legation I have my desk, I have the post to open, your answers to send.'

'You are bored, then?'

'No, not with you, ever.'

'Well, we have cooks in the Legation, Hermann to look after us — '

We are sitting in the Sunbeam before the door of Prince George's lodge, each waiting to snare the other into submission. 'It is nothing to do with any of that,' Xenia says, and turns away from me to gaze into the empty space below the trees.

'So what is it?'

'There was a letter for me in my room that I found while you were at the Electric Telegraph office.'

The more interest I seem to show in this letter the less she will tell me about it. 'Turn back, Xenia, please.' When she turns she shows her smile, believing I've submitted. 'What was in your letter?'

'You think I am an only child?'

'I believe you said so.'

'No. Mr Dillon told you this, when he asked all the questions before you gave me work.'

I take her hand and turn it in mine. 'We have to look into the background of the Legation staff you know, recruited locally. But when I saw you, I felt — '

'I know you are happy here with me. But I would like to be in Belgrade, in the Legation, please.'

'In Belgrade I lose you every night when you go home.'

'No, I will stay with you.'

There must be some reason. 'What is it then, Xenia? You can tell me, it won't make any difference.'

'I will still be your stenographer?'

I laugh. 'Yes, at least until the new Minister arrives. He may wonder why you're sleeping in the Legation, too.'

'You see, I have that little brother and he has no father to look after him.'

'Why does he need a father to look after him?'

'He has nowhere to go. He is a student and because of his cough he has been sent away. If our father was alive he could go to him.'

'Is this what was in your letter waiting for you?'

'Yes.'

'But you saw him at the races, you didn't need a letter to tell you that.'

'You don't believe me. You think I have a lover.'

'No, I 'm sure you haven't.' But I'm not as sure as I say I am.

'If my brother was in the Legation with me I could look after him.'

That, then, is the snare. 'I'm afraid the new Minister wouldn't approve.'

'I don't believe there is going to be a new Minister at all.'

'Why do you say that?'

'Because I don't think there is time.'

THE TOPČIDER idyll is over and we are back in the Legation. That rent handed in cash to Prince George looks as if it's down the drain and Xenia's little brother is expected at any moment. I am standing in the morning room window, overlooking the street and the steps to the door, with Hermann just behind me. Since the assassination of the Archduke, Hermann seems loaded with hatred. 'What population of slaves, *Exzellenz,*' he says as we watch the anxious people of Belgrade in their light summer clothing pass along the street and below the windows. Xenia with a young man holding on to her arm appears round the corner of the house, moving quickly, almost pulling him along towards the steps and the entrance. 'Bring some plum brandy and three glasses, please Hermann. That young man looks to me as if he could do with it.'

'*Schmutz,*' Hermann swears as he rolls away.

The brother is lame. Even the few steps to the door exhaust him and his face is white. The cough Xenia mentioned is probably consumptive, in which case we're all putting ourselves in danger of infection.

'Mr Harris, this is Milan.'

'Good morning, Mr Ciganović,' I say in Serbo-Croat but he doesn't respond.

'Milan, Mr Harris has spoken to you.'

Milan looks up at me, raises his right hand which is bandaged, then his left to be shaken and smiles like a man awaiting surgery. At this moment Hermann returns with the plum brandy. 'We will help ourselves, Hermann.'

'If you drink twice, use the same glass *Exzellenz,*' Hermann advises before he goes.

'In the British Legation should be a British butler, I think,' Xenia says.

'Your better health,' I say, raising my glass. By the time I've taken a sip, Milan has drained his and looks slightly better, still chalk white but with a bit of glow in his eyes. 'What are you studying, at the University?' I politely ask.

'History,' he mumbles. 'Old history.' He is holding the empty glass away from him like a begging bowl. I refill it. I don't have the impression that more questions about his studies would be welcome. Probably for reasons of health they have been broken off, or he failed his last examinations and is ashamed. I begin to feel even more sorry for him, but my Serbo-Croat is limited and if Milan is doing history he may have no other language.

'Very interesting,' I say. 'Greek history? Xenophon?' I don't expect an answer and I don't get one.

'Like other students in Serbia, Milan does work as well as study,' Xenia says. 'I know at Oxford it is different because all your fathers are rich.'

I can't deny it, the gap is vast, but if Milan the orphan son of a Serbian peasant can be at the University then things have progressed further here than with us. 'What work does he do?'

'He is night clerk in the railways.'

'And attends meetings of the Narodna Odbrana?'

'Like all students.'

'We must look after him here till he gets better and goes back to work,' I say, knowing well that if Milan is consumptive he isn't likely to get much better very soon. In a day or two I will send for our doctor and then with tact Milan can probably be moved somewhere, a hospital for example, but for the moment Xenia's fears must be lulled. Why am I doing this? I need only look at her and into myself for the answer. 'Feed him up a bit. Plenty of plum brandy, I can see that's good for him.'

'I will look after him,' Xenia says, 'he must go to bed now in that little dressing-room near to yours and I will prepare his food so Hermann can't poison him.'

I hadn't bargained for Milan being separated from my bedroom only by a wall and I look from Xenia to him and back again, trying to see what the understanding between them is. Their expressions are blank; but friction within the Legation may soon cause sparks, while the smallest spark will ignite the fires of Europe. Are we to be the match box?

Among the many calamities incidental to the human frame there are few so distressing to the sufferer and so annoying to his friends as confirmed stammering . . . It is a melancholy spectacle to see a youth, born to a good position, of refined intellect, seemingly destined to adorn society, and yet unable to give oral expression to his thoughts without inflicting pain on those who listen to him, or subjecting himself to ridicule; for, while the deaf-mute is pitied, the stammerer is generally laughed at.

Stammering and Stuttering, Their Nature and Treatment. James Hunt, PH.D., F.S.A., F.R.S.L.: 1863.

'MY BOY PREVAILED on me to remove him from school, Mr Selzman, because the others were making his life wretched with their cruel laughter. You may think me weak, but Theodore is now our only child. I am unhappy if he is unhappy.'

'I understand you, Mr Harris.'

'He must study at home. I will make sure he studies, but the impediment — free my poor Theodore of it if you can, Mr Selzman, so that by the time he goes up to Oxford he can express himself as well as his father.'

'You must accept that your son will never shine at the bar, or in a professorial chair,' Selzman pronounced weightily, his twisted hands and knuckles wrapped round the head of his stick. 'He must strike out for himself on some new path, such as his talents and improvement in his speech will allow him.'

James Harris was unused to being lectured but this Selzman, a scholar and leading authority in the lonely field of the stutter and the stammer, was about to enter his employment as Theo's tutor. He seemed to James, despite a rather old-fashioned didactic manner, to be a man of open mind and flexible views. Striking out on new paths (with a certain income behind one) was quite in harmony with James Harris's feelings about the world.

'You may wish me to tell you a little more of Theodore's history before you meet him,' he said.

'I would rather make my own discoveries. I can help him more in that way.'

SO THAT WAS how Emanuel Selzman first came into the Harris household. Theo took to him immediately. He liked his ears, which were large, fine, and pointed, and his abundant untidy hair standing out from the sides of his head. He even liked the twisted knuckles and the stick. They made Theo feel that Mr Selzman, whose ankles were probably in no better state than his knuckles, would not manage to catch him with that stick and to a Victorian child, coddled at home but not at school, this was a valuable consideration.

'Good morning, sir,' Theo said, looking at the ears.

'Good morning, Harris. I prefer that you address me as Selzman, sir engenders an illusion of inequality. We are equals but for the fact that I, being older, for the time being know more than you do.' Mr Selzman smiled at Theo in such a way that his large pointed ears seemed to slip round towards the back of his head. His teeth were strong and good, which was by no means true of all schoolmasters.

'Thank you, sir. I mean, thank you, Selzman.'

'What would you say to us making better acquaintance on our first day over the way in the park? The sun is shining. We will have enough rainy days of Greek and Mathematics indoors later in the month.'

'I think that's a first rate idea, Selzman.'

'Shall we take your dog with us? Would your father approve?'

'She's called Juno, and my father always says she gets no exercise. Come on Juno, rabbits. Rabbits, girl. You know she's really a gun dog, Selzman, they shouldn't chase them but this is London.'

'So we'll stroll in the park without guns. With my joints and stick I won't keep up with Juno but you can do some running. It will do you good. Exertion is excellent.'

'Juno and I adore exertion.'

'I can see you love this dog, Harris.'

'I do.'

'Very well. I'll hold your coat while you exert yourselves. By the way, do you notice that so far you have made not a single hesitation of speech?'

IN THE AFTERNOON Selzman went to his other pupil, and in the evening to a third. Theo never knew the names of these others nor where, exactly, they lived, but it wasn't long before they became objects of jealousy, an unreasoning jealousy which ate into the confident relations of tutor and boy. Selzman observed this process and by his reticence about the other pupils seemed to foster it. Theo didn't know if Selzman had a family of his own or not, and jealousy was exacerbated by ignorance. One day he asked his father.

'I think that if Mr Selzman wanted us to know about his personal life he would tell us,' said James.

'Didn't you think to ask him Papa, before you put him in charge of me?'

'Theodore, I am in charge of you. Mr Selzman is a specialist equipped to help you, he is not a policeman.'

'Are you my policeman, Papa?' They both shed a tear or two while this misunderstanding was cleared up and it was explained to Theo that his father and mother, however distant circumstances might sometimes make them appear, were his best friends in the world.

Meanwhile, there was a worsening in his relations with Selzman so he would stare at the tutor in deliberate silence while the tutor watched him with the steady, grey gaze of equals temporarily at odds. But didn't that grey steadiness imply an inequality, when Theo's own gaze was so troubled? He met the inequality in his own way — fluent one moment, seized up in his stammer the next.

'You know there are many repetitive vocal exercises we can go back to, Harris, if your stammer gets worse again. Indeed we would have to go back to them for want of any other resource. But that would be very tedious for both of us, don't you think?'

'Yes,' Theo said in a surly manner.

'You must have suffered doing them as a small boy.'

'Yes.'

'I have known other boys who were sadly teased within the family while they tried to follow that discipline. At least, even if lonely you had no one to tease you.'

Theo looked at Selzman in surprise. 'But there was someone.'

'Who?'

'Did Papa not tell you?'

'No. Who was it tormented you?'

'My parents always said he meant no harm.'

Selzman, leaning forward over his twisted wrists and knuckles resting on the handle of his stick, started to guess at what was being hidden from him. 'You had a brother? A James like your father?' Theo didn't answer but passed the back of his hand rapidly across his eyes. 'When I go to my other pupils who are neither of them, I may honestly say, anywhere so much in my affection as you — ' Selzman paused for some time — 'you are angry with them?'

'I hate them.'

'And me?' Theo laughed without humour. 'Did James fall ill?'

'He drowned.'

'Bathing?'

'Sculling.'

'Sculling — so he was alone?'

'I saw him go over the weir from the bank.'

Selzman left another long pause as though he had to weigh this up for judgement. 'So you stood there on the towpath watching James drown? And when you struggled to speak about it your parents had no patience to listen — is this how it seemed?'

Theo's hand closed about an ink pot on the table, he saw Selzman's pointed ears and his smiling mouth curled back as if laughing at him. He stood and threw the ink pot with all his force. It struck below the eye and there was bleeding from above the cheekbone, running down in a scarlet stream towards the chin. Selzman remained in his chair, dabbed his cheek with a silk handkerchief, patted his eye. 'I am glad this has happened,' he said, almost at once. The calm of his deep, even voice made Theo sit again, hands cupped together on the table.

'We should send for some iodine for the cut on your cheek,' he stammered painfully.

'Thank you for your concern, Harris, my handkerchief is perfectly clean.'

'I am very sorry to have hurt you, Selzman.'

'It is perfectly superficial. Let us return to Aristotle, the *Nicomachean Ethics,* Book 2. Moral excellence is the acquired rational capacity to choose the mean between extremes. Would you agree?'

'Yes, I would.'

'And that parents can be misunderstood?'

'Altogether.'

'I think the worst of your hesitations may be over.'

SELZMAN'S SOCIAL VIEWS went a good deal further than those of James Harris, advanced as they were for the time.

'Your father's book on population control for the masses is a very respectable work,' he said one day, 'but I think the solution reaches only the surface, important as it is. At bottom, our society is cruel, corrupt, decadent and repressive. Our humanity is crushed by it.'

'Shall we soon have a revolution, do you think?'

'I have said more than I should. But no, I don't suppose we will have any revolutions here.'

'I haven't yet been allowed to read Papa's book,' Theo said. 'I believe it touches on matters I am thought too young to understand.' He looked at Selzman in a sideways manner, then more directly.

'It touches on reproduction. You are familiar by hearsay at least with that process and its means?'

'Very vaguely.'

'Well, Harris, this is not in our curriculum but if, during our next walk with Juno in the park, you have any question to put to me I will answer as well as my own experience allows me.'

'Could we go over to the park this morning, do you think, Selzman?'

BY THE TIME he went up to Oxford, Theo's stammer had become no more than a delivery with a slightly broken rhythm to which people listened carefully as if they might miss the essential. The drawback was that they always thought they remembered exactly what he'd said, and this made him cautious. He was the conscious master of his own speech and chose his words knowing they were likely to lodge in shaky memories.

'You take with you my highest hopes, Harris,' Selzman said at their last meeting. 'You have my address in Pembroke Villas if ever you feel like a talk — I will miss our meetings.' Selzman wiped his eyes rapidly with the same silk handkerchief he had used ages ago to mop the blood on his cheek. 'Remember that your way of speaking singles you out. It is a very fine way, a disciplined way, the result of patience. But it will always be noticed.'

'I will never forget your tolerance, Selzman.'

'You could give me no greater thanks.'

The Dual Monarchy will have the sympathies of the whole of Europe with her, if she takes severe measures against Serbia. Even Russia would approve a campaign undertaken against a nation tainted with the guilt of regicide and the rest of Europe would certainly stand by Austria in a war of self-defence against murder and outrage.
Neue Freie Presse, 14th July 1914

'REGICIDE? HE WAS an Archduke, not a king.'

'I think the journalist is referring to the reigning pair who were chucked out of the palace windows in 1903,' Oliver points out.

'Yes, of course. For Vienna, all Serbia is tainted with guilt.'

'We withdrew our Minister too, remember.'

'And then sent Ramsay.'

'To teach them a lesson.'

Since Kosovo Day Oliver has brightened up considerably, and in fact seems sober almost all the time. Oliver needs a woman, but romantic alcoholics tend to fritter away the summer of their age on yearnings. I don't suppose Kitty, victim in a way of her own beauty, ever gave him any more encouragement than she gave to all — probably just what Browning called 'much the same smile' — but it was enough.

From the dining-room of the Legation you see over the terrace and beyond and below it the clear green water of the Save flowing side by side with the yellowish Danube, then gradually merging. On the Hungarian shore two small gunboats are moored under the willows. The armament they carry is nothing to the famous Austrian artillery, said to be the most potent in Europe, but they're probably well able to lob shells across the river onto the buttresses of Kalemegdan and the Legation standing almost next to it it, shoulder to shoulder. 'We'll be in the firing line if anything goes wrong,' I say, handing the field glasses to Oliver and pointing to the gunboats, small, grey, innocuous, tethered among pleasure steamers threading a way upstream to Zemun and Novi Sad and Vienna, between islands covered with bathing cabins and market-gardens, maize and melons, girls bent among the summer crops.

'The crisis will pass,' Oliver says cheerfully, 'just a summer storm. Huffing and puffing of emperors and kings.'

'I'm not sure.'

'Diplomacy will do the trick and you're in charge of that here, Theo. For the moment, you *are* Britannia. I don't envy you.'

'If the Legation should be in danger from shells we must think of the archive. It would have to be moved to safety. I want you to make immediate preparation for that eventuality Oliver.'

'Where on earth would we take it?'

'The German Legation is in the safest part of the town, behind the University.'

'And I would keep the archive company there?'

'That could be your duty.'

'Perhaps Prince George will come home now.'

'Perhaps.'

'If he can tear himself away.' Beyond the Danube nothing stirs in the heat of the morning. A faint haze drifts here and there above the river like a cloud of insects in mating ritual, rising, shifting. Apart from that, silence and stillness seem to stretch across the flat plain to the horizon, beyond which all roads and thoughts lead to Vienna. 'Dead calm,' Oliver says. 'Long may it last.'

'We can only wait and see, like the excitable and fatalistic people of this country.'

'You know them more intimately than I do.'

'Can one ever know enough to generalise?'

'As you just did?' Oliver scoffs at things on the surface; deeper down he is conformist, believes with all his heart in the values of the Foreign Office, and considers me a subversive. 'I forgot to mention that the Russian Minister has summoned you again.'

'When?'

'His catamite telephoned at ten this morning.'

'I mean when does he expect me to call on him?'

'At once.'

'It's midday and you think of telling me now?'

'I have new worries about the move of the archive to the German Legation.'

POSHA PUTS ME to wait in an ante-room where the pictures are crude portraits of boyars, popes, czars, inspiring no confidence in history, a tribe of war makers issue of the Asiatic horde.

'How crisp your linen suit is!' Hartwig booms as he comes in. 'In that I would melt in ten minutes, I have to have air, plenty of air between my body and its covering.' Today he is dressed in a toga-like garment and wears his great brush of hair wrapped round itself and fastened with something like the thin leather chin-strap of a helmet. 'We will drink champagne this morning,' he says. The long window of this ante-room looks on a courtyard with a fountain, and when Hartwig opens it the sound of trickling water and the cooing of doves comes into the room with the rush of hot air. The birds, small and pink, flutter feebly about in a big aviary to one side of the courtyard, watched by a cat whose tail sweeps the dust behind it from side to side. 'It's cooler here than in the library,' Hartwig says. He is sweating and his eyes have a burnt-out look but he seems in good spirits. He raises a hand to the chin-strap. 'As the shadows lengthen one likes to experiment a little with appearances,' he says by way of explanation.

'I'm sure no shadow lengthens for you, Hartwig.'

'It is already long, very long, Harris.' He stretches his hands towards the open window so the sleeves of the toga fall back, revealing plump arms like those of the women in Ingres' painting of the Turkish Baths, only older and less, much less, appetising. 'And what then will become of my ring doves? They will die pining for their master.' I don't believe in this — those shadows, the doomed doves out in the aviary, the epicene manner — Hartwig is an indestructible man, he must be, I depend on him. 'Here is Pósha, now we can have a serious discussion of the international crisis.' He laughs joyfully as Pósha fills his glass the size of a small flower vase. 'Leave us, Pósha, and don't allow anyone to disturb us on any excuse whatever.'

'Very well your Excellency,' Pósha says, bowing low.

'Well hurry up and get out.'

A pair of upright, black wooden armchairs faces the window and the fountain and the aviary. Hartwig waves me to one of them as he sits down on the other. There is a thin horsehair squab cushion on the wooden seat and the carving on the back digs into the kidneys, but Hartwig looks comfortable and has the champagne bottle on a stool near his feet. 'You realise, Harris, that for the moment you and I *are* the Corps Diplomatique in Belgrade?'

'There is Boppe.'

Hartwig waves the idea of Boppe away with the back of his hand. 'Be serious, Harris. In the greatest crisis the world has ever faced, here at the hub of Europe, there are just two of us.'

I can't be sure how literally he means to be taken. Hartwig is political to his bones so if he exaggerates now it's to alarm and pin me into a corner, signifying that his government has turned its sights on Westminster. 'Luckily we have the friendliest of relations, Hartwig.'

'We have, we have.' A long silence follows this, while Hartwig refills his glass. 'You are drinking nothing.'

'I enjoy every drop.'

'I have always said, Harris, that you drink like a girl. Never mind. Thank heaven you are not one, so we can understand each other. You agree? You are *un homme à femmes* and there are no flies on you. But you have distracted me from my purpose.'

'I hardly see how, Hartwig?'

'With your talk of women.'

'I am sorry.'

He looks at me sternly. 'You are still quite a young diplomatist who must learn to detach your thought from the imperatives of nature when professional concentration is required and the stakes are high.'

'Thank you for your advice, Hartwig, which I will take care to remember.'

'I am sure you will.' Having established authority Hartwig turns to surface matters. 'Pašić is on his way back from Greece where he has been plotting with Venizelos, without my sanction, which he may come to regret. He will be in Belgrade by tonight.'

'You will be seeing him?'

'Tomorrow morning at nine. And so will you.'

'What were they plotting about?'

'How can I know, Harris? Secrecy is the essence of plots.'

'But you have an idea, I'm sure.'

'I see what you're doing. You postpone the moment of consent to my wish and use the delay to extract information from me. Well, I can tell you that Pašić hoped to embroil Venizelos in some scheme to gain for Serbia an outlet to the sea. Pašić is an old fox, Venizelos still a fox in his prime.'

'A little like you and me, Hartwig,' I say, laughing and holding out my empty glass.

'No. Tomorrow we will act as a bull deals with an old fox. We will drive him into a corner.'

Outside in the courtyard the big fat cat is still there, hypnotising the doves with its tail movement and yellow eyes. The water trickles down the green sides of the bronze or iron fountain and into a stone basin where aquatic weeds flourish in the general neglect. The Russian Legation is for politics, not horticulture.

'I hardly think His Majesty's government wishes to drive the Serbian Prime Minister into a corner you know, and I have no instruction —'

'To the devil with governments and all the old women in them. I am thinking of you, of your unique position.'

'In relation to the Narodna Odbrana? I have no information about them.'

'Harris, Harris! It is they who have information about you! And that's why you will join me tomorrow in urging on Pašić the one course possible — he must submit to whatever Austria demands. He must hold nothing in reserve. He must question nothing. Vienna will walk into the trap because he will deny them the pretext to do anything else. Precious time will be gained while my countrymen prepare and yours make up their minds. The strategic railway will advance with giant pace towards our western frontiers. Our millions will mass and then we will be ready.'

'But London — ' I begin to object.

'St Petersburg and Paris will work on the feeble spirits who govern your island and a new balance of power in Europe will be created. This is the only way to avoid war, my dear Harris, and in the end you will be praised for the part you will have played, if you know on which side of your bread the butter is spread.'

This specious argument has attractions. The new brutal diplomacy which Hartwig is taking to like a duck to water has long days ahead of it, and there's Xenia sheltered under H.M's roof, and her brother; if, as I now begin to suspect, they know more about the assassination at Sarajevo than I have been told, then no one in Europe, not even Hartwig with his million men and strategic railway, has greater need to gain time than the British Chargé d'affaires.

'Shall I come to you here in the morning, Hartwig, so we appear together?'

'That is a good idea, Harris. We will rehearse our arguments further at eight o'clock. And now tell me how the little Ciganović is faring? They say you hold her captive in your Legation. This is perhaps a somewhat archaic way of keeping a young woman under one's eye but we know how the English love tradition, and secret power.'

VI

Vienna, July 5, 1914

I had some conversation with M. Schebeko, Russian Ambassador, who cannot believe that Austria will allow itself to be rushed into war. A Servian war meant a general European war . . . No nation could abhor more than the Russian the hand of an assassin, for Russia had greatly suffered from political murders. But to make the country in which a plot was prepared responsible for its execution was a new doctrine, and he did not think the Austrian Government would be induced by a few violent articles in the press to act upon it . . .

de Bunsen to Grey.

Minute

I doubt whether Austria will take any action of a serious character <u>and I expect the storm to blow over.</u> M. Schebeko is a shrewd man and I attach weight to any opinion he expresses.

Sir Arthur Nicholson, Permanent Under-Secretary, Foreign Office.

EVEN AT FORTY (or a little over) you can miss a father's quiet presence in the background. My father went into the final sleep in his armchair by the fireplace, my mother watching over him as his breathing slowed and stopped and his head fell against his shoulder. The Eugenics Education Society had to manage without him and so must I.

I believe he would have understood about Xenia; 'The real importance of sex lies in its power to create unhappiness through physical incompatibility,' he liked to say. In other words happiness depends on choice and timing and a sensible man draws his conclusions and acts accordingly.

Do I mean that my father James was not a true Victorian? No, I mean that Victorians were as various and sensual as anyone else.

Word has come that Prince George is on his way back and though I've paid rent for the lodge he'll demand instant possession, so I must go to Topčider and remove any of our belongings still left, the sheets we used, for example; not work for H.M's Chargé d'affaires, but I'm more compromised as the calendar ticks off the days.

Milan Ciganović has hardly stirred from the bedroom since his arrival. I sometimes pass along the corridor but I hear no consumptive coughing. I might drop in on him now, knowing from Hermann that Xenia has gone to buy fruit. Why buy fruit, when the Legation orders all that's needed? Because, apparently, the brother has a hankering for water melons — flesh the colour of diluted blood. I enter without knocking. He is lying on on his side turned away from the door, and his immobility tells me he's in pain. Should I speak in German, or use my few words of Serbo-Croat? I settle for German.

'Are you feeling better? Do you make good progress?' I ask.

'*Ja, ja danke schön, mein Herr,*' Xenia's little brother answers as if this phrase has been learnt by rote.

'So when will you be up?'

It isn't a kind enquiry and the boy doesn't answer it. We stay silent while the uncertainty of our situation grows. I walk round the bed so I am between it and the window and can take a harder look; he lifts his head and returns the hard look and I feel sure, seeing him at close quarters for the first time, that he is not consumptive, but injured. He's not here in convalescence, he's in hiding. And what, I wonder, does he make of me? His eyes are close-set, penetrating and black. I dare say he slots me into the category of Englishman not hard to dupe though not easy to buy. Poor fellow, with what could he buy anyone? Suspicion uncoils in my head.

'My sister — she will answer,' Milan says, and from compassion if nothing else, I leave him alone with his pain.

'NOW WE MUST tidy up before we go so the prince finds things as they were,' I tell Xenia.

She has an arm behind her on the pillow so her head is raised up. The hair under her arms is less tawny than on her head, and is now moist in the sunlight slanting in through the half-closed shutters.

'I want to stay longer here,' she says. 'There's no hurry, I can do what you call tidy up in only a few minutes.'

'If you hadn't dismissed the prince's servants you wouldn't have to do it at all.'

'But they would have been listening at the door.' She brings the arm round to draw me down. 'We have all the afternoon left.'

'What about your brother, if he needs something?'

'He needs to sleep. And I have given him what he needs for that.'

'Did a doctor prescribe it for him?'

She doesn't answer but puts her free hand on my mouth and the question gets forgotten.

THE MESSENGER has passed the bag to Dillon from the train window on his way to Constantinople, and there's a letter from Kitty.

Vence, 6th July

Dear Theo,

I think I will stay here where I have found a pretty house to rent and some land, I'm not sure how much but you can see the Mediterranean in the distance and you know how that matters to me.. I feel I must say Theo that I am afraid you don't think much about what Father Darcy calls the disembodied love, the highest sort. If only you ever had we could have been happier, you and me. But I know what goes on in your head, Theo, and I prefer to remain here in Vence, and you in Belgrade.

People in France say there is going to be a war but I expect if there is it won't last long — anyway it will be good for those Russian railway stocks I have — Anglo-Russian Trust four and a half percent Debenture Stock whatever that is — don't you think? And that will be good.

I was truly sorry your father died last year, but your mother hasn't ever been very kind to me and now that I have those Russian debentures and things and you will soon have a Minister's salary I don't want to be in any way beholden to your mother, she has always hated me I honestly think. So I don't want to go to Rutland Gate or Orchard Harris in the rain but stay here where the olives ripen and the almonds blossom in February.

I send you affectionate and loyal wishes and hope if the worst comes you will be able to drive or take a train in good time out of Serbia to safety so I will see you again.

Prince George who was great fun here these last weeks has left, which is sad.

Your devoted, Kitty

IT'S A TOUCHING letter and it makes me laugh. She's so simple, absolute and self-deceiving. But it also makes me sad, very sad, for a few minutes. I don't think she believes in the disembodied love any more than I do, and what she says proves the truth of my father's remark about unhappiness and physical incompatibility. Is it always the man's fault? For a long time I blamed myself, remembered Havelock Ellis on man evoking music in woman, and felt ashamed to have called up so little, or none at all, from Kitty. What else did my father say about marriage? that if your minds can be freely opened, you are home. I'll write back and advise her to sell those Russian debentures while the going's good.

But first I'd better ask Hartwig, who often mentions the growth of railways in his country, how good he thinks the going is. Hartwig insists that I must accompany him this morning to the Austrian Minister on a visit of condolence. It seems that some reptile who was present in the Russian Legation on St Vitus Day saw Hartwig return from the telephone, glass held high and face charged with glee as he made the tragic pronouncement, and then resume the Kolo. The reptile informed the Austrian Legation where serious offence was taken and now Hartwig is ordered to make amends. That's why he wants me to go with him, to show that such good allies as Imperial Russia and England could never be wanting in consideration for another crowned head on the death by revolver bullet of the Heir Apparent. Actually, I think Hartwig is nervous about the interview with the Austrian Minister because he has difficulty controlling his aggression. 'We will go to Pašić together afterwards,' he said on the telephone. 'We will gauge the sentiment in the Austrian Legation and tell him about it. It will add urgency to what we have to say.'

'Who will request the meeting with the Prime Minister's office?'

'Oh, Pósha can arrange all that,' Hartwig said.

Vienna, July 3, 1914

Why the German Emperor has not come after all, I do not know. The official reason is that he had an attack of lumbago. My own idea was that he had been made to understand that foreign Sovereigns and Princes were not expected . . . or welcome. Thus within a week of the crime the funeral honours for the murdered Archduke and his Consort have been brought to a rapid close. Complaints have been heard that these honours were perfunctory . . . at the last moment a contingent of notables, who had not been honoured with invitations, contrived to attach them-

selves to the tail of the funeral procession which arrived in the dead of
night on the Danube.
  de Bunsen to Grey.

THE INTERIOR of the Austrian Legation is a piece of Vienna transported. There is a staircase with twin arms which carry you up under a dome of stars and cherubs and angels. Hartwig goes up one arm, I go up the other and we meet at the top where they join like handcuffs.

'My God,' he whispers, 'such decadence.'

'His Excellency the Minister of His Imperial Majesty Tsar Nicholas II to the court of His Majesty King Peter,' roars the major domo into the echoing spaces of the first reception chamber; 'and you sir, if you please, whom should I announce?'

'Mr Harris, British Chargé d'affaires.'

We advance towards double doors at the far end of this empty room, and into a second reception room full of plaster work and gilding where Baron Giesl von Gieslingen, the Austrian Minister, awaits us. He doesn't come forward and he doesn't extend a greeting hand but stands at attention.

'My dear colleague, my most profound commiserations,' Hartwig cries in his heavily accented German, insincerity loud and clear. I know he detests the Austrian Minister who detests him even more. 'His late Imperial Highness is a great loss to all Europe which will be felt for many years, and by none more deeply than myself as we shared many of the same aspirations for the future of the Balkans.' It isn't a tactful introduction to the excuses he has been commanded to make. The Archduke was distrusted by the Austrian government, and hated by his uncle the Emperor because of the aspirations shared with Hartwig. 'I only wish I could have been present at the obsequies for the unhappy couple,' Hartwig adds, 'unfortunately I was prevented from travelling in the train as I had hoped by a sudden attack of lumbago, and the obsequies were, so I understand, held without delay.'

Baron Giesl bows again and gestures us towards a couple of small, straight-backed gilt chairs. He sits on a third chair, facing us, waves his hand behind him whereupon a tray of coffee cups is hurried forward and passed around. The coffee is excellent but I can see that Hartwig needs something more bracing and I notice for the first time that his breathing is shallow and fast.

'His Imperial Highness and the Duchess were accorded ceremonies following the Spanish rites of the Court,' Giesl says defensively.

'Yes indeed,' Hartwig says, building up to something. 'It is reported that on the Duchess's coffin only a pair of gloves and a fan were placed, to mark her low-born status.'

'I am unaware of what other insignia might have been put there.'

'Any of the orders so freely distributed among the idle classes of Austria-Hungary, I should think,' Hartwig says.

'Offer his Excellency some more coffee,' the Austrian Minister orders, and the flunkey circulates like clockwork with newly filled cups. 'I will convey your words of condolence to the Ballplatz, where their sense will be appreciated,' he says.

There is a long cold silence. 'I was acquainted with that poor little duchess when she was only Sophie Chotek,' Hartwig goes on remorselessly. 'She was an extremely pretty girl who would have done better if the Archduke had never laid hands on her.'

'I too saw the late duchess in Vienna,' I break in hurriedly, 'a charming lady to whom, I believe, the Archduke was a devoted husband.' The longer I remain in the Service the more my tongue seems to move in treacle, uttering these formulae. They emerge, I don't stammer, but a gulf of bad faith opens as I speak.

The Austrian Minister inclines his head vaguely in my direction without saying anything. I'm only a Chargé d'affaires and known to be carrying on an inappropriate affair with a Serbian stenographer. My well meant remark may have seemed presumptuous, I'm afraid.

Hartwig hasn't finished yet. 'I'm told there was a tremendous thunderstorm as the coffins were ferried over the Danube and they had to be hurried into a station waiting-room with what there was of a cortège to accompany them. Perhaps the heavens were warning of the rage to come.'

'Even King Cnut the Great of England couldn't command the elements,' says Giesl, and suddenly smiles.

We all laugh with relief and Giesl murmurs something to the servant who then hurries away. I think I caught the word schnapps and if so it will come as a life-saver to Hartwig whose breathing, still rapid and no longer so silent, is beginning to worry me. A glass or two of schnapps might calm him.

'If you will excuse me a moment, gentlemen, I will bring my wife to you who I know would wish to join us for a minute before you take your leave.' Giesl, short and stout, waddles off towards a pair of doors at the side of the room.

'I believe I managed to smooth things over,' Hartwig says, and the little gilt chair creaks alarmingly under his weight. He is slumped on the seat and his colour is not good.

'Do you feel quite well, Hartwig?'

'Of course. Why?'

'You look to be . . . under some strain.'

'I am under some strain Harris. My uniform is tight, my feet are hot, I am in the house of the enemy and this coffee decidedly does not agree with me.'

'We'll soon be away from it.'

'Oh yes, thank God, and then we will go to my Legation where you will show me the steps of that tango — I would love to learn it.' He puts a hand on my arm and I feel a light pressure from his fingers, like a farewell.

The Giesl couple are back. Baroness Giesl is hardly distinguishable from her husband so similar are their outlines, their eyes and mouths, their colouring.

'My dear,' says Giesl as they stand in front of us, side by side, interchangeable, 'I present the Russian Minister Monsieur Hartwig, and the British — '

At this instant, just as Hartwig should take a step forward to kiss Baroness Giesl's plump little hand which is held out ready, he takes a step backward and lets out a great gasp and a cry, stretching his arms up; then collapses to the parquet in the awful silence following.

'Is he drunk?' hisses Baroness Giesl.

Giesl calls for help and a troop of servants and secretaries begins to fill the room. I am on my knees beside Hartwig's unconscious mass and attempting the motions of life-saving I remember from the fencing school at Oxford — seize the arms of the subject, having first reassured yourself that he is not wounded, and pump them vigorously back and forth from behind his head to his waist in order to revive breathing and so the action of the heart. As far as I can see, no action of any kind is being revived. Hartwig's colour is grey, his eyes stare ahead, his mouth is open, the lower jaw dropped.

'Here is our Herr Doktor,' Giesl says in the high excited voice of panic as a sombre, bearded individual, exuding temporary authority, advances on the form of Hartwig, unbuttons his tunic and shirt and puts an ear to his chest.

'This patient — who had unhappily no time to become formally my patient so I could question him — is dead,' he announces.

'Are you sure, quite sure, Doctor?' I ask.

'Do you question my ability to tell a dead man from a living?'

'No no, by no means, I meant, can nothing more be done?'

'Nothing whatever. The heart is silent as the grave. It has certainly been diseased for some time past.' He feels about Hartwig's abdomen with the palms of his hands. 'Also the liver, in lamentable condition. The pancreas bloated also. I would expect to find haemorrhoids, incipient cancer of the oesophagus, and gastric ulcers.'

I feel tears in my eyes. Diagnosis like this, general and devastating, is not how to say goodbye to a friend who was, as he said himself, in a way a father. But the diagnosis of death is the only real moment of farewell, afterwards are the formalities. The flame has guttered in the socket and is out, Hartwig, doyen of mischief-makers, has rejoined the master of mischief in the sky.

Belgrade, July 11, 1914

Very confidential

I have the honour to report that by a strange fatality M. Hartwig, the Russian Minister to Servia, succumbed to heart failure within the precincts of the Austrian Legation on the evening of the 10th instant. This sad event has greatly perturbed his friends here.

It appears that M. Hartwig was desirous of offering to the Austrian Minister, who had returned to Belgrade from Vienna the same day, a personal explanation in regard to certain rumours which had become public concerning his behaviour and attitude subsequently to the assassination of the Archduke Francis Ferdinand.

(1.) The 'Reichspost' of Vienna had recently published an article attacking the Russian Minister for holding a party at which dancing took place on the evening of the Archduke's murder. It is true that M. Hartwig was quietly entertaining some colleagues that evening but, under the circumstances, the article in the 'Reichspost' seems to have contained some very unnecessary animadversions.

(2.) I regret to state that M. Hartwig had recently been heard to use ill-advised language in regard to the character and private life of several members of the Austrian and Hungarian governments and even of the Imperial family itself. I do not know whether his remarks were repeated at the Austrian Legation, but if this was so, I can say from first-hand knowledge that the interview must have been, on M. Hartwig's side, somewhat emotional, sufficiently to hasten an end which, according to doctor's evidence, could in any case have been only deferred a short time.

On news being received in Belgrade of the strange circumstances attending the Russian Minister's death, sinister reports were at once circulated to the effect that M. Hartwig had taken a 'cup of coffee' at the Austrian Legation. I mention this as an indication of the somewhat mediaeval morals prevailing in this city.

Harris to Grey.

EVERYONE HERE says that his coffee was poisoned and that Vienna would stop at nothing to deepen the crisis. This morning there's to be the state funeral for Hartwig in the Cathedral, immediately after which his remains will be entrained for Constantinople for enshipment (urgent by now in this heat I should think) to Russia. I will be in the Cathedral and my heart will be heavy but my thoughts elsewhere, because I have received this day from F. Jones, Consul at Sarajevo, a copy of the 'Bosnische Post' and of his despatch sent at the same time to London.

An article in the 'Bosnische Post' declared that the murders were proven to have been organised and instigated by the Servian Narodna Odbrana; that a certain Ciganović distributed firearms and bombs in railway station near the frontier to young men who expressed willingness to carry out the murder of the Archduke, and that Major Tankosić, of the Servian General Staff and Secretary of the Narodna Odbrana, supplied Ciganović with the pistols and explosives.

I DON'T BELIEVE a word of it, needless to say. Someone, under torture, has given the first name he could think of, and the tortures used by the Austrian police are famous all over Europe. But I wonder if Consul Jones out at Sarajevo in the depths of Bosnia has somehow got wind of something and is decently trying to warn me? I ring for Hermann.

'*Exzellenz?*'

I begin to wish he'd stop calling me that; ever since St Vitus Day I hear in it a hint of contempt. 'Tell Mr Dillon I would appreciate a word with him.'

Hermann bows and goes in silence. Do we really need a butler here? I think I may give Hermann the sack and warn the new Minister to bring a man of his own from England, which ought to delay his arrival still further. Hermann is becoming a nuisance, but what is much worse, he could become dangerous. What if a copy of the 'Bosnische Post' fell into his hands? Would he carry tales at dead of night to the Austrian Legation?

'You wanted to see me, Theo?'

'Yes, Oliver. Sit down. Have you been away?'

'I took a little trip into the country for a day or so.'

'Where did you go?'

'Into the Fruška Gora to see some Roman remains I'm interested in. And the vineyards — the wine from there — ' he spreads his fingers before his lips.

'You took a train?'

'Of course.'

'And did you at all think of continuing your journey across the frontier into Bosnia, for a night or so?'

The eyes look shifty. 'Perhaps I did. You threatened to have me seconded to the Consulate at Sarajevo. I thought it might be a good idea to have a look at the place.'

'You know quite well that wasn't seriously meant.'

'Once upon a time I was second secretary, now I'm an archivist. I can't take threats to pack me off to Sarajevo as a joke.'

We smile at each other, old friends with a lot to lose. But now I must have an answer to my question. 'Did you see Consul Jones?'

'Yes, I did. Not exactly a bright star.'

'He sent me this.' I hold out the copy of the 'Bosnische Post,' pointing at the item which Oliver reads carefully and slowly, his finger tracing the words across the paper as if German is not his strong point. He is here for his Serbo-Croat, as he was in Peking for his Mandarin-Chinese; Oliver specialises in double-forked tongues.

He laughs as he reaches the end of the marked passage. 'Under obvious duress,' he says.

'I wonder why the Consul sent it to me.'

'He must have thought you needed to know. He's an easy-going fellow who hoped for a quiet life on his last posting and all of a sudden he finds himself at the centre of a world crisis. He's terrified of not doing the right thing. He sends off dozens of telegrams a day.'

So that's all I'll get from Oliver; if he committed an indiscretion in Sarajevo he won't admit it now. He has put the 'Bosnische Post' back on the writing table between us with the item face down. Did he actually take in the details, the name, make the connection? I think on the whole he didn't. But I am in a dilemma through which Hartwig might have guided me. Now I see him again lying like a shot bear in uniform on the parquet of the Austrian Legation, his limbs at awkward angles to his trunk, his rapid breathing halted. Silence, stillness.

'Sorry about Hartwig,' Oliver says, 'you and he were complementary.

You'll feel the loss.'

'Yes, I do. Are you coming to the State Funeral in the Cathedral? You should, Oliver.'

'You can represent King George better on your own. You look well in uniform and funerals put me in a melancholy.'

'All right, all right.' It comes to me that Oliver is playing a careful hand. His pretence of ignorance about the 'Bosnische Post' was meant to be seen through, but left no opening. His difficulty in reading German was to mask recognition of the name Ciganović, and its implications. And his silence about it all puts me at his mercy, because of course he knows. He can converse with the sick Milan in his bedroom at any time, in Serbo-Croat. He won't do it, I think, because latent knowledge is a deadlier instrument than verified detail; Oliver has the background information, hazy as it may be. I go up to my bedroom with an uneasy mind to climb into uniform for the funeral.

IT WAS VERY MOVING, at least I was moved, not by incense and bells and chanting and dignitaries but by Pósha, in a pew far back among the unconsidered class. Out on the steps of the Cathedral we watched the feathered catafalque roll away behind horses towards the railway station and I saw tears on his unshaven cheeks.

'You were his only friend of all these big people,' Pósha said.

The big people certainly didn't look as if they grieved much. I saw the Italian Minister laughing heartily in conversation with the German Minister Von Storck, a couple with whom I must remain on good terms. Well, now Hartwig has left on his last journey into Holy Russia. They will put him in the black soil of his native Belgorod where two crops a year rise from the earth; may his spirit bear harvest!

'I am sorry Pósha, that you lost your master so suddenly.' This is inadequate, not only to his feelings but to mine. I try again. 'We who were fond of him should remain — ' What? Friends? 'If you have any . . . difficulty with the new Minister, you may come to me and I will see if I can help in any way,' I say lamely.

Pósha embarrasses me by grabbing both my hands, there in public on the Cathedral steps, and kissing them as if I were a bishop. 'Nicholas Vasiléevich was right to love you,' he says.

As I reclaim my hands an idea comes into my head. There is more in Pósha's effusiveness than grief — there is gratitude. That means my suggestion offers him a way out of some difficulty at which I can only guess; probably he fears that his relations with Hartwig make him unwelcome in the new Minister's household. Pósha expects at best to be demoted to the kitchens. At worst, he will be sent home under guard for knowing too much. 'Remember what I said. Don't telephone, come to the back entrance of the British Legation and ask to see me. Don't give your name, just say I sent for someone to look at the engine of my Sunbeam.'

'Your sunbeam?'

'My motor car.'

'I understand,' Pósha says.

'We could perhaps be useful to each other.'

'I understand.' And I'm sure he does after years working at the Russian Legation where informants flow back and forth on the tides. But I think Pósha may prove worth more than that.

THE FRENCH MINISTER, Boppe, accosts me at the corner of the street after the crowd has dispersed, as if he and I were already reduced by the world crisis to exchanging information in whispers under lamp posts. He is pale and I notice a tremor in the hand held out to me.

'I must see you to talk to you, Harris.'

'Would you like me to call at your Legation?'

'Yes, I would. Come tonight. The matter is too urgent to allow delay.'

'Shall I bring the foils? Shall we be scattering chalk on the parquet and practising the Counter-disengagement and *Prises de fer* where we left off last?'

'No, Harris. Even an Englishman must see that the time has come for seriousness and that play is at an end.'

'Certainly, Boppe, you're right. Nothing could be more serious, and I am in constant communication with the Foreign Office where Sir Edward Grey and Sir Arthur Nicholson and Sir Eyre Crowe bend their minds to the seriousness of the situation night and day.'

'Ha,' says Boppe, 'you speak with irony of your hierarchical superiors. We will discuss more of all that this evening. *A ce soir, Harris.'*

'A ce soir, Boppe.'

Paris, July 8, 1914.

The visit of M. Poincaré to Russia is taking place at a moment when the extraordinary awakening of Russia is manifesting itself . . . in all fields of human activity, only comparable to that of the United States of America thirty years ago, amid measures for bringing about a huge increase in Russian military power. By the winter of 1916 the Russian army on a peace footing will have progressed from 1,200,000 to the colossal figure of 2,245,000 men. Russia will then, thanks to new strategical rail-ways, be able to mobilise as quickly as Germany. But she is animated, like France, with pacific intentions, and the Emperor Nicholas said a short time ago to the French Ambassador: 'Nous voulons être assez forts pour imposer la paix.'

Lord Granville, Counsellor of Embassy, Paris, to Grey.

THE FRENCH LEGATION is perhaps more elegant than ours, though a lot less imposing and much worse placed, tucked away in a side street off the rue du Prince-Miloche. The interior has charm and the Empire furniture reminds you, as it's meant to, of France's great hour in the world with which no one will ever compete again. Actually, Boppe has pointed this out to me more than once while we relaxed after our prac-tice. 'Yours is a parvenu among Empires,' he likes to say, 'and devoid of universal mission.' I'm struck again tonight by how he looks, jaw and hands trembling, eyes fleeing contact, shoulders sagging. He leads the way into his study.

'I am glad we've seen the last of that scheming scoundrel Hartwig,' he says. 'I hope they now send a more responsible diplomatist.'

I know better than to rise to this, and of course it is true that Hartwig hardly stood for what's most emollient in diplomatic practice, and that he despised Boppe and often said so. 'Boppe is a *con,'* he said, not mincing matters.

'You of course have an alliance with Russia, we have only an entente, so the personality of the Russian Minister must weigh with you more than with me.'

'I believed the personality of Hartwig rather to your taste, Harris. I don't refer to his private proclivities, naturally,' he adds.

'I was fond of him, yes.'

Boppe produces a bottle of Armagnac and splashes out two generous doses, the bottle rattling against the side of the glasses as he does it. 'He would have spent his time better pressing you from mere entente into alliance than in provocations, as he did.'

'Don't you consider the entente represents our best interests, Boppe?'

'I think it represents nothing but the pusillanimity of your government,' Boppe says, his mouth pursed forward. 'Our Ambassador can naturally not say so to Sir Edward Grey in such terms, but I can say it to you and you can remind your Foreign Office — for better or worse Great Britain holds our future in her hand.'

Boppe looks sicker by the minute; I wonder if his coffee too has been poisoned? 'In what sense precisely do you mean that?'

'In the sense of time won, Harris, the simplest and most vital in diplomacy. Another year of Russian preparations and we will encircle the central powers in a vice. Meanwhile England's decision decides for us all.' I know what's coming next. Boppe's shaking hand seems to obey his brain no longer, the Armagnac is spilt on the carpet. '*Sacré Albion.*' His head falls forward as he surveys the broken glass while the wool absorbs the spirit into the pattern.

I feel nothing will be gained by staying with him; what he needs is skilled attention. I reach for the bell beside his chair and in a moment a secretary arrives. 'His Excellency seems not well,' I say.

'I will send for Mademoiselle Clotilde. It is not the first time,' says the secretary, and I leave before she appears. I have seen the type — severe, competent, with a hint of playfulness in the presence of foreign gentlemen — and feel no urge to see more. But I'm sure she'll know exactly what to do.

SO BOPPE and Hartwig are both struck off the diplomatic map and I'm alone. The Italian Minister is in league with the Austrians, the German is at arms' length; and who knows where Germany stands, as we all await an Austrian vengeance for which those tragic fools of assassins have offered a pretext served up on a dish, like caviar black as shot?

VII

Every fencer has one or two strokes in which he has confidence. At some period or other of his fighting he has tried them and brought them off successfully. Unfortunately, he has not realized at the time that these strokes were successful, not so much because they were well performed, as by reason of the fact that they happened to be the right strokes to use against the particular form of defence adopted by the adversary.
Fencing with the Foil. Roger Crosnier.

JAMES HARRIS, Tribonian Professor of Roman Law in his old university (with occasional lecturing but no administrative duties) took his son on a tour of the colleges to see which one would suit him best. It wasn't a question of the most brilliant, the smartest, the most sporting; it was an architectural question. Theodore was obsessed by the ideal of mediaeval architecture as sanctified by Ruskin and William Morris. The more modern notions of the Century Guild Hobby Horse were for later, he said; if he was to be an undergraduate at Oxford then the true mediaeval was all that mattered, and James bowed to his wish. So it was on Merton that the accolade fell. The chapel tower, Theodore told James, was the most perfect of all Perpendicular towers in England, built in 1450 and far superior to that of Magdalen dating to 1504. At this time, dates were all important to Theodore and he often easily crushed his father in argument thanks to details still in recent memory. James himself was a fellow of St John's, but the early buildings there were too much altered to be acceptable to Theodore. At Merton he felt no reservations as he surveyed the mediaeval library, the Treasurer's roofscape, the unviolated windows and doorways of Mob Quad. So it was settled.

'This is where I shall come, Papa,' Theo said, allowing himself a momentary, threatening hint of a stammer.

'Of course, if that is what you wish my boy.'

'It is.'

But as it turned out, not for long.

FOR THEO WAS soon bored by Oxford. Thanks to Selzman he was mature for his age, had read and discussed the works of Flaubert, and Stendhal, and more recently Huysmans. *A rebours* had no risky novelty for him even before he came up. He surfed through tutorials on a wave and after the first long vacation, spent improving his Spanish in Madrid, he wrote a bull-fighting story, 'The Stones of Salvador Guerrero,' which was nervously taken by Blackwood's Magazine.

His mother was overjoyed and pressed a copy of Blackwood's on Mr Hardy. 'Theodore has broken into print,' she said.

'First great mistake of the deluded boy's life,' Hardy said gloomily, stuffing the magazine into the pocket of his baggy tweed suit.

After all that excitement, returning to Merton was anteclimax. The fencing school was Theo's recreation and soon became his solace from college life. Fencing demanded just those qualities of swiftness and control that he felt slept in him all day long among a thousand undergraduates who still hadn't started to live. Take the most brilliant of them, a dandy of the name of Beerbohm, Theo's neighbour in Mob Quad. Beerbohm knew how to bring to the social life of the university the qualities Theo brought to the fencing school, but Theo knew almost at once that there were aspects of the life outside that Beerbohm ignored. And it was those waiting aspects which made Theo so impatient that he sometimes asked himself if he was in some way disordered. He decided to consult his father. 'Papa, I have to put an important personal question to you.'

'Are you short of money, Theodore? I warned you to keep accounts. You know that I am not close, but you must discipline yourself if you are to have the control a man should have of . . .'

'No no,' Theo said impatiently. 'Nothing to do with that.' He softened a little. 'But it's thoughtful of you to mention it. This is more theoretical.'

'Ah,' said James who liked theoretical questions of any kind. 'Go on. My knowledge, such as it is, is at your service always.'

Theo smiled at his father, because what he said was true. James had never hesitated to share opinion on all subjects, even the most sensitive.

'I want to know if you think I may have a tendency to place an exaggerated importance on the physical aspects of natural affection, Papa.'

'You mean, I presume, a leaning to lascivity?'

'Yes.'

'Well, I believe I can answer your question,' James said, looking at him fondly. 'My answer is that the importance can hardly be exaggerated, though greater for some men than others, the difference being certainly genetic. I think the Harris family is genetically disposed to be needy in that department. Before my happy marriage to your mother I myself was — '

Theo interrupted him. 'The fact is, Papa, that I find monastic conditions make me very restless, mentally. I mean that I feel *intellectually restricted*. Which I believe you would *not* approve of.'

'Indeed no,' said James. 'It is said, however, that the capacity for postponement is the first sign of maturity. And maturity is a lifelong aim, Theodore, never fully achieved, never lost.'

'And don't you think that one should arrange the conditions of life to fit the maturity one has reached, allowing for what you said?'

'Yes,' James said cautiously, 'I agree with you, in principle.'

'And when you were following your brilliant career at Oxford, Papa, how did you manage the genetic disposition?'

James rose and closed the library door. 'In my day,' he began, 'the university was more tolerant. Those in authority were born in the 18th century or during the Regency at the latest. The ideas of Lord Chesterfield to some extent still obtained. In the town . . . there were young women . . .'

'Are you saying, Papa, that you had girls in your rooms?'

'I believe this happened.'

'To you?'

'That was what I meant to convey, Theodore.'

'And now you are a Fellow for life.'

'We are discussing nature, not tenure.'

It was only when it came to things like dates that Theo could hope to defeat his father in debate; with quibbles over words he always came out on top. No. It was really through emotions that he could be reached, like most people, even Victorian intellectuals. The emotional argument, that was the way to go in dealing with him.

'Well I can tell you that what you admit you did would be absolutely impossible now.'

James laid down his cigar and cleared his throat. 'The century we live in has seen great changes and some of them not for the better,' he said. 'Unnatural restrictions have grown up and I have spent my life combating them.' Theo knew from this that his father was feeling cornered. 'But during your vacations, Theodore . . . your allowance is quite liberal. I don't pry, but in Madrid, or Paris, even London, you have little to hinder you. It may not be something to discuss with your mother but I assure you she understands. You are not held to account.'

Possibly Theo was less mature than he thought; visionary parents find their children looking for new grounds of resentment and this was what happened now between Harris father and son. 'You want me to content myself with prostitutes, Papa,' he accused, the stammer returning so the consonants were shot out like bullets. 'What did Johnson say about Lord Chesterfield? "The manners of a dancing master and the morals of a whore." Not to mention love, or keeping faith.'

'Have you anyone to keep faith with, Theodore, apart from your parents?'

'Yes, Papa, I have.' A long silence followed while both parties thought hard about what they had said and would say. James, indulgent but not used to being crossed, was by now as angry as Theodore. They sat in their armchairs glaring at one another.

Then James, having more to lose and less time left to lose it in, laughed first; 'If so, then naturally I back you and ask no questions. But you are still very young.'

'I want to come down from the university,' Theo said coldly.

'You haven't made some girl — you haven't committed the indiscretion of — ?'

'Ignoring your views on population control? I don't think so. But it could happen, who knows. What I do know is that you ought to think of my unhappiness as I am.'

This was enough. James Harris authorised Theo to leave the university at the end of term, and enrol at the crammers Diptitch Scoones in Garrick Street with a view to entering the Diplomatic Service, for which he seemed well suited, as soon as possible. The girl Theo thought he was keeping faith with was soon forgotten, or replaced by another, while at Diptitch Scoones he gained access through a friendly tutor, short of cash, to the text of lectures for diplomatic candidates, copied them out in the shorthand method which he had mastered while idling at Merton, retired to Orchard Harris with his notes and successfully entered the examination four months later. Admittedly Haldane put in a good word for him, but his interesting delivery, so poised, so timed, made an excellent impression at the interview with Lord Lansdowne who was subject to a speech defect which no Selzman had ever come to grips with. 'This young man should be useful to the Service,' Lord Lansdowne noted, and no one contradicted him.

So in 1894 Theo entered the Foreign Office doors as an unpaid attaché, and in 1896 he went as third secretary to Madrid. He always felt that his father had stood by him in difficult emotional times, and although occasional requests for extra subsidy were frostily received he thought of James as having shown himself very decent in that respect too. When his father died in 1913 Theo was bereft. He was first secretary in Tokyo at the time, and grieved for several weeks, looking out on the cherry blossom of the Ambassador's garden.

The outrage was planned in Belgrade; the murderers were trained in their handiwork in Belgrade; they were provided with money and instruments of destruction in Belgrade; Belgrade and all Servia are the home of an idea which ever aims at the destruction of our Monarchy and consecrates its most adept pupils as national heroes.

Budapest, 'Pester Lloyd,' July 17, 1914: 'From the Servian Witches' Kitchen.'

HERMANN TENDS the geraniums on the Legation terrace and this summer, one by one, the plants are dying off, flowers bled dry, while across the Danube you can descry the movement of uniforms at nightfall, a shifting of grey against grey, multiplying in the dark.

Xenia has come on to the terrace looking for me. 'I am going out,' she says.

'Yes?'

'There are things I must buy.'

'Are there? More water melons?'

She approaches. 'You don't like me to go out any more from the Legation?'

'I need to know what you're doing, Xenia. You're safe inside the Legation. Outside no one is safe.'

'I know.'

'Are you going out to buy things for your brother?'

'Perhaps.'

'Medical supplies?'

'Several things, Mr Harris.'

'Shall I come out with you? I'd like to.'

Xenia lays her hands flat on my shirt front so the elbows rest at about the level of the solar plexus. 'I don't want you to come with me to carry parcels. You have work.' Is truth, in her mind, stretched across several dimensions and to be read accordingly? Especially the sexual dimension? Or is the mystery deeper?

'I didn't mean to carry parcels, only flowers perhaps.'

'I forgot — an English diplomat never carries parcels, Oliver explained this,' Xenia says, laughing as she goes out.

MILAN'S CONDITION has deteriorated and there's a sickroom smell of disinfectant and bandages and lingering excrement. I know that home nursing in the Legation is not enough for Milan's case and he needs a doctor. I go to the bedroom window and draw back the curtain so the July sunlight pours into the room, and after a hard look at the man on the bed I close the curtain again. He has no blanket on him, presumably because of the midday heat, his face is haggard and unshaven, eyes blacker than ever against skin as white as his sheets. Xenia says he's eighteen years old but he looks like a man of thirty in a bad state.

'Should we not bring you a doctor?' I ask slowly in German. 'The Legation has an excellent doctor on call. I think you should allow one to see you. What do you say?'

He says nothing. Faintly from beyond the closed window the noises of the town, hoofbeats on wooden cobbles, occasionally a motor car, raised voices, a woman singing, come into this darkened silent room. Apprehension of pain comes in waves distinct as sounds from the still figure on the bed. There is a stain on the upper sheet, to one side, which may be blood, may be anything. Perhaps that smell which seems to grow the longer I stay in the room is the smell of pain itself.

'Will you let me send for the doctor?'

'Xenia — is all the doctor I need.'

'Are you wounded?'

'My lung is sick. Next week will be better.'

'Are you sure?'

'I am sick like my country.'

'Are you in much pain?'

Milan shakes his head slowly like an ox teased by flies. 'It is nothing,' he says.

Returning to the study and its broad, sleeping windows, I wish more than ever that Hartwig was still here. He would have known how to deal with sick or injured hostages. Russian Embassies and Legations all over the world have for long hidden the living or dying remains of agents, traitors, *provocateurs*. Milan would have been child's play to Hartwig; but Hartwig has struck camp and stolen away.

IT SEEMS THAT the women behind recent protests have blown up the Coronation Chair in Westminster Abbey. They say it's the symbol of masculine oppression, the seat of dominance, they claim it stands for all that won't do. The explosion was a small one, more noisy than destructive, and historically illogical since Mary, Elizabeth, Anne, Victoria were all anointed with their behinds resting on this angular piece of furniture.

But in international terms it's deplorable because foreign powers will take the Liberal government for an impotent old pensioner incapable of standing up for itself or anything else. Let's hope the guilty women are soon caught so one can claim that Liberalism is not the end of civilisation. But what if they're not caught soon, what if they continue their explosions, their revolver shots like the assassins of Sarajevo? Will we be reduced to executing them too?

Perhaps because of the incident in the Abbey I've received no instructions at all. Sir Edward Grey has nothing to say to the Servian government. He will brief the new Minister Des Graz but I don't believe this new Minister will reach here before the balloons go up, as Hartwig put it; in this diplomatic hiatus I'd better request an interview with the Prime Minister to reassure him of London's concern for the fate of his little country.

It turns out that Pašić doesn't wish to receive me, and I know what this means. The new Russian Minister will soon be here and until he is, Pašić won't know what support he can count on, and has no idea what to say to anyone else. I don't suppose Boppe has seen him either — wherever we are, in whichever capital, we're all in the dark but everything is expected of us; the history books are waiting, blank and open.

I go down to the archives to see Oliver.

'Hallo, Theo.' The sound of the voice with a hint of laughter behind it is comforting, in a way.

'Hallo, Oliver.'

'At a loose end?'

'Too busy to be at a loose end,' I say, and now he does laugh.

'What are you going to do?'

'I am going to see the Foreign Secretary Grujić tomorrow and the Prime Minister as soon as he'll receive me, and I shall urge caution.'

'Yes,' Oliver says seriously, 'that sounds prudent.'

'It's no joke, it's a historic crisis.'

'Ireland has lived in historic crisis for centuries.'

As soon as he mentions Ireland I know there's nothing more to be got out of him. I wonder if all over Europe men are hiding fear in conversations as trivial as this? Oliver and I, with a clear view of the gunboats swinging lazily on the Danube stream, may feel even more fear than Sir Edward Grey, and M. Poincaré, and Prince Lichnowsky the peace-loving German Ambassador in London as they go through their telegrams. If we were military men we might find the ballistics involved in firing ordnance from the water too engrossing to leave room for fear but we are diplomatists, the swords we wear with our uniform are polished toys.

'What for God's sake is going to happen ?'

I take the question literally. 'We both know the archive's a fetish for the Foreign Office, and we'll have to move it somewhere as soon as the Austrian artillery begins to bombard, or sooner if we get wind of it.' I hear Hermann's heavy step on the stair, he reaches the bottom step, straightens up and marches forward, soles slapping the floorboards.

'Yes, Hermann?'

'His Highness Prince George is in the drawing room, *Exzellenz.*'

'Good heavens. He arrived unannounced?'

'What do you expect?'

'I will come at once. Did you offer the prince something to drink?'

'No,' says Hermann. 'He is only a Servian so-called prince, not someone to fill up with whisky. He should be offered tea.'

'You had better come too, Oliver. The prince will tell us the news.'

'Of the Riviera?'

Not insensitive to Oliver's feelings, I turn back to him. 'News of the palace — King Peter's reactions to the crisis — the army.'

'I'd rather stay down here.'

'All right, but we need our wits about us.'

'Do you really think the governments of Europe wait on our wits, Theo?'

I mount the stairs three at a time, Hermann pounding the flagstones after me. 'Highness, If you had thought to telephone I would have received you at the door.'

Prince George's arms open wide and he kisses me on both cheeks. 'Theo!' he shouts, as though I might have forgotten my own name, 'there is no time left in Servia for telephone calls and politeness. The Austrian knife is at our throat! The enemy is at — '

I look round for Hermann and see him marching towards us with a tray of glasses and bottles and a ferocious expression on his old face. 'Put the tray on the table,' I order him. 'I will serve his Highness myself.' It seems a sensible precaution. I offer the prince a glass of whisky to remind him of happier days at Sandhurst; he accepts it, drains the whisky and holds out the glass at arm's length for more.

'We will slaughter the swine. You have seen them, gathering like maggots over the Danube? We will crush these maggots in their carrion! Your butler, Theo, is he an Austrian spy?'

Will more whisky calm him? Probably not. These days almost everyone is a spy for someone and servants in Embassies and Legations have always spied. It's the new agent, the unrecognised, who may be valuable — Pósha, for example, would only learn what is thought useless to the Russians, but anything he learned might be very useful to me.

'I trust you found all in order at Topčider, Highness?'

The prince laughs in a hearty manner, fearing I am about to ask for a refund of rent. 'Of course, of course,' he says. 'But I have no time for such details. My country needs me too much. My father is too old, my brother too young. But I have returned.'

I know George is no fool; his eyes flash dangerously but I see the fear in them, as in the eyes of every man and woman in the street. 'What is the feeling of His Majesty about the present situation?' I ask. The poor old man is probably terrified as any peasant on his patch of earth.

'My dear father has surrounded himself with priests and he is praying for Servia and our house.'

'And for his government, I hope?'

'His government, the King leaves to me.'

'If I may say, Highness, very great circumspection is what the Servian government is going to need.'

'You have said it, Theo, and I respect your advice,' the prince says, brushing it aside. He passes his free hand over the golden buttons of his uniform. 'But above all, we must be men and prepare ourselves for the attack. I will have another glass of your whisky.'

'Have you yet seen the Prime Minister?'

'Pašić has not been a friend in trouble to me,' the prince admits sombrely, as if this failure on the part of Pašić was about to come home to roost and the Prime Minister would have only himself to blame, 'but I have seen Grujić.'

'And how do you assess the Secretary General's opinion and feeling as regards the menace hanging over Servia?'

'You mean does he think the same as me?'

That isn't actually what I meant but maybe it's the best that can be hoped for. 'Naturally.'

'Well, he doesn't.' Without warning, the prince subsides into depression. His eye is dull, his voice hollow. 'These politicians, they are the sons of shopkeepers. At least my grandfather's father was a man who dug the earth and tended his pigs and killed his enemies. I think you understand this Theo. You are not a bourgeois like Grujić or Boppe or an intellectual like Pašić but a peasant really like my father the King, and me.' Tears come into his eyes as he sinks his third tumbler of whisky. 'You drink nothing but you are of the soil.'

I suppose it's a compliment. The long ago Harris, sower and pig minder, now equals Karadjordjević the grandfather of the king. My mother might approve the idea but she's beyond such fancies these days, her mind wandering with my father's spirit.

Back on earth the echo of guns may soon sound and history will want to know what one did to prevent it. The last days of peace will seem like those moments before sleep when the unconscious warns you that your dreams will be terrible and you fight to stay awake. 'The heat of these days is hard to bear. On the Riviera you had cool breezes off the sea?'

'All this is forgotten,' the prince shouts. 'Olive groves, casinos, nightingales — many, many of us will never know these joys again.' He weeps, mopping his eyes with a silk handkerchief and overlooking the fact that extremely few Serbs have ever known them at all. Nightingales, yes, they sing inexhaustibly in the woods of Topčider.

'May I ask, if the Secretary General's view doesn't coincide with your own, what you believe his view is?'

'He thinks what all these yellow-livered shopkeepers think, that we can only wait. Vienna decides, we wait like women at the street corner. When I say attack at once, remember glorious 1913! the Secretary General crawls into his shop and pulls down the blind as if his blind would stop the shells.'

I can see that for a Karadjordjević, politician's prudence seems effeminate. The last of the Obrenović, stripped and defenestrated in 1903, had been thought prudent by the international community and King Peter Karadjordjević was not at first taken into the charmed circle of crowned heads. Now he is. If you think about it, the European royal houses are open to recruitment from all classes but I fear that for many of them their day is nearly done. The gunboats on the Danube are only the beginning.

'Perhaps you would like news of your wife, Theo?'

'She writes me quite regular letters.'

'I had the pleasure to escort her on one or two occasions in Cannes recently. My news may be fresher than the post brings you.'

'I have no doubt.'

'She is resplendent, she reigns on the Riviera. There is no one to touch her. There are women more fashionable, richer, there are archduchesses, but for beauty, Madame Harris is queen.'

'The ice queen.' I regret it as soon as said.

'Ice yields to the sun.'

I see the prince out of the door and watch him clanking with sword and boots down the steps of the Legation and out on to the cobbles. There is no car or carriage waiting for him, he is a disinherited prince; a nonentity, waiting to die for his country.

VIII

Belgrade, July 18, 1914. 11 a.m.
I gather from Austrian Minister that he is not personally in favour of pressing Servia too hard, and he does not view the situation in a pessimistic light.

Minister's leniency and optimism may result from his belief that the Servian Government is in too weak a position to resist.
Harris to Grey.

Foreign Office, July 20, 1914
I asked the German Ambassador to-day if he had any views of what was going on in Vienna with regard to Servia.

He said that he regarded the situation as very uncomfortable.

I said that the more Austria could keep her demand within reasonable limits, the more chance there would be of smoothing things over. I hated the idea of a war between any of the Great Powers, and that any of them should be dragged into a war by Servia would be detestable.

The Ambassador agreed wholeheartedly.
Grey to Rumbold.
Repeated to Belgrade.

GIESL VON GIESLINGEN caught me on the steps of the French Legation where I'd gone to ask after Boppe. I wasn't taken in by Giesl's declaration of leniency towards the Serbs; what he wanted was to pump me about Prince George.

'I believe the prince has returned from his Mediterranean cure,' he said, 'and I was hoping to hear from you that he is now in the best of health?'

'He seems well.'

'Before he left he appeared febrile — we know what febrility makes him capable of — so I wondered if calm had returned?'

'The situation of his country hardly induces to calm at the moment.'

'That was what I feared,' Giesl said.

'I think you might be advised to give the prince quite a wide berth.'

'A wide berth?'

'Keep out of his way.'

'Yes, I had thought of that also,' Giesl admitted, thinking nervously of it now. 'Would you consider that the prince's opinions are lent much weight by the Servian Government in the light of his personal history?'

'Do you mean, will he whip them up?'

'Yes.'

'I believe the prince's first concern is for his father.'

'Ah. That's good. A good son. But a dangerous adviser.'

We leave it there. Perhaps I should send a despatch putting the Austrian Minister's remarks more in context, but my connection with Prince George is not for Foreign Office eyes. Someone in those gloomy rooms overlooking St James's Park might mark my despatch with the damning words, 'wanting in detachment,' and they would figure for ever after on my record and even Lord Haldane (as he has recently become) couldn't get them erased.

Foreign Office, July 22, 1914

It is possible that Servian Government have been negligent, and that proceedings at the trial at Serajevo will show that the murder of the Archduke was planned on Servian territory. I hope every attempt will be made to prevent any breach of the peace. It would be very desirable that Austria and Russia should discuss things together if they become difficult.

I have instructed Chargé d'affaires to urge caution on Servian Government, while avoiding any appearance of too great an interest on our part. We need not involve ourselves in others' quarrels.

Grey to Sir George Buchanan, Ambassador, St. Petersburg..
Repeated to Belgrade.

BREACH OF THE PEACE — things becoming difficult. The Foreign Secretary sounds like a village constable while the investigation at Serajevo yields such answers, betrayals, lies, as great pain can force from the helpless. Only the luckiest will hang.

I call through the open communicating door for Xenia.

'I am coming Mr Harris.'

And there she is, smiling, Slav, solid. I hold out a hand. 'Those young men in Serajevo — I'm afraid they're being tortured.'

'We can't help them,' she says.

'But I think about it.'

'You must not. It does no good.'

'Perhaps at this moment — '

She pulls her hand away. 'You only make sick pictures in your head . Some prisoner tortured — it's bad but we are here, not there.'

'And if it was Milan in that prison?'

'It is the same.' I don't believe her.

'But it could be?'

'How? Milan is sick with his lung'

Later I ask her to telephone the Servian Foreign Ministry for an interview with the Secretary General, Grujić. 'Please tell me when you are speaking to the responsible person.'

'And here in the British Legation we are how many, responsible people?'

'Two. Me and Oliver.'

'At the Foreign Ministry perhaps a hundred.'

'You are giving way to extravagance as you say I do to imagination.'

'Then we must both learn,' Xenia says, and this gives me great comfort, though I don't know why.

GRUJIĆ IS an old man, and that must be taken into account. Old men's anger, when roused, is more dangerous because they have less to lose. He was Prime Minister in 1904; earlier in life he was a soldier and became a General, and no one can say that a Servian General has never seen blood spilt. One look at Grujić is enough to convince you that he personally has spilt plenty. Hidden in his beard, his long yellowing teeth like those of an ancient crocodile shoot in and out when he opens his mouth. Now he is Secretary General of the Foreign Ministry and after Pašić, the most powerful figure in the government, like Sir Edward Grey after Asquith. But Grey and Grujić would not, I feel, mix well. An angler wouldn't take to a crocodile.

'Ha!' Grujić exclaims as I enter his office, 'Mr Harris!' For some reason he laughs. 'Tell me what are your government's intentions, please. We all wait to hear — Servia, Russia, Austria, Germany, even France. And no one knows.'

'For the present moment, General, His Majesty's Government are exercising patience.' Perhaps patience wasn't a very well chosen word — 'they are inclined to wait a little longer on events and developments.'

'Patience! The gentlemen in Westminster sit in their striped trousers on their leather armchairs while the foundations tremble!'

'They are not the cause.'

'You wish to see us crushed — '

'On the contrary, General, we hope to see the quarrel settled without bloodshed.'

'Bloodshed — ' With a wave of his hand the former General expresses his contempt for detail. 'Mr Harris, I apologise, I should offer you first something to drink, then after a few toasts we would speak more calmly.' That's another side to an old man's anger, it quickly subsides. He rings an electric bell on his desk. 'You are right. We must all be patient.' We remain standing, Grujić swaying slightly with knees bent, and wait for ages for the manservant to arrive; then there is an outbreak of shouting and banging from the ante-room. The door bursts open and Prince George bursts in.

'Sava! General! My dear friend and beloved companion of arms!' The prince is in the excited phase of his cycle.

Grujić attempts to click his heels together but his knees prove too shaky; he takes the prince's hand and steadies himself on it, then bows low. I recall that Grujić was the chief advocate of Prince George's destitution, urging that Servia stood in need of respectability; the demise of King Alexander and Queen Draga and all the sordid details being still fresh in the international memory. The crown of Servia, Grujić argued, could not afford to be associated with another royal scandal.

'And Theo too!' The greeting seems less ecstatic, but I'm a civilian. Still, I believe the prince is fond of me in his way, if with a dose of guilt.

The windows are wide open and street sounds blow in with the hot air, with the dust and flies and that odour all-pervasive in Servian towns of inadequate sewage systems which no Serb ever notices. On the General's desk is a wide silver bowl of roses in full bloom whose scent mixes on the air with that of the sewage. 'To our hopes for a hundred years of peace!' I say raising my glass.

'Mr Harris,' Grujić begins. 'We think your government is being like a woman who will not say no, or yes, but will not say anything at all, yes or no, perhaps, tomorrow —'

'Britannia is the greatest lady cock-tease in the world,' the prince says in English in his high voice.

'You do His Majesty's Government an injustice.' I stop. The General is, on the contrary, doing the government no injustice at all. He is being as patient with it as they say they are with him, and more so. 'I have instructions allowing me to advise you of my Government's views.'

'Ah,' the General says. He holds his glass of plum brandy up in front of him as if studying the effect of light through the purple-red liquid. 'Tell us, Mr Harris.'

'Sir Edward Grey is of opinion that if things become difficult, the governments of Austria and Russia should enter into direct discussions. We, here, although in a sense at the centre of events, should remain quiet.'

'Quiet?' says the prince.

'Sir Edward recommends it.'

'And what is your recommendation, personally, to the government of our country?' Grujić demands to know.

'I have to recommend the greatest caution.'

'Caution?'

'Prudence.'

'Prudence?' The General may never have heard the word before. On the other hand, this seems to be dragging on and usually when that happens it means that the other is trying to trap you. He thinks that by ironically repeating your last word he will surprise from you what you hope to conceal. What do I hope to conceal? Certainly not any secret intentions of the British Government who, it seems to me, are behaving like a clutch of hens when a fox comes sniffing around. They have no secret intentions, they are frightened out of their wits. Europe wants assurances from them? From our Liberals who have inherited the earth and its powers? Smooth things over, clear things up, is the sum of Sir Edward Grey's wisdom for a world on the brink of war.

'Shall we say that we should all be careful to lie low until at least the Austrian Government issue their notice?'

'You propose to lie low, Mr Harris?'

'I think it best.'

'In your Legation?'

I catch a glance between the prince and the Minister. 'I have returned to the Legation in Belgrade from summer quarters at Topčider where his Highness — '

'I know all about that,' Grujić interrupts. 'I mean is it your intention to pursue — ' he pauses a moment and wipes his eyes — 'Sir Edward Grey's counsels of precaution here in the town? Naturally in a time of crisis I need to know.'

'I think my duty requires it,' I say, and the prince and Grujić break out into that kind of laughter which tells you that you have added to the great stock of English absurdities an irresistibly amusing instance.

'Mr Harris, you are an example of lying low that I would dream of.' The General rocks from side to side as if mirth, like loose ballast, threatens his stability. 'You preach caution to us but we think you are being most incautious — very incautious indeed — with your stenographer Xenia Ciganović.' All of a sudden the General is serious, his crocodile teeth have retreated into hiding, his eyes are hard as bullets. 'And with her associates.'

SERVIA IS FULL of spies and I think Prince George is not the friend I took him for. He has leaked my private affairs though I counted on him to keep quiet because of his own, which concern me, after all. The prince is, let's face it, a blackguard. On my walk back to the Legation I pass the cafés which it would now be unwise for me to enter, the Green Crown, the Golden Sturgeon, cafés where friends or members of the Narodna Odbrana gather; and the girls on flower stalls, and the peasants come in from the country to sell cheeses or wine from their holdings. Fear hangs in the air like dust. I stride past them all resolutely, looking neither to left nor right. At the end of the street, high up beside the rock of Kalemegdan, the Legation looks out over the Save and the Danube while its rear windows, smaller than those that face the terrace and the Dual Monarchy, peer inward onto the guilty town.

Minute
It is difficult to understand the attitude of the German Government. On the face of it, it does not bear the stamp of straightforwardness. They are in the best position to speak at Vienna. All they are doing is to inflame the passions at Belgrade and it looks very much like egging on the Austrians when they openly and persistently threaten the Servian Government through their official newspapers.

It may be presumed that the German Government do not believe that there is any real danger of war and so are flirting with it.

Sir Eyre Crowe, Assistant Under-Secretary, Foreign Office, July 22.

'THERE IS A person who says he is here to look at your motor-car, *Exzellenz.*'

'Where is he?'

'He is with the motor-car in the stable-yard.' When this Legation was built the Minister kept horses and a carriage to convey him to the other Legations and the Foreign Ministry, and the Palace, and the races at Topčider.

'I will go down.'

'He could be ordered to wait for you beside the entrance, in the street.'

'I need to consult him about the engine. It's more convenient in the stable-yard.'

'Very well, *Exzellenz.*'

'I don't want any interruptions. The engine of a motor-car is a very delicate instrument.'

Hermann bows, looking suspicious. Well let him. I know what will happen one day soon — Hermann will go without a word. A Legation butler is always in the pay of someone or other but I believe the end of that world may be drawing near. The servants of Europe today will be the independent workers of tomorrow — at least those who come through whatever is on the way for all of us. Pósha is waiting in the stable-yard and his ignorance of the internal combustion engine will soon be obvious to Hermann, spying through his pantry window, and even to Xenia whose little office also looks out over the yard, seeing Pósha gaze at the gleaming paintwork and polished leather of the Supreme Silent Sunbeam. 'I will open the bonnet, you will look inside, and then after a word or two we will go out for a drive,' I tell him in a low voice.

'Very well, your Excellency,' he says.

I open the bonnet and we both lean in over the engine. 'It is a 16 horse-power four cylinder Sunbeam engine, 80 mm bore, 150 mm stroke, cylinder cast *en bloc.* You have something to tell me?'

'We have made no arrangement,' Pósha answers.

Something tells me that he is in trouble at the Russian Legation or more probably has already left it. He is both crestfallen and defiant. 'Get in after me.'

We issue cautiously from the Legation yard, held up every few paces by mule-drawn carts, or pedestrians still living in the pre-motor age, wandering all over the place. But I don't blow the horn because I am an envoy on mission, in a sense. We advance at a snail's pace through the crowded streets.

'His Excellency would have ordered his driver to run some of these peasants down,' Pósha says.

'Perhaps. But I doubt it.' Death creates a certain equality among survivors. Pósha and I can speak of Hartwig from such different points of view as if the three of us were brothers. 'He was humane, for a Russian.'

'What you call humane,' Pósha says, 'for a Russian of Monsieur Hartwig's rank is the same as gilt on an iron lamp. You rub it hard and you see the iron back in your hand.'

Well, Pósha knew Hartwig better than I did. But we aren't sailing over the heads of the crowd, rumbling along on the wooden cobbles in the direction of the open country, in order to talk about Hartwig and his relations with Pósha. I take a sideways look at him as he leans forward and watches the road rock and skim past us as we gather speed. He looks hungry, to me. 'You need some money?'

'I need food.'

'You're no longer in the Legation?'

'I ran away when the new Minister was announced.'

'Why?'

'He was an enemy of M. Hartwig.'

'So where are you sleeping?'

'Anywhere,' Pósha says. 'I don't sleep, I am too hungry.'

Poor fellow — in Hartwig's day he lived off the fat of the land, vast unfinished dishes and half-empty bottles passed through his hands several times a day and at night he wrapped up warm on sheepskin or cool in silk from Tashkent or somewhere, and looked forward to the coming day in all the security of the man who prepares clothing for the master to cover his nakedness. 'You could have come to see me sooner.'

'I was afraid they follow me.'

'Who?'

'The new Minister's secretaries.'

'And today?'

'They have all gone to Novi Sad in the train to meet his Excellency Monsieur Schebeko and Prince Koudachev.'

'From the Embassy in Vienna?'

'Yes.'

'I wonder why an Ambassador has come all that way to meet a Minister?'

'Monsieur Schebeko is going to the Black Sea for his holidays. Novi Sad is on the way.'

So Ambassadors go to the seaside while Europe waits. 'Do you know why they're meeting?'

'The new Minister brings secret orders for the Ambassador. Too secret for the telegraph.'

Pósha seems to know quite a lot of what's going on in the Russian Legation, even if he's wandering the streets and starving. He must still have an informant within doors. 'Do you know anything about these secret orders?'

He doesn't answer. We are approaching the downs of Topčider, there's no one about, the countryside sleeps, the trees give a deep inviting shade. I stop and get out to stretch my legs. If Pósha is hungry he will answer in good time. Everywhere the grass is brown and worn through as if dead, even the oak leaves are curled up in the long blazing drought. The sky is bare, white with heat, motionless, as peaceful as an African sky might be had the greed and rivalries of Europe never existed. Pósha is standing a little behind me; I turn to look and see tears in his eyes. 'I don't know any more,' he says, and I understand. He thinks I may pay him nothing for so little information, his patron has gone and he is hungry, terribly hungry.

I touch him on the arm. 'Don't worry Pósha, I think you will be very useful to me and here's some money to keep you going for a week or so, but stay in a village outside Belgrade where no one knows you. You speak some Serbo-Croat?'

'Oh yes.'

'Buy a mule and come into the town as if you were selling fruit or flowers.' I look at him again. He hasn't shaved for a few days and his beard is red. 'Let it grow,' I say pointing at it, 'but blacken it with something and always wear a hat. Have you got a hat?'

'Only for winter.'

'Well wait, I think this will do.' In the car is an old Panama of mine, so dilapidated that any Servian peasant could wear it on his way to market. 'Where have you left your belongings?'

'In a sack at your Legation, Excellency.'

That, for a newly recruited spy, was an error. Let's hope Hermann hasn't confiscated it. 'Get back in the car. We'll find you a room in a village. Don't come to the Legation any more, it's certainly watched. I'll come to you and tell you what I want you to do. Do you know how to blacken your beard?'

'I will use the stain of walnuts, Excellency. It is what my mother does for her white hairs.'

I'm not sure how useful a spy Pósha is really going to be; he was at the height of his powers while Hartwig was alive but left to himself he's an amateur, and perhaps a child. I take the road to Niš and after the first village stop in the lee of a wood. I give Pósha all the change I have in my pocket and a couple of notes, enough to keep him for a week if he's careful. 'Don't show the notes at first, just coins. And don't talk more than you have to. You can change one of the notes buying the mule.'

'What do you want me to do then?'

'Go into some of the cafés in Green Crown Square and keep your ears open. The Golden Sturgeon, the America, the Acorn Crown. But wait for the beard to grow a bit. Be patient. I want to know anything you can learn about Milan Ciganović, a student. The Acorn Crown is always full of students. Listen first to what they're saying about Princip, then gradually get round to Ciganović.'

'Trust me, Excellency.'

'When you have something to tell me, telephone the Legation and say the spare part for the Sunbeam has arrived. I will meet you at Topčider under those big trees. Will you find the place?'

'I think so,' Pósha says, and I can only hope he's right. 'Excuse me, Excellency, but I don't think the money you've given me will let me be patient for very long.'

I've let myself in for this, and hand over another note.

THE RUSSIAN MINISTER, Strandtman, has invited himself to the British Legation to put whatever pressure on me his new instructions order him to put. He is one of those Russians of German extraction who rise to power in the Petersburg bureaucracy, in medicine, in the University. After a few generations they are more Russian than German but something remains — in his case it is an exterior polished as an iceberg, behind which you can sense a nervous terror of independence. He was all right when he was getting his orders in St Petersburg but here he's on his own.

'Very honoured by your visit, Monsieur Strandtman.'

'I too am very honoured to know you, Mr Harris.'

We consider one another uncomfortably, with polite smiles. 'Do you care for a whisky, Minister?'

'Ah! A whisky! I have been once to Scotland myself.' This is always said as if the memory left in the mind of the Continental diplomat must be matched by an impression, equally indelible, made by his visit on the Scottish mind. This assumption is especially noticeable with the French. Hermann shuffles forward with the decanter of Glenmorangie and the seltzer water. 'Enough!' It seems to me that the new Russian Minister is in a nervous state bordering on panic, or is it just that the best informed are the most alarmed? I'm not one of those, so I wait for the whisky to take effect and for Strandtman to expose what he has in his instructions.

Vienna, July 23, 1914

Prince Koudachev is instructed to concert with French Ambassador and myself to warn Austro-Hungarian Government against sending in a note to Servian Government in terms which latter could not accept.

Under-Secretary of State, Count Forgach, told me that the note to be presented at Belgrade was a stiff one; he hoped, but hardly seemed to expect, that Servian Government would yield to peremptory demands which it contained.

I fear that serious crisis may now be at hand.
de Bunsen to Grey.

I CAN WELL imagine that Strandtman and Hartwig were enemies. What Hartwig despised was a man who couldn't let his weakness show, and it was for this sincerity that I was so fond of him, but I'd better keep quiet about it with Strandtman. 'Have you any indication of when the Austro-Hungarian note will be delivered, Minister?' I ask, to break the silence. I know, of course, that he hasn't because no one has. The Ballplatz are playing on the world's nerves.

Strandtman doesn't answer the question directly. 'You realise, Harris, that the Austrian Empire holds a theory according to which Servia cannot exist by itself. It must be under Turkish or Austrian rule, one or the other.' This sounds like a lecture and shows the new Minister's inexperience. 'Nearly every nation in the heart of Europe has won its freedom by a struggle against Austria — Germany, Greece, Italy, the Netherlands. This is perhaps the last struggle; but for so small a prize the stakes are so much deadlier.'

'They certainly are — high explosive shells against unprotected cities — the Austrians have a giant howitzer called *Schlanke Emma* — '

'Never mind cities, do you realise that the Russian army, when fully mobilised, will number *three million* men ready to swarm over frontiers? Not well trained perhaps, but drilled to savage obedience?'

'Come, hardly savages — '

'You have seen St. Petersburg and perhaps a few Russian country houses near Moscow, you have read Turgenev and Tolstoy who write about the landowning class, not the brute humanity with bayonets in their hands.'

'They describe them.'

'From above.'

I see what Strandtman most fears; the horde terrifies him, the horde that war will let loose from the soil only for it to turn back one day and finish the good work at home. He trembles for his kind more than for himself, I see his vision and feel a certain sympathy.

'Perhaps it would be right for us to concert our view of the crisis?' I suggest.

'We must urge the Servian Government to yield to the Austrian demands when they are made known.'

'I think that's done. I had an interview with Grujić, not wholly satisfactory, but I know your predecessor, too — '

'Hartwig was a thorn in the side of the Foreign Ministry where I was personally in charge of the Balkan Section.'

'You think the Servian Government must accept whatever is required and you will tell them so?'

As I foresaw, there's a hesitation. This is the only question left in Europe — not the relative size of the British and German Navies, not Alsace-Lorraine, Dublin, the Baghdad Railway — just the dying throes of the Holy Roman Empire. 'I think they must attach few conditions to their reply.'

'Russia will stand behind them?'

'The panSlav notion is no longer so well viewed in St. Petersburg, but the Servian Government will be assured of our support, within reason.'

'And the three million men?'

'Let us think of them ploughing in their villages on the Steppe.' Strandtman shudders. 'Otherwise, the abattoir, the slaughterhouse. And the British Government alone,' he adds after a heavy pause, 'can keep them there. The railway lines will reach the frontiers tomorrow, the day after tomorrow. The brute of the Steppe can be brought into the heart of Europe in a matter of hours. Your reluctant Parliament will put out no burning cities.'

Luckily there's a knock on the door which then swings gently open. Xenia in her cotton dress is framed in the rectangle of strong light from behind her. 'There are races again at Topčider today,' she says. She turns to Strandtman. 'Will his Excellency come with us?'

'Will you, Strandtman? We would be pleased.'

Strandtman makes a rapid mental adjustment; at first he'd taken this girl for a clerical worker, now she's suddenly the Legation hostess. 'I would be pleased — ' he says gamely.

'Then Hermann will put a basket and some champagne with ice in a bucket and we will have our lunch in the shade of the trees and watch the races all afternoon.'

Strandtman, for the moment, looks too beguiled to worry about nerves. 'I should first telephone my Legation,' he says, his eyes fixed on the shifting folds of Xenia's dress as she leaves.

'Tell them peace and war can wait for the races. Tolstoy would say the same.'

'He might, Harris,' Strandtman agrees, 'which is why he wept in his old age. But just for today the races will be enough for us all.'

'Hermann!' I call.

'Exzellenz?' He must have been just behind the door.

'Please tell Mr Dillon that we're making a party to the races at Topčider. We leave in twenty minutes.'

'The *Herr* archivist is to accompany you?'

'Of course.'

'A person telephoned, *Exzellenz,* saying he has procured some mechanical part for your motor-car.'

'Yes, very well, Hermann.' This means that Pósha will be waiting under the very trees where Xenia plans to lay out our picnic. He and the Russian Minister will be in the same patch of shade. 'No. Tell the mechanic I can't see him today.'

'He didn't wait to hear if you would see him. He spoke with a foreign accent and replaced his instrument like all those Servian swine who make insults at a safe distance.'

'Go and give my message to Mr Dillon.'

'Very well.'

'Your butler seems like one of those who infest Russian country houses and abuse their freedom,' says the Russian Minister.

'Butlers are not easy to live with. One can only really be comfortable in a house with women.'

'I don't think your militant suffragettes in London would like to hear you say this, Harris.'

'The lady who blew up the Coronation Chair in Westminster Abbey was making a protest on behalf of women servants, you think?'

Strandtman and I are laughing together when Xenia returns. 'Oliver is changing into his Irish horse races suit,' she says, looking at us suspiciously.

'SO WHERE does one place one's bets?' Strandtman asks, viewing the crowds and dust and disorganisation of the Topčider gathering in the heat of the afternoon sun, the white of the women's dresses, the horses and riders running all over the place, chased after by boys, watched by girls with fearful longing.

'There's no betting at Servian races,' I tell him.

'The fools do it for the joy of the thing,' Oliver says.

'Of course,' Strandtman says, 'the joy of our Slav peoples.' He sounds quite depressed all of a sudden so I signal to Oliver to open the picnic hamper. I can see Pósha leading a mule along the irregular line of trees connecting the track to this grove of ours, Xenia is looking that way too, curious about what attracts my attention. I'm familiar with this — for Kitty it was always a woman I must have my eye fixed on in the middle distance.

I sit on the grass before the hamper and pour wine for everyone. 'To peace!' I say loudly, raising my glass.

'To peace!' they agree.

'I won't be a moment. Oliver, I leave you in charge.' I walk quickly in the direction where Pósha disappeared, then dodge into a clump of hawthorn bushes and wait. I neither see nor hear him arrive but there he suddenly is. Pósha is warming to the work.

'Well?'

'I have passed two nights, all night, in those cafés.' The flesh around his eyes is haggard and the beard of a fortnight's growth is gingery black as if he'd been in the rain and the walnut had run.

'Yes?'

'I have learned a lot.'

Clearly, he won't share what he's learned until he feels sure of continuing support. Well, any other spy would do the same. I put my hand into the inside breast pocket of my jacket, and leave it there. 'Go on,' I say.

'The mule was expensive and it too must eat.' I wait for him to go on. 'They talk and talk in those cafés, Excellency, all night long, and drink and make plots, and weep for the boys in the Austrian prison.'

'I can believe it.'

'Princip is consumptive, he won't last long, they say his arm is rotten with gangrene already in that stone pit.'

I see this may go into details I don't need to know about, however pitiful, and there isn't much time. A call of nature has a reasonable duration. 'Tell me if you learned anything about Ciganović. Be quick.'

'I had to listen and not ask many questions. But in the end when they get drunk enough on their firewater it doesn't matter any more. Ciganović works on the railway. He is a clerk.'

'In Belgrade station?'

'No one knows where he is now, but he was somewhere on the frontier.'

'Which frontier?' The information drops from him bit by bit but Pósha can't be hurried, he's tired, he may be ill.

'The frontier with Bosnia.'

The Austro-Hungarian newspapers have all said that the assassins crossed from Servia. 'The Pester Lloyd' in Budapest was particularly virulent on that point. 'The line to Serajevo?'

'Yes.'

'So he could help someone without papers to get over that frontier?'

'From what I heard people cross back and forward over the frontier all the time. His work on the railway was not what they say he did.' I wait without saying any more. Pósha's prize piece of information must come of its own accord. I do no more than withdraw my hand from the pocket with my notecase in it. 'Everyone, all say the same thing. Ciganović, they say, is the man who gave Princip and the others their bombs and the revolvers.' Pósha looks hard at me with his exhausted eyes still sharp. 'Where Ciganović is now, he better hide himself very very well, Excellency, or he goes where Princip is.'

When I get back to the picnic party I see that Strandtman, cross legged on the grass, is showing a side of himself which Hartwig would have approved. He is laughing, pink in the face, his voice is raucous as he starts to sing a phrase of some folk song, probably. 'It is Turgenev's rendering of the nightingale,' he shouts.

The Serbian government have not taken any steps against the Serbian accomplices in the crime of 28th June; on the contrary, they have attempted to wipe out the existing traces.
Austrian Red Book.

IX

Dr. Klencke observes: 'The habit of thinking and speaking only by fragments gives to the character of the stammerer a capricious disposition . . . 'This may explain why some stammerers defy a world whose fluent rule seems to keep them, and their tongue, in chains.
Hunt: Stammering & Stuttering, 1863.

And the tongue of stammerers shall speak readily and plain.
Isaiah, chap. xxxii, 4.

EYRE CROWE nested discreetly at the top of the Foreign Office and kept an eye on fledgling diplomats, and above all, on applicants. One day in 1895 he asked Haldane, then only an M.P. but rising fast, to call on him.

'I want to ask you about your nominee Theodore Harris whom I interview tomorrow.'

'He's the son of the Tribonian Professor.'

'Yes. The fact is, I'm told there was an incident some while ago — involving a magistrate.'

'A magistrate? At Oxford?'

'It seems Harris came down and went to his father's place in the country to work for the entrance examination. He was alone in Dorset and got into a spot of trouble.'

'Not awfully unusual, surely?'

'This particular trouble involved a woman caught lifting a piece of jewellery, some trinket or other, in a shop in Bath. Harris stood bail for her.'

'He'd have done better to buy the jewellery.'

'He wasn't with her at the time and the young woman, who was French, hopped it back to France. It seems that Harris, who had picked her up at the Theatre Royal in Bristol, put her aboard a ship bound for Brittany and told her to make herself scarce.'

'Well, he forfeited bail. A lesson to him but I don't suppose his father was pleased.'

'There's more to it. Harris told the magistrate to his face that he'd made an elementary error of judgement, the girl should have been released for want of evidence. He said it was a miscarriage of justice which he'd taken on himself to rectify.'

'Not tactful, I admit,' Haldane said.

'He may have been right but the incident leaves something of a question mark over Harris's head,' said Crowe who appeared, to Haldane, to be looking for a way out.

'Mind you — initiative in a public servant — self-reliance — not such a bad thing. There's plenty of dead wood in the Diplomatic Service as you know, of all people.'

'I see some difference between initiative and taking the law into your own hands.'

Crowe evidently needed something more. Haldane, tipped for the War Office in the next Liberal government, felt it would cost him little enough to do an old friend a favour. 'James Harris is a brilliant and independent spirit, Constance too, in her way, and we — I mean, of course, the next Prime Minister — will want to attract brighter spirits into the service, after all.' Haldane drew breath, feeling he had shot his bolt.

'Harris is bright.'

'Oh he's bright all right.'

'But is he safe?'

'Safe as a Tribonian Professor of Roman Law could make him.'

Crowe laughed. 'And Byzantium lasted a thousand years.' So the discussion of Theo's brush with the judiciary ended, judgement going more or less in his favour.

'HOW DID you get on?' Oliver asks.

I don't answer him, confirming his suspicion that I have something to hide. I'm studying Xenia from above as she leans a little towards the Russian Minister, smiles at him, her forearm and the brown hand holding the wineglass horizontal at breast level, the Russian Minister plainly under the spell. I think Xenia has decided she may some time or other need him as an ally, should I fail her, that is. But what does she know? How much has she hidden from me, and about what has she lied? Of course I keep reminding myself that Ciganović is a very common name, while Milan is as current as Jack. But those wounds of his, if wounds they are?

'The first race will be in a quarter of an hour,' Xenia says, laughing. 'We must eat our picnic or we'll miss it. And if there's to be war it will be the last race for a long time.'

The race is started by the firing of a pistol which excites everyone. The course is roughly laid out with flags planted here and there, and judging by the line of crowds who know the way it runs across the dome of the down, round a small wood of oaks, along a shallow valley in full view from all around and then onto the home straight, to end up before the only stand in sight, reserved for King Peter. The king, as everyone knows, lives a hermit's life on his estate in the country, is decrepit and perhaps senile and unlikely to attend race meetings where an assassin passes unnoticed in the throng. In his place on the royal stand is Prince George, eyes flashing, the starting pistol held aloft.

'And for sure loaded with live rounds,' Oliver says. 'That's one bet you can safely make.'

'He is romantic,' says Xenia.

'Xenia,' (I have never heard Oliver use her Christian name before), 'you talk like a convent girl, the prince is a retarded ruffian.'

'The Karadjordjević are all heroes to us.'

'Watch the race,' I say.

The runners have passed behind the oak wood and out of sight but shouts and cheers float over the air from the far side. Someone fires another couple of shots and louder cheering follows. Suddenly the first horse appears round the edge of the wood, far off across the sweep of brown grass, and charges down into the valley, followed by the field. The riders are bare headed, some in uniform, some in breeches and coloured shirts, knees and elbows pumping the air, heads thrust down and forward. Xenia takes my hand and holds on tight as if her fortune's on the race.

'Is he the one you want to win?'

'No,' she says.

'Which, then?'

'The one with a blue scarf. He must still be behind the wood.'

'You know him?'

'No,' she says again.

'Why him?'

'I had a dream. The blue scarf was for peace. If he wins the first race there will be peace.'

'He'll come round the wood in a second and make up along the valley, and then get the lead in the straight. I'm sure of it,' I tell her.

I lower my head and she puts her mouth firmly on mine. 'If he doesn't, we still have some time,' she says. The world will be reduced to that and perhaps it should be.

WELL, HE DIDN'T reappear at all. After a while, a stretcher party brought from the other side of the wood a body which moved no more, the blue scarf trailing along the grass. By then Prince George had fired into the air again and also into the crowd, hitting no one, and been led away by the officers accompanying him. No one offered, or sought, an explanation of his conduct. The prince is accepted for what he is, a natural hazard.

'Omens are not to be believed,' I say to Xenia.

'But we all believe them, even men.'

The situation seems too tragic to worry any more about truth, or lies. The crew of the gunboats, prow into the current, range their sights on the buildings of Belgrade with the Legation in the front line. The tragedy is for the people who have no escape. The crowds at Topčider in their cotton clothing and straw hats may never see more free horse races about the down and along the valley. So what does it matter who lies? But I must confront it.

Vienna, July 18, 1914

The suggestion that Servia will be given only 48 hours in which to accept the Austro-Hungarian demands seems unlikely to be well-founded, for the Servian Prime Minister is reported to be absent from Belgrade on a ten days' electioneering tour, whilst the harvest in Austria and Hungary will not have been got in for another 3 weeks, before which time it cannot be desired to bring on a crisis.

de Bunsen to Grey.

GRUJIĆ HAS telephoned in person demanding to speak to me, an unusual step for a Foreign Minister but not, as it turns out, intended as an honour. He makes himself objectionable from the first word.

'You are walking a perilous tightrope, Mr Harris,' he says in an angry voice.

'It happens, General, that I have a proposal of my own to make to the Prime Minister as soon as he returns. An initiative which may help us all.'

'The Prime Minister is on his way back to Belgrade and when he gets here I shall have other things than your proposal to tell him concerning the British Legation.'

I decide to stall. 'I feel, with all respect, that the initiative I have in mind must be first put to the Prime Minister himself.'

'I am not talking about your ***** initiative,' Grujić shouts, using a German military colloquialism better left off record. 'I am talking about your stenographer. She is known as a member of the Narodna Odbrana and even its inner circle.'

'The Narodna Odbrana is a respectable society, General, many prominent citizens belong to it, who love Servia. If I were not in an official position I would apply to join it myself.'

'Would you, Mr Harris. Well it's fortunate for your career that you haven't. They were respectable once, now they are a rabble associated with the forbidden Black Hand who will end by destroying us all. Narodna Odbrana has fallen into the orbit of young nihilists who will stop nowhere.'

'I am sure that Xenia Ciganović has no connection — '

'You are wrong. She is in it up to her neck. And tonight my agents will call at the British Legation to take away your pretty Xenia Ciganović for questioning.'

This means she can no longer safely leave the Legation building. The terrace will be her exercise yard. But why should she leave it anyway? Her responsibilities are here — if she has clandestine relations with secret societies it's too late to do any good, or more harm. Now is the time for closing the circle. If Milan and Xenia are a danger to themselves, to me, better they remain guests within the walls.

When the agents from the Foreign Ministry present themselves at the door of the Legation I open it myself. It is eleven o'clock and above the parapets of the royal palace opposite a harvest moon hangs in a smoky sky. The men are respectful.

'We are sent to take Xenia Ciganović to the Foreign Ministry for an interview with the Secretary-General, Excellency,' their leader says.

'The person you name is employed in the Legation and has no mind to leave it.'

'We have orders to apprehend her.'

'You cannot execute them on His Britannic Majesty's premises. You may not enter.'

'The Secretary-General, that is, General Grujić, will be angry.'

'You have my sympathy over that but the King of England would be even angrier if I let you in to arrest a woman under his protection.'

They salute, in a ragged kind of way, obviously terrified of Grujić's reprisals. 'Thank you, Excellency,' their leader says. 'You would do four ordinary serving men a good turn if you telephoned the Secretary-General and told him the refusal yourself.'

'I will do that. And good luck to you if you have to go to fight.'

'Good luck to you too,' they say in unison as they turn about and lumber away.

THERE'S NO MORE pretence of not sharing the bedroom. Humans, like sheep or cattle, huddle together at the approach of the storm and Hermann shows no surprise when he brings the morning coffee.

'So I must stay inside?'

'We have the terrace.'

'You said this already. The terrace is small. I am a woman who must move and breathe.' This is true, and not only for her. Her motion and breath have become my own.

'The government has prisons without terraces where they do bad things to help people answer questions. Especially women.'

'And I must choose between you and the government.'

'Xenia, you must answer them or me.'

'Why must I answer you?'

Doesn't she understand? It's because I must protect her. Must? The question to my own mind carries its own answer — with Xenia I'm beyond the turning back, the stage of inclination, desire, first possession. I am in love with her. I have lost the freedom I no longer want. 'Because we must be true and choose.'

'I choose you,' she says, turning in the warmth of bedclothes and pillows, with the curtains still drawn shut. 'While there's time.' I yield to the offer and the hope.

OLIVER BRINGS the bag to my office where I sit gazing across the junction of the rivers and the plain beyond, where Austro-Hungarian ants swarm in woods and fields.

'The Messenger said he hoped we were keeping our end up.'

'This was his comment on the international situation, coming from London?'

'He said he attended the Smith versus Carpentier boxing match at

Olympia. He'd never seen so many excited women in one place in his life before.'

'If they like spilt blood they'll soon get their fill.'

Among the despatches is a letter from my mother, the handwriting a little wilder, more random each time she writes.

Dearest Theodore, (she has never called me Theo).

I know you would wish to know what Richard Haldane said to me last night. He said that Sir Edward Grey thinks well of your despatches from Belgrade. Grey considers that you have an insight into affairs and Haldane is proud of having nominated you!

If only you had used that insight more for literary ends! As I wished and longed for! But of course your father rightly said that (here the sentence breaks off unfinished).

It seems that some Irish are gun-running in spite of the Home Rule Bill. Had I been born Irish and after so many broken promises I might have run guns myself —

Kitty came to see me in Rutland Gate, how beautiful she is in all her furs — even in London, in July! She brought Theodora but the child seemed strangely subdued in her mother's presence.

I worry for your safety, Theodore, there in Belgrade! What is going to happen to us all?

Remember your

Mother — life's mainspring broken, only the helping of others, now, still left.

MY MOTHER'S MESSAGE is a warning, but what good is a warning now? Oliver is back, with a letter in his hand. 'What's the matter?'

'Look at the postmark.'

When did anything with a Dublin postmark last bring good news? 'More troubles?'

'The King's Own Scottish Borderers opened fire on the crowd in the street, on passers-by, on women.'

'Who is your letter from?'

'Desmond. Our sister was shot on the steps of the Gresham.'

'Oliver, I'm most sorry, believe me I am. All my condolences.' I put a hand on his arm. 'Sit down, you look done in.' I guide him to a chair and ring for Hermann. I feel, naturally, terrible about Oliver's news. 'That will take the Government's mind off the crisis here on the continent. Did your sister have children?'

'She was a nun of the Sacred Heart.'

What was she doing on the steps of the Gresham? Was Oliver's sister a spoiled nun come from the races in Phoenix Park? It wouldn't surprise me. 'Do you feel you should go over? Does your brother suggest it?'

Oliver doesn't answer the question, making me suppose that his brother suggested nothing and reported as little as possible. 'Do you think of taking leave?'

'I do not,' Oliver says after a decent pause. 'I'm needed here.'

'Yes of course you are. I need you, Oliver, and in the coming days we may all need each other more than we know.'

'Exzellenz?' There he is at last, I'd almost forgotten him.

'Whisky for Mr Dillon.'

'Usually the *Herr Archivar* pours for himself, he knows where it is,' Hermann says insolently as he leaves the room, but it proves to be the right antidote; Oliver laughs out loud.

'Old Hermann — what a bugger.' He goes on laughing, but who, in Dublin or anywhere else, will laugh and forget the firing on women in the street?

I AM SUMMONED by the Prime Minister, with whom the interview may be difficult. Reproaches could be levelled, complaint sent to the Servian Minister in London, but is that likely? Pašić, with so little time left, needs all the friends he can keep. He has a fine long head with a high brow tilted backward, a powerful nose, and a mass of white hair and beard. His eyes are opaque as the circle of water at the bottom of a well.

'Mr Harris, I stand here in great need of your help.'

Well, it gets us off on the right foot. 'Most honoured to be of service to your Excellency, in any way possible.'

'Sit down.' We sit in silence for a full minute before he looks at the clock on the wall opposite his desk. 'You know what is going to happen?'

'We are still waiting.'

'The Austrians desire war at any cost, the game is to deny them. For Vienna, we are a subject race. You know well what is a subject race, even in your own islands you have one, I believe.'

'We are traditionally in sympathy with peoples numerically inferior to their aggressors. We have usually been numerically inferior ourselves — '

'To whom?'

'To the French.' We both laugh because this is one of the few reliable jokes of European politics. 'I believe the Emperor Francis Joseph is no more favoured by London than King Peter.'

He leans across the table, extends an arm and puts a cold hand on the back of mine before I have time to withdraw it. 'Define your attitude,' he says in a low urgent voice, 'Servia begs you, Russia begs you.' His hand tightens on mine. 'Your country has never been afraid to weigh in the balance, it should not fear now.' I entirely agree with him, and when he removes his hand I leave mine where it is. 'Why does your government hesitate?'

If a subordinate minister or a difficult deputy disagrees with Pašić, something unfortunate will soon befall them. With us, such people have to be led by stages. 'Because Parliament is divided. No government in the United Kingdom can go against the will of Parliament.'

'How admirable!' Pašić says with irony and feeling. 'Speeches, parties and paralysis.'

I smile, I have something to say, but not about that. There's a long pause with Pašić tapping out a rhythm on the table top with his fingers. Clearly he has something to say too and is considering the best way to say it. 'You have seen the monitors across the Danube, Mr Harris?'

'They are moored at no distance, with binoculars one can see the barrels of their guns sweep as they rehearse their aim.'

'Rehearse.' There is another long pause. 'You are somewhat exposed, I think, in your Legation.' His voice is quite gentle. 'Prince George was here this morning.'

'I saw him a day or two ago. He suffers by being out of the centre of things.'

'I am aware of that, and it's his own fault. However, the prince — ' the tapping of the left hand fingers is now more drumming than rhythmical — 'spoke of you in warm tones.'

'Too kind — '

'Though he has fears about your professional detachment for private reasons.'

'Prince George may not be quite dependable — since his removal from the succession. His views may be unsafe.' Pašić watches me with a disillusioned eye. I am busy blackening the witness but he doesn't know what's coming next. 'If I may,' I say in a firm voice, 'I would like to put forward an idea for your consideration and that of your Government.'

Pašić sweeps the Government away with the back of his hand. 'Speak your mind with no more *beating around in the bush.*'

'My idea, Prime Minister, is that you should start investigations into the alleged conspiracy. Make it known everywhere, inform every Embassy and Legation in Europe and all your free newspapers, also correspondents of leading European newspapers represented in Vienna.' I pause to see how he's taking it. His expression is illegible, his left hand now flat on the desk. 'We are perfectly aware that Vienna's accusations of Servian complicity in the murder are absurd. No one doubts it.'

'The absurdity?'

'The lie. It has even emerged that all the accused were Austrian subjects.'

'We have plenty of those in Servia, they are Bosnians.'

'Investigate them. It will yield nothing, but international opinion will make the Austrian Government hold its hand.'

'Nothing? And you yourself, Mr Harris — should the investigation reach as far as your Legation — what then?'

'I can assure you I would cooperate in every way.'

'To the extent of admitting our agents into the building?'

'For that, I would need authority.'

'And have you authority for the proposal you make?'

'I make it of my own motion. Let us take the wind out of the opponent's sails. It was Nelson's method. '

This time it's Pašić who smiles. 'We are a landlocked country, Mr Harris, we need to annexe Albania, then we would have an outlet to the sea. I must reflect,' he says, and I know his mind is made up. Perhaps he's too wily for something so simple. 'We have an election on our hands. The Radical party fights for its future and the Commander-in-Chief is on leave.'

'Where?'

'In an Austrian watering-place.'

'Recall him.'

'We have reason to believe that restraint will be exercised on Vienna by Berlin.'

'What is your source?'

'I think from a Chargé d'affaires the question goes too far.'

'And my proposal?'

'Investigations are dangerous things. Have you ever turned over a rock in the forest? Until the results of the Sarajevo proceedings are published we have no material on which to base an enquiry of the kind you suggest.'

'You don't wish to find your own?'

'I think the rock is best left lying. Even the rock of Kalemegdan, and the buildings beside it.'

The Prime Minister rises, the interview is at an end, his mind returns to the Radical party and the election. I've done my duty, put my head on the block, and there will be no investigation. I buy a flower for my buttonhole, a small yellow rose, from a girl with bare brown feet which I feel, suddenly, a desire to take into my hands.

Belgrade, July 18, 1914

In the course of a private conversation with the Prime Minister this morning, I urged that the wisest course for Servia would be to undertake herself and of her own motion an enquiry into the alleged South Slav conspiracy on Servian soil. M. Pašić pointed out the impossibility of adopting any definite measures before learning the findings of the Serajevo Court which had hitherto been kept secret.

Harris to Grey.

Minute
A golden opportunity lost.
Eyre Crowe, Assistant Under-Secretary, Foreign Office.

OLIVER REPORTS hearing sounds of delirium in the night from the bedroom next to his, occupied by Milan. 'That poor fellow should be got to a hospital,' he says.

'Was his voice raised?'

'He was shouting and moaning.'

'Did you make anything out?'

'My Serbo-Croat doesn't run to ravings.'

'Send for the doctor.'

'Xenia won't have it.'

So he's already spoken to her. Oliver is the kind of man women often confide in because he will never blackmail them as sober men do. 'What did she say, exactly?'

'She said you are in charge here, not me.'

'Well that's right.'

'You don't think it's more a warning?'

'To whom? And of what?'

'To you, Theo, to you.' He offers no answer at all to the second part of my question before he goes.

I press the electric bell on my desk which communicates with Xenia's little office. 'Oliver tells me he thinks your brother is getting worse. We must talk about it honestly, Xenia.'

'I am always open with you.'

'You're open but what you say is perhaps not the same as what you say to Oliver.'

'You are jealous, of Oliver?'

'Of anyone.'

She approaches. 'I am glad you're jealous.'

'I think we should go and see your brother, now.'

'Yes.'

She stops outside his door and turns to me. 'You think Milan has a wound?'

'I'm sure he has.'

'A Servian man thinks nothing of wounds in war. Milan was among the *komitadji* in 1913.'

'So you told me before, but his wound must be newer than that.'

'I want you to look at this wound. You must have courage.'

There is a smell of corruption in the bedroom and the man on the bed is moaning and restless and, I should think, sweating heavily in the heat of the afternoon. The window is shut. Xenia pulls back the sheet, gently turns Milan onto his left side, holds him steady with one firm hand while with the other she neatly removes a dressing from his right thigh. It's a nasty sight. The flesh of the leg is bluish and grey and gaping, with a pale bloody liquid trickling from it and signs of inflammation about the edges of the wound. I lean down and peer into the opening. The interior is torn enough to rip at one's nerves but I feel quite sure there is something in there which should be removed at once; something smaller than shrapnel and larger than a dart. A bullet, then. 'You see?' Xenia says. 'We must remove this.'

'How?'

'You are a man, all surgeons are men and you must get it out. We will pass the blade of a knife through some flames and you will do it. It is simple.' If the situation wasn't so alarming I would laugh at her. Whatever she wants is simple, she has set her mind on it and difficulties melt away. 'Show me you're not afraid,' she says, and at this I do laugh.

'I'm afraid of killing your brother and causing him a lot of pain for nothing. I'm going to send Oliver at once for the Legation doctor. Only you and I and Oliver will know anything about it. The doctor is very discreet and he'll come with chloroform and clean instruments.'

'You are being despot, not like an Englishman.'

'So you say.'

Much against my will I have to assist at the operation, so there I am, holding the chloroform pad in one hand and the bottle in the other. 'If he shows signs of coming round, sprinkle a few more drops on the pad and hold it close over his nose. You won't kill him,' the doctor says. 'And you,' he goes on, turning to Xenia, 'you will hold my instruments, do exactly what I tell you to do, and at once. Don't hesitate. He will feel nothing.'

The whole ghastly thing is over in a few minutes and the bullet lies in the enamelled bowl beside the knives and needles. 'This wound must close from the inside,' the doctor says. 'He will have a lot of pain in the next few days. Cleanliness is primordial and his worst pain will be the iodine. One doesn't use iodine in wounds as a rule but here there is risk of gangrene. The man should be in hospital but I understand that's impossible.'

'I will see to everything. I thank you for what you did,' Xenia says, and I can see that this doctor is afraid of her.

I take the poor man into my study and offer him a whisky. He accepts at once and I fetch it myself so that Hermann should know nothing. 'You have been extremely good to us, Doctor,' I say, 'we are all most grateful.'

'I have already forgotten, it's the safest,' the doctor says, and quickly drains his glass.

'Perhaps you would like your fee settled now rather than sending an account?'

'There is no fee for what has never happened We have both taken a great risk,' he says, and hurries away into the night.

Milan is still asleep and Xenia settled in an armchair with a blanket pulled up to her chin and a lamp burning on the table beside her. She looks exhausted even by this dim light, the heat is intense and the window still closed.

'You need fresh air in here.'

'No. Fresh air is bad for open wounds. All the germs come in from the town. Everyone knows you can only recover with windows shut.'

REPEATEDLY OVER the next two days, as Milan's cries under iodine resound through the building, I try to reach the doctor by telephone but without success, and in the end I go round myself to his house. A girl opens the door.

'I must see the doctor, please.'

'He is away.'

'Where has he gone? When will he come back? How can I find him?'

'Doctor has gone away. In the country, perhaps,' says the girl looking frightened, and quickly closes the door in my face.

PART TWO

X

Each July morning is hotter than the last; you wake sweating in the knowledge that the day will be hard even in the shadow of darkened rooms. On the island known as War Island the bathing cabins are open, early bathers already entering the Danube under the willows. Further upstream the colder, cleaner water of the Save runs green; with field glasses I can see citizens of all ages wading in from the bank, among the swallows. From Vienna to the Iron Gates the Danube collects the sewage of every town but the Save flows through oak forests and vineyards, over filtering stones and sand, past white farmhouses at the foot of empty hills.

Can an acting Minister slip out through the stable yard, borrow a boat at the Semlin Bridge and row up to the green water for a bathe? Who would ever know him for what he is? I can feel the wash run over my heated body, my head, cooling, calming. But of course I can't do it, I'm needed, I must be.

BOPPE HAS SENT a note in a shaky hand, the sequence of ideas shaky too, but what he has to say is clear enough. We have all waited for the moment of verdict which passes, returns, hangs over us. I go down myself to the Electric Telegraph Office with my coded telegram for the Foreign Secretary.

Belgrade, July 23, 1914
I am informed by my French colleague that a note was handed in last evening giving the Servian Government forty-eight hours within which to comply with the Austrian demands. I have not yet details, but I am told that the conditions imposed are exceedingly harsh.
Harris to Grey

I KNOW ALREADY it's an ultimatum, the six-gun monitors on the Danube tell me that.

Foreign Office, July 24, 1914
I said tonight to the Austro-Hungarian Ambassador that the note seemed to me the most formidable document I had ever seen addressed by one State to another that was independent.

It was solely from the point of view of the peace of Europe that I should concern myself, and I felt great apprehension . . .
Grey to de Bunsen.

WITH THE ULTIMATUM in his hands, Pašić does what power and reality demand — he turns to the British Chargé d'affaires.

'Mr Harris! You at least I can reach by telephone. We are seated on the powder keg, you and I!'

'May I say, I think we all are.'

'Say what you like, but come at once to see me at my office.'

Pašić is grey as a hanging dawn. I suppose he loves his people and his people count on him, the poor king being only a distant figure surrounded by priests and candles and anachronism. King Peter is hardly even recognised by those crowned heads who in coming days will exchange cousinly telegrams: 'Dear William — Nicholas — George — Henry.'

'You are informed of the content of the note?' Pašić asks.

'I hope for a chance to read it word for word in the original.'

'I will show it to you later — but it's quite clear.' He pauses, moisture from his eye running into the thicket of his beard. We're still standing just inside the door of his bureau, face to face; the Prime Minister pulls himself together. 'Let us be seated like gentlemen.'

'The time limit is a make-believe,' I say. 'Every government in Europe will sympathise with you.'

'We need more than sympathy. We need the British Government to climb off the fence where they love to sit.'

'We must help them, Prime Minister.'

'How can I help Sir Edward Grey and Mr Churchill with his fleet at Spithead?'

'At Spithead, exactly — and ordered not to disperse as it usually does for the summer.'

'So?' He is interested. Power speaks, the Navy always speaks.

'It means our Government is poised to act. To weigh in the balance.'

'Those are your instructions?'

'I anticipate, as even a telegram can go astray.'

'You are audacious, Mr Harris.'

'I have warm feelings for Servia.'

'Private feelings?'

'Perhaps.'

'I understand,' the Prime Minister says; I think that in a way he does and my plight seems natural to him.

'Although I haven't seen the text, I'm sure I know what you should do.'

'Go on.'

'Think of the fleet, accept the note, whatever the detail. Your acceptance will seem an act of faith in the community of nations.'

'The what?'

'The powers, Prime Minister. My government, I'm sure, will rally when it's seen in Parliament that a strong power is bullying a small one. And when you accept the note, what can the Austrians say? Months will elapse and the strategic railway will reach the Russian frontiers.' As once before, Pašić has put a hand on mine on the edge of the table. 'So will you do it?'

'Are you alone in making this recommendation?'

'I think the French Minister is of the same mind.'

'*Ce pauvre Boppe.*'

'The Minister and I are fencing partners.'

'Ah,' says Pašić again, eying me curiously. 'How apt.' An idea for one last joke seems to occur to him. 'Did you meet Madame Boppe, before her return to Paris last year?'

'No, I had only just arrived.'

'A pity. She had appetite and temperament and might have saved you from yourself. And the fatal trap of time,' he ends a little sadly.

'We're all trapped, Prime Minister, but making no conditions will create sympathy for you, and give it room to grow. Unconditional acceptance — '

'Of every demand?'

'Yes.'

'And this, in particular?'

Pašić turns over a page of the Austrian note lying on his table. He holds it up to his eyes and peers at it as though his sight is blinded by the tragedy to come and then passes it to me, watching.

I read rapidly . . . *it is to be gathered that the Servian civil servant Ciganović, who is accused . . . by the criminals whose affidavits agree with one another . . . was still in Belgrade on the day of the outrage . . . while the Prefect of Police and the director of the Servian press declared that he is completely unknown there.*

'What do you say of that, on which apparently the peace of Europe depends, Mr Harris? What is your advice about this accused, Ciganović?'

'There's another name here, Major Tankosić, who sounds a more likely agent. But naturally these men, whom we must think innocent until proved guilty, should be questioned. An enquiry is what I recommended.'

'And if Ciganović, as I fear could be the case, is in a safe haven somewhere?' Pašić insists obtusely.

'The name is a common one.'

After a long pause, Pašić says, 'I think I see what you may be suggesting.'

'I don't presume to suggest anything, Prime Minister.'

'Yet a moment ago you recommended a course of action.'

'On behalf of my government.'

'You anticipated them. Who are you anticipating now?'

We are on dangerous ground. 'No one.'

'I see what has happened to you, Mr Harris. Your *morale* is corrupted by emotions that some say the English have mastered.' The Prime Minister is standing so I stand too. He bangs himself with closed fist. 'The groin, Mr Harris, you are a Scorpio, governed by the groin.'

My mother, acquainted with Madame Blavatsky and a believer in all that could take apprehension beyond normal limits, often drew attention to the Scorpio connection. 'You are a slave to the sense, Theodore,' she said, 'and given your sign I see no other choice for you.'

MILAN'S BED and belongings must be immediately taken down from the first floor. I can forbid entry to the Legation if I'm faced with government agents at the door but our windows face those of the palace, empty and accessible to government spies. We are certainly watched already, and not only from the street.

'Oliver, we must help Xenia carry the bed, and the boy if necessary, downstairs to the cellars.'

'Why, what's he done?'

'A Ciganović is named in the Austrian note. They demand he be arrested and handed over to the frontier police.'

'For interrogation?'

'I don't think Xenia would want that.'

'Don't you? It would get rid of him.'

'I couldn't do it.'

He looks at me in wonder. 'If it's your duty, Theo? If it was best for all in the end — for us, for the Service, for the nations?' I was forgetting the hard realism that Oliver, like all his countrymen, is capable of.

'I give up a wounded boy to Austrian mercies? I couldn't.'

'Lucky in that case I'm a reliable old friend who knows how to keep his mouth shut.'

'That's just as well for both of us.' I prefer to question Milan myself before deciding whether or not the Austrian claim has substance; if they questioned him, what would be left after they'd finished? 'Come with me, please.' The cellar, with the bed and a couple of chairs installed and a small cupboard for medical necessities, doesn't seem at all grim. On one side, the racks of wine bottles, on the other the table with the oil lamp and the cellar book kept by Oliver.

'He is tired,' Xenia says.

'He seems much better, don't you think? I'm sure the doctor would be pleased.'

She ignores the mention of the doctor. 'He is improving, but moving him has hurt his wound.'

'I'll be getting back,' Oliver says.

'Stay with us please, I need your Serbo-Croat.'

'Serbo-Croat is Xenia's mother tongue.'

'Her German has certain gaps in it.'

'You don't trust her?'

I waste no more time on him but sit on one of the wooden chairs near the head of Milan's bed. His face is thin and the line of cheek and jaw and neck still hard.

'Are you comfortable? In less pain?'

'I am in great pain.'

I don't believe it. His eyes are too bright. 'We have brought you down here for your own protection, chiefly.'

'Chiefly? I don't understand, please?'

I think Milan is beginning to show signs of resistance to hospitality. That always happens in the end, even with guests who invite themselves. 'Your presence in the Legation is dangerous for everyone here.'

'Yes, I understand, it is because of Xenia.' He looks me in the eye as he says this, a sign of complicity however shameful. Many men would sell their sister for their own skin, and not only in the Balkans.

'I think of you and your wound. I need to know how you got it.' His eyes retreat into a fog of incomprehension and pain and then close. 'Well?'

He says something in an undertone to Xenia which escapes me.

'He needs the bedpan, after this removal which has upset him. This is urgent,' Xenia says, and Oliver and I retire.

'You know they're fooling us?' Oliver says.

'She's a woman, Oliver.'

'You mean you're not fooled?'

'With eyes open.'

'Oh my God,' Oliver says, 'and what do you see?'

'I think the boy has a lot to tell us, and he must tell it.'

'DON'T BE AFRAID of us. Mr Dillon will translate your answers in which I hope you will be truthful and complete.' I look up at Xenia. 'Xenia is here, you are safe with us.'

Milan strains to sit up higher and takes my hand to pull me down closer to him, speaking in a whisper. 'You, a Minister, you love Xenia?' The hold of his hand is clammy but hard as a vice.

'Yes.'

He lets go and falls back on his pillows. 'Bad pain, very bad,' he says.

'In your leg?'

'My soul,' he says in German; does he mean his heart, since *Seele* can signify either? Perhaps he's still delirious.

'Loving the same person can be the start of trust,' I say, also in German. 'I want to know if you ever met Princip in any of the cafés in Green Crown Square — the Acorn Crown, the Golden Sturgeon, the America?' I feel no hostility; I accept Milan's importance to Xenia without fully understanding it, and therefore his claim on me too.

'I must tell the truth?' he asks.

'You must tell the exact truth and nothing else, or I will turn you out onto the street tonight.'

'You are so sure you will know?' Xenia asks.

'I can find out.'

'Then why are you asking the poor boy all these questions?'

'Because we must all understand each other.'

'And Hermann? Must he understand, and report?'

'I think Hermann will soon be gone.'

'I think he's gone already,' Oliver says.

'Why d'you think that?'

'He was afraid. Someone came with a message and it frightened the wits out of him. Next thing I knew he was scuttling away from the yard with a couple of bags.'

'When?'

'An hour or two ago,' Oliver says vaguely.

'Did you see the messenger?'

'Yes, I think so.'

'Well?'

'An individual, somehow familiar, I don't know why, leading a mule and selling water melons.'

I return to Milan.

'When did you last meet Princip?'

'I haven't said I met him.'

'The man who sells water melons has told me that you did.'

'Princip was a poor type, a scarecrow,' Milan says.

'He was a student. They're often hungry.'

'He has bad lungs.' Milan coughs, as if reminded that he's meant to have them too. 'He spits blood.'

'I think in the Austrian prison he loses blood in more places than his lungs.' The daylight reaching the cellar by an aperture in the vault is failing fast as the sun drops behind the old-rose-pink fortification of Kalemegdan. Grouped about the bed with the wounded Milan prone under a sheet, only his head showing, we're like figures from *The Anatomy Lesson of Dr Tulp* or Wright of Derby's *Experiment with an Air Pump*. 'So you know him well?'

'Like a lot of others in those cafés, no more, no less.'

'I am not trying to trap you,' I say, and this time it is Xenia and not Oliver who translates.

'Princip sweated all the time, and trembled like a frightened girl but he wasn't frightened. He was impatient. He wanted to do some noble deed before he died so that all Servia would remember him like the martyrs of Kosovo.' I think I hear contempt in Milan's voice as he becomes more

— 134 —

loquacious. 'He thought the red flowers of St Vitus would ever afterwards be in memory of him, Gavrilo Princip.'

'And you helped him?'

'Yes, I listened to him.'

'They had bombs and pistols. The bombs were not very effective but Princip's pistol was. Did he get it from you?'

Milan groans and turns on his side towards the wall as if pain, or the truth, is growing unbearable. I don't think he'll answer any more questions but he hardly needs to. Pósha's information was obviously correct; I am harbouring the man named in the Austrian demands.

'What are we going to do?' Oliver asks.

Xenia has a hand on my arm, her thumb in the crook of the elbow. Milan groans again more softly, to signal exhaustion. 'We must think of everything,' I say 'and first and foremost we must get that water-melon seller off the street and make him butler before he sells his information to anyone else.'

Xenia has followed me into the study. For a moment I thought she might express gratitude but I underestimated her. She sits in her usual chair for taking dictation, hands crossed one over the other with fists clenched. I am struck by the thought that a man with his hands in that position would have the palms downward, knuckles uppermost, while hers are the other way, ready to uncurl.

'I think he is getting better,' I say gently.

'Yes.' She is making some silent calculation. Of which factors? Power, love? Love won't enter into the equation for Chancelleries and War Offices; men called to march on shell-torn ground must put love aside. But the focus of Xenia's thought is narrower, more intense. Death is closer here than in Ministries, it hovers near the cellar door. Now she is studying me. 'Who is your spy?' she asks.

I tell her, and she laughs. 'Poor man,' she says, 'he will be lonely.' She laughs again, a low laugh. 'Mr Harris, you are going in deeper and deeper. Is it all for me?'

I must keep a level head now and answer later. 'How did Milan get that bullet in him?'

'I will tell you now,' she says. 'Before, I was not sure you would be on the side of the heroes of 1913.'

I take her wrists and hold them. 'I'm not on any side about 1913. 1913 will soon be forgotten because of 1914. We will all be forgotten. But I am on the side of the individual human while we're still here.'

'Even Milan?'

'Even him.' A motive which I had forgotten now surfaces. 'I can't stand a second time on the bank and watch a brother go down.'

'I don't understand that but you're a good man, Theodore.' She has never used my first name before.

'I don't think I'm very good, I am selfish.'

'Oh yes, you are selfish. But you share.'

'So I will shelter him.'

'You need shelter too, men needed this in 1913, 1914 is not so different.' She's convinced there will be war whatever anyone does.

'What about that bullet?'

'Milan was working on the railway at the frontier with Bosnia.'

'When he wasn't in the Belgrade cafés.'

'The train travels from the frontier to Belgrade in an hour or so and employees of the railway ride on it for nothing.'

'All right.'

'So he was there, at the frontier, when Princip and the others went over.'

'Did Milan go with them?'

'No.'

'You know there was shooting in Serajevo that day. He could easily have received the bullet the doctor took out.'

'No.'

'What has happened to our doctor, Xenia?'

'It's better you don't know.'

'You mean the Black Hand has taken him somewhere?'

'He is alive, and when the war comes he will be with the soldiers. That's where he will be needed.'

'And meanwhile?'

'What do you mean, meanwhile? You forget I am a prisoner here in the Legation.'

'I would like to be sure that Milan was not with the assassins that day, Xenia. Please think of me too. I must meet the Foreign Secretary and the Prime Minister and tell them lies I have to believe in. I only do it because I can't give up an innocent man to the torturers.' This statement of honourable motive is incomplete. 'And because of you.'

'I think so.'

'I know it.'

She moves next to me. 'He was at his little station by the frontier. It was the frontier guard on the Bosnian side who fired into the darkness. It happens often, because men pass back and forth over that line in the night all the time.'

'Why didn't Milan get looked after by the railway authorities?' I ask, my arm on her shoulder.

'Because he still had one of the bombs in his coat pocket.'

'Where is it now?'

'You will be angry, Theodore.'

'How could I be?'

'It is hidden in Oliver's archive cupboard.'

'Good God, does Oliver know?'

'You think God doesn't even exist so we can leave God alone. No, Oliver doesn't know.'

'He must be told at once. The bomb must be — ' What? Thrown in the Danube, buried in the foundations? 'Perhaps,' I say slowly as the thought forms, 'we ought to send the archive and the bomb to some safe place before the shelling begins.'

Foreign Office, July 24, 1914

The German Ambassador said that . . . Austria might be expected to move at the expiration of the time limit. Servia must not reply with a negative . . . I said that if the Austrian ultimatum to Servia did not lead to trouble between Austria and Russia I had no concern with it.

Grey to Rumbold.

Grey thought it impossible to stop Austria from invading Serbia but she might be appealed to not to advance too far . . . it was a policy which showed Grey's complete lack of understanding of the situation created and revealed by the ultimatum.

Albertini: The Origins of the War of 1914.

WHAT YOU EASILY forget is the scale of force. In St Petersburg there are two or three men commanding millions conscripted on the steppes where their fields are. With us it will be from villages, lads from cottages, a handful to volunteer; and if they're given bayonets and taught to kill — they will kill. Have we millions in waiting? Perhaps we have. So a wounded youth in Belgrade will count for very little when the graves are level with the earth; a diplomat's scruples for still less.

The summer rain has passed and the sky is brazen again; the swifts make the last shrill rounds about the roof and terrace before gathering for exodus; the frenzy of their circuits is over. 'Oliver is back and the Prime Minister is on the telephone,' Xenia reports.

'Has he come back alone?'

'No. He has a man with him.'

'Bring them in.'

'And what shall I say to the Prime Minister?'

'I will go to the telephone.'

Of course it's only his office, but one has to be careful. 'His Excellency wishes to see you at once, Mr Harris.'

'I will come immediately.'

'Shall I say you will be here in twenty minutes?'

'I will be there in fifteen.'

I meet Oliver with Pósha on the stairs on my way down. The rough life has not improved Pósha's appearance. He is thinner, unshaven, and looks ready to burst into tears. 'What have you done with the mule?' is all I can think of saying, for the moment.

'It's tethered in the stable yard,' Oliver says. 'I'll find it a home.'

I should know by now you can't impress a politician by arriving early at his bureau. They have no sense of time, only urgency. I kick my heels in the anteroom, a bleak, barely furnished, windowless chamber on the first floor in the rue du Roi-Milan.

'Mr Harris?'

It is time to go. Pašić, father of his country, is waiting behind his beard and ready to lean, to push, to threaten as fathers must, generation after generation.

Belgrade, July 24, 1914

Prime Minister who returned to Belgrade early this morning is very anxious and dejected. He begged me earnestly to convey to you his hope that His Majesty's Government will use their good offices in moderating Austrian demands which he says are impossible of acceptance.

I have seen the note, which is curt and peremptory. The time-limit of 48 hours, which expires on Saturday at 6 in the evening, was given verbally.

Harris to Grey

Foreign Office, July 25, 1914

You should remember it is not our business to take violent sides.

Grey to Harris.

THIS EXCHANGE of telegrams hides almost everything. Grey's hides the truth that the Cabinet are pacifist, and have their heels dug in.

He can't carry them with him. In mine, I naturally skipped the detail of my conversation with Pašić.

'Be seated, Mr Harris,' he said. 'It is time you read this from beginning to end. Read carefully.'

'It's a violent message,' I said, and handed the terrible paper back across the desk.

'It means war.'

That's one of those statements which echo down the history books because the men who make history feel the need to mark their day with the seal of cliché. It's like love, there are no new things to be said, one says the old and lets the action drown the words. 'We still have a little time — '

'For only one thing, your country must declare that you stand with your friends. You know who it is you face across the water? The same who face us over the Danube.'

'I will send a despatch, Prime Minister — '

'A despatch? How many days for a despatch? Send a telegram, Mr Harris! The ultimatum is for Saturday evening! When will the English awake from the 19th century? What can rouse them?'

'We are, believe me, alert to what the world expects.'

'So what will you write in your telegram?'

'A Chargé d'affaires is not a Minister, his advice is limited.'

'But you are in a special position. You were intimate with Hartwig — '

'Intimate, not quite — '

The Prime Minister laughed, probably for the first time in weeks. 'No, not quite.' A blazing sun was pouring in through the high window but he didn't seem to notice. I felt the sweat trickle down the side of my chest. 'Let me put words in your mouth. Remind London that Tsar Nicholas is weak; his generals are impetuous and will mobilise at his command or without it, as Hartwig knew and always told me.'

'You mean our government should tacitly consent?'

'I mean that perhaps the threat will be enough to wake them up.'

'The Ambassadors in St Petersburg and Berlin will send the information, if it's true.'

'Only you had the advantage of knowing Hartwig — you know more than any of those Ambassadors can ever know, even by their spies.'

A manservant arrived at this moment with biscuits and white wine. 'Would it be possible, Prime Minister, to have the curtain drawn?'

'The light is too strong?'

'The heat — '

'I understand. You have not the tradition of the sun. Your island is covered by icy fog. Draw the curtains,' he ordered.

'Thank you.'

'You need not thank him, he is paid to draw curtains and pass wine and biscuits.'

I was feeling distinctly better. Still hot, but more carefree. 'If the Russian generals are so headstrong it seems all the more reason to accept the Austrian note without condition. The generals will calm themselves; Sir Edward Grey will respect your statesmanship, and the Russian railway engineers will continue toward your eastern frontier. When they reach it, no one will think of attacking you any more. You have only to accept — '

'Every condition?'

'Every condition.'

'And how, without the missing man Ciganović?' I have no answer. 'Illusion is impossible, Mr Harris. Whatever man we produce will be confronted with the Serajevo prisoners. They say it was he who gave them capsules of cyanide to avoid torture. Perhaps it was only water capsules Ciganović gave them, as they are still alive, it seems. Just alive.'

XI

Berlin, July 25, 1914

Large crowds are collecting before the newspaper offices. Incessant cheers for Germany and Austria arise among the crowd, which to a great extent consists of the educated classes.

A German whom I saw this evening confessed to me that it was feared that Servia would accept the whole Austrian Note, reserving the right to discuss the manner in which effect should be given to it, in order to gain time and to allow the efforts of the Powers to develop before the rupture.

I see in England the only Power which might be listened to at Berlin.

M. Jules Cambon, French Ambassador, Berlin, to M. René Viviani, Foreign Minister, Paris.

'LISTEN, PÓSHA, keep out of sight. Don't answer the front door.' I leave him polishing in the pantry beside the dining-room.

'The plot thickens all about,' says Oliver.

'It does. I have a letter from Des Graz. He was on his way via Vienna.'

'Let's hope he gets held up.'

'We must make sure of it.'

'How?'

'It could be a mission for Pósha when I know where Des Graz has got to. How is Milan?'

'Up. He'll soon want something to do. A young fellow can't be kept for long in a cellar.'

Oliver is right. Our guest is dangerous in every way, but one thing I'm sure of is that as long as I don't let Xenia out of the house, she won't let him out of her sight.

PASIC IS PREPARING the Servian reply and must give an answer on every point unless he rejects the whole, which is unthinkable. The Russians are watching over his shoulder. I meet Strandtman coming out as I go in.

'Well, Harris? Downing Street still in its ancient dreamless uninvaded sleep?' he says in his almost perfect English.

I recognise this. 'Until once — ' I hesitate for effect, 'he shall roaring rise — '

'And on the surface die,' Strandtman winds up. 'But let us hope it doesn't come to that.'

The Prime Minister is pacing slowly up and down his room, followed by a secretary to take down any phrase deserving of rescue in the day's growing panic. When he sees me, Pašić waves the secretary away. 'What I must say to you must be said alone.' He is by the window and below in the courtyard the sentries march back and forth, dressed now in field grey with boots and belts and their odd, four-sided caps, as during the war of 1913. 'You see? The days of our European fancy dress are past,' the Prime Minister says.

'They will come back.'

'A charade, the heart will not beat any more under the fancy dress.'

'Need we regret it?'

Pašić turns toward me with a quick movement. 'You are a subversive, Mr Harris, I always thought this but now I see you in the open.'

'Perhaps, but my late father taught me that duty came first.'

'You have sons yourself?'

'No.'

'I thought not. Every father repeats what your excellent father told you because a father's first duty is to instruct. Only a man without sons can afford the luxury of subversion.'

'A father also protects, Prime Minister.'

'I see.'

'Isn't that a duty too?'

'My duty is to four millions, I believe you have set yourself up as protector of a single man. You see those soldiers in the forecourt? Their duty is to march up and down, and presently go and get killed or maimed. What is the duty of your protégé, do you consider, Mr Harris? And yours?'

— 142 —

I could put up an answer in serpentine sentences, but I respect him too much. His hand is on my arm and I feel the cold of his fear for his people. A diplomatic answer would seem worse than silence, so I say nothing. The answer you don't give creates a vacuum soon filled by something else, some other question, some other approach.

'Two men are named in the Note. One of them, Major Tankosić, we have handed over. He willingly went the way of his fellows — Princip, Cabrinović, the other wretches torn to pieces in Austrian dungeons — he said he would sustain them in torture and die with them as slowly as the Austrian wished.'

'A brave man.'

'Indiscreet and dangerous but if he was a countryman of yours, I think you would say *a gentleman.*'

In England the word has a constant if tired value, like a currency expensively maintained at its original exchange rate. In diplomatic circles abroad you hear it all the time, always in inverted commas, always meaning something different.

'If all these men have given under torture such testimony as they have to give, what is there to add?'

'You mean what could the surrender of the last man add?'

'Yes.'

'You see the clock over the soldiers' heads? It is about to strike eight. We have twenty hours left, you and I and Sir Edward Grey; then — it begins. Strandtman and yourself and Boppe, you all tell us to concede, agree, accept on every point. Time, you say, play for time. *Je veux bien.* But I must have a last piece in my hand to play.'

'Your Excellency,' I say formally, withdrawing my arm so his hand drops back to his side, 'I will weigh every word you say and faithfully inform the Foreign Office of your views.'

'I think you will, Mr Harris. I think you will. I believe the lovely Mrs Harris is on the Riviera?' he says, leading me towards the double doors of his vast, soulless room. 'His Highness Prince George is an impetuous character. You however have a bright career before you, a beautiful wife, a gentleman's reputation. And I have twenty hours.'

'I am honoured that you receive me — '

'It may be for the last time. You realise that the British Legation, standing between the river and the town, will be the first building in Belgrade to come under bombardment? You would do well, Mr Harris, to evacuate your women, your wounded, and your archive.'

Foreign Office, July 25, 1914
I have urged upon German Ambassador that Austria should not pre-cipitate military action.

It seems to me that Servia ought to promise that, if it is proved that Servian officials, however subordinate, were accomplices in murder of the Archduke, she will give Austria satisfaction. For the rest, I can only say that Servian Government must reply as they consider their interests require.

Grey to Harris.

DO I GO back to Pašić and say, 'do as you consider your interests require, your Excellency?' He could telegraph his Minister in London to inform the Foreign Office that his Government no longer had confidence in the British Chargé d'affaires, and give the reason. What I do is encode another telegram myself, and take it down to the Telegraph Office where I am received by clerks who have never before seen a Minister on their premises.

Belgrade, July 25, 1914
It appears that Russian Government have already urged utmost mod-eration on Servian Government.

Reply to Austrian note is now being drawn up. Prime Minister informs me that it will be in most conciliatory terms and will meet Austrian de-mands in as large measure as possible.

The ten points are accepted with reserves of insignificant character.

They agree to suppress Narodna Odbrana and have already arrested officer mentioned in Austrian note. In prevailing state of alarm, some misunderstanding caused by fact that a man also mentioned has same family name as stenographer employed in the Legation. She is sheltered here and misunderstanding is being clarified. Opinion of Servian Gov-ernment is that, unless Austrian Government desire war at any cost, they will accept full satisfaction offered in Servian reply.

Prime Minister begs me to convey to you his appreciation of your sup-port to his beleaguered country.

Harris to Grey.

THE OPERATION is known in hunting circles as drawing across the scent, I believe. Pósha appears in Hermann's uniform which droops from his wasted shoulders like a coat hanger.

'Ask Mr Dillon to come and see me at once.'

'Mr Dillon?'

'Oliver.'

'Oh yes Excellency, Oliver.'

'You should try and remember that his name is Mr Dillon.'

'Very well. Mr Dillon, but Oliver when I must put him to bed.'

'Thank you. That will do.'

'The boy in the cellar is a brave boy and a patriot but there is something you ought to know, Excellency.'

'I'm sure I know it already. Go and fetch Mr Dillon.'

'I will tell you later.'

I'm beginning to feel that Pósha is going to become a nuisance but he may have one last use. If war comes, he will be a responsibility too many; Des Graz, on the other hand, a bachelor stranded in some remote frontier village between Bulgaria and Hungary, could find him invaluable. Once the bombardment starts Des Graz's retreat will be cut off, he will have to withdraw into Russia, and then Pósha will come into his own.

'You wanted to see me?'

'Yes, Oliver. I have a dangerous mission for you.'

'Am I paid for dangerous missions?'

'The Foreign Secretary will be informed of your exploit.'

'Yes?'

'The Prime Minister has warned me that the guns of the Austrian monitors are trained on the building. You must take the archive to a safer place.'

In a word, I send Oliver with the archive containing Milan's last bomb to the German Legation, a solid building in the lower town and a long way from the Danube, with orders to remain there until further notice. I have telephoned Von Storck to warn him.

'Your archive will be safe with us, Harris,' Von Storck says.

'And Dillon — he's of the temperament Boppe calls *fragilisé.*'

'You mean this man is a drunkard?'

'No, I mean that I feel answerable for him as a friend and not only as his chief, for the moment.'

'I understand you, Harris. This Mr Dillon is what you call a sensitive plant and we in the German Legation will be careful to see that he does not dry out.' Von Storck gives a booming laugh into the instrument. And what right have I to stereotype it as humourless?

'Thank you, Von Storck.'

'Our countries are friends and our peoples cousins,' Von Storck reminds me.

WHEN XENIA LEARNS what I've done she's outraged. 'You have sent Oliver away with a bomb?'

'And what would have happened to us with the bomb still here when the shells begin to fall on the house?'

'Does he know the bomb is wrapped up in his archive boxes?'

'Yes. I told him to take it out when he gets there and put it somewhere in the Legation garden. The Germans have a big garden down there, full of laurel bushes.'

'What did he say?'

'He was very happy to do his duty.'

Actually, he turned white as a sheet when I explained the delicate part of his mission. 'A bomb?'

'Quite a small one I think, Oliver. The one they threw at the Archduke as he drove over the bridge didn't even go off.'

'But if it had, it would have blown the bridge to bits.'

'That, admittedly, was the idea.'

'And you want me to handle this thing and bury it in the Germans' garden?'

'I have told you the facts, Oliver. You must draw the conclusions.'

'When I reach the German Legation?'

'That's right.'

'You will be in my debt to the end of your days, Theo.'

'We are in each other's debt.'

St Petersburg, July 25, 1914

Minister for Foreign Affairs told French Ambassador and myself that Emperor had sanctioned mobilisation of 2,100,000 men. His Excellency assured me that Russia had no aggressive intention until forced on her.

French Ambassador then gave his Excellency formal assurance that France placed herself unreservedly on Russia's side.

Minister for Foreign Affairs turned to me with the question 'And your Government?' I replied that you did not yet despair of the situation. His Excellency said that unfortunately Germany was convinced that she could <u>count upon our neutrality.</u> If we took our stand with France and Russia there would be no war. If we failed them now rivers of blood would flow and we would in the end be dragged in.

French Ambassador said with great vehemence he could not believe
that England would not stand by her two friends —
Sir George Buchanan, Ambassador, St Petersburg, to Grey.
Repeated to Belgrade.

THE TELEGRAMS and despatches will be published one day, and men who weren't there at the time will argue for generations about where the responsibility lay. Here in the British Legation we have responsibilities nearer home. 'Pósha, I must tell you I have learned there is general mobilisation in Russia. You have family?'

'A mother and sisters, *Exzellenz*.'

'Your father?'

'He was valet to Prince Pavel Dolgorúkov, president of the Committee of Literacy,' Pósha says with pride.

'And he is alive and well?'

'Oh no. He accompanied the prince on his tour of villages beyond the Urals to tell about literacy and they were not always well received.'

'So your mother and sisters will need you by them if there's a war.'

'Need me? They work as prostitutes in St Petersburg. And if there is war,' Pósha adds grimly, 'the work won't fall off.'

He is from a world where two million men are mobilised at the Imperial initial on a page of paper and I may be sending him back to it. Being butler in a Legation, even the British one, is Pósha's zenith, and I must return him to his native soil where his sisters survive as whores. 'You understand, Pósha, the Legation will soon be vacated. The shells will fall on it and I have to obey orders from the Foreign Office. We must disperse.'

'The boy in the cellar? You have orders for him?'

'All of us must disperse.'

'And what will happen to me?' His body in the uniform too big for him droops still further.

'I have something to propose to you.'

He brightens up. 'I will bend myself to your requirements, Excellency.'

'I have an idea that may help you return to Russia where you must go, as I think you know — '

'I will be put in prison.'

'Why should you be put in prison?'

'I ran away from the Russian Legation to become your Excellency's spy.' In my father's day it was more straightforward. You gave a reference or a pension and escaped with your Victorian conscience free from feelings of guilt. 'This is what you will do. I've heard by telegram that the new Minister from London is held up at Tsaribrod in Bulgaria. You will go there by the last train tonight from Belgrade, cross the bridge on foot and present yourself to him. He is Mr Des Graz, a kindly bachelor. You will know what to say to him and how to offer your services. You will tell Mr Des Graz that the bombardment will start at any moment, Servia will be invaded, and he would do better retiring to Sofia with you to look after him. I expect Mr Des Graz would be reluctant to see you sent back to Russia, into prison, if he likes you enough.'

Pósha is looking me straight in the eyes. 'This is because of the boy in the cellar and your secretary,' he says.

'I'm thinking also of what may happen to you.'

'No. You throw me in the gutter.'

It's an injustice. Or is it? At the moment of enrolling a spy or servant you are in the dominant position. At the moment of sacking, the boot is on the other foot, morally speaking. The spy has been used and you are withdrawing from the contract and he can make you feel it. 'Mr Des Graz is Minister Plenipotentiary. When I leave the Legation I have no authority to take staff with me.'

'But you will take the secretary and the boy.'

'It is a personal responsibility.' Why do I explain? 'An emotional responsibility.'

'You mean of love?'

'Yes, that's what I mean.'

Pósha's expression changes. 'I told you that I had something to inform you.'

'This is your last chance to do it.'

'Your Excellency, like Monsieur Hartwig, is a man of education and from a high family.'

'Not so high.'

'I think so,' Pósha says firmly and speaking from experience of high and low.

'Well?'

'So you don't know much about the peasants.'

'Perhaps not. But I am familiar with Ivan Sergeevich Turgenev's *A Hunter's Notes.*'

'Another man of high family,' Pósha says, 'also looking for peasant women for his pleasure.'

'Listen, you must be on the Budapest train in thirty minutes — '

'In peasant families in Russia the women are for the use of the men, and the boys. I am from a peasant family and I saw this. It is the same in Servia. The girls marry another peasant perhaps, but first they are used in the family.'

The rigmarole is unpleasant and behind it I sense something worse. I take a step towards the door. 'I have your money and safe-conduct. I will drive you to the station in the motor car.'

Pósha doesn't budge. 'Your Excellency's secretary is from a peasant family.'

'I believe so.'

'She is educated but education only changes peasant ways after two generations. Perhaps three. Ivan Sergeevich Turgenev's mother was the granddaughter of peasants and she was terrible. Terrible.'

'Mademoiselle Ciganović — '

'Has your Excellency taken the trouble to observe her with the boy in the cellar who they say is the brother?'

'Yes, I have.'

'I have done more than observe.'

'Yes?' There are lies one should never hear but one always listens.

'I owe thanks for your goodness to me. But you do what Monsieur Hartwig would never do — you shelter bad people against your duty.'

I open the door of the study. 'Fetch your belongings. You may keep the uniform to convince Mr Des Graz that you are what you say.'

There are tears in his eyes. 'What I told you is true.'

'Hurry up.'

'All I have is in my pockets.'

'Very well.'

'Can I have the money now, please?'

It's the traditional rule and I give him over a month's worth of Hermann's wages.

'Your Excellency is generous, as I would expect.'

'I think we have been useful to each other, and I will forget what you were saying a minute ago.' We are already on the stairs with the front door open ahead of us. The money has vanished into his uniform; Pósha remains silent during the drive to the railway station and still says nothing when I hand over the ticket I've bought him for the Budapest train which will take him no further than the last station on the Servian side. I hold out a hand towards him, because war is coming and he will very probably be slaughtered in it, whatever Des Graz does with him.

Pósha doesn't take the hand. 'Monsieur Hartwig used to read to me from those stories of Ivan Sergeevich sometimes, when we were alone and I had no work to do. He shared his pipe with me because he loved the people, he wasn't afraid of them.' Now he is weeping openly. 'There was one story, I think, about leeches that kill a man by hiding in a part of his body he doesn't see. Because you understand Excellency, however well you wash yourself you don't feel a leech, sucking blood away.' His voice has become a droning sound. 'And any man has only so much to give.'

Driving back to the Legation I feel sickened, but whether from revulsion or doubt I'm unsure.

Belgrade, July 25, 1914

I hear answer to our Note is to be delivered to me before time-limit expires. Packing-up is proceeding at the Russian Legation while British Legation as usual seems concerned with other things — my British colleague, whom I met by chance at the railway station today invited me to a déjeuner à l'herbe on the occasion of the next race meeting at Topčider!! With young women!

Ammunition depots in the fortress are being evacuated. Railway station thronged with soldiers. In pursuance of the advices which have reached me while I write, we intend, in the event of a rupture, to leave Belgrade by the 6.30 train.

Baron Giesl von Gieslingen, Austro-Hungarian Minister, Belgrade, to Count Berchtold, Foreign Secretary, Vienna.

I COME BACK to a haunted Legation, yet there are quite a few of us still here. Ourselves, the women who cook and clean, the boy in the cellar. When does a boy stop being a boy and become a rival ? When you start to suspect him. Xenia is standing by the pillar in the entrance hall, one arm against the veined marble surface. 'I am tired of not being allowed to go out,' she says.

'You want to be arrested?'

'I want to see the grass at Topčider one more time.'

'Why just one? The crisis will pass.'

'I think you know it will not pass.'

I have never seen her sad before. Feelings, sentiments, develop in the dark, you think you know your feeling for a woman while all the time it has been changing and growing. I know I could never give her up, no government could make me. 'We could go on to the terrace and have coffee in the shade of the vine.'

'And watch the Austrians beyond the Danube? I'm a prisoner without them.'

'You know why, Xenia.'

'Because of the Narodna Odbrana.'

That's a disingenuous answer though it may not be so on purpose. 'No, because of Milan. He shouldn't be here and if he wasn't you and I would be free to go anywhere — Topčider, Smédérevo, anywhere. In the last hours we could take the road to Salonika.'

'There. I said you knew these hours are the last. Let's go on the terrace.'

There's a short flight of stairs to the main floor; the dining-room feels uninhabited, dark, the table unlaid. Her hand is still on my arm and I feel the touch of her leg against mine — together, apart and together. 'There's no one to bring us a glass of cold wine or some coffee,' I say, holding the curtain back for her to pass into the sunlight.

She doesn't answer. Well, it wasn't a question but I have questions I dare not put. Watching Kitty's jealousy over the years I believed I was above such a feeling; but it seems I'm not. 'You see where that wood of firs and willows comes down to the bank of the river, there on the other side?'

Xenia narrows her eyes even further. 'There are thin funnels like black cigars in the trees.'

'Yes. And look harder at the boats under them.'

'They have guns.'

This is her country, I can lift the telephone at any moment, tell the Prime Minister's office, 'Ciganović is here. He is a guest in the British Legation. Your men may come at once.' I should, perhaps, but I won't. 'I believe the Austrian Minister will leave Belgrade by the 6.30 train to Vienna unless the answer is accepted and we know now it won't be accepted. Those guns are waiting to fire on us.'

Xenia is leaning on the balustrade, looking upward at Kalemegdan. 'There are men carrying things out of the fortress.'

I take her arm and move toward the dining-room doors. 'They're taking the ammunition away. You must stay out of sight.'

'Would it blow up if the Austrians send their shells?'

'Of course.'

'Then it's a good thing they take it all away.'

'Yes. You wouldn't want Milan blown sky high.'

I mustn't let her suspect me of jealousy; the jealous are always at a disadvantage. We are at the dark end of the dining-room and she turns, holds both hands towards me. 'He is only a boy, he thinks he's a man because he followed the soldiers last year and worked on the railways and met students in cafés who planned tricks — '

'They gave Austria the excuse she was waiting for.'

'Austria would find the excuse whatever a lot of student boys did when they were drunk.' Why deny it? Dying empires are dangerous. 'You can give him to the government men, Theodore.' She lays both hands on the lapels of my coat and moves them gently, as if unaware of it, against my chest. 'They will offer him to the Austrians and say it was to save thousands of our Servian lives. But will it save them? The guns over the river — you think one wounded boy will stop them? Don't their orders come from somewhere too high up?'

So the Milan question is left ticking but I know that she has nothing closer to her heart than the decision I must take about him.

'The future has everything to give us,' she says.

Budapest, July 25, 1914

General opinion here is that Servian Government cannot accept demands, and that Servia's day of reckoning has come.

Probability of Russian intervention is denied or disregarded, and Government apparently expects that war will be localised . . . monitors are already on the Lower Danube.

Mr W. Max Müller, Consul-General, Budapest, to Grey.

A MESSAGE has come by hand from Prince George, written in pencil on a sheet of exercise book. His conscience may have suffered one of its rare wakeful moments but the thought is kind. I hurry down to the Telegraph Office.

Belgrade, July 25, 1914

I hear from a sure source that in the event of war no attempt will be made to defend Belgrade and that Government will proceed to Niš. In view of exposed position of British Legation, all cyphers and secret archives have been removed to safety in the German Legation. We expect a good many refugees applying to the Legation for shelter.

Harris to Grey.

IF THE GOVERNMENT goes I must go too; what then? If the Legation is shelled who will still be in it? I know Xenia won't abandon Milan, because in her mind and heart (as in mine) we're linked together in a pattern like pinpoints in the night sky. Locked, perhaps, would be the most fitting word.

XII

London, July 25, 1914

In Foreign Secretary's absence.

This morning Servian Minister raised with me question of your stenographer's homonym. On assurance that misunderstanding was clarified I said this was a matter for your responsibility on the spot. Clearly a nervous atmosphere.

Crowe to Harris.

Paris, July 25, 1914

I do not think that if Russia pick a quarrel with Austria over the Austro-Servian difficulty public opinion in France would be in favour of backing up Russia in so bad a cause.

Consequently the French Government will probably advise the Russian Government to moderate any excessive zeal that they may be inclined to display to protect their Servian client.

Sir Francis Bertie, Ambassador, Paris, to Grey.

OLIVER SAYS they're looking after him in the German Legation. 'Have you had a chance to admire the German Minister's garden?' 'Yes.'
'You planted a souvenir with H.M. Government's compliments?'
Oliver laughs. 'I've done my duty,' he says.
Well I'm sure he's safer than we are in the front row. How will it feel, when shells smash through the tiles of the roof, the timbers, the plaster and planks? I find Xenia teaching Milan to walk again on his wounded leg. They have an arm about each other's waist as they lurch forward

across the cellar floor, like a couple attempting a dance step heard on the gramophone. They don't see me straight away, and when they do the music seems to go out of them. 'You see, he will soon be running. Then he will be very useful to you.'

'The ultimatum expires in three hours.'

'What will the answer say?'

'We must hope it gains some time.'

'For what?

Milan is now walking on his own back and forth across the cellar floor, rapidly, like a bear in a pit, turning at the wall. Xenia says something in a low quick voice, but he doesn't stop his bear-circuit. 'He is exercising the muscles,' she says, 'when he is strong he will help us. You will see that and be glad you keep him safe here.'

In the British Legation the menace to the world is reduced to this — a girl's possessive feeling for a wounded boy, and my need to keep her. But if all is about to be split and felled and burned like the giant oaks in Turgenev's tale, who are you if at the end you possess no one at all?

5 P.M. The Prime Minister has asked me to go with him to the Austrian Legation. He says that only the presence of the British Chargé d'affaires might temper the Austrian reaction to the reply which will, though he doesn't say it, include an admission that the railway clerk Ciganović is not to be found in Belgrade and has never been heard of by any intelligence service. I accept the Prime Minister's invitation.

Giesl von Gieslingen receives us very insolently, I think, considering that Pašić has come in person. 'You have the reply in writing?'

'It is here,' says Pašić.

Giesl accepts the letter, opens it and scans it briefly. 'I will read this in the light of my instructions and give an immediate answer.' He struts from the reception room where we are left on our feet to consider the view from the windows or the cherubs on the domed ceiling. He isn't gone long. 'It is five minutes before six. I take this as your last word and find I am not satisfied with it. I will leave by the Vienna train at six thirty with the staff of the legation. Diplomatic relations must be considered as broken off.'

'You understand what you have done?' Pašić says to me as we reach the street where the Sunbeam and his hearse-like official carriage wait. The sky is black with thunder clouds and the first violent rain is falling.

'Ciganović — ' I begin, shaken by what has just happened.

Pašić searches his politician's store for some image to express his despair and I place a hand on his arm as we stand side by side on the hissing cobbles. 'Your Empire encircles the globe like an old man who once possessed her, and is now too impotent to lift even a finger,' he says.

'I'm sure when the time comes you will find us — '

'It will be too late for my people.' Pašić impatiently shakes my hand away as he climbs into his hearse. 'And probably even for yours.'

Vienna, July 26, 1914.
The Royal Servian Government have refused to comply . . . very much against our will, we find ourselves obliged to compel Servia by the sharpest measures to make a fundamental alteration in this hostile attitude.
Count Berchtold, Foreign Secretary, Vienna, to Embassies.

Berlin, July 26, 1914
Austro-Hungarian Embassy here consider localisation of crisis between Austro-Hungary and Servia will depend on whether, and , if so ,to what extent, Russia and France think that they can reckon on active support of His Majesty's Gouvernement in the event of a general complication. That is we would exercise a restraining influence by holding back.
Rumbold to Grey.

I HAVE A COPY of the Servian reply. Only the faintest shadow of reserve falls on acceptance of the demands. Like Pašić in person at the Austrian legation, his Government openly humbles itself; but the missing man is declared unfindable. Local diplomatic autonomy in the Hartwig mode has become a burden I can't carry alone; I telephone the German Legation.

'May I speak to the British archivist?'

'At once, Excellency.'

Perhaps the title is meant to sound ironic. At the German Legation they must already know that the Austrians are waiting on the railway platform for the 6.30 train to Vienna.

'Theo? Hallo?'

'Yes. I want you to — ' without warning, my stammer strikes me down.

'Return to the Legation?' Oliver asks patiently.

'Yes,' I say after an effort.

'Go and pour yourself a whisky, Theo.'

He may be right. I ring for Hermann but nothing happens, then I remember. The decanter must be in the sideboard in the dining-room; I go down there, find a glass, follow Oliver's prescription and presently feel a slow untying. By the time I hear the hooves on the cobbles I feel better, and pleased to see him, with his pink face from which the blue eyes glare forth, pugnacious, boiled, and kind. I take the bull by the horns. 'We may have been too hospitable for the good of Europe, Oliver,' I say.

'We?'

'I may have.'

'The Serbs have returned their answer?'

'Yes. It was a very emollient response but in the circumstances it could not satisfy on every count.'

'On which counts?'

'The question of Austrian participation in police enquiries on Servian soil.'

'And Ciganović?'

'Yes.'

'So our hospitality has something to answer for?'

'Very little when weighed against what's coming.'

'One life against thousands — hundreds of thousands maybe?'

'But a life we can preserve.'

'You mean a love preserved.'

I am in his hands and he knows it, and also that I trust him. 'The Austrians are boarding the train at this moment. Their Legation is closed.'

'How long before the shelling starts, do you think?'

IT STARTED just before dawn. Milan was first up and I wake to find him with Xenia in her nightdress standing over me.

'It has begun,' she says.

I raise my head and listen for the sounds of firing or crashing masonry but the silence of house and town is complete. 'When?'

'Ten minutes ago. Milan was on the terrace and he saw flashes the other side of the river.' So now he's getting outside on his own. Perhaps I could point out that his young countrymen are being mobilised; but if he turned himself in he wouldn't be put in camp with them, he would be rushed across the Danube to the gunboats.

'Perhaps a gun was fired by mistake,' I say, stupidly.

'They are only little guns they have over there on the water,' she says, and laughs.

Peering into the shaving mirror, I hear a sound like the limb of a tree snapping, then a shrill whistle and a crash from the direction of the terrace. It's oddly undramatic, for the start of a war, but I know that's what it is and I run down and out through the dining-room window. The damage on the terrace is considerable. Queen Victoria is in fragments and the balustrade is smashed all along one side. 'Come in quickly,' Xenia says, just before another crash wipes out the remains of the balustrade and Prince Albert with them. 'We should draw the curtains because of flying glass.'

The sky over the far-off Transylvanian Alps is slowly filling with the whitish light of another roasting day; there have been no more explosions, no gunfire, Belgrade is hardly yet awake but cook and maids have already deserted us. The rambling, dusty, shabby little capital city which has become the eye of the cyclone seems at peace. Oliver and I sit at the long scrubbed table in the kitchen with the coffee pot between us. 'If the government removes to Niš I may have to leave you in charge here, Oliver.'

'You mean I'll be Chargé d'affaires?'

Xenia appears carrying a pointed metal object held in a face towel. 'You see what I found in your bedroom?' she cries, and lays it on the table. It appears to be the head part of an unexploded shell.

'Where's the rest of it?' says Oliver.

'This is all.'

We study it like a snake under a rock. Is it dead or alive? Does it contain explosive or is it only a cone of iron?

'Don't pick it up again,' I say. 'We must send for a gunnery expert. I will get a message sent to Prince George's headquarters.'

'Leave him alone,' Xenia says with contempt. 'We will show it to Milan and he will tell us.'

I can hear Milan stumbling up the cellar stairs with a coal bucket; he notices the small shell head at once and smiles as though his 1913 memories bring back the scent of victory. We watch him fill up the stove with coal, clouds of black dust rising to the ceiling, and wait for his opinion. He picks up the cone, turns it in his hand, sniffs the jagged lower end and says something to Xenia. They both laugh, with the low sound of Slav laughter.

'Milan says they use toy guns. Pop guns. They are not men over there on their little boats.'

'Nevertheless it did a lot of damage on H.M. Government property.'

'This is a strong building,' Xenia points out, 'it would need a big gun to knock it down. Now we will make some glue with flour and water and stick paper on all the window panes on the side facing the river,' she says. 'Oliver will help me.'

'We'd better be quick about it,' Oliver says. Between the three of them they seem to have things in hand.

Vienna, July 26, 1914
Servian reply not considered satisfactory. War is thought imminent. Wildest enthusiasm prevails in Vienna. Russian Embassy is being guarded by troops to prevent repeated attempts at hostile demonstrations on part of the vast crowds parading on the streets.
de Bunsen to Grey.

Cadogan Gardens, S.W., July 26, 1914
I lunched with Stamfordham. He told me Prince Henry came over from Germany yesterday and breakfasted with the King this morning. Prince Henry said if Russia moved there would be an internal revolution and the Romanov dynasty be upset. This is nonsense — but it shows how anxious they are to make out to us that Russia will remain quiet — a foolish procedure — (Prince Henry has gone back to Germany).
Nicolson to Grey.

Belgrade, July 26, 1914
Government is leaving for Niš. Special train is placed at the disposal of Diplomatic Corps this evening. I am leaving with my other colleagues — Vice-consul remains in charge.
Harris to Grey.

I NOMINATED OLIVER acting Vice-consul though I doubt the augmentation of salary will ever reach him — some pen-pusher in the Foreign Office will discover that I was acting *ultra vires* and rescind the appointment, war or no war. As I leave I can see Xenia standing just behind him, then she dashes out on to the steps.

'Go back!' I dismount and follow her in. 'Don't you understand the Government agents are everywhere?'

'You think I still interest them?'

We are safely in the hall, the door closed behind us. 'What did you want?'

'How could we say goodbye properly with Oliver there?'

'It isn't for long..

'And when the real war starts?'

'There's been no more shelling. I'm sure there'll be no real war.'

'I know this is not what you believe.'

'Then I'll come back for you.'
'You promise this?'
Our hands touch.'I promise it.'
'You should trust me more than you do.'
'I'll do my best, Xenia.'

THE ROAD to Niš is appalling. Since the historic fight of the Balkan League against the Turks the Serbs have no resources to take care of things like roads. They are a military and agricultural nation, farmers and armies can make do with dirt tracks. I suffer on account of the Sunbeam and her springs as I bounce painfully along in low gear, hoping that the motor will not over heat nor the radiator boil. That would mean a delay of hours while my colleagues of the Diplomatic Corps bag the only habitable accommodation in the God-forsaken town of Niš.

I suffer no more than two punctures on the way and have two spare wheels; at last the road takes us into the outskirts, a dismal assembly of huts and hovels and the yards of smallholdings, not a tree, not a garden to be seen. Boys, who before long will be left alone to defend their homes when the fathers go to the front, watch with fascination as the motor car passes. One of the chief duties of a British diplomatist these days is to counter hostile fascination so I wave in an encouraging fashion and squeeze the rubber bulb of the horn a few times, which seems to have some effect. These hungry looking boys bare their teeth in what may be a grin so I draw up and ask one of them the way to the Palas Hotel which is where I have been told Boppe is going. I feel Boppe and I should stick together as the world crisis unrolls. The boy doesn't answer but stoops to pick a stone from the road which he hurls at the windscreen, hitting the brass headlamp. The shock of this attack strikes silence into me and I drive on without help through the dust and pot-holes in search of the Palas hotel, aware that it will be some time before speech returns.

WHEN JAMES Harris had to report his fourteen year old son missing, the matter was taken up by the Home Office because James knew about the dangers of publicity in kidnapping cases. Haldane was then only a member of Parliament and James not yet a professor; however they were rising men and between them they saw to it that the forces of order were mobilised and the press kept well out of it.

Two days later, with the forces of order still drawing blank, Theodore reappeared in Rutland Gate. He had nothing to say, appeared incapable of saying anything. The brougham was sent round to Selzman's lodgings with orders not to return without him. Theodore's mother, less indulgent than her husband but still full of careful attentions, inspected him as he waited.

'His clothes and person are dirty,' she told James.

'He has had some bad experience.'

'We must be very careful.'

'I am always careful with Theodore.'

'Neither I nor the world could find any fault with you, James,' said the other half of the mutual admiration society.

When Selzman arrived, calm as always, James took him into the library, closed the door, and explained the circumstances in a few words. 'Theodore left here to attend his drawing tutorial with Mr Mackmurdo in Fitzroy Street on Saturday morning. I should never have left him to go through London alone but Fitzroy Street is in a respectable district. Since his return an hour ago he hasn't spoken.'

'He has had some great shock, I fear.'

'Yes.' There was a long silence. 'I have not sent for the doctor.'

'I think that was wise.'

'My wife and I both believe he may talk more readily to you than to either of us, once he recovers his speech with your help.' Another silence. 'Whatever has happened may leave him with a sense of shame which he wishes to hide from us. We would therefore be the worst people to try and find out what it was.'

'I understand,' Selzman said, 'I won't even try to find it out. When confidence returns I'm sure he will tell me if he is hurt.'

'I trust you entirely,' said James, and they shook each other warmly by the hand for the second time. 'It would, I believe, be better if you spoke to me about whatever transpires, rather than my wife.'

'Yes.'

'Theodore has taken a bath and is in his room.'

Almost as soon as he was alone with Selzman, Theo began painfully, unsuccessfully, to stammer out some words.

'We are in no hurry, Harris. By the way, I should like to see those verses you mentioned you were working on to offer Mr Selwyn Image at the Hobby Horse. I'm sure you have made progress.' Theo handed over his notebook with obvious relief for Selzman to read. 'I can see a more ordered discipline here in your stanzaic pattern,' Selzman said kindly.' 'Let us look at the patterns of the map of London.'

When any map is spread out, the eye tends to look for the last site visited there, and this is just what Theodore's now did. It travelled northward from Fitzroy Street towards St Pancras, then onward to Pentonville and seemed to hover above the blue stripes on the page marking the Regent's Canal and its adjoining basins. Not, Selzman, thought, too safe a corner of London's hidden life. He put a hand on Theo's shoulder. 'You make advances in drawing under Mr Mackmurdo's eye, Harris?' Theo nodded. Selzman leaned forward to take a couple of pencils and a sheet of paper from the table. 'I have to leave you for a minute or two, I must walk off my indigestion. Would you draw an impression of your last subject with Mr Mackmurdo, while I'm gone?'

Selzman judged that fifteen minutes would be enough; he limped out with his stick into Rutland Gate and across to the Park where he saw the Life Guards go past, all spit and polish and rattling harness. He liked the horses best, remembering the equestrian statues of Lisbon. When he returned he found Theo folded in on himself in a chair on the dark side of the room. The drawing on the unlined sheet of paper had nothing to do with the last subject in Fitzroy Street but told Selzman all he needed to know about Theo's lost days.

'I hope you are not physically hurt, at least, Harris?' he asked.

'Not physically,' said Theo, speaking for the first time.

'The mind is so made that it has a tendency to cure itself far better than one might think from the accounts of unhappiness in novels,' Selzman said with a smile; 'on condition that nothing is hidden away in the dark. And your drawing hides nothing. You are already a man of some courage, Harris, at fourteen.'

Listening from the library door on the ground floor, James Harris rejoiced to hear his son's voice, light and hesitant, saying goodbye to Selzman at the end of the afternoon. He tried to persuade the tutor to accept a ride home to Pembroke Villas, but Selzman preferred the journey by omnibus.

James asked no questions, then or later, about Theodore's experience; Constance for her part had decided to rise above the incident entirely and the life of tutor and boy resumed as before, but everyone understood that Theodore wore in him a mark, not so much a scar as a difference.

THE PALAS HOTEL proves to be little better than a hovel and there is no sign of Boppe. The town of Niš, once the capital of Constantine, can hardly have seen such crowds since the Emperor departed. The members of the Skuptchina assembly, convened at a day's notice, throng the streets and asphyxiate the hotels and quarrel noisily in the few cafés and restaurants. Eventually I run Boppe to earth at the Europa Hotel whose relative comfort convinces me I ought to leave the Palas immediately.

'There are no rooms here any more for anyone,' Boppe tells me. 'Albion arrives at the eleventh hour. You should have come with common mortals in the train.'

'Thank you Boppe. *Vive l'entente.*' Next I find Von Storck drinking a cognac in the reception hall, flanked by two secretaries of Legation and a military attaché in uniform, a far larger contingent than any other representative here. 'Ah, Harris!' he calls. 'You have good rooms I hope?'

'The hotel is full.'

'How many are you?'

'I am here alone.'

'With no stenographer? But I have good news for you, Harris. My military attaché here tells us there is a woman who lets lodgings only to important visitors. What is the address, Wolfgang?'

'Number 3, Prince Michael Place, Excellencies,' Wolfgang barks.

'I should waste no time, Harris,' says Von Storck, 'you will be comfortable there, though I fear lonely, at first.'

The landlady in Prince Michael Place has let me two well furnished rooms and sent up a maid with a bottle of white wine within minutes of my arrival. The maid indicated that this was not the only service she was there to provide to travellers, I thanked her and gave a small tip. The next thing is to locate the Telegraph Office.

Niš, July 27, 1914

Government and Diplomatic Corps have taken up quarters here. Prime Minister expected tomorrow.

My French colleague again expressed apprehension lest H.M. Government should hesitate to manifest their full support for French Government as promptly as the latter might hope and the situation, in their view, demands.

Harris to Grey.

THERE'S AN INWARD telegram also, and I take it back to Prince Michael Place for decoding.

Budapest, July 27, 1914

Budapest was last night scene of popular demonstrations of wild enthusiasm for war with Servia.

*General Putnik, Chief of Servian General Staff, was arrested last night
by military authorities at railway station on the way to Servia.*
Max Müller to Grey.
Repeated to Niš.

GENERAL PUTNIK is Pašić's closest friend and adviser so this provocation shows that the Austro-Hungarians have already, in their own
mind, declared war. Those three isolated shells on the fortress and the
Legation were forerunners. I try to reach Oliver by telephone but in the
end, after a long struggle with officials at the postal office, it is Xenia
who answers.

'Are you in a comfortable hotel?' she asks.

'I have taken rooms in a private house recommended by the German
Minister.'

'It's probably a brothel,' she says and laughs, the laughter sounding
hollow as a reed down the line of the primitive Servian telephone system.

'I need to speak to Oliver.'

'He is too drunk to speak to you.'

'Put his head under the cold tap and I'll telephone again in an hour.'

'Milan must do it. It is not suitable for a woman to do that.'

'The police haven't come to bother you?'

'No, but there are refugees.'

'British subjects?'

'There are many British subjects,' Xenia answers carefully.

'But not all?'

'Perhaps.'

A straight answer is unusual in diplomatic complications and unknown
in private ones. 'You are an employee of the British Legation, Xenia, and
I wish you to find out if these refugees are entitled to the protection of my
Government, and if not, who are they?'

'Very well, Mr Harris,' she says and I can hear, as usual, the laughter
in her voice.

'I miss you, Xenia.'

'I just wish we lived, you and me, on a lovely farm in the English
country with horses and cows and vines, and no diplomats,' she says.

'And no war. But now tell me what I asked to know about the refugees.'

'I will try.'

'Well?'

'Not everyone here in Belgrade has a passport, you know. Some of the people who have come here for protection do not have them in their pocket so it is difficult to know what is their nationality.'

Getting a reply as opaque as that you may lose heart, and this happens to me. 'You are not to admit anyone else to the Legation who cannot present a British passport or safe-conduct, please.'

'So if there is a war you will send me away because I don't have one?'

'No, I will never do that, Xenia.' I hang up the instrument before she has time for her next question because I know what it will be.

Paris, July 28, 1914
Russian Ambassador last night declared his belief that war is inevitable and by fault of England; that if England had at once declared her solidarity with Russia and France, and her intention to fight if necessary Germany & Austria would have hesitated. He said that Austria's objective is to extend Germanic influence and power towards Constantinople, which Russia cannot possibly permit. He said that HMG by inaction had encouraged Austria.
Bertie to Grey.

VON STORCK has sent round asking me to dinner on the terrace of the radio-active mineral baths at Niška Banja; one can drink champagne under the linden trees, he says, and look down from the hillside on the valley of the Nišava and the heights of Suva Planina beyond. I have no desire to share a mineral bath with him but in diplomacy you must not refuse a colleague's invitation. On the way, I stop at the Telegraph Office.

Niš, July 29, 1914
Considerable panic in Belgrade, in consequence of which more refugees are crowding into British Legation to seek protection of our flag.
Harris to Grey.

XIII

Schönbrunn, July 29, 1914
A halt must be called to these intolerable proceedings. In this solemn
hour I am fully conscious of my responsibility before the Almighty. I trust
in my peoples and in the might of the Fatherland, and in the Almighty to
give victory to my arms.
Emperor Francis Joseph.

BOPPE, TOO, has been taking the baths, but I fear it has done him little good. He caught sight of me seated under the trees with the Germans
and made a gesture of despair and contempt. I rose at once to go to him
but he had already vanished into one of the bathing cabins.

'Boppe is not in the best health at the moment, I must see if he needs
help.'

'Kingdoms stand shoulder to shoulder against republics, make sure the
entente with France doesn't turn to alliance,' Von Storck says.

'These terms denote little more than varying frequencies in the spec-
trum,' I say, and the German party present the closed faces of those who
understand the idea well enough but haven't yet worked out the implications.

I knock on the cabin door. Boppe, attended by two secretaries of Legation, is trying to re-knot his bow-tie in the small, cracked looking-glass
hung on the wooden partition wall. His hands shake so that the knot fails
to hold, sags beneath his collar stud or flaps about like an injured moth.
I long to lend a hand but that would be badly received — French diplomats are prickly customers.

'What passed between you and the Germans, Harris?' Boppe asks.

'Nothing but an insignificant Prussian joke.'

'But surely for the English a joke is a serious communication?'

I take this as a sign of mental confusion and say nothing. The first secretary, a man of my own age, is watching me in a way which I think must mean he expects to take over the French Legation at any moment and then report to Paris on my attitude and conduct. Their training equips them for work as conceived at the Quai d'Orsay, a ceaseless striving after hegemony. '*Son Excellence souffre d'une légère fatigue,*' this man informs me, and I see no reason to contradict him.

'Have you your motor-car here, Harris?' Boppe asks.

'I have.'

'Perhaps you would be kind enough to drive me back to my hotel? I believe it is a two-seater?'

Obviously he is attempting to escape the secretaries. 'Yes it is. But it has what we call a folding dicky-seat, that is, an outside place for two passengers.'

'A sort of pillion, in a word?'

'Exactly.'

'Excellent,' says Boppe, cheering up considerably. 'You two can sit in the British Chargé d'affaire's folding dicky-seat. We will erect the hood, for privacy.' He laughs for the first time in weeks and looks much better at once. 'Dicky-seat!' he repeats to himself several times as we walk over the dust and weeds to the Sunbeam. He's still laughing, with a trickle of saliva from the corner of his mouth.

In the driving compartment he seems to me to be reaching the end of his tether. I hear it in his muttering voice and turn my head to look at him. 'Are you quite all right, Boppe?'

'Naturally I am not quite all right, Harris.' His voice is broken; problems of speech arouse my fellow-feeling, and in a language like his they arouse pity. 'I have a vision of a million Frenchmen dead in the fields.'

'That's only a bad dream, Boppe.'

'I have two boys in the army.'

'There is still hope, our rulers will draw back from the abyss.'

'France is a republic and we rule ourselves as adults.' This is said with such anguish that I slow down and halt by the side of the road. We are on a slope on the outskirts of Niš, a tram labours uphill towards the mineral baths, crowded with citizens who have yet to take in the significance of the Government's move from Belgrade to here. Are they on their way to the baths for the last time? Or fleeing the town altogether? Going downhill, a troop of scrawny horse precedes a couple of pieces of artillery, the men in charge hauling back on the brakes as the guns lurch from side to side of the road. I draw further in under the shelter of the trees.

'Have you consulted your doctor, Boppe? We know each other well and I think you'll allow me to suggest that a sedative might be indicated — to ease the stress I know you feel?'

'Don't take us directly to Niš, Harris. I want to talk to you in private.'

'I see your secretaries of Legation behind us, gesticulating.'

'Let them gesticulate.'

Paris, July 30, 1914

President of Republic is convinced that preservation of peace between Powers is in hands of England, for if His Majesty's Government announce that, in the event of conflict between Germany and France, resulting from present differences between Austria and Servia, England would come to aid of France, there would be no war, for Germany would at once modify her attitude.

Bertie to Grey.

Foreign Office, July 31, 1914

I told French Ambassador that we had come to the conclusion that we could not give any pledge at the present time. The financial situation was exceedingly serious; there was danger of a complete collapse that would involve us and everyone else in ruin; and that our standing aside might be the only means of preventing a complete collapse of European credit. This might be a paramount consideration in deciding our attitude.

M. Cambon expressed great disappointment at my reply. He repeated his question of whether we would help France if Germany made an attack on her. I said that we could not take any engagement.

In view of prospect of mobilisation in Germany it becomes essential to His Majesty's Government to ask whether French Government is prepared to engage to respect neutrality of Belgium so long as no other Power violates it.

Grey to Bertie.

Is the word 'honour' to be abolished from the English language?

M. Paul Cambon, French Ambassador, London, to Wickham Steed, diplomatic correspondent, The Times.

'WHERE WOULD you care for me to drive you, Boppe?'

'Follow the road up that hill over there, you see it? With the small white building on the top? The bigger building below is the military hospital, for the wreckage of war against Bulgaria. Soldiers without tongues.'

'Without tongues?'

'A Bulgarian speciality — linguectomy on prisoners.'

The winding road is not hard to find in this country of few roads, and on the way up we pass a mosque in whose minaret, the only one still active in Niš, a crier stands waiting for the sunset. I press the accelerator pedal to the floor as we pass by the military hospital's gruesome precinct. 'What is that white building, Boppe?'

'You will see.'

When we reach it, I do see. It's a mausoleum open on one side, the interior like a stone beehive. 'What on earth is it for?'

'It shelters the Tower of Skulls from the elements,' Boppe says. 'Stop here.' The city of Niš, more a sprawling suburb of single-story houses than a town, lies spread below us; I can hear the secretaries of Legation hurrying to get out of the dicky-seat. 'We will remain in your motor car, Harris,' says Boppe and waves the secretaries away. With suspicion printed on their features they walk off round the side of the hill, in step, casual but regular, expressive of the republican idea — equal, free, conformist.

'Are you thirsty? Your voice is hoarse, I have a bottle of Seltzer here.' I take it from the door pocket and hold it out.

'From what am I supposed to drink, Harris?'

'For God's sake, drink from the neck of the bottle.'

Obediently, the French Minister drinks from the Seltzer bottle held to his lips. 'You were right, Harris, to insist as you did,' he says. 'You are not a bad fellow, after all,' he adds in English, 'but you have too quick a temper for a good diplomat. Possibly your impediment enervates you. I have known other instances.' What seems to be happening is that he oscillates, like Europe herself, between native lucidity and a state bordering on breakdown.

'I should not have spoken as I did.'

'You apologise?'

'If I must, I apologise.' We both laugh and he hands me back the Seltzer bottle.

'You asked to be informed about this Tower of Skulls,' Boppe says. 'After defeating the Serbs near Niš in 1809 the Turks, according to Oriental custom, erected a rude tower, now enveloped within the mausoleum you see before you, composed partly of lumps of rock and partly of their enemies' heads to commemorate the victory.' The precise, measured pedagogy of his voice is beginning to crumble and break up into component parts of distress and fear. 'Old people in the neighbourhood relate that there were originally twelve hundred skulls embedded there — twelve hundred skulls in this little tower!'

'Is this reliably corroborated?'

'What is reliable corroboration? I can only tell you that when Lamartine visited the tower which was then open to the sky, many of the skulls still had hair clinging to them, grinning in the rocky façade.'

'Perhaps we should drive round the other side of the hill and pick up your colleagues there?'

'No, Harris. I have something to say to you, much to say, in fact. A great deal to say which you must hear carefully and relay to your superiors.'

This news is not unexpected. Boppe, stuck in his Legation with a couple of secretaries eager to take over his job and too young to sympathise with his nervous troubles, has chosen me. Because I regularly let him score at foils he imagines himself preeminent.

'You will allow me to ask you, Harris, whether as Chargé d'affaires you are kept well informed by London?'

'Events are unfolding very fast,' I say.

'I think your answer means that as you are not a Minister, your instructions are more peremptory than illuminating.'

'The Foreign Office with the best will in the world is often not very illuminating.'

'I understand. You refer to what Zola called *les ronds-de-cuir* — the gentlemen with circular bottoms seated on circular leather cushions in the offices of the State.'

'My mother is a great admirer of Zola and helped to get him published in Victorian England.'

'Possibly, possibly. But you don't answer my question.'

I'm no longer sure what it was, but what I am sure of is that Boppe is going downhill. His speech is still rational but his eyes are not. They are dilated and twitch in their sockets like stranded fish. 'I believe I am sufficiently informed for my responsibilities,' I produce, without much hope.

Boppe attempts a *redoublement,* renewal of attack against an opponent who parries and delays. 'Now I will tell you what will happen in the family of Europe while your Liberals watch from behind their half-open door.' He's trembling, diplomatic discourse may be about to disintegrate, but what can I do? Call those secretaries and have him carted off, padded up, shipped back to Paris? What would Selzman do? He would attempt to restore the sense of worth.

'We need to know what intentions are in the French official mind and there you could help me. I will be discreet in what I relay and how I relay it to the Foreign Office, where sympathy and regard for French interests is almost the first concern, as you know.'

The trembling is worse. My words were either ill-chosen or they came too late to do any good. The engine, which I have left running in the hope that Boppe would soon agree to be driven back to his hotel, gives a cough, a kick to the universal joint in its leather gaiter, and stops. I have never seen a nervous breakdown before and feel I can do nothing to help except keep the secretaries away and listen as the temperature rises in the front of the car. I take the Seltzer bottle and have a long swig. There's not much left.

'The official mind — I invite you in to see what happens while I, a humble functionary, carry the weight of the Republic in this . . . this small state peripheral to European civilisation.'

'It wasn't peripheral when Niš was Constantine's capital,' I ill-advisedly say.

'Constantine! His mother was English and he was born at York! Charlemagne's empire was bounded by the Danube and the Save and he possibly never knew of the existence of Servia; better had it never existed!'

'Please go on with what you were about to say — the official view — '

'It is cold in your automobile. Have you no rug?' Boppe seems to wrap himself round, fold his arms about his chest and shoulders. 'Now we will consider the historical aspect of our crisis,' he says in a measured voice. 'Your Government under Gladstone gave a guarantee to Belgium to which the Powers subscribed, reinforcing the Treaties of 1831 and 1839.'

'Yes, indeed,' I say.

'And Clarendon in 1867 defined your country's guarantee as individual, not collective.'

'That is my understanding.' Boppe looks at me sharply to see if if my understanding is as clear as I say it is, and he is within his rights to do so. These details which have lodged so well in his head that he still commands them even on the edge of breakdown, leave in mine only a vague, anachronistic impression of British policy as being that of gentlemen of their word.

'It follows that England must spring to the defence of Belgian neutrality whatever the other Powers may do, the guarantee being individual.'

'No lawyer could put it better than you do, Boppe.'

'This, Harris, is the fact on which the future of the world hinges. Not Europe, the world.' His voice is uneven, discontinuous. 'Your people are walking open-mouthed — ' his shaking has become spasm, 'we will never forgive you if you don't come in.' He thinks a moment. 'Nor, I fear, if you do.'

'Why on earth do you say so, Boppe?'

'Do you understand nothing? It is because France cannot live under obligation.' I put a steadying hand on his shoulder but he continues. 'The old Flanders whore must be raped before your Liberal ministers will awake. Very well, she will be raped. You will see.' One of the secretaries, having completed the circuit of the hill of skulls, raps at the window. His eyes are fastened on his Minister trembling on the polished leather of the seat. 'You will see,' Boppe cries, 'France knows how to attend to this — the Flanders whore — and individual guarantee.' He begins to laugh in his nervous disarray. I push away the side screen and call to the secretaries to hop in the dicky seat.

Paris, July 31, 1914

French Government are resolved to respect the neutrality of Belgium, and it would only be in the event of some other Power violating that neutrality that France might find herself under the necessity, in order to assure defence of her own security, to act otherwise.

Bertie to Grey.

Minute
The Cabinet are discussing the question. Wait.
Crowe.

I am not sure that we should inform German Government of French reply. The two countries may very shortly be at war and we should not pass on anything from one to the other. And if France asks us we can say we have had no reply from Germany either on the Belgian question.
Nicolson.

CRIPPS HAS somehow reached Niš with the bag, passing via land and water through Trieste and Dubrovnik and the mountain passes.

'Decent billet you found for yourself here, Minister, and caught sight of a girl peeping from a doorway on the stairs — I must say I wouldn't mind — '

'You should waste no time finding somewhere to lay your head tonight, Cripps, the town's bursting. Try the Palas Hotel. And now, if you don't mind, I must open the bag. Come back and have dinner when you've found a lodging.' I hear Cripps's tread on the staircase, then his voice, low and suggestive, and that of the maid.

The bag contains out of date despatches repeating the Government's difficulties with their electorate ever since the Boer War. And there's a letter from my mother in a black-lined envelope. I open it with mixed feelings — her handwriting when I was unhappy lifted the heart; these days the strong but erratic characters have a different effect because I see signs of weakness. She will need me, in the end, even more than I needed her because then my strength waxed; hers is on the wane.

Richard Haldane came to my Thursday afternoon and I thought you would like to know what he told me. It has become so rare for a n y o n e to tell me anything, since your Father died. For another year or two she must be allowed to go on claiming that life holds no more meaning or purpose but in fact she recovered quite quickly from grief because life in her burns so strongly.

Just now half the Cabinet, after roasting for hours in the heat of a Downing Street forenoon, fled to the Automobile Club in Pall Mall to drown themselves in the green waters of the Swimming-pool, below the Ionic columns, with masseurs in waiting. (Do you picture them? Haldane with his paunch, Churchill on his short legs, Asquith and his — what has Asquith to distinguish him from other men? Oh yes, his mind).

So there they are, floating about like Balloons, and still discussing, discussing What? The Fleet at Spithead — should it disperse or remain in the Channel to strike terror everywhere? The Dublin riots — ought more Irishmen be mown down in the interests of the Crown, or fewer, or none at all? The suffragettes — there it seems there was unanimity. These women must be placed out of danger to themselves in Prison and in the opinion of some members of the Cabinet, be whipped by Beadles pour décourager les autres. According to Haldane, this idea occasioned a certain commotion in the green Automobile Club waters.

Then last of all, and vaguely, those difficulties in Servia. These, I believe, did not detain them long. Powerful governments, like Victorian fathers, fasten their protective instinct on some object too insignificant to do them harm; for our Government, it seems that Servia is not the chosen Beneficiary. The pampered, graceless favoured child of our rulers is Belgium.

Lonely and useless as I now am I still try, dearest Theodore, to bring my drop of information to your notice.
As always, your devoted,
Mother.

I THINK she understands the world so well that it's no wonder Haldane still patronises her afternoons. 'Constance has the clear unspoilt apprehension of a relatively uninstructed mind,' I once heard my father say, out of her hearing.

What should I do? This picture would have fascinated Boppe, but what difference could it make? Well, as the minutes tick off almost anything might make a difference. The French Government might wait before letting the military make some fateful step; around the short Belgian frontiers the forces will mass and Grey and the rest will come off the fence before a shot's fired. It's a small if forlorn hope. I set out for the Hotel Europa.

'*Son Excellence a subi une crise de nerfs, une véritable crise,*' the secretary tells me excitedly, his eyes bright and pitiless. 'He will travel on the hospital train tonight to Salonika.'

'A doctor has seen him?'

'But naturally, Monsieur, a doctor has seen him. The former Minister will be sedated and will travel with Mademoiselle Clotilde who is instructed in his care.'

'May I, perhaps, see him for a few minutes?'

'I regret, this is not possible.'

'Why is that?'

'It is because the former Minister's mental condition precludes it.'

'You know, of course, that I must report this state of affairs to London?'

'Do you not think, Mr Harris, that we are beyond the stage of reporting individual vicissitudes?'

DOES ANY individual still count at all, as the machines shift and rumble towards collision? When I get back to my rooms I find a message from Pašić and return to the Telegraph Office where everyone knows or guesses at everyone's business, impotent as we are.

Niš, July 30,1914
Information received here that war declared by Austria.
Harris to Grey.

THEN I telephone the Legation. 'Oliver?'

'Yes, Theo.'

'What's happening?'

'Another shell or two fell in the garden below the terrace.'

'No damage?'

'Only frightened the wits out of half the population of the town. Everyone says the shelling proper will start tonight.'

'What about the refugees?'

'What indeed,' says Oliver.

Niš, July 30, 1914

General bombardment of Belgrade expected tonight. I have instructed vice-consul to hoist flag over Legation. He will order refugees to leave.

Prime Minister tells me that he has now left it entirely to military authorities whether Belgrade be defended or not.

Harris to Grey.

AROUND MIDNIGHT and long after the Telegraph Office is shut I realise that I didn't ask for Xenia; perhaps I carry her in me where she can come to no harm but first thing in the morning I telephone again. 'I must speak to Xenia.'

'Ah,' says Oliver. 'Well. She went out.'

'You allowed her to go out?'

'I'm not her keeper, Theo. She was of the opinion that the agents of the Foreign Ministry now have better things to do than arrest her. She has gone to fetch provisions for the growing population.'

'The refugees are still there?'

'Quite a crowd. You should see it. And there's been more shelling.'

'Were we hit?'

'Most of the windows are well and truly busted.' Oliver laughs.

Niš, July 31, 1914

I am informed that several shells have fallen on portion of Legation exposed to Austrian fire, doing considerable damage.

Minister for War states that Servian frontier has not yet been violated.

Harris to Grey.

BUT IT WON'T be long. In this makeshift town, officials of Ministries dash hither and thither, conveying instruction, rumour, denial. The latest is that King Peter has risen from his bed and is about to arrive though there are no troops to review, no court to hold. His kingdom is disintegrating before our eyes and only Hartwig might have held it together; but Hartwig is gone, and with him all the old diplomatic play. Now I see Von Storck marching along the street towards me, his shoes throwing up little puffs of dust from the uneven ground.

'Harris! I have something to tell you.'

'I am keen to know it.' We are near a kind of public garden or open space ornamented with uncared for bushes, desired by no one, despaired of as soon as planted. Von Storck takes my arm and draws me into the no man's land.

'Boppe did well to get himself carried off in a hospital train. He would hardly have dared to face me after what I have learned,' Von Storck says, and I feel fear at what's to come. 'A French aircraft has violated the Belgian border, flying by night in the direction of Aachen.'

'Aix-la-Chapelle?'

'Aachen, Harris.'

'If the aeroplane was in the air, in the dark, can we be certain in international law that a border exists to be violated? Are we not rather referring to an imaginary vertical extrapolation from the ground which can hardly be held to — '

'Enough!' Von Storck says in a voice echoing about among the dying bushes. 'You are playing with me. This French aircraft then proceeded over our territory towards Aachen and grenades were tossed from the cockpit onto a populated area.'

'Was anyone hurt?'

'We are not speaking of individual hurt, Harris, but of the right of peoples.'

'Of armies and Marshals, Von Storck?'

'In the Channel your Admirals hang along the French coast.'

'One must hope that this trivial incident in the air will not be taken too seriously in the Wilhelmstrasse?'

'It is not in the Wilhelmstrasse that it will be taken so seriously. We diplomatists must make way for the military men.'

'The men of war?'

He doesn't answer and without another word swings away from me and marches off through the dust in the direction of the Hotel Europa. I think there's nothing in what he said that calls for another telegram to

London where they must know all about the air incursion; but what it does call for is a reappraisal of the safety of our archive in the German Legation building in Belgrade. Cousinly peoples can become enemies.

I'M CERTAINLY NOT the only one awake, all Niš shifts restlessly in the stifling night heat — men and women, horses tethered in the streets, the Prime Minister and his aides, King Peter himself if he has arrived. Probably only Von Storck sleeps heavily, his mind at rest for eight hours — and I may be wrong about that too.

I get up from the wide, hard bedstead with its coarse woven flax sheets and dress. The full moon is high in a clear sky and its light falls evenly as snow over the roofs, the earth of the street and the wooded hills; standing at the open window I watch the night life of this big ugly village, at each window I can see a figure doing the same and along the street, on the ground, are those without walls or windows.

I must face the responsibility waiting hidden among the refugees in the Legation at Belgrade. Before the moon pales and fades and vanishes I must decide — one way or the other.

St. Petersburg, July 30, 1914
In this serious moment I ask you earnestly to help me. An ignominious war has been declared against a weak country and in Russia the indignation which I share is tremendous. I fear that very soon I will be forced to take measures which will lead to war. To prevent a calamity such as a European war would be, I urge you, in the name of our old friendship, to do all in your power to restrain your Austrian ally from going too far.
Tsar Nicholas II to Emperor William II.

Foreign Office, July 31, 1914
It is, of course, too late for all military operations against Servia to be suspended. But if Austria, having occupied Belgrade and neighbouring territory, declares herself ready, <u>honour satisfied</u>, in the interest of European peace to cease her advance, I hope that Russia would also consent to suspension of further military preparations. It is a slender chance —
Grey to Buchanan.
Repeated to Niš.

SO IN THE DAWN light, back from the Telegraph Office with cypher in hand, I learn something new about honour, though whose honour the Foreign Secretary doesn't exactly say. The Servian Government has provided the Diplomatic Corps with a secretariat without which we would wait at the Niš post office where there are three telephone instruments for the population; I must speak to Xenia and call up the courage for what I think I have to do. I am the first to arrive as the night birds begin to tire and the doors open.

This time it's she who answers and I picture her before the bookcase in the ministerial study where the instrument stands, her cotton dress falling over comfortable hips. Her voice is even and cautious.

'The British Legation. His Excellency is absent.'

'This is me, Theodore.'

'Mr Harris.'

'I haven't slept all night.'

'Your thoughts came — ?'

'Of course. But not only because of that. I must make a decision.'

'No one anywhere sleeps in Servia now,' she says, more guardedly. Her intelligence speeds ahead of my intentions before they form. 'Perhaps you should return to Belgrade,' she says. 'Niš is too far away, it's not a good place to make decisions.'

'The Government is here, and the other diplomats.'

'All those men with positions and seats in this and that are not important now,' Xenia says in a low voice, almost a whisper, 'now the only important thing is faith between people like us.'

'I think so too.'

'Come back to Belgrade.'

FROM THE DIPLOMATIC secretariat opposite the Hotel Europa to the Turkish comfort of 3 Prince Michael Place is a ten minute walk, but in a motor car it's nothing. So in Vienna, Berlin, St. Petersburg, between Embassies and offices from where commands go out to mobilise, to march, to begin what everyone is waiting for, the distance is nothing. As soon as I get in I ring for coffee which the maid brings on a tray with cakes. I touch her hand, due to simple solitude. I'm sure she understands that, she smiles and goes.

Lying on the ottoman I read Grey's telegram a second time. 'Cease her advance and discuss how a complete settlement can be arrived at — ' as though one arrived at peace by settling the bill.

And who dare reduce the chance of a settlement, even the slightest? Not me, I think. The Austrians demand the arrest and surrender of Ciganović; if they have him, will it be harder for them to refuse Grey's proposal? Xenia is right, I should return to Belgrade. But when I get there I must call the officials from the Foreign Ministry — she will grieve, her heart which I can feel through the beating of my own will contract and hide but she's young still, and has me. Milan will be handed over to some high authority of his own people; perhaps Prince George, leaving the dirty work to him. Betrayals great or small may succeed where the old diplomacy is failing. My mind seems made up, though I'm not proud of it.

XIV

Potsdam, July 30, 1914

According to my opinion it is perfectly possible for Russia to remain a spectator in the Austro-Serbian war without drawing Europe into the most terrible conflict it has ever seen. Naturally mobilisation by Russia would accelerate a calamity which both of us desire to avoid.

William to Nicholas.

Minute

It becomes more and more absurd for Germany to pretend that her hand is being forced by French and Russian mobilization. Germany is always mobilized. The German Government is throwing dust into our eyes for the purpose of hindering those preparations which alone would enable us to take part in the struggle when the Cabinet eventually recognize that we have no choice. Haldane, accused of Germanic sympathies, knows this.

Crowe.

Foreign Office, July 31, 1914

It is most important to know if you have acted on my instructions and whether cyphers and other highly secret documents left at Belgrade have been burnt.

Grey to Harris.

NIS IS A day's journey from Belgrade. So what do I do? I know there are trains because I hear them in the night, but if I reach Belgrade as bombardment turns to invasion? Trains would cease, the frontier would shift; I could get away via Vienna in a diplomatic coach if the Semlin Bridge still stands, and so could Oliver. But not Xenia. I can only take Xenia out of Belgrade, and keep her, if I travel by road.

The German Legation is naturally the one building the Austrians and their allies will respect and enter, and so is the wrong place for British cyphers and archive to be sheltered; I have committed a blunder. Grey's telegram is proof that the war is hours away and then the Belgrade archive may not matter much — but cyphers in German hands — by my fault —

No one in the Prime Minister's office cares any longer who is present in Niš and who has left it, telegrams will still fly about and be washed away in the bloody tide. I warn Oliver that I'm starting. 'I hope to be in Belgrade tonight. Telephone the German Legation and say you will sleep there. I will call tomorrow to take away the archive.'

'Do you think that wise, Theo? Don't you think they'd go straight off and open it?'

Oliver always surprises me with his practical side. 'You're right. We'd better decide what to do when I arrive. Tell Xenia — ' I hesitate, not sure what she should be told.

'Tell her what? That you're coming for her? That Milan had better disappear for his own good?'

'Just say I hope to get through safely some time tonight.'

TROOP AND ARTILLERY movements have still further wrecked the road to Belgrade. About half way, a bridge has been destroyed and the river is higher than the running board and full of rocks. Halted on the edge I watch the current break around them, and feel the force of what's to come. Boppe's sons and other boys from villages everywhere will be sent to die in that flat land along the Belgian frontiers, and my problems seem not much in comparison. I step down and remove my coat and trousers in the heat of the afternoon sun. This motor car must somehow be pushed through with the engine running and roll on along the ruined Roman highway. The stones inflict two punctures so with both spare wheels in use I have to crawl the rest of the way, all movement of people and animals going in the opposite direction, southward from the frontier and the coming battles. A single motor car comes towards me round a bend in the woods, jerking along uncomfortably. I flag it down and explain about the broken bridge ahead.

'How did you get over?' asks the driver, an officer of the Servian army, eying my suit with contempt. 'Get your motor car out of my way.' Here in Servia, after we have gone, what will become of civilians? Of wom-

— 180 —

en? In a village with one shuttered inn and no sign of life, I draw up and sound the horn which echoes along the road between the walls of deserted houses.There is a long wait.

'Yes?' The landlord, standing guard with a single-hammer shotgun, has appeared in his doorway.

'I would like supper and some wine, and water for the radiator of my motor car.'

'Where are you going?'

'To Belgrade.'

'Why? Belgrade is bombarded.'

'I am the British Minister.'

'Excellency, enter my honoured house.' He shouts behind him for support and I imagine that no meal is ready for non-existent travellers along the ruined roads. 'You are wrong to return to Belgrade,' the landlord presently tells me as he opens a bottle. 'It will soon be destroyed. It's new and built of poor stone by Austrian architects and will fall down under Austrian shells. No one will still be living in it.' He puts two glasses on the table and wipes his eyes with a napkin. 'My mother is there. I must go for her. What do you think of my wine?'

'The wine is good, thank you.'

'Can you see that, an old woman alone among the explosions? What should I do?'

'Will you join me in a glass? Is your mother alone?'

'She is the most unhappy old woman in Servia.'

Probably I will get no more details; the landlord refills his glass from the long green bottle between us. His wrist is like the branch of a tree. 'I could perhaps take you in my motor as far as the centre of Belgrade.'

'My mother is in a side street behind the Town Hall.'

'The British Legation is near the Town Hall.'

'Yes,' the landlord says as if he knew that well enough already.

It's a makeshift supper — ancient sausage and cabbage served with sour cream. But appetite hardens you. After that's over the landlord arrives with a Turkish pudding of sugar added to honey and whipped up in plum brandy; a coffee pot, and a bottle of more plum brandy. He sits facing me and I know the moment of settlement is here.

'You are a good man,' he says, smiling on me with the affection of one about to take advantage of this fact. Goodness has no place in the training of a diplomat; one tries to deploy certain virtues, that's all.

'I can only say I feel sorry about your mother, with you here so far away.'

He extends a hand towards me across the table. 'Where is your own mother, Excellency?'

'In London.'

'Not with bombardments.'

'No.'

'And not in a hovel of one room.'

I find no answer. The landlord's mother lives in a hole in a Belgrade wall and mine in a high house in Rutland Gate. 'You can come with me, if you like,' I say in the end.

He takes my hand in his and crushes it painfully. 'I am ready at once in very few minutes.'

Waiting at the wheel I wonder what's keeping him, and when he appears I can see it was his armament. He has a rifle slung over one shoulder, a shotgun over the other, a pistol, a leather ammunition bag, and in the failing light of sunset he mounts onto the seat beside me. 'At night the roads are full of bandits. I am Branko Branković, and now I am ready.'

A couple of miles from Belgrade the road rises along a low wooded hill and then comes into the open with a distant view of the capital. The streets of Belgrade are lit by electric lamps in white globes of glass which still shine on through the night on white buildings; from the northern bank of the river comes a regular flash of artillery fire as if the white globes are taken for targets. The road is deeply cut about by all the retreating wheels and hooves of the past days and thinking of my tyres I take a turning for Topčider from where the last stretch downhill will be smoother. For the steep descent I use the handbrake. It is three in the morning.

'I will leave my mother till daylight,' Branko announces. 'Let the poor woman sleep.' Throughout the slow night drive, with the road ahead of us clear in moonlight except under trees through whose deep shadows the acetylene headlamps threw a soft uncertain beam, he kept still and quiet, his eyes fastened on the road in front and his rifle, laid across his knee, at the ready. Every now and then the figure of some fleeing citizen appeared beside the road and watched in wonder as we passed, Branko raising the rifle just in case. The Belgrade cafés which used to stay open till dawn are shut, even the market place and the streets around it are deserted yet you feel that the population doesn't sleep and from time to time the buildings shake in the explosion of shells. But this will seem nothing beside the coming bombardment from howitzers still lining up beyond the Danube, the famous *Schlanke Emma*, pride of the dying Holy

Roman Empire. When that starts the new white buildings will shake to their foundations.

'The people are afraid,' Branko says, 'but animals afraid are angry.'

Our Legation sleeps without lights; I realise I am in the absurd position of having no key to it. Why should I have? I put my legs over the gear lever to dismount, and then tug at the bell pull for a long time.

'What is it?' a woman's rough voice shouts at last in Servian from behind the door.

'Harris. I am the Minister. Fetch Mr Dillon.'

The locks turn and the door swings open. 'You forget my voice?' Xenia asks, standing in the moonlight. Behind her I make out dim figures lying about on the floor of the entrance hall like forgotten luggage. She puts a hand to my shoulder.

'Didn't Oliver tell you I was on my way?'

'Oliver has one of his bad days.'

'He's unconscious?'

'He is sleeping. Why are you so cold?'

I seem cold because I've come back to give a life away. 'I am not cold, Xenia.'.

'Who is that man?'

'He keeps an inn in a village forty miles to the south, Branko Branković.'

She laughs; 'We need an inn-keeper in the British Legation?'

Branko gets down, the rifle banging on the shotgun and against his groin. 'Let's go inside.' In the fluctuating electric light I see a lot of huddled sleeping figures, with piles of luggage.

'British subjects,' Xenia says, not expecting me to believe it; not knowing what I'm about to do to her.

'All of them?'

'You know Oliver is in charge of passports and safe conducts.'

'Where is he?'

'With Milan in the cellar.'

'Is he unconscious too?'

'I think they both sleep tonight.'

'It's the morning already.' So Oliver and Milan are drinking partners. 'Mr Branković had better doss down here for an hour or two, I am going to bed.'

'Shall I come?'

'Yes. Yes.'

WHEN I AWAKE at nine it's to a darkened world. The first thing to do, even before I lift the telephone to denounce poor Milan, is to send Oliver to the German Legation for the archive. I should have warned Von Storck before I left Niš; I try to do it now.

'There is no line to Niš at present,' I am told by the exchange operator. 'There has been damage.'

'I am the British Minister. Is it being repaired?'

'The men have gone in search of the place.'

'Somewhere between here and Niš? How are they travelling?'

'They have horses.'

Other plans must be made, and at this moment, Oliver presents himself, looking terrible. 'You are to go to the German Legation and reclaim the archive. Foreign Secretary's orders.'

'Does the German Minister expect me?'

'He's at Niš, and no, he doesn't expect you.'

'This has the makings of an incident.'

In diplomacy, an incident is one step worse than a complication, but I keep my head. 'I think affairs are moving too fast for an incident to make any difference.'

'It's more awkward than you realise.' Now he looks really ill; 'I need a drink.' I give him time.'Primo, the Prussians locked the archive in the cellar before I left. Secundo, when I passed by there yesterday I was received in an unfriendly way by armed guards. There are no officials left in the German Legation. I'm sorry, I can't do it.' He cheers up considerably. 'Down in the hall I saw an armed brigand leaning against a pillar. Send him.'

I hear a slight sound near the doorway. 'I know what to do,' Xenia says, 'now I understand.'

'Do you?'

'Yes. Milan will go to the German Legation and while you talk to the guards he will go into the cellar. They won't shoot you in your uniform.'

'How would he get into the cellar?'

'This I don't know,' Xenia admits; 'Oliver will help.'

'I don't think Oliver can help anyone today.'

'You're wrong there,' Oliver suddenly says, 'I know just how to get into that cellar. In the alley at the side of the Legation there's a hole — a chute for coal.'

'Is the archive in the coal cellar, Oliver?'

'You've got it,' Oliver says, and his eyes begin to close.

— 184 —

I turn to Xenia. 'Could Milan get down that coal chute into a pitch dark cellar and find it?'

'Yes, I think.'

'Please bring him here to me.'

From the hall rises a noise of voices and every now and then the bark of dogs. The Legation is a refugee camp where no one has seriously examined credentials as the shells fall. I call down the stairs for Branković.

'You have a big house here in Belgrade,' he says. 'And full up.'

'Too full of people who may not have a right to protection. And I have no one to separate them out.'

'I see. What is that man there?'

'He is an official of the Legation who has fallen ill.'

'I can smell his illness, I am an inn keeper,' says Branko brutally.

'Listen. I need your help.' I pause for this to sink in. 'Soon we will bring your mother here to safety, and when it's possible for me to do so I will drive you and her in my motor car back to your house.'

'Yes,' Branko says, looking wary. We both wait for the other to speak again.

'You can help me if you found out which of those people are not British refugees but other nationals, because I can't look after everyone.'

'Not all the population of Belgrade.'

'Exactly.'

'And you want me to drive these others away?'

'Discreetly, if you can.'

'Discreetly?'

'Politely.'

'I will see to this,' Branko says, and like a gorilla slips away about his business.

By the time Xenia returns with Milan I can hear orders barked in the hall, querulous cries but obedient shuffling of feet and removal of packages, effects, domestic animals. 'You have found a better servant than Hermann,' she says, 'but Serbs are never servants so you must have bribed him.'

'I am helping him.'

'How?'

'By sheltering his mother'

'Here?'

'Naturally.'

'When he has finished driving Serbs from the house?'

'Not all of them, Xenia, not all.'

'Not me, then?' she says with a smile.

'Certainly not you.'

'And Milan?'

Milan, white-faced, is seated on a small chair near the door with his leg stretched in front of him. He listens to what's said but apparently has nothing to say himself. I get up and walk over to the window from where I can see the trickle of expelled refugees as they leave the front door and make their way towards the great market place, the railway station, the poor quarters where the town turns into neglected countryside. They are people who sought protection where they could, some of them hoping for a meal in the chaos. A shell hits the palace, then another, sending a shower of rubble and splinters of white stone out among the refugees. I turn away.

'I will drive to the German Legation and you will telephone to warn them of my arrival. Milan will travel in the dicky seat of the car with the cover closed but not fastened. I will stop the car at the entrance to the alleyway beside the Legation.'

'How will he get out?'

'I said the cover won't be fastened to the bodywork.'

'If there is a mistake he will have no air?'

'There will be no mistake.'

SO THE RESCUE of the British cypher from the German Legation at Belgrade, changing Milan's fate for ever, was carried out on the eve of war. He left by the back door into the stable yard, dragging his wounded leg. We'd had a brief exchange with Xenia interpreting, her hand on his shoulder.

'When we stop, you'll know if there are any German guards standing near because you'll hear them move.'

'Why will they move?'

'From curiosity. The guards are young and the Sunbeam's bright.' There she sits in the yard, mud-spattered blue paint and steel and brass, shining in the hot morning sun.

'Yes,' Milan said, his eyes bright too with curiosity. 'I have never been in a motor car before.' Neither, I'm sure, had Princip and the others, when they threw their bombs and then later, bombs failing, opened fire on the Archduke's ponderous Teutonic motor carriage with the artillery wheels. Xenia peered into the well of the dicky. 'There is not room for Milan with his bad leg.'

'I can lift out the seat.'

'Then he will be in a pit like a bear.' Milan brushed Xenia and her objections aside, curled up in the dicky and closed his eyes.

'Afterwards, get back in and shut the cover behind you. You see?' He made no response and I closed him in.

At the German Legation armed officials said their orders were to forbid entrance to everyone. I mentioned my conversation with the German Minister only yesterday at Nis, enquired whether their Legation had yet been hit by shells; played for time until I heard a couple of shots from inside the building. The officials, hearing them too, vanished. I could have walked in after them but I returned to the Sunbeam, taking my time, admiring the flight of the swifts against the blue above. The dicky was closed and I saw a dark trickle of blood where the sun beat down on the coachwork. I wound the engine and stepped into the cab.

'Excellency! Wait!' came a shout from the German Legation, but I accelerated up the rue du Roi Milan, reaching forty miles an hour on the empty street, and swung round the gates and lodges of the deserted palace and into our stable yard; there I found Xenia seated on a mounting block as if she'd known all along how everything would turn out.

Belgrade, July 31, 1914

Cyphers and all highly secret archives were carefully destroyed by fire this afternoon in my presence and that of the acting vice-consul.

I have deferred my return to Niš until such time as the presence within the Legation of refugees not entitled to H.M. Government protection is satisfactorily resolved, meanwhile I remain when necessary in telephonic communication with the offices of the Foreign Secretary, M. Grujić.

The bombardment, I regret to report, has just recommenced on a larger and fiercer scale.

Harris to Grey.

MY CONSCIENCE is not clear. Here I have responsibility for individual lives; in Whitehall, lives are draughts pieces. But on my return from the Telegraph Office I enter the Legation from the stable yard to avoid the refugees and go straight up the back stairs to Xenia's office from which there's a small door leading to the bedroom where I slept, in the days now so distant, when I was only first secretary. As expected, she is in there with Milan. They are side by side on the day bed under the window, his head on her shoulder, his leg bandaged from the new wound he has acquired in my service. I watch them for a moment and they both watch me with their awakened eyes.

'Is it bad, the wound?'

'It's nothing, a little hole in his calf where the bullet went in and another little hole to come out,' Xenia says.

'Nothing,' says Milan.

'The wound must be kept clean.'

'I have poured in iodine.' They both laugh heartily, their eyes now bathing me in approval, trust, hope.

'I'll go to my office and then with Oliver's — ' there's an explosion somewhere in the roof above us, the sound of crashing masonry, a searing as the plaster above us splits and the end of a beam comes through, then subsides to rest in a cloud of dust. 'We must go to the ground floor. The shelling's getting heavier.'

'More all the time,' says Milan. They wrap their arms round each other and limp towards the stairs. I feel lonely, following them.

Minute
This bombardment of Belgrade gives the impression that the object is the destruction of the Servian capital as a form of punishment. It will, however, be better that we should not be the first to raise protests. Mr Harris must 'grin & bear it' while doing the best he can for those who have put themselves under his protection.
Crowe to Grey.

Foreign Office, July 31, 1914
Ensure that only British nationals are afforded the shelter of H.M. Legation as occupation of Belgrade approaches.
Telegram received by German Embassy from German Chancellor states that Russia has proclaimed general mobilisation and that in consequence of this, martial law would be proclaimed for Germany.
Grey to Harris.

THE POPULATION in the hall has thinned out, and those remaining look up with fear and trust in their eyes. 'I have to tell you that both Russia and Germany have mobilised. We know that for Germany mobilisation is a word, followed immediately by the blow. Belgrade will shortly be occupied by the Austro-Hungarian forces and there will be fighting in the streets and hills around us. I will do what I can for your safe departure from Belgrade before fighting becomes general throughout Servia. My staff will try to see to your needs but you must show patience in the difficulties. If anyone here has not proof of his status as British subject, will he please come forward.'

— 188 —

There is a long general silence and the expression of the faces turned towards me seems less trusting. My speech was not of a stirring character, but it wasn't meant to be. If they feel less blind dependence, so much the better. I turn to Oliver. 'We're instructed to verify the identity of all those still remaining under our roof. I leave this to you. The situation is developing very rapidly.'

'Only proven British subjects may remain?'

'And employees of the Legation.'

One of the refugees, an elderly man leading a woman with one hand and a couple of whippets with the other, comes towards me.

'What will the British Government do to protect British property, Minister?' he asks in an angry voice. 'I am the owner of a vineyard on the best slope of the Fruška Gora and five hundred acres of forest above it. I have a house there. The revenue from the vineyard is my income. What is going to be done?' he demands again, his voice rising.

'The international situation is too precarious for the Servian Government to guarantee property against violation, and still less H.M. Government hundreds of miles away.'

'So what are you doing to help?'

'I am giving shelter and if things get worse I will advise that a special train be sent to evacuate British subjects in distress, like yourself.'

'If things get worse,' he says furiously, 'what can be worse than the whole year's grape harvest lost and my trees chopped down for army fire wood in the winter?' There are tears behind his fury and I agree with every word he says.

'It seems to me the misfortunes of war may pass the Fruška Gora by and leave your land in peace. You'll return there and the world's thirst for your white wine will only have redoubled.' Some of the other refugees laugh at this. 'And today I see there's a barrel of wine here in the hall provided by H.M Government and I hope you will all go on taking advantage of it.' Much better they be fuddled than unhappy; enough unhappiness is on the way.

Potsdam, July 31, 1914

I have communicated what you were so good as to say to me at Buckingham Palace last Sunday to William, who was very thankful to receive your message.

William, who is very anxious, is doing his utmost to comply with the request of Nicholas to work for the maintenance of peace. He is in continual telegraphic communication with Nicholas, who has today con-

firmed the news that he has ordered military measures which amount to mobilisation.

We have also received information that France is making military preparations, while we have not taken measures of any kind, but may be obliged to do so at any moment if our neighbours continue their preparations. This would then mean a European war.

Prince Henry of Prussia to King George V.

Buckingham Palace, July 31, 1914

Thanks for your telegram. I am very glad to hear of William's efforts to act with Nicholas for the maintenance of peace. I earnestly desire that such a misfortune as a European war — the evil of which could not be remedied — may be prevented. My Government is doing the utmost possible in order to induce Russia and France to postpone further military preparations.

George to Henry.

The 'Gerard Telegram':-

Potsdam

King George empowered Prince Henry to transmit to me verbally that England would remain neutral if war broke out on the Continent, involving Germany and France, Austria and Russia.

His Majesty asked me if I would transmit to Vienna the British proposal that Austria was to take Belgrade and a few other Serbian towns and a strip of country as a mainmise to make sure that the other Serbian promises on paper should be fulfilled in reality.

I was happy at the peaceful outlook.

William to President Woodrow Wilson.

BRANKO, HAVING DRIVEN off most if not all the non bona fide refugees, is waiting for me at the door of the ministerial study.

'My mother, I wish to bring her here now as you promised me.'

'Don't come to the front door. Slip her through the stable yard.'

'Why?'

'Others would follow you. It is hard to refuse entry while shells fall around.'

Branko seems in no great hurry to go. He follows me into the study which he examines from wall to wall with great interest.

'We are very few aristocrats still left in Servia,' he says. 'The others have run away to Hungary.' He sits in a leather armchair. 'You have Servian employees?'

'I have one.'

'The stenographer?'

'Yes.'

'What will you do with her?'

'I think that's a question for me, Mr Branković.'

'Excellency, you will take her with you when you go from Servia. I have seen her brother. If you leave her, she will be killed because of what must stay secret. Servia will look for sacrifice and if they don't find the man to sacrifice they take a woman.'

'I may soon have to give them the man.'

'No,' Branko says forcefully. 'No, because of her.'

Crisis breaks down barriers. I always meant to take Xenia away from Belgrade if she was willing, though how to regularise the situation I have no idea. Counting, I suppose, on love — its exchange rate, its purchasing power — I've taken success for granted. And now there's Milan wounded in the service of H.M. Government; and not least there's Grujić whom I must reach on the telephone in his offices at Niš. I see present and future knotted like the strings of a kite brought to earth.

XV

Prince George is here, his head wrapped in a bloodstained bandage, his voice hoarse. His country is already at war while ours watches the stock market, and swings at anchor with the Fleet.

The prince was with a regiment under canvas near the Hungarian frontier which was treacherously assaulted an hour before the declaration, so he says. 'Imagine the cowardice, Theodore. With my friends we were drinking in our tent — and there were some women — and we drank a toast to the King — and these swine with no warning crossed the river Drina and attacked us in the night.'

'Had you no lookout posts?'

'You are not a soldier, you know nothing about military things.'

I can't argue with an ex-Crown Prince straight off the battlefield, from whose bandages a trickle of blood runs down the side of his unshaven face; but this doesn't sound to me like good organisation. The Servian army fought in 1913 with a spirit which since Waterloo we've forgotten, at least in European affairs; it may be exhausted but what matters more is that its heroes are very few in face of the giants striding over frontiers, as we go on pouring oil on the waves and hoping for the best. Luckily, perhaps, the telephone calls me back from military things to the world.

'We have established a line to Niš,' the exchange tells me. A long silence follows, then a crackling, then a series of buzzes.

'Mr Harris?' Grujić asks.

'Yes, General.'

'What have you to tell me?'

'The bombardment continues and the British Legation, including the façade, continues to suffer damaging shell fire.'

'I know this already. Besides, what do you expect me to do about it? The building is where it is and the Austrian batteries are where they are — in the Semlin fortress.'

'It was not for this that I hoped to speak with you, General.'

'For what, then?' The moment has come. Prince George whom I'd thought of, with his subversive past, as the right person to receive my denunciation and surrender of Ciganović, is here beside me. The Foreign Minister is waiting on the line. Yesterday I believed history waited on me also. 'For what, Mr Harris?'

I must do it now; but my history, my nature, Xenia's voice in my head, all cry no. It's my duty, a moral obligation in the crisis. But does nature's imperative not override it?

'Mr Harris?' The decision is ready, waiting like a letter to be picked up and opened. 'For what, Mr Harris?' I allow a moment — a last look at the unopened letter. 'Mr Harris?'

'Only to ask if you require my return to Niš, General.'

'I think the Prime Minister wishes for friends about him.'

'I will come as soon as possible.'

'If personal affairs detain you — we will be patient.'

'His Highness Prince George is with me and has suffered a wound to the head.'

'I envy you the company, Mr Harris.'

'And we have a number of British subjects sheltering here. I must do what I can for them.'

'I think you should know that Belgrade will soon be abandoned.' Grujić checks himself, probably aware there may be listeners on the line. 'A tactical temporary withdrawal from the city seems inevitable.'

'Then I must request the sending of a special train from Vienna to Belgrade.'

'You are not at war, the train could be preceded by an engine carrying the Union Jack and followed by another with another. But do it quickly, before the Semlin Bridge is blown into the Danube.'

'May I ask, General, whether a new French Minister has yet reached Niš?'

'He has not.'

'My respects to the Prime Minister.'

'I won't fail you, though you have failed me,' says the Foreign Minister, and the line goes dead.

The charge, if true, is overtaken by the facts. The Government in London is waiting to be forced by events; I have decided this event for myself. I turn back to the prince.

'The Foreign Secretary warns me that Belgrade will be evacuated, Highness.'

'He's an old man and when he was a General he was no good. The King is in Belgrade — the capital will never be abandoned. I will have some more of your whisky, Theodore. No, continue pouring, you are too parsimonious, your own wife says so.'

'She makes this criticism from her residence in the hills overlooking Cannes and the sea?'

Paris, July 31, 1914

Confidential.

'Times' correspondent here believes that Ministry for Foreign Affairs wishes him to prepare public opinion in England for mobilisation which may be ordered at any moment, and to induce it to consider such a measure as forced upon France by German preparations

Bertie to Grey

Belgrade, August 1, 1914

It is urgently necessary that train be allowed to approach Belgrade under white flag to convey away non-combatants, British subjects in principle.

Harris to Grey.

EQUIVOCAL WORDING, but this may be one of the last buttons we can press on the international scene so I press it in favour of the unfortunate, those sheltered downstairs in the hall or in the cellar or with their pitiful livestock in the stables. And for Xenia and Milan, if I can get them out in no other way.

Meanwhile the prince is talking to himself or to anyone willing to hear him. 'They will abandon Belgrade, our army will fight in the hills but it will be crushed. My father, old and sick, will walk with his soldiers in the hills and the forests, he will defecate beside them in the ditches.' Would anyone dream of talking like that about George V? 'He will starve with them in the snows of Albania.' The prince weeps. 'We will never forgive the supposed friends of Servia who betray us. I will return now to the army.' He rises unsteadily. 'Now I will go.' He stops at the front door of the Legation, looking round at the curious, scared faces of refugees. 'But you had something to say to me, I think. Something you wished me to do for you.'

'No, Highness, I had nothing more to say to you. Thank you for your visit.'

'You may tell Kitty that I remembered her on the field of battle,' he says with the aimless benevolence of the crazed, and at last turns to go. I'm glad to see the back of him though he's not a man you can dislike, just a casualty of the fate, two or three generations ago, that brought a mountain peasant to an invented throne after five centuries of Turkish despotism.

'Here's hoping it's his whole royal bloody head that goes next time,' says Oliver's voice, reminding me that they are rivals. The lovely, life-less Kitty, like an angler dozing on the bank of a pond, nets them without even having to wake up.

Foreign Office, August 1, 1914
Ask Government to give immediate order to allow train to approach Belgrade under white flag to convey away British subjects and other non-combatants.
Grey to de Bunsen.

Luxembourg, August 1, 1914
German troops have entered south of Grand Duchy. Armed train arrived station of Luxembourg.
Mr N. Le Gallais, Consul General, Luxembourg, to Grey.

Minute
It is impossible for the German troops to get out of Luxembourg with-out crossing Belgian territory except through a narrow bottle-neck into France which the French have taken good care to close. Which of them set the trap? And for whom, in the final analysis?
Crowe.

MOTHER BRANKOVIĆ has refused to leave her home in the town wall, she says an old woman's virtue will be respected by the soldiery and she hates the village where her son keeps his inn. Branko argued with her long and hard but she was adamant. 'Persuade her at least to come into the Legation. The walls are thick.'

'Not as thick as her wall,' Branko says, 'nor her understanding.'

'So what will you do?'

'I must stay. I will help you too.' With what, he doesn't say and per-haps doesn't need to.

'There's a train tonight to Niš, it's probably the last and I must go on it,' I inform Oliver.

'How will you get back?'

'I don't know yet.'

'And I am to join the white flag train steaming to Vienna?'

'If you put the refugees safely aboard and then wait here for me with Xenia and Milan, I hope to leave Servia in the Sunbeam. There's room for four, just.'

'And going where?'

'Salonika, the sea.'

'Better than Victoria Station.'

Xenia is displeased when I tell her that I'm returning to Niš. 'I thought you came back to look after all the people here.'

'The Servian Government need a British representative, Xenia.'

'They can do nothing — they are old men who say everyone must listen to them, while the shells fall. You are needed by real people, not ghosts of the war of 1913.'

Isn't that what Milan is? I don't say it. We are standing on the railway platform under one of the white electric globes while a red full moon sails just clear of the smashed glass of the station roof, hit in today's bombardment. Steam from the waiting locomotive drifts between the light of the globe and the light of the moon, stained by each in turn like liquid in coloured glass. 'I think if there's a war — '

'What do you mean? There is a war.'

'I mean if we join it.'

'You mean when not just a few hundred Serbs are killed or wounded.'

'If what I'm talking about happens, it will be hundreds of thousands.'

'So, if — ?'

'The Government in Niš will quickly be nothing, as you say, and I will be recalled, and I will come for you.'

'You will?'

'Yes, I will. And until then you have Oliver and Branko to protect you.'

She laughs. 'He is like any Serb with all his guns.'

I feel unhappy too, leaving her, and I draw her behind one of the iron pillars that formerly held up the glass roof of the station. We stand close as if for the last time.

'You can ask me for anything, Xenia.'

'Then I think there is no need to ask.'

The locomotive blasts a final warning as the whistle of a shell, then its impact, comes from the street behind us. 'Run back to the Legation. If you hear that whistling, get into a doorway.'

'I feel like you, just the same as you. But like you I have others.'

'I haven't any others.'

'Oh yes, but you forget them and that's the difference.' Whatever she means, I decide not to take it up. I mount the three steps into the waiting coach with my heavy case containing cyphers and files of telegrams and much else that's unnecessary now, and useless. I wonder what an enlisted man takes with him as he marches the miles through countryside to the front.

'I BELIEVE, Prime Minister, that the Government in London will come round to the position you hoped they would take at an earlier moment.'

'It will be too late. We will be crushed.'

'Not too late to prevent much worse.'

'Mobilisation? For Russia, this means calling peasants from their black soil and giving them rifles with no bullets in place of their hoes. For Germany, to mobilise is to strike.'

'Sir Edward Grey understands this distinction.'

'Why then, according to my Minister in London, were the pleas of the French Ambassador, with tears in his eyes, refused?'

'Parliament, Prime Minister, was not ready.'

'And Parliament doesn't obey?'

'Parliament is sovereign.'

'How can anyone govern such a country?' the Prime Minister asks in despair.

'Sir Edward Grey, as you will see from this speech a day or two ago, has attempted to prepare Parliament for the commitment they must make.'

'I will read it when I have time, Mr Harris.'

Niš, August 1, 1914

Sprit of this country is now fully aroused, and optimism has supplemented dejection first noticeable. Firm attitude of Russia and reports received as to solidarity of England have encouraged this feeling. I have endeavoured to reassure Prime Minister as to our concerns for his country and he asks me to express to you his deep gratitude for your statement in the House of Commons.

Harris to Grey.

THESE PRETENCES are pitiful, mine most of all. Perhaps I shouldn't have schemed against the arrival in Servia of the new Minister whose faith in the order we represent has never been undermined by doubts. On an evening of splendour I walk out of the teeming dusty shambles of Niš and up the hill to the Tower of Skulls. I find the place deserted, not a living soul, no dog or goat, only wooded hills grey as old men; but the remaining skulls glow warmly in the light of a setting sun and in the round air. I'm suddenly carried a long way back, I feel off balance and I sit on the parched grass. It's the voice of Selzman discussing a sonnet we've been studying; I hear the tone of warm, full, slightly nasal instruction with the same pleasure as always. Why did his tone never irritate me as other instruction does? Perhaps because the nasal quality was like the note of some instrument at the back of the orchestra you never suspect till it releases its contribution. He would have liked the comparison. 'When music moves me I let the tears run, it's human, indeed manly and I recommend it,' he once said, leaning forward so his hair fell across his brow.

I went to call on him a week or so before his death, then living alone in two rooms on a ground floor in Marylebone High Street. 'My wretched joints,' he said; 'but don't worry about me, Harris, the lame don't die, they only fade away.'

'I've brought my wife to meet you, Selzman.'

He sat up on his pillows, eyes bright in the skull behind the yellowing skin. 'Bring her in, if she has no objection.'

I had never before seen Selzman with a woman other than the late Mrs Selzman, silent and gaunt, and my mother whom he skirted round, keping a distance like a *cordon sanitaire* between them. At the sight of Kitty he showed the traces of a once irresistible charm. 'I'm very glad to meet you, Mrs Harris, your husband was my brightest pupil and his career is always close to my heart which rejoices that he has found so lovely a partner for his life.'

'I am delighted to meet you too, Doctor Selzman,' Kitty said, looking perfectly lost. 'Theodore has spoken awfully well of you, often.' She was so exquisite wrapped in the furs I couldn't afford that I thought no suspicion of her silliness could cross the mind of an observer, but I saw that Selzman was on to it at once. The pupils of his eyes, always dilated at a first meeting, were closing.

'This is an old man's sick-room, Mrs Harris,' he said, 'not a place for you. Your husband and I will say our farewells for a few minutes and you will find in my sitting-room plenty of books, some illustrated, to amuse you. Goodbye.'

I knew then he hadn't long to go; I'd seen in my father's last days this kind of abrupt transition which means that the echoes of youth are drowned out by the din of death, marching and filling the ears. 'What do you think of her, Selzman?' I stupidly asked.

'A moment's ornament, Harris as we both know,' he said with the candour of the dying.

'I couldn't resist.'

'I'm determined to live to see you an Ambassador, Harris. How many years? Three, four?'

'Longer. Ambassadors in place have to retire and you know how old men hang on.'

'I may not hang on long enough, then.'

'I didn't mean — '

'Of course. Of course. But look at me, here,' he said angrily, surveying his own limbs. It was a hot afternoon and under the single blanket you could make out knotted knees and twisted hips. Then his voice altered and he continued more lightly. 'Changed from what I was when like a roe I bounded o'er the mountains, wherever nature led. I elide, Harris, as you recognise, but the bounding roe is done for.'

'You mustn't say it.'

'Why should I spare you? You pay me to spare you? You buy the image of what you think I should be?'

Crossing Portman Square with Kitty in search of a cab (she doesn't care to walk far) I realised that though I'd come with the intention to give, as usual with Selzman I had taken, and he would always be the stronger.

THE LIGHT DRIFTS off, the birds go quiet, the skulls lose their glow; beyond Niš the plain and the wooded hills stretch away for ever towards the panSlav world and Asia. The incoming stream of men and horses with civilian following which began when the Government settled here has dried up in the last day and now the current is reversed. The same men are being marched back towards the Austrian frontiers where the general mood of manic optimism under Prince George the firebrand will send them into some desperate counter-attack. More smashed limbs, crushed heads, but tonight, from up here, central Europe lies in silence. A single late nightingale tunes up from a bush behind the tower, a bit off the note.

Foreign Office, August 1, 1914
I still believe it might be possible to secure peace if only a little respite can be gained. His Majesty's Government are carefully abstaining from any act which may precipitate matters.
Grey to Goschen.
Repeated to Niš.

St. Petersburg, August 1, 1914
With the aid of God it must be possible to our long-tried friendship to prevent the shedding of blood.
Nicholas to William.

Berlin, August 1, 1914
I have shown the way through which alone war may be averted. No telegram has reached me with the reply of your Government, I have therefore been forced to mobilise my army. An immediate, clear and un-mistakeable reply is the sole way to avoid endless misery. Until I receive this reply I am unable, to my great grief, to enter upon the subject of your telegram.
William to Nicholas.

Paris, August 2, 1914
State of siege declared in Paris and Algeria.
Bertie to Grey.

AS THE NIGHTINGALE pauses I hear a shuffle of many feet along the sandy path approaching the monument which is, I should have re-membered, a historic icon. I feel uneasy about my presence here. A care-ful diplomat doesn't go for an evening stroll where national memories are hallowed and have life breathed into them by patriots; the diplomat's job is rather to lull all that into a harmless sleep — not forgotten, coma-tose. I would like to slip round the back of the tower and out of sight but it's too late, the first of what seems a long procession have arrived; at least I'm no longer sitting on the grass, leaning on the wall with my back to the skulls. I bow and call out good evening but no one answers. They are forming up, dozens, a hundred or more figures thrown from the wave of darkness washing in from the east to stand in a semicircle facing the tower. Very soon only the starlight will still show us each other, then perhaps I won't be noticed at all.

They seem all to be men, and when they sing, the impression is confirmed. Are they old soldiers, mourning fellows lost on the fields of Kosovo among the peonies? Are they fathers of the young men now tramping back towards the Danube and the death waiting there? Their song is like a chant with a martial response at the end of verses. The voices are deep, sad, and the beats fall irregularly, but it's a text they know by heart, the responses mark time. The music is as mournful as if it issued from the skulls ranged before them like a choir of monks.

Just as they arrived, simply and silently, they're drifting away again. The song is sung, the plaint made. Whoever they were, they were right; a cry must be sent up and god, if he exists, placed before his responsibilities. But these pilgrims will go home empty-handed and the young men be smashed as before.

THE DIPLOMATIC CORPS at Niš is reduced to Strandtman, Von Storck, and myself. The first two are no longer on speaking terms and Strandtman, only a pale reminder of the fame that was Hartwig's, now avoids me, perhaps because of that. The French have still to get their new Minister here by rail, road, or horseback; Des Graz, as far as I know, is stuck on the frontier. Von Storck, then, is the nearest I have to contact with the outside world, and he keeps me in his sights. In relations between diplomats at isolated posts there's always a point where policy has been exhausted, the little power you had is out of your hands, history takes over and the men on the ground are left with nothing but personal feelings to keep them busy. Between Von Storck and me that point is reached. He is waiting for me in my rooms when I return, with the pilgrims' song still in my head.

'Harris! It is night! Have you been out spying from the hills around us?'

'I'm glad to see you, Von Storck. There's nothing left for any of us to spy on.'

'No. We must sustain each other, Harris, in brotherly fashion. I think you too feel this.'

He means it, his eyes are misty. Diplomatists bring native qualities to their work: the Germans bring suspicion and periodic emotional overflow; the French, consistency, tension, rigidity. What do we tell ourselves we bring? Soundness, soundness. And there's my Achilles' heel — I am not sound; but Von Storck may not know that. 'I appreciate your confidence.'

'What are your people doing, Harris? Do they still believe they can sail away from Spithead to another world?'

'We can only wait.'

'For what? We in Germany cannot wait. You have water, we have frontiers.'

He wants to act out with me a charade of confrontation, and it's tragic to see. At least I have the refugees in the Legation, and Xenia and Milan and Oliver Dillon to think about, but Von Storck is tormented by a sense of uselessness. 'A little more whisky, Von Storck?'

'A lot more, Harris.'

Potsdam, August 1, 1914

For technical reasons the mobilisation which I have already ordered on two fronts — east and west — must proceed according to the arrangements made. But if France offers me her neutrality, which must be guaranteed by the English army and navy, I will naturally give up the idea of an attack on France and employ my troops elsewhere. I hope that France will not be nervous.

William to George.

St. Petersburg, August 1, 1914

In this solemn hour I wish to reassure you once more that I have done all in my power to avert war. Now that it has been forced on me, I trust your country will not fail to support France and Russia.

God bless and protect you.

Nicholas to George.

WITH SURPRISING EASE, I reach Oliver by telephone at nine in the morning. 'How about the bombardment, Oliver?'

'Getting heavier.'

'And the refugees?'

'Numerous.'

'I've demanded a train.'

'I know that. So do they.'

'I hope they appreciate all that we, and H.M. Government are doing for them?'

'I think they'll appreciate it when they draw into Victoria Station.'

'You're able to get supplies for them and yourselves?'

'Food and wine? Oh yes, Xenia sees to that.'

'Has Branković expelled the impostors?'

'I do believe he has, the fierce man.'

Potsdam, August 1, 1914
I have gone to the extreme limit of the possible in my efforts for the
preservation of peace. It is not I who bear the responsibility for the mis-
fortune which now threatens the entire civilised world. It rests in your
hand. No one threatens the honour and peace of Russia —
William to Nicholas.

VON STORCK IS permanently on the lookout; he sends secretaries or
bodyguards to watch my windows so that when I do emerge, there Von
Storck is, waiting for me.

'Ah, Harris! Let's walk together to the Foreign Ministry or wherever
it is you're going.'

'I'm actually going to the baths.'

'I will accompany you and we will take the baths together.' He signals
for a secretary who comes at the double. 'Fetch my dress and requisites
for bathing.'

Arm in arm the German Minister and I march across the town to the
bathing establishment, watched with wonder by the citizens and a kind
of imploring hatred by the wretched remaining soldiers who have slept
on the ground for weeks, far from their families, hungry, afraid.

'We will have good discussion in the baths, far from the noisome pop-
ulace,' Von Storck promises.

'They're men on their way to die.'

'Nevertheless you are on your way to the baths, where you pay.'

'Payment has nothing to do with it.'

'You are right — washed or fouled, we're all equal when the bullet
strikes.'

Each bathing apartment has two baths, sunk into the floor with steps
leading down to them and fitted with hot and cold douches. There is no
ventilation so the heat of the air is appalling. Von Storck with his high
colour seems to me at risk in this atmosphere; he surfaces in the bath next
to mine, submerges, resurfaces.

'So, Harris, the Royal Navy remains ready. The Fleet is not dispersed.
What is this Expeditionary Force we hear of? And the Territorial Army,
what is that?' I wonder if these questions are rhetorical ones. 'You have
no real army, seriously, that is so?'

'Lord Haldane at the War Office worked very hard to produce one.'

'But it is nothing, we are informed. And he is despised because of
his love of the German philosophers. I too love them, the philosophers,
though I am too busy to read them.'

'Perhaps he should have made greater study of your military methods.'

'Yes, perhaps. Together, we would rule Europe.' For a time, nothing but the sound of lapping waters about the limbs of the last representatives in Servia of the Diplomatic Corps breaks the silence of the baths. 'With Hartwig you played the son but it was Hartwig who deferred to you, actually. He looked in your direction to see what you were thinking, I noted this many times. Not what was thought in London — we all know soon enough what London thinks — but what you thought yourself. I wonder why?'

'I think he felt his strength grow less as he grew older.'

'Hartwig saw in you something ruthless, something of the Goth, Harris.'

I splash noisily to show suitable derision of this idea. 'What nonsense, I'm a mere Chargé d'affaires and Hartwig, in the Balkans, was a great man. Some said a dangerous one.'

'We will leave this now,' Von Storck says heavily. He soaps his calves, turning them this way and that in admiration. 'But there is nothing of the Goth about your Liberal Government in London. I think they will remain quiescent. We must hope that it will be so.'

Leaving the baths, he follows me to the Foreign Ministry. I stop in the road and turn to study him for a moment; it's not curiosity or the German passion for spying that is making him attach himself to me like this. Behind the brazen surface of his blue eyes is something quite different — isolation, guilt, need to be led. What did Nietzsche say — 'to submit, that is the German virtue; to achieve obedience to a person is the cult.' Well, I must remain detached. Von Storck may be troubled by a national guilt, I by a more private one.

'We will go in, decode and compare our telegrams,' he says.

Niš, August 2, 1914
Information has just been given to me at the Ministry for Foreign Affairs that Germany has declared war against Russia.
Harris to Grey.

THEY SURELY KNOW already but I send it because it's my duty to send it. Then I turn on Von Storck.

'You hid this.'

'I have no instructions.'

'Do you deny the information?'

'I am sorry for it.'

'Let's agree that we have nothing to lose by being perfectly open with each other.'

'Naturally, Harris, naturally.' It's still only eleven in the morning but the sweat rises on his brow and cheeks. 'We must be as open as brothers.'

'Very well.'

'And you will have luncheon with me at the Europa.'

'I have no wish to lunch at the Europa.'

'Then I will take the meal with you at your lodgings.'

I consult my watch, though I know what time it is. 'Come at a quarter to one, if you will.'

Von Storck looks relieved and happy to receive these rapped out orders. 'As you like, Harris.'

There is also a telegram whose contents, vague as they are, worry me rather at the personal level when one's mind should be all on the march of the public hours.

Foreign Office, August 2, 1914

Train for British colony at Belgrade. This has left Vienna under the white flag. Mr Des Graz signals through Budapest that he is obtaining transport by road and will make his way to Niš. He is accompanied by vice-Consul. When and if he arrives, you should consider your mission at an end.

Grey to Harris.

Note

You have acquitted yourself well. As there is no longer an archive, Mr Dillon is relieved also.

Crowe.

THERE'S NO TIME to lose. When the Legation at last answers, it's Xenia's voice. 'They are shelling the water near the Semlin bridge,' she says.

'The train is on its way. The Legation must close. I am recalled.'

'To where?'

'To London.'

'We will lose each other.' Her voice is firm, without any note of protest.

'No.'

'Where can I go to be with you if you are sent back to London in that train?'

'I won't go in the train, I never even thought of it. Please find Oliver for me.'

'Listen,' I say when I hear his voice. 'The Legation is to be evacuated. Have you prepared safe conducts for those travelling by road?'

'Yes I have.'

'I'll come to Belgrade as soon as I can.'

'Won't you wait for Des Graz? It wouldn't look well — '

'Yes, unless the train comes sooner. Evacuating the Legation is my first responsibility. You must warn me.'

'I understand,' Oliver says, and I just hope he does.

Berlin, August 2, 1914

Minister for Foreign Affairs tells me that French have already commenced hostilities by dropping bombs from an airship in the vicinity of Nuremberg. His Excellency begged me not to mention this to any of my colleagues but he himself had told the Belgian Minister.

Goschen to Grey.

Foreign Office, August 3, 1914

German Minister for Foreign Affairs telegraphs today that all French news respecting German troops crossing French frontier are complete fabrications.

Grey to Bertie.

VON STORCK IS waiting at the door for me. 'Lunch will be sparse, Von Storck.'

'Please don't apologise, Harris.'

The maid is laying out the dishes, and Von Storck watches her as if he may never see another woman bent forward like that over a white tablecloth. 'Shall I pour the wine?' the girl asks in her suggestive voice.

'No thank you. I will do it.'

'I trust you have comforted yourself with that girl, Harris?' I don't answer. Is comfort all there is to it? 'Strandtman saw us discussing in the street, Harris. He turned his back on me when I said good day. This is undiplomatic, you must agree.'

'You have declared war with his country.'

'A formality soon put right.'

'And by going to war with Russia, you are at war with France, it seems to me, because of the alliance.'

'With you, we remain at peace.'

'You have an adversary on both your frontiers.'

'Harris, you have made no military studies, I can see. German diplomatists must do this, in order to understand the relations between states. You study international law, you would do better to attend lectures on strategy. France will be rapidly crushed while the Russians slowly mobilise. Their aristocracy is worm-eaten, France is mesmerised by fear. It will all be over in weeks.'

He may be right, they were right in 1870. 'Rapidly crushed? How?'

'Think of the map.'

'Your forces are in Luxembourg in a bottleneck.'

'There are other ways into France.'

'You know, Minister, that my country by the Treaty of London guarantees the neutrality of Belgium?' As soon as I've said this a tide of futility washes over me, drowning reason, treaties, honour. The two of us here, connected to the outside world only by a frail unpunctual telegraphic service, are not much more futile than the ministers and emperors. The neutrality of Belgium and the guarantee have been a by-word for obsolete ineffectiveness throughout Europe ever since 1870 — if four of the guaranteeing powers decided to partition the wretched little country among themselves, the fifth would have to fight them all. And now the beast wakes and stirs and who dare say the waking beast is futile?

Berlin, August 3, 1914

Chancellor begs me to bring following to your notice: 'French aviator who must have flown over Belgian territory was shot down today during attempt to destroy railway at Wesel. We must state it as an undeniable fact that there have been breaches of peace and violation of Belgian neutrality on the part of the French.'

Goschen to Grey.

VON STORCK HAS a draughts board with him which he brings to my rooms where we set it up in the window overlooking the street so as to keep an eye on the world as we play. I sense that he's better at draughts than I am, he has made a study of it, he leads and I follow until we find ourselves at a critical point; then he lets his hand hesitate and makes some fatal slip. At first I thought this was loss of nerve but soon understood what he's doing. He is losing deliberately, as I did with Boppe and the foils, but for a different reason. With Boppe I was honouring the tradition whereby France expects and is given the first place; with Von Storck it's guilt at work. 'There is a strong smell of sewers in your lodgings, Harris.'

'You don't have that at the Europa?'

'It is less pronounced. This is a mediaeval building, the Europa was built by good Austrian architects.'

'The new British Minister may prefer to join you at the Europa then.'

'There is a Minister on the way?'

'He's trying to get here by road.'

'I regret this. I enjoy our games.'

Paris, August 2, 1914

Dear and Great Friend,

It would seem that war would be inevitable if Germany were convinced that the British Government would not intervene in a conflict in which France might be engaged.

It is, I consider, on the language and action of the British Government that the last chances of a peaceful settlement depend.

President Poincaré to George.

THE REARGUARD of the Servian soldiery has quit Niš on their starved horses, making for the frontier and the counter-attack about to begin. May some god watch over them, Xenia's countrymen, so tired and hungry they seem held together only by their breeches and leggings, their leather straps. Without them the dusty streets under a furious sun are empty, dead. The horse droppings, unswept, rot gently beneath a cloud of insects. There is general silence, as recommended for times of mourning. General Grujić has sent for me.

'Mr Harris, hope is dying across Europe.'

'My Government is still not in despair of the conflict remaining localised.'

'You mean with only Servian blood spilt?'

'I hear your army is counter-attacking valiantly.'

'One cannot nourish some hundred thousand men on a diet of illusions,' says Grujić.

'I believe, General, that it won't be long now.'

'What do you mean?'

I know I'm losing professional detachment, sympathy is taking charge. 'I think the Belgian frontier will soon be — ' what was Boppe's verb? — 'violated.'

'And then, Mr Harris?'

'Then, General, I believe Parliament will awaken from its torpor.'

Foreign Office, August 2, 1914

The French Ambassador repeated his question whether we would help France if Germany made an attack on her, and then asked me what we should say about the violation of the neutrality of Belgium. I said that was a much more important matter; we were considering whether we should declare violation of Belgian neutrality to be a casus belli, *Mr Gladstone having declared in 1870 that defence of Belgium was required by policy and morality independent of time or circumstances.*

Grey to Bertie.

AS I LEAVE Grujić's room a message comes that Mr Dillon is trying to reach me on the telephone. I hurry to the Diplomatic Corps office. There is no one else there, as if the futility of international communications has come home at last to them all.

'Yes?'

'Des Graz has telephoned from Bucharest.'

'How did he get to Bucharest? He was coming here,' I say, stupidly relieved.

'He bought a motor car in Hungary and they broke down and had to walk thirty miles to the nearest town. He took the train to Bucharest where he's installed at the Legation. He doesn't expect to reach Niš at all soon.'

'You said they. Who has he with him?'

'That Russian.'

'I don't think there are any trains running from Bucharest to Niš.'

'And none to Belgrade.'

'One could say the Minister is stuck.'

'It seems one could, Theo.'

'And until he arrives we are stuck too.'

VON STORCK LOOKS as if he knows something I do not. He is a Minister and the Wilhelmstrasse may keep him better informed than the Foreign Office keeps me.

'Black, or white, Harris?'

'White.'

Sitting opposite him with his large, blond, not unhandsome face a foot or two from my own as we concentrate on the board, I realise that I have become almost fond of Von Storck. You have noticed the animal in the Zoological Gardens who offers his backside as a gesture of submission? Metaphorically, this is what Von Storck has taken to doing; the other animal always responds with careless acceptance, showing how many of our reactions are innate. His country and mine may at any hour be at war, yet I warm to him simply because of innate response to a submissive posture.

'What has happened to your new Minister?'

'He has trouble with his transport.'

'Where is he now?'

'Does the Wilhelmstrasse ask to know that?'

'I would like only to know how much longer I may enjoy your company, Harris.'

'Until the Belgian frontier is violated.'

He reflects for a long time on his next move, how to lead me to the trap where he can sacrifice himself and present his backside. 'By whom, that is the question, Harris. You are aware that in 1870 the Marquis de la Valette, a minister of Napoleon III, urged the elimination of small states to allow the expansion of larger neighbours?'

'No.'

'France has always been the threat to Belgium. It seems unnatural to the French that the fertile cabbage growing lowlands are separated from them.'

'They are vulnerable to the north.'

'Unless they have a powerful friend beside them.'

'That would make a difference.'

'That would indeed make a difference, Harris, measured in blood. I will lay the board for another game.'

Brussels, August 3, 1914

Remembering the numerous proofs of your Majesty's friendship and the friendly attitude of England in 1870, I make a supreme appeal to the diplomatic intervention of your Majesty's Government to safeguard the integrity of Belgium.

King Albert of the Belgians to George.

Note
Diplomatic assistance, not military aid, implored.
Crowe.

'I HAVE NO appetite for another.'

'A quick game, with a limit of time on moves.'

'Not today.'

'Please, Harris?'

'No.'

'You deny me my revenge,' Von Storck says.

I look hard at him. The pleading voice is belied by an expression of secret triumph in his eyes. He knows something. 'Let's not speak of revenge.'

'Let's speak then of other things. Let's drink some of your whisky. Let's compare the experiences we have with peasants on our lands at home.'

'I have a bit of land but the people on it are not peasants.'

'What are they, Harris?'

'Agricultural workers.'

Von Storck laughs genuinely for the first time in my acquaintance with him. 'When you have a shoot, these agricultural workers work at driving your partridges and pheasants towards you?'

'They're paid to do it.'

'And do you also call peasant women agricultural workers?' Von Storck is still laughing as he goes down the short flight of steps and out into the street.

I feel in need of a female presence, a different voice, so I ring for the maid; she will probably be surprised to find so little asked of her.

'What is your name?'

'What name would you like best?' She stirs herself about. 'Your mother's name? Your sisters' names? Your wife's?'

'Your own.'

'It is Katarina.'

'Sit down please, Katarina.' She obeys, warily. 'I want you to tell me about your family. Do you come from a farm?'

'Yes, from a farm. In the mountains. But my brothers told me to go.'

'Why?'

'Because they had wives, I couldn't do a man's work but they said I was good enough for woman's work here in Niš.'

If the house of cards falls and scatters, will the plight of this woman be any better? Has it roofed her over? 'You worked on the farm?'

'I slept in the straw with my brothers.'

'So their wives wanted you to go away?'

'No. The brothers wanted it. I was no more use.'

I regret this conversation but she is dry-eyed, hard, ready for whatever comes next, and in her experience what comes next probably doesn't vary much. 'You know there is war, Katarina?'

'Oh yes, there is always war and there are always men passing through Niš who have heard too much of other men's voices.'

The sorrow I feel for Katarina and the girls like her is swollen by sorrow for the men in their sweaty uniforms, their bloodstained leggings; and by sorrow for myself, one of the elect, reading telegrams from Emperors and Czars — yet lonely, extremely lonely, because of that perhaps.

'You have a soft voice, Katarina, the men must like it.'

'And a soft tongue.'

Foreign Office, August 3, 1914

German Ambassador knew nothing, he said, of the plans of the General Staff: but it might be for German troops to go through one small corner perhaps of Belgium. If so, they could not alter that, now that they have received definite information that France intends to invade Germany through Belgium.

Grey to Sir Francis Villiers, Ambassador, Brussels.

Brussels, August 3, 1914

Ultimatum states Germany fears Belgium will be unable to repel French attack without assistance and she therefore declares that if Belgium will adopt attitude of benevolent neutrality towards Germany in coming war, Germany will on conclusion of peace guarantee Belgium and Belgian possessions in Africa, and relations of friendship between the two nations will become more close and durable.

Villiers to Grey.

I GO ROUND to the Hotel Europa to see what I can find out about Von Storck's inside information. He has a suite of rooms at the rear of the hotel, round a bare courtyard — no flowers or grass, all the windows open in the heat, and sounds of music floating along the corridor as I approach, familiar from a long way back. The instrument is a 'cello, playing a short passage over and over, as a student repeats. But that isn't why this player is doing it, I know; each time at the end of the passage he trails off as if much more is to come if one can only wait — a year, a decade, a century. I lean against the wall to listen once again although I already know the secret. Selzman, in the days before his wrists and fingers were bent in until the nails almost dug into his palms, was a 'cello player and in Pembroke Villas could still perform this little passage I hear now floating around the court of the Hotel Europa.

'Haydn noted it in his *Entwurf-Katalog* as the opening theme of a concerto in C, Harris, but no one has ever discovered the score. This is all we have, and I can still manage it.'

'You manage it beautifully, Selzman.'

'You are not a musician, you can't know that.'

'But it moves me.'

'Imagine what the concerto would do, if we could find it.'

'Please play it again.' of course the fingering was slow by now but he drew a full tone from his 'cello and it gave pleasure to watch his concentration.

I was unaware till now that Von Storck was a musician and I'm surprised; perhaps it's not him playing but one of his acolytes, which would surprise me still more though with Germans and music you can never know. The door of the room is half open and I pass inside; the player is Von Storck. 'Ah, Harris! Do you care at all to hear music? Or is all fencing with you? You will never have heard this little passage — '

'On the contrary, I know the passage well. Haydn mentioned it in his catalogue of 1765. The concerto has never been found.'

'My dear Harris, you are a surprising man.' His eyes glow with approval. 'I have no whisky but I can offer you some excellent cognac.'

'A glass of white wine would do very well, thank you.'

With the door closed on us, Von Storck sits opposite me, the 'cello standing on its pin between his knees, his arms around its neck. 'You have heard news? You have received a telegram?' I say nothing. 'You have spoken to Secretary Grujić?' This is a time for silence, forcing the other side to stop asking questions and start providing information. 'The white wine — it is good enough, Harris?'

I have to answer that. 'It is very agreeable.'

'Since Waterloo and our famous victory we are allies, are we not, Harris?'

'We're certainly friends, Von Storck.'

'And so Haydn wrote his London symphonies — and Handel! Think of Handel! Handel lived and died in London!'

'That's true.'

'We are one people, really.'

'All mankind is one I dare say.'

'Ah, you sneer at us Harris, from the safety of your island.'

'I assure you — '

'But still we never quarrel, one family without any quarrels. A good family where no quarrel is possible, eh, Harris?' He plucks with his forefinger at a string, then at another and the two notes fill the room.

It seems to me that Von Storck has a rosy picture in his head of family life. 'I only hope you're right.'

'You say very little, Harris.'

'I am without instructions for the moment.'

'In this case, you are somewhat in the dark?'

'For the moment.

Now he can either tell me what he knows, or not tell me. I see the dilemma in his eyes, the personal element between us softening them; then they turn slowly to stone. 'We demand free passage for our troops through Belgium. We are obliged to do this, the French are preparing to do the same.'

I stand, putting my wine glass on the table. 'How many hours is your ultimatum?'

'Twelve.'

'They have run out?'

'They have run out.'

'Belgium is violated?'

'Violated, violated! You are obsessed with the word.'

'We observe treaties.'

'Scraps of paper, Harris.'

One may discuss but one must never argue. 'I'm sorry to hear what you tell me, Von Storck. I must go to the Telegraph Office.' He doesn't insist on accompanying me and on this afternoon of August 3rd, the two hundred yards between the Europa and the Telegraph Office are coals in the sun. There is no telegram waiting for me.

Reichstag, August 3, 1914

Gentlemen, we are in a position of necessity and necessity knows no law. The wrong — I speak openly — the wrong we now do we will try to make good again as soon as our military ends have been reached. He who is threatened as we are can only think of how to hack his way through.

Chancellor Von Bethmann-Hollweg.

Paris, August 3, 1914

German Ambassador leaves Paris tonight.

I am not surprised at H.M. Government declining to send a military force to France. I think it would be of advantage to us to give naval aid in the war for it would bring it to an end sooner by starving Germany and give us a locus standi *to determine the conditions of peace which we would otherwise lack.*

Bertie to Grey.

SENDING POSHA to intercept Des Graz may turn out to have been a mistake. H.M. Government must at all times be represented where there's advantage to be won or disadvantage avoided, and when the new French Minister gets here this will be all the more desirable.

The girl at my rooms is waiting for my return. 'I need nothing, thank you, Katarina, and I am very busy.'

'I will sit quietly, if you like, and then if you want something you tell me.'

'No. You must leave me alone now.' I take her hand for a moment, then let it go. 'You understand, Katarina, I was all of a sudden very lonely and everyone now is afraid.'

'You don't need me any more?'

'It was something I won't forget.'

'You will go away and leave nothing for me.'

'No, no. I will find something.'

'At night I sleep in the little cupboard under the stairs.'

'Yes, I understand.' All I have to give is my father's pocket watch which doesn't work any more; why should the girl not have the watch?

'It's nice,' she says.

'Good.'

She grips my hand firmly, holding it for a moment, and I hold on to her hand firmly too.

AUGUST 4TH IS born beneath the same burning sky as the days before, but with a new dread. I dress and make my way to the Government offices. Niš is far inland but its single storied buildings rest on short stilts with steps down to the sand and dust of the street as if a tide might any moment come in. Well, the tide's coming. No one in the Government offices requires my presence and I haven't anything to say. There's no sign of Von Storck; Strandtman, I'm told, has gone to attend a council of war at Bucharest. I go to the Telegraph Office. If Strandtman can get to Bucharest from Niš, Des Graz, who will surely meet him there, can get back with him; all the resources of the Russian state will be behind them and the sooner they come the better. The train from Vienna for the Belgrade refugees will have crossed the Semlin bridge by now and must be sitting with steam damped down in the main railway station; the Sunbeam awaits in the Legation coach house.

There is a telegram which I decode in the deserted premises of the Telegraph service.

Foreign Office, August 4, 1914

His Majesty's Government have asked Imperial German Government for assurance respecting Belgium by 12 o'clock tonight. If not, H.M. government feel bound to take all steps to uphold a treaty to which Germany is as much a party as ourselves. You should inform Servian Government who have for so long and earnestly begged for our commitment.

Grey to Harris.

SO IT'S HERE, and no prevarication could stop it. I return to the office of the Foreign Minister and wait for him to receive me. He does so immediately.

'Our Government has sent the German Government an ultimatum, General. I'm glad.'

He looks at me without speaking, for a full minute, leaving me to share his silent thought — an ultimatum, so late, so much too late. 'Belgium?'

'Yes, Belgium.'

'How strangely the English mind must work! Not for Luxembourg, certainly not for Servia — but for Belgium! A little fiction occupying huge stretches of Africa where I'm told their rule is the most ferocious in all the colonial world! More ferocious than in Siberia! Can you explain it, Mr Harris, to an old soldier?'

'I think I can, General. Since the reign of Edward III it has been a principle of English policy that the Low Countries and their ports must never fall into the hands of a great naval or military power. We have fought battles over them through the centuries. Waterloo was the last.'

'And you long to fight again over the same ground?'

'Not against the French, General.'

'No. They are no threat to your rule of the seas.'

We fall back into silence, more peaceable this time. Finally, I feel obliged to break it. 'I think it likely the new Minister may arrive at Niš after all,' I say.

'You are right. I have heard that he left Bucharest with the Russian Minister yesterday. They may already have crossed the Danube at the Iron Gates.'

'Then this may be our last meeting, General.'

'No, no, Mr Harris. We won't let you go so easily. The Prime Minister will insist on meeting you before you leave and may have a little surprise for you. The King himself is aware of your efforts on behalf of our country.' He claps me on the shoulder as I take my leave. 'This new Minister of yours may never get here. Our roads are bad and there are no policemen anywhere any more now. I think you will be with us for a long time.' He laughs unkindly. 'We hope not to lose you, Mr Harris.'

There is now no one at Niš with whom I can pass the long, hot, light evening. I wonder about Kitty in the hills behind Cannes, and the company she keeps. Do the lemon trees of Vence give enough shade to the peach of her skin? An alarming thought surfaces. Should war by any chance make life uneasy on the Riviera she may decide to install herself at Orchard Harris; she might even try to do it in Rutland Gate, though I believe my mother could hold her at bay. I stop by again at the Telegraph Office.

Niš, August 4, 1914

Situation looks most unsettled. Strongly advise you purchase house at Vence for security reasons at reasonable price. For funds consult Harris solicitors.

Theodore to Kitty.

NOW, WELL NOW, in my loneliness, I would even not reject the company of Von Storck. Some hours remain to midnight. We're not enemies. Shall I seek him out?

No need, he has had the same thought and is waiting for me in the street. 'I have the board.'

'Have you dined?'

'No.'

'Let's go in then.'

I think he wants to escape the Hôtel Europa and has come to look on my rooms as a second home. I ring for Katarina.

'His Excellency will share my supper, Katarina.'

'He need not share it,' she says, 'I will bring two suppers.'

'A good clean servant.' Von Storck sounds dispirited; I have a bottle of white wine already open and pour two glasses. 'Excuse me Harris, but tonight I would prefer some of your golden Glenmorangie. His voice suddenly grows round and sonorous as his 'cello: *'Kennst du das Land, wo die Zitronen blühn? Im dunkeln Laub die Gold-Orangen glühn —* '

I'm standing near the window, hearing the voice of all the women who will pass their spinsterhood in war-torn lands.

'I'll drink a whisky with you, Von Storck.'

Katarina's supper is copious as always but we eat very little. 'What time is it, Harris?'

'Eleven.'

He holds out closed fists and I tap on the left. 'Black. So, I open,' Von Storck says. 'An hour still before us.'

Little by little as the hour runs we capture, block, and huff. We take our time, clear the board and play again. I look at my watch — five minutes before midnight. It is Von Storck's turn, he hangs over the board as it might be the map of Belgium. 'What time now, Harris?' I lean back in my chair. 'Midnight?'

'Yes.'

We sit in front of the unfinished game and the empty bottle and I can read on Von Storck's face and in his posture the despair we feel. He is slouched forward, his hands between his knees.

'For a treaty long ago forgotten by everyone,' he says.

'Remembered by Parliament.'

Von Storck throws up his hands at arms' length above the board between us as if to close his fists and bring them down on me. 'So you honour the treaty of 1831 and your members of parliament go home to their country houses while Belgium — *Belgium* — sucks our peoples into war.'

'They believe they've done their duty.'

'At what cost? At what cost, Harris?'

The cry, repeated several times along the corridor, echoes back from the street like a night watchman rousing the town as Von Storck leaves with his draughts set under his arm. 'At what cost!'

NO SLEEP; between four and five there was a time when memory stopped work, but that's all. I ask for coffee at six, dress carefully and go first to the Telegraph Office.

Foreign Office, August 5, 1914

War declared Germany. Act.
Grey to Harris.

I GO STRAIGHT to the Prime Minister's office. 'Mr Harris, I was expecting this visit.'

'I have to announce that my country has declared war on Germany. I have the telegram in my hand.' I pass it to him, with the decoded words. It isn't a long one, after all.

'I too have a telegram, from our Legation in London. It tells me that Germany has declared war on Britain. We are all in the hand of God.'

'Who has never shown much mercy.'

'God has purposes obscure to us.'

'Your Excellency puts it very well.'

'Yes. Well now, Mr Harris, I am going to invest you with the Order of the White Eagle of Servia in recognition of your — ' he hesitates in the citation and tries again — 'to show our appreciation of your — feelings for our country.' Pašić takes from the drawer of his desk a chain and pendant in silver gilt and enamel. 'You offered advice which was not taken. But we know in the end that one man more or less would have stopped nothing.' It is the first decoration I have ever received and I can imagine Selzman saying, 'The god of honours moves like all gods in mysterious ways. Take it.'

'I am honoured, Prime Minister.'

'Prince George has spoken highly of you and Mrs Harris to his father the King.'

So perhaps the White Eagle round my neck owes more to Kitty's qualities than mine. 'I think Mr Des Graz, the new Minister, may reach Niš at any time, in which case this will be my leave-taking.'

'He is already here. I wished to offer you the decoration while you are still officially Chargé d'affaires.'

'Where is Mr Des Graz?'

'He arrived at the railway station on a military train. The station master telephoned half an hour ago. Mr Des Graz awaits you there.'

'If there are military trains, I would like to reach Belgrade, Prime Minister.'

'I have no doubt, and we will arrange to put you on one.' I can see that Pašić finds my situation humorous in spite of all. Somewhere far within his beard the amusement stirs and rises like gas from the depths of a pond. 'But soon now there will be nothing left to laugh about, and the days of diplomatists' peccadilloes will be forgotten. The next generation will be dull fellows.' As I reach the door he seems to remember something he meant to say. 'One moment.'

'Yes, Prime Minister?'

He pauses before going on. 'My friend General Putnik tells me his information is that France is unprepared against attack from the north. Does that not seem strange?'

'It does; particularly as it's the condition on which British entry into war depended.'

The Prime Minister is watching me with wonder. 'He would be a very cynical historian to suggest that the one explained the other,' he says.

'That Germany — '

'Was wilfully enticed.'

Berlin, August 5, 1914

Last night a noisy demonstration was made outside the Embassy and stones were thrown at the windows. The crowd seemed mad with rage, howling, 'Down with England! Race treachery! Murderers!'

This morning, one of His Majesty's aides-de-camp came to me with the following message: —

The Emperor regrets these occurrences but you will gather from them the feelings of his people respecting the action of Great Britain in joining with other nations against her old allies of Waterloo.

Goschen to Grey.

XVI

'The refugees?'

'Pulled out from platform two at nine last night,' Oliver says. We walk up the last slope of Prince Michael Street in silence. Shops and cafés are shut, windows smashed, the Hôtel Impérial deserted, but the sound of continual Maxim gun fire comes from the direction of the Danube or the Save; every few minutes a deeper roar splits the air, and then an explosion somewhere near the railway station we've just left.

'The Legation's safer than the street,' Oliver says.

'If the Austrians bring up *Schlanke Emma* even the Legation would be blasted off the face of the earth.'

'Who is *Schlanke Emma*?'

'A 305 mm howitzer. I've been hearing about her from the German Minister over the draughts board.'

I go into the stable yard and there she is, gleaming in the sun, woodwork and brass and leather glassy with polish. The Supreme Silent Sunbeam's wire wheels are cleaned of mud. I walk slowly about her, watched by Oliver. 'You're putting something off,' he says.

'We must organise and equip and take enough motor spirit to reach the frontier.'

'Come inside,' Oliver says. 'Xenia will think you're planning to leave her behind. She already suspects it.'

She has come out of the shadow of the interior into the heat of morning, her dress like a smock hanging away from her by bands at the shoulders. 'All is made ready for you to go, Mr Harris.'

'Oliver says you think I'd leave you behind, Xenia.' We are in the doorway face to face. 'I don't believe him.'

'We go together?'

'Yes.'

'And when they make you a Minister?'

'It'll be the same, just the same.'

She moves away. 'Everything is packed — I am ready.'

'Milan is fit to travel?'

'He is ready also.'

'Let's go in then.'

In the hall of the Legation is a pile of luggage which I can see won't fit into the car with passengers, and there stands Branko with his rifle and revolver. Is he coming too? He steps forward and embraces me.

'Excellency! My friend! You will need a guard and I am the man you need.' Probably he has some good reason of his own to reach the frontier and cross it but that's no business of mine; what concerns me is how many people with luggage and tins of petrol the Sunbeam can carry across hundreds of miles of fearful roads to the sea.

'Two bags in the dickey, one in the front, and a few parcels. The rest stays here.' There's a silence. 'We should leave in an hour.' From not far away comes an explosion which makes the marble floor shake. 'Repack everything and bring it outside. I will see about our petrol supply.'

At twenty four miles to the gallon and three hundred and eighty miles to Salonika I must start with twenty gallons. Petrol stocks will be commandeered by armies; we need two four-gallon tins strapped to the stepboards. I find the filling up already done, the instruction handbook which I keep in the pocket of the door open at the page of diagrams with the lubrication chart. 'Magneto: 6 drops thin oil each 200 miles. Universal joint at tail end of propeller shaft: replenish grease every 500 miles . . . One look at the magneto tells me that this has been carried out; drops of fresh oil are visible on the casing. I close down the bonnet and find myself face to face with Milan. 'It was you, who — ' I raise the lubricating manual in my hand.

'Yes.' He's a man of few words, in any language.

'You understood the instructions in English?'

'Xenia helps me.'

'Do you know how to drive a motor car?'

'Now I do.'

'I see.'

'It is a wonderful machine,' he says.

'It has to take us a long way on terrible roads. We will often have to change the wheels and mend the tyres.'

'Good. I will do this.'

'We'll do it together, we must work together to get Xenia and you safely out of the country. You understand?'

'You too, you must get out safe and reach the sea. We Serbs fought a war for a way to reach the sea, perhaps this one will give it to us.' A long speech, for him, and I smile and nod.

I must go warily with Milan, he doesn't want to owe anything like thanks for shelter or rescue, he's an injured man who will accept and never give, as if the world were his nurse. I could of course surrender him, somewhere between Belgrade and the frontier, to the Servian army who would put him into uniform and drag him with them to extermination in the Albanian snows when Servia, sooner or later, is overrun. Poor Prince George foretold that. But now as before, I would have to watch Xenia's grief. 'I want to see you drive. I'll swing the engine.'

'The engine is warm.'

He climbs up, pulling his bad leg after him; I stand back, he drives easily round the yard, stops, reverses back beside me. He knows how to manage the car and treats gear box and engine with respect.

'This will be a very hard journey,' I tell him, 'we will drive in turns, you and I.'

'I thought this,' Milan says, and smiles at me for the first time since I've known him. 'And I learn to speak English.'

It is she who has organised this but he has gifts and lets her exploit them. I open the dickey. With two passengers no suitcase will go into the footwell, that's certain. We must reduce our interior luggage to bundles.

'I tell Xenia all those boxes impossible,' Milan says.

'We can tie two or three to the stepboards.'

'I have the ropes ready.'

'We need a strong one for towing.'

'It is here.'

'We should take a spade.'

'I have it.' He seems to have thought of almost everything.

'Well,' I say, fixing on something he can't have thought about, 'we must study a map.'

'All my maps from the army are on your table.'

He follows me in to the cool interior of the Legation, up the first flight of stairs and then into the study where his military maps lie spread out, like plain and mountain to the White Eagle's eye. I call down for Oliver.

'Your consul Mr Dillon is a thirsty man,' Branko says, arriving with a supporting arm round Oliver's shoulder. 'In my inn, I would look after him.'

'We are going to study the maps to see our best route,' I say.

'Sofia,' Oliver says indistinctly, 'I knew a Roumanian princess there — mind you, princesses in Roumania — all over the place.'

'Des Graz warned me Bulgaria may any day enter the war on the side of Germany. We can't go there.'

'Is that your only reason?'

'And Milan fought against them last year. They are not good to prisoners.' I turn to the spread out maps. 'We will go to Niš and southwards across the plain and into the valleys to Skopje.' A finger running over the folds of a map, following contorsions of rivers and the string of villages and towns can make a journey seem simple, clear.

'Those mountains in Macedonia — many, many bandits,' Branko says. 'They steal everything and slit the foreigners' throats.'

'From Skopje we will climb to the watershed at — ' I peer down at the map whose printing, though German, is a far cry from the Ordnance Survey showing every field — 'near Gevqelija and these lakes, here.' The silence following shows that no one else either has the remotest conception of what Gevqelija or the lakes in its vicinity can be like; Milan's map can't draw representation into reality, but its contours and soft colouring, the pink and green washes, the stain of wooded height and cleft are all we need for now. Reality, we will learn to deal with, and perhaps get through to Salonika in spite of all.

EVERYONE FEELS SAD to leave the stone mansion for the last time. It has taken bombardment and given us protection which we won't have among Macedonian bandits. I put the ring of keys into my pocket for delivery to Des Graz as we pass through Niš where Dillon and I will take official leave of him, after which we will no longer be diplomat, inn-keeper, terrorist or stenographer, but a party of motorists attacking a journey no car may ever have attempted before. Sleeping under the sky, cooking on fires, drinking from streams. Xenia's hand is in mine and I feel ten years younger than the Chargé d'affaires decoding telegrams these last days

I put Oliver and Branko onto the unsprung folding dickey seat, load them into place with packages, and warn Oliver about dust and flies and corrugations in the road.

'This will be all right, don't worry about Oliver or anything,' Xenia says.

She is between Milan and me, her thigh and hip, pressed against mine on her right side, are equally pressed against Milan's on her left. And when Milan drives it will be the same but the other way round. Would I rather she was pressed against Branko or Oliver? The car floats down the deserted street just as another shell falls on Kalemegdan behind us, earth shattering this time.

EVENING CAMP. DAY ONE. Des Graz received us with a mixture of envy and suspicion. Envy of our getting out and leaving him in the middle of a war which we failed to prevent; and suspicion because someone has talked.

'So, Harris, our Legation is wrecked?'

'Pretty well, yes.'

'You leave no staff there?'

'None.'

'What have you done with them?'

'They have been dispersed.'

'Yes. I was told to expect that.'

Did I want to know who told him? Had I even time to wonder? At this moment the door of the Minister's room opened. It was Pósha. 'Your Excellency's coffee,' he said, and put a single cup on the table.

'You and Dillon are leaving by road alone?' Des Graz persisted.

'We are,' said Oliver in a firm voice. I felt no need to add anything, but saw how our future is pledged by our debt to him, and his, by his knowledge and his lie.

'The proceeding is unusual. Very unusual,' Des Graz complained.

'War is an unusual state,' I said.

'And I hear you have even been given a decoration,' said the new Minister resentfully.

Later we picked up the others where we had left them, in a wood outside the town. Hamlets deserted, people fled to the hills. First puncture. Milan and I changed the wheel but when we reach a pool of water the puncture must be mended. After four hours of driving I put Milan behind the wheel and he is, I admit, a capable driver, will soon be as good as I am. 'You see,' Xenia said, 'we can't go without him.'

'We don't go without him.'

A few hours' sleep at the edge of an oak wood. Owls.

DAY TWO. South of Niš the road is still more terrible, deep holes, rocks, sudden ditches where wheel ruts were. The thermometer on the nose of the radiator will warn of us of overheating; the danger, I think, is from stones thrown up that could puncture the oil well without our knowing. It's a huge, empty, featureless plain, vegetation burnt by the sun. The car crawled along, then reached a good stretch lasting a mile or so until at a turn in a wood the track was abolished. The torrents of spring took it away, so Xenia said; we crossed a dry ford between alders into a sere pasture land, a better surface than the road and inhabited by a donkey which followed us, curious, hopeful, patient, lonely, as far the outskirts of a village.

'That poor ass needs a horse for company,' Oliver said.

'All the horses are gone to the war.'

'We haven't a drop to drink.'

'We're sure to come across a running stream sooner or later.'

'The liquid of a stream,' Oliver said, leaning forward over the folded hood and speaking clearly, 'is not the juice that made the Britons bold. Dryden, you know.'

'We're not having the juice you mean in this motor car.'

'You should let him drink something or he'll be ill,' Xenia said and of course she was right.

'Stop in the village,' I told Milan, and we drew up before one of the many single-storied, shuttered white houses.

'That one is an inn,' Branko said.

'We'll go in together,' Oliver said climbing out of the dickey.

'Let him go, sometimes I think he is your better half,' Xenia said in German.

'Better half?'

'I mean you are gentle with his weakness because once someone was gentle with yours.'

After that I found nothing to say but sat watching her until Milan announced he needed to get out, his bad leg hampering him from climbing over the gear lever on the driver's right side. Xenia and I made way and stood together, leaning against the petrol tins and boxes, metal burning hot to the touch, the two of us alone in this treeless village street. 'You think I'm kind from weakness, when I'm kind?'

'No, then you wouldn't drive us to freedom through the mountains of Macedonia.'

'We haven't reached them yet.'

'You see? Over the roofs there? That blue line like a wave is the mountains.'

Hot and dirty as we are, I put an arm alongside hers so they touch on the folds of the hood; 'I'm driving to freedom too.'

'I think you can never be free, now.'

She was right, but I won't think about it. 'We must reach those mountains before dark.'

'Why so much hurry?'

'The Greek Prime Minister Venizelos is in Salonika, but not for long.'

'You know this Mr Venizelos?' Xenia's voice speaking of a foreign potentate was full of wonder, though any mention of powerful men in her own country is with contempt.

'Venizelos was good enough to notice me at Athens — '

'You mean he liked you?'

'He invited me on his yacht. And if we reach Salonika while he's there everything will be all right. Our papers — yours and Milan's — won't be questioned.'

'On this Greek yacht, did Mr Venizelos show how much more he liked you than you thought?'

'Venizelos is a brave man.'

'We are all brave now, men or women,' Xenia said.

DAY THREE. We reached the foothills after dark, everyone exhausted by fourteen hours of road, gullies, fields, the stifling heat. We had the hood raised to shield us from the sun but Oliver's face was brick red under the day's crust. This region even more deserted than the plain we've crossed — but the night warm and we had bread and cheese and fruit and wine hidden by Branko in the dickey. I was glad to see it, and when eventually we lay down to sleep on the grass I felt a happiness lost since those moments in childhood when reality and all its fears slip away and you live under your own rule.

A regrettable thing happened, perhaps on account of that. Thinking about it by daylight, I feel more astonished than ashamed that the years of discretion slipped from me like the reality. We were lying scattered about in the open, the nearest trees ten yards distant, a small spring discovered and cleared by Milan now trickling among stones, the night brilliant with stars. So on waking, it was diamonds I saw spread on the breast of the sky as I lay on my back. Xenia was on her side, a light blanket over her and turned away from me, a few feet off. Everyone seemed asleep, quite still.

For a minute or so I reflected on the war just beginning; but Xenia's outline was within reach and war thoughts receded into the dark.

'You must keep quiet,' she said in my ear.

'I will.'

The regret was later. Above the plain to the east was a thin line of lighter sky, we lay side by side, murmuring words of affirmation and relief. It was just when Xenia dropped off again that I looked over towards the others and saw that Milan was awake and watching, and I knew that something irreversible had happened. I looked away.

We had to get on. Skopje was fifty miles uphill, across escarpments fallen into the chasm where the Morava thunders northward. Milan was silent all day; he took the wheel when told and gave it up when told but said nothing. The damage was done. We pursued the long climb through the mountains, reaching the watershed by midday; behind us the Morava flowed to Niš and Belgrade and the Danube. From here on every spring was tributary to the Aegean. Xenia, like most Serbs, has never seen the sea.

'Did you have wind for the sails of Mr Venizelos' yacht?' she asked me.

'It was a steam boat.'

DAY FOUR. We came to Skopje, a pleasant town undisturbed since history began, in the late afternoon. There was no sign of war — boys bathed in the river among women washing their linen on the stones; in the narrow streets the country commerce continued; along a boulevard between the station and the river Vardar with the citadel and minarets just above, crowds of citizens without a care wandered in the sunshine, a musician here and there playing a violin or zither. It was market day, you could buy a goat, a foal, a rug of brilliant colours; more to the point, provisions for the road.

'If we hang around here,' Oliver said, 'you'll have to present yourself to the local *Ban,* and if you want my opinion, he won't let your diplomatic passport, if he can read it, stop him enquiring about the rest of us.'

'We have papers.'

'Not Branko.'

A pity he was right because there was a clean hotel with a courtyard shaded by vines and a deep-arched brick cloister. Clothes could have been laundered and returned in the morning. But the crowds watched the car move among them and the news would be in the office of the *Ban* within minutes. I told Milan at the wheel to hurry on.

ACETYLENE HEADLAMPS throw light enough for streets but not for Balkan mountain roads and by midnight I knew we must stop. 'We'll sleep where we are.'

'On the ground?' Milan asked.

'We will take turns watching.'

Xenia curled up on the seat with her head against me. 'I am not worried about bandits.'

The place was in a woody gorge above a stream, the cliffs outlined against a sky almost as dark. In the evening when we entered the first of these gorges by sunlight the stone walls were ochre and rose, with narrow terraces growing maize and vines and tobacco, and rough paths twisting up the cliff face and striping the stone with earth colours. Now you could hear the stream and make out the stars but all else was black. Sleep came almost at once.

My watch was due from three to six. I woke with Branko's hand to my shoulder. 'You can sleep on.'

'No, give me the rifle.'

'It is loaded.'

I sat with the rifle butt between my knees, the pistol resting on them. Xenia had moved without waking and her head now was against Milan's shoulder on the passenger side instead of mine. The strong smell of horses close by alerted me. I breathed in, waited for the sound of drinking, heard a shout like an order out of the dark, another, then Branko's voice from the dickey seat. 'Give me the rifle.' The horses were trampling on the track and along the river bank, but no shot came.

'What's going on?' asked Oliver, and the question was followed by a flash in the dark.

'Fire the pistol in the air,' Branko shouted from somewhere above. As I raised it, a hand closed round my wrist.

'Now I can do the thing I want,' Milan said in German in my ear.

Under the cliff a spark struck, flew and fell on the track a pace or two from the car where it flared up so we were lit as targets in the dark. A volley of shots followed, while from a few feet away Milan emptied the pistol as Princip had on the bridge at Sarajevo; then came the sound of hooves receding. It seemed that the attack had been repelled.

'The petrol tins — we must smother that flare,' I called out.

'I'm doing the thing,' said Oliver, out on the ground with a canvas sheet. A last shot came from the wood above the gorge, the canvas sheet fell over the flare and darkness returned.

'I think Oliver is hurt,' Xenia said.

'No, he's there.'

'But I heard something.'

'We must light the acetylene lamps.'

'He is hit,' Xenia said.

He was sitting with one knee drawn up, the other leg stretched before him; the light of the lamps was just enough to make out a dark stain on his trousers at the level of the knee.

'Are you in pain?' I asked.

'Well, I feel something down there.' Xenia was crouched beside him. With the trouser leg cut away, blood could be seen running freely from a point on the inside near the kneecap, and I thought of the journey across the worst roads in Europe to a hospital beyond the frontier.

Milan appeared out of the darkness, looking down at Xenia. 'Branko is killed, I think,' he announced flatly.

Branko was lying at the foot of a tree with his rifle beside him, peaceful in death for a man so lively. We waited for first light to lift Oliver into the Sunbeam without hurting him more than we had to, and to take care of Branko's remains as well as we could. With tyre levers and the spade Milan and I dug a shallow opening near the stream where the ground was soft, and lifted the body in. He had no papers in his pockets but a sum of Servian paper money equal to about two thousand pounds sterling; for an escape or mission into Greece he was well supplied. I put the money with my own papers; later I would contact Des Graz at Niš and ask him to find Branko's old mother, though whether when this cash reached her it would still be worth anything much was a hazard of war.

Xenia bound up Oliver's wound and we lifted him into the front seat, his leg supported on bundles and bags. 'We must cut up the dicky seat and put part of it under his leg to cushion it,' I said, and so we did. Xenia and Milan sat behind and as the light grew stronger we edged forward. Progress was slow, bleeding continued and pain grew worse.

In the miles before Veles the river valley widened, the Vardar ran sweetly over stones between pastures, buffaloes bathed in the waters and storks watched beside them. The sky was more southern every mile, and softer. But not for Oliver. 'Ah God,' he cried, 'take me, take me.'

At Veles we learned that the only doctor in the town had gone to the war; there was a pharmacist who sold us bandages, iodine, and morphine. Peasants in Aegean costume thronged about the car, more in disbelief than admiration. We bought a day's supply of food and some wine.

'You have a wounded man?' the pharmacist asked.

'An accident on the road,' I said.

We crept over the wooden bridge crossing the torrent of the Vardar, then took the road for Salonika. From here the surface was better, the countryside cultivated, donkeys trotted along with peasants on their backs, water systems irrigated the fields and trees shaded the road. It was a matter of endurance to reach Salonika along the meandering valley beside the railway line, between these gentle hills. In places, with Oliver half conscious, we reached fifty or even fifty five miles an hour.

Not far from the frontier near Bogdanci the road ran beside a lake, reflecting the sky and with oaks and alders growing down to its edge. 'I'm going to bathe in that lake,' I said.

'I will also,' Xenia said.

We went behind the trees and stripped. The car was out of sight, the world was deserted, we entered the water naked.

'When we pass the frontier, we're free,' I said to her.

I turned my head to see Milan standing on the bank. 'Mr Dillon is not asleep,' he said, 'he is in coma.'

We crossed the border with Xenia in front and the fugitive Milan folded into the dickey in darkness, airlessness and heat. He looked up at me from the well of his eyes as I closed the cover on him.

SALONIKA. They've saved Oliver's life in the hospital here but at the cost of his leg. Milan and Xenia and I are in an hotel on the Aegean edge, tied together, for better for worse, from now on.

Just after lunch on a brilliant day, all sides having declared war in due form and committed their peoples, the sky darkened; slowly the birds fell silent, cicadas slept, a purple light filled the world. 'It's an eclipse. You mustn't look up at the sun,' I told Xenia and put my hand over her eyes.

XVII

Back from a visit to the first Dublin Horse Show since the ending of war to end war, Colonel Proby found a note from Oliver.

As you see, Boppe has had his way and his Legation and ours have moved to Antigua Guatemala, much pleasanter than Guatemala City where rebuilding for the new population seals into the masonry the unhallowed corpses of the old.

I planned writing you a line, kept putting it off hoping you might turn up again some time soon. I've had a couple of warnings around the heart these last months, but I dare say I can hang on till your next trip. Theo sends regards —

THE MESSENGER due for the American tour was Stewart, to whom Proby had recently advanced a loan to get him out of a hole. Stewart arranged to be unfit to travel and Proby arranged to be in the chief clerk's office when the news of it came.

'How would you feel about Guatemala at short notice, Colonel?'

'More than willing.'

The chief clerk looked amused. 'The ancient Maya civilisation? The principle of the zero?'

'I might take a few days leave in the forests.'

'Archaeological searches?'

'Let's say to work a few things out.'

'In yourself?' Proby didn't answer this undiplomatic question. 'We have a slightly perturbing report from an unofficial source, Colonel Proby. Some anxiety is felt here.'

'Concerning the Legation?'
'More the ancillary personnel.'

THIS TIME he agreed to be met at Puerto San José by the Legation motor car instead of travelling on horseback through the coffee and banana plantations, because he felt worried about Oliver and wanted to lose none of the days he had. The driver was the man named Igman, surly and perhaps mentally disturbed Legation hanger-on. Proby could think of no other designation for him; what did he do, whose interest did he serve, who paid him, if paid he was? The eighty mile journey was likely to be heavy going, Proby thought.

But Milan gave him a polite smile. 'My mare is very well,' he said.

'Good, good. Does Mr Dillon go out riding with you?'

'Oliver is not strong now.'

The car was a big, heavy, slow Talbot in which six or eight people could be carried at a comfortable snail's pace. 'This car is nothing,' Milan said. 'In Serbia we had a Sunbeam.' The road from the coast showed signs of recent work, surface holes mainly filled and decent ditches on either side carrying rain water which fell without cease, heavy and warm and splashing noisily on the outspread banana leaves. Proby smiled and saluted at peasants along the way who had to clear the road of their animals to let the Talbot pass, but they didn't smile back. 'Peasants here are afraid to smile,' Milan said, 'those are Indians. Ladinos sometimes smile but not much. You know a Ladino because he wears shoes.'

'I expect they all laugh at us well enough among themselves, shoes or no shoes,' Proby said, but Milan either didn't understand or didn't think this humane assumption worth following up.

Colonel Proby was content to let his mind rest as they rolled along; the scenery of coast and then plain and then gently rising ground through wealthy coffee plantations didn't interest him. What interested him was the home of the Maya in the vast, roadless forests of the interior, and the task that he believed duty dictated. The thing to do was to assess Oliver Dillon's state of health and issue morale-bracing encouragement to him with nostalgic reminders of the Dublin Horse Show, then take a long ride into the forests. He might even make some archaeological discovery in there which would put his name in the textbooks for ever. Proby's Dig, it could be called, a more impressive memento of existence than a simple mention in the roll call of King's Messengers — and of duty well if painfully done.

'This is Escuintla,' Milan said as they came into the outskirts of a town in the foothills. 'There is a prison here called *El Infierno*. It is a hell where no one escapes.'

Proby had the military habit of caring for the welfare of men to the last, though he carried it further than most. 'You have a girl somewhere?' he asked. 'It would be lonely without.'

'I have nothing to do with girls,' Milan said, and they drove on toward the ring of smoking volcanoes in silence as if *to El Infierno* itself.

The cones were cultivated almost to the crest, leaving a corona of forest rising from bare ground to the top. Looking down from the shoulder of the pass, islands of clouds floated below you over the vast, rich valleys of the interior. 'Is that Antigua?' Colonel Proby asked, pointing at a layout like a Roman town, a grid work of streets, churches and palaces far below and in the distance.

'Antigua Guatemala,' Milan corrected sombrely. 'We have a puncture.'

Proby watched him change the wheel. With his sleeves rolled up he showed himself robustly constructed; his forearms were thick, his back, under exertion, powerful beneath his shirt. 'Have you ridden much into the forest, Igman?' he asked when they got under way again, jolting down the long pass where the road was rougher, between forests and grazing land, clouds light as smoke rings below you, then level, then above.

Milan turned his head towards the Colonel and his smile was different from the one he'd given at Puerto San José, more aroused. A man who rarely smiles betrays more than he knows. 'It is a long way, too far, but there are things in there,' he said, 'so our wars in Europe are nothing.'

PROBY HAD consulted a handbook in the Foreign Office library about Antigua so he knew that in 1773 it was almost as much destroyed by earthquake as Guatemala City a couple of years ago. The difference was that no one had ever seriously tried to rebuild it; they just went on living there. In the same year of 1773 one of the volcanoes erupted, pouring out clouds of poisonous gas which fell on the surviving citizens sheltering in crypts and cellars. It seemed that the hatred of God for humankind was manifest here at the surface of the world whereas in Europe it showed itself more in the heart of man himself. The outskirts of Antigua, after a hundred and forty years, were like those of Amiens on 12th August 1918. In Proby's mind the mixture of horror and earlier memory produced the familiar sorrow beyond remedy.

'There is the Catedral de San José,' Milan said, jabbing a finger at a stupendous ruin occupying one side of a square. 'This is the Plaza Mayor. Here there were bullfights and hangings and tortures for the happy people to watch.'

'Your English is very good now, Igman.'

'I talk with Oliver.'

'Does he talk to you about Ireland?'

'No. But I hear him talking about it to the Minister, to make him feel bad.' Milan laughed.

The Legation now occupied an upper floor of the Hôtel Casa Santo Domingo, the French Legation monopolising the piano nobile of this ancient building. It was Xenia Ciganović who opened the door.

'Colonel Proby! A good journey with Milan? Not too many punctures? Not too much of his black thoughts?' She gave her free and open laugh, so open that it could hide almost anything.

Any free woman, after a certain time in all-male company, becomes more florid, adamant, perhaps more reckless. So it was, to Proby's eye, with Xenia. She moved her hips more liberally, by every movement she seemed to give more of herself.

'Mr Harris is here?'

'He is visiting a house of American Protestant nuns. They are starving but they don't complain, it's their vocation to starve, naturally. But Theo is worried because one of them is from Scotland.'

The British rooms in the Hôtel Casa Santo Domingo were smaller, less airy, and far less grand than those of the Legation building in Guatemala City; was this why the French Minister had urged the move to Antigua? 'Is Monsieur Boppe quite well?'

'Poor man. Theo is cruel to him, he won't let him win at foils any more. They are less young than they were and Theo has not so many victories in front of him.'

His bedroom was well-appointed and lonely. From the windows he had a view over the ruins of the cathedral, its former dome excised as by a mastectomy (the colonel was a surgeon's son), leaving spandrels, pillars, and a voided disc, below which the weeds grew and flourished on pavings where homeless children set up their brutal model of an adult world. Proby unpacked his case and went to the Minister's study with the bag to await his return; after that he could enquire about Oliver Dillon.

He heard the Minister in conversation with Miss Ciganović, the sounds coming from the entrance hall, their voices low but insistent with the rapid, even note of intimacy. 'My dear Proby — delighted to see you!' Harris did not look in too good condition. He had lost weight so his suit hung about him, his face was thin and deep lines had appeared in it from the nose to the corners of the mouth; he had remorse, or something very like it, written all over him. 'What about the Peace Conference?' he said. 'It will never hold. Sykes-Picot is a dead letter; the Italians have already occupied Fiume; how can we claim to rule in Baghdad, or the French in Damascus? What have we done, what on earth have we done?'

Proby took all these questions as symptomatic of Harris's ailing frame of mind which physical signs already betrayed. Hadn't Dillon told him last year that Monsieur Boppe, in 1914, cracked up from his responsibilities in Belgrade? And if Dillon's manuscript meant anything, Boppe's responsibility was nothing to Harris's. 'So many men can't have died for nothing,' he said.

'Oh yes they can,' said Harris. 'You know the total? On all fronts?'

Proby shook his head. Totals were for those who weren't on the ground. On the ground it was the man next to you, or yourself.

'Ten to twelve millions.'

'Surely not for nothing?'

'What do you think? Perhaps a small emancipation of morals and manners and a liberalisation of politics which would have come in its own good time.'

'I recall that Miss Ciganović told me on my last visit, when we spoke a little of your time in Belgrade, that you had done everything any man could do to prevent the catastrophe, Mr Harris. And the king decorated you.'

'She said that? Everything possible?'

'I think that's what she said.'

'Ah.'

Proby felt his attempt to bolster the Minister's morale — apparently not enough — was as much as his position allowed. 'I would like to leave the bag with you and go and find Mr Dillon who I hear has not been well.'

'Oliver is in bed. I'm unhappy about him but he refuses to leave us. There are doctors here but he should go home.'

'To Ireland?'

Harris laughed for the first time. 'Try suggesting that,' he said.

'I understand it's his heart in cause?'

'Oliver's heart has always been his weak point.' Proby could tell the depth of their friendship from the flippant tone of Harris's voice, failing to hide the sadness. Dillon's state must be bad.

'Which is the way to his room?'

— 236 —

'The archive is at the end of the corridor. There's a sign on the door. He won't leave that either'

PROBY WAS NOT afraid of sickrooms and anyway he didn't expect to stay long in this one. If Dillon was nearing the end, reality and fiction might no longer be quite separate in his mind, if they ever were. So, an account to give him of the Dublin Horse Show, and then a look at Milan's mare. Where was the stable, by the way? 'Can I come in? Proby.'

Oliver was more on the bed than in it, under a sheet like a body in the morgue but propped almost upright by cushions. He seemed to be fully dressed, his shoes sticking out from the end of the covering. There was no smell of whisky. He signalled the colonel forward, indicating a chair placed near the head of his bed. 'Haven't much puff,' he wheezed.

'Sorry to hear it.'

They sat in silence for a moment or two; Proby was quite comfortable with silence, in a ward of wounded men you were often glad of it.

'How do you find Theo?' Oliver asked.

'A little thinner.'

'That's right. Gnawed by conscience.'

Proby considered it was too late in the day to know more about the Minister's conscience. 'I thought of taking a tour on horseback in the forests,' he said.

'Wear good boots,' Dillon whispered, 'they're alive with snakes.'

Proby wasn't sure how much of the wheezing and whispering and shortness of breath was theatrical; sometimes a man exaggerates his symptoms as a kind of magic to bring the date of release a bit closer. 'Don't worry, I always ride in good boots.'

Oliver's eyes were closed and his mouth slightly open. Proby stirred in his chair and shuffled his feet on the wooden floor. 'The manuscript you gave me — I have it with me. I read it over several times.'

Oliver closed his mouth and pulled himself up. 'You did? I won't ask you what . . .' he paused. 'Milan should have gone the way of Princip and the others.'

'He escaped a bad end.'

'I think there was no escape in the trenches.'

'Certain men went willingly. For some it was an escape.'

'Yes.'

'What did you intend — for that manuscript?'

'For you to do whatever you think you should,' Oliver said as he had before.

'I will.'

Oliver pushed himself back into his pillows and gave out a small sound between a groan and a whimper. 'Ghastly pain,' he said.

'Whereabouts, Oliver?'

'Guts. I think I'm bleeding.'

Proby stood, looking down at him. It seemed to him that Oliver's colour had changed, he appeared greyer though the light in the room was the same, and there was a dark ring round each eye. 'Your doctor should come at once. I'll tell Mr Harris.'

'Tell Xenia.'

OLIVER DILLON was carried that night to the infirmary of the University of San Carlos Borromeo, and opened up. The surgeon's report, which Harris gave Proby to take back to the Foreign Office for eventual transmission to Oliver's family, whoever they were, stated that the rectum was almost occluded by a tumour, the removal of which would have left Mr Dillon with severe handicaps during what remained to him of days. He was spared these by dying of heart failure under the anaesthetic, the surgeon giving as his opinion that chronic alcoholism had weakened the organ of life and no doubt contributed to the principal symptoms of the late archivist of His Majesty's Legation in the Central American Republics.

NONE OF THE DOZENS of churches or convents in Antigua was intact; most were a heap of carved stones with an arch or two, a pillar here and there, a decorated façade which if stripped of ornament could come straight from Palladio's Four Books of Architecture. Oliver's funeral service was held in the safest of the surviving remains, the chapel of La Recolección, with the Bishop of Antigua, aged about a hundred, officiating for the obsequies of this distinguished Catholic member of the diplomatic corps.

'Many of the architects of the old city were French . . . some possibly Italian,' Monsieur Boppe murmured in Proby's ear with a reverential nod of the head. 'Hence the excellent quality of the ruins. Have you noticed that Monseigneur is of mixed colour? I think naturally of the black Virgin of Le Puy on the road to Compostella. You know it, I imagine?'

The burial was in the cemetery of the Calle Del Espirito Santo; Xenia and Milan stood side by side, their faces like stone, but Mr Harris was obviously deeply upset. As the coffin was lowered into volcanic earth he wiped his left eye with an almost imperceptible motion of the forefinger before attending to the other with his handkerchief.

But Proby's sympathy for Harris occupied only one side of his thoughts this morning; the other was fixed on action to be executed. The Minister was coming towards him as he waited beside the Legation Talbot at the entrance to the cemetery.

'You'll be leaving us, Proby,' he said.

'I have a few days free, if you have no objection I might stay on a little? Even make myself useful clearing up Mr Dillon's affairs?'

Mr Harris was considering him with the look that Proby found the most unsettling; the one telling you that your thought was an open book. 'Of course, of course,' he said.

The day passed like the day of any burial, time suspended by the will of each to spare the others. In the Legation, Xenia had arranged a lunch.

'Is Boppe coming?' Harris asked. 'It would be unkind not to invite him.'

'No need to invite him, he announced himself. To take part in our pain. That's what he said,' Xenia answered.

Milan had chosen to return on foot from the cemetery and didn't appear for lunch. The three — Harris, Xenia, Milan — had been joined and held together by the relative neutrality of Oliver; now they were merely attached by common fear, and common history. After lunch, Boppe withdrew. 'Poor Monsieur Dillon was victim of his country's past,' he said before going; 'now if the Bantry Bay attempt of 1796 had with our help brought liberty — '

'It was a bungled, vain, interfering adventure,' Harris said.

'France, as herald of universal values . . .'

'Thank you, Boppe, for coming to share our sorrow,' Harris said in a lower voice.

After he had gone, Minister and Messenger sat peaceably at the table for a minute or two, saying nothing. Then Harris broke out again. 'Do you believe that we — civilians, ministers — led you into all that?'

'I think the forces at work were greater than ministers.'

'Greater than any individual?'

'What do you mean?'

'What any individual did, within conscience.'

'I believe that isn't for others to know.' Proby smiled; everyone in 1920 had a theory, except those who thanked their stars for being alive.

'If Grey had declared at the outset that England would stand aloof, dissociated us from France and Russia, war would have been averted. It happened because they drew us in.'

'Germany would have become the master.'

'I believe everyone — everyone — carries blame,' Harris said with sudden bitter vehemence, 'but most of all — ' he left the sentence unfinished and said no more.

Proby put out his cigar stub and rose. 'May I take it you have nothing against my staying some days in Guatemala?' he asked.

Harris repeated what Oliver had twice said, in much the same words. 'Do what you think you should.'

PROBY LOCATED the stables in a ruinous building next to the Casa Santo Domingo, with a blank wall on the street. You passed through a double wooden door and found yourself in a courtyard surrounded by pillars and inward facing windows. The building was roofless, crumbling, uninhabited even by children, but two rooms were in use as a stable. And this was where he found Milan, as expected, with his horse.

'That's a nice mare.'

'She is a child for me.'

'Yes, I understand that. But you ride her.' Milan had the mare's offside hind hoof between his knees and was busy filing it. 'Tell me something, Milan. You are Miss Ciganović's brother, I believe?' Milan looked up, his expression changed. Severity seemed to ease away as if release had come and he nodded. 'So your real name would be Ciganović, not Igman?'

'Igman is a mountain where the Save is born, near Sarajevo. We were born there too.'

'Why do you call yourself after a mountain and not after your father?'

'When Oliver made a passport for me, he said I must choose another name.'

'To leave Serbia?'

'To live anywhere.'

'If that was necessary, why admit the truth to me now?'

'You are a soldier. An officer.'

'And you have been a soldier too?'

'Yes.'

So Dillon's manuscript was a tale of real events and a mere change of name on a passport wasn't going to be enough for safety. Proby wasn't thinking of the safety of the man but of the Diplomatic Service, from the inquisition of historians; it was under enough fire already, he thought, for failure during those summer months of 1914. Milan had finished with the offside hoof and moved on to the near, filing away in silence. And if

historians got onto this it wouldn't be only the Service, it would be public honour. Proby was not a man given to large generalities but this one
seemed to impose itself — the manuscript must be destroyed, of course.
Living, breathing, speaking witness is not so easily done away with.

'I'm thinking of taking a few days' ride into the forest of Petén,' Proby
said. 'Looking for lost cities, perhaps. I have some maps and I'll need
to equip — a rifle and pistol, among other things.' Milan's eyes lit with
interest. 'Hammock, tent, cooking gear. Where d'you think I could find
a horse?' Milan was back to his filing. 'What about yours?' Milan shook
his head, not looking up this time. 'You ride out a lot?'

'Every day.'

'Not far, then.'

'I must come back.'

'Mr Harris orders you back?'

'Xenia is nervous.'

'Of what?'

'Of the forest.'

It seemed odd that a man of Milan's age should worry about his sister's
nervousness of the forest, but of course that wasn't it, it was something
else she feared. What would be left for Harris and Xenia if Milan escaped again, this time to freedom? What would the world still have to
give them, these refugees, with Dillon's story testified? How long before
the newspapers found him, the speaking witness?

'How do you feel, Ciganović, about making an expedition; you and
your mare and me with a horse which you can help me find? And a
couple of rifles, into the unknown? There are leopards there, I've seen a
Mayan sculpture showing a man being eaten by one.'

'Someone has a stable in the old cloisters of San Francisco — '

'And your sister?'

Milan barely smiled but anyone could read his feelings, Proby thought.
'We are three men. Not even Xenia — ' with a shrug he seemed to take
his leave of her.

IT WOULD BE dishonourable to take any advantage of Miss
Ciganović's absence after dinner, so Proby waited for her to come back
from her briefing of the women in the kitchen. But she didn't come back.
'Xenia was very fond of Oliver, you must excuse her,' Harris said.

'They were friends since Belgrade days and your adventures together?'

'I think a woman and a man can be friends without going further.'

'Of course, of course they can,' Proby said. 'And Dillon may have been somewhat detached from the emotions. Committed elsewhere, perhaps. Or perhaps he wrote them out of his system.'

'Oliver wrote? To you?'

Decidedly, Harris was quick on the uptake, and the last thing Proby wanted was to confirm a doubt best left dormant. 'Oh no.'

'Oliver's emotions were deep like Irish anger.'

'I had Irishmen under command in Flanders and they were blown to pieces the same as all the others.'

'But you survived.'

'I survived.'

Harris leaned forward slightly over the table. 'Do you wonder about the right to survive? I mean being there still after the sun has gone down for so many others.'

'I don't consider it a right.'

'For yourself?'

'For anyone. We are subordinate — '

'To fate?'

'To role and to duty, a more comforting way of putting it.'

Harris seemed to turn this over in his mind. 'And you think your role and duty take you into the forest?'

'It's reported that Americans are exploring for petroleum. My interest is purely archaeological but if I learn anything of their activities, the news might be welcome at the Foreign Office.'

'It will be a long ride.'

'Cortés did it. His horse became an idol of the Indians.'

The Minister's mouth stirred in silent, reluctant amusement. 'Ah yes, Cortés,' he said.

'I HAVE THE HORSE for you, Colonel,' Milan said. 'Come to San Francisco and bring some money.'

What still remained of the church and monastery of San Francisco was decidedly post-Palladian — barley sugar columns and broken voluted pediments containing statues of the Jesuit saints. The church, so Proby had been told, was destroyed several times over by earthquake and now looked unsafe for occupation even as a stables. Segments of spandrel like ripped parachutes overhung the interior, and in the cloister and monastery garden the walls were leaning, split from top to bottom. Milan stood by a well in the centre of the cloister with a fair looking bay up to Proby's weight. He held the horse by a halter and caressed its nose, speaking Serbian words of comfort.

'Where's the owner?' Proby asked.

'It is the priest,' said Milan.

'How much?'

'I have paid, you will repay me.' He smiled. 'When we come back.'

'Saddle and bridle?'

'You must buy those from him now, I didn't have enough. Pay only half what he says.'

The padre, a Ladino, was affability itself, delighted to take whatever Proby offered which made the colonel suspect that Milan, with whom the priest seemed on friendly terms, had paid over the odds for the horse before he arrived. Never mind. They walked the horse back to the crumbling stable of the Santo Domingo and when he had it tethered, Milan turned, tense as a spring.

'When will we go?' he asked.

'You're ready?'

'Yes.'

'For whatever happens?'

'For what will happen.'

'Tomorrow, then,' Proby said with decision.

'WE KEEP a pistol and a rifle here, you take them. The French Legation's an arsenal by itself.' Harris laughed as he had after Oliver's burial — laughter quickly snuffed out.

'Miss Ciganović won't worry?'

'For whom?'

'For her brother.'

'Oliver told you this?'

'Yes.'

Harris spread out his hands in an uncharacteristic gesture. 'We who are left, what right have we to live and grow old? We buy time with our losses. Any of us may do that.'

Proby had no idea what he meant, what he could mean; nevertheless, some message got through to him since he felt less concern for Miss Ciganović and her worries. She was likely to be well treated, on the whole, by life, whatever the accidents lying in her way. Perhaps that was all Harris wished to convey, really.

'WE WILL CROSS the mountain by the train to Puerto Barrios,' Milan said. 'We will order them to stop where we wish and then ride on to Flores. This will save two days.'

'Will they stop it?'

'We will pay them, not much, and show them the guns.'

The railway line, owned by the United Fruit Company of America, was narrow single gauge on which the train climbed between the volcanoes and steamed across forest and watershed from the Pacific to Atlantic shores. They travelled with the horses in an open truck and dismounted on the Atlantic slope where the locomotive halted for watering. The night had been cold and the early morning, under a clear sky, was sharp, with a white frost on the ground. A track led over a wide cultivated valley to the fringes of forest stretching northward towards Mexico and containing hidden somewhere within it the Lake of Petén Itzá, once the most densely populated of the Maya regions. What had driven the people away so their cities were lost and buried? Some authorities claimed that around 800 AD rain ceased to fall, the wells became empty pits in the earth, the network of canals dried to the bare bone, the penises of the men shrank to invisibility under this curse from heaven. It was a landscape where no animal, even the fiercest like the leopard, survived long. Colonel Proby was familiar with landscapes like that.

XENIA SAID NOTHING, but she need say nothing. 'Perhaps I'll leave the Service,' Theo said, the day after Proby and Milan took the train. 'A divorced Ambassador is frowned on. We would never be invited to Buckingham Palace.' Xenia, instead of laughing, looked through to the well in his head as if to read there what depth of betrayal she must expect. 'Proby will be back in a few days.'

'And Milan?'

'Milan must leave us, some day.'

'Yes, I think so,' she said, but this apparent acquiescence settled nothing between them.

FLORES ON THE LAKE of Petén was an island village at the end of a causeway, like a polyp on a stem, rotting in the tropical rainfall which had resumed some time soon after the first millenium and never ceased. There was a little café and the Hotel del Norte with a stable; the King's Messenger looked forward to one decent night after the long ride here, before going on into the heart of the forest beyond the lake where the site of Proby's Dig might be there for the finding.

Milan was opposed to stopping a night in the hotel. 'We can buy what we need and not lose any time,' he said, as if his ear filled with the sound of sifting sand.

'We will stop the night,' the colonel ordered.

His bed was unclean and he was woken by the slithering sound of a snake. He sat up, pistol in hand, and shone his dry cell flashlight round the wall.

'Leave it alone,' said Milan who was curled up on his pack and the folded tent in a corner of the room; 'it doesn't want us, it will go, in an hour it is dawn and we go too.'

AFTER LAKE Petén Itzá the known world ceased. Proby's maps indicated tracks and rivers and hills; nothing gave any idea of the blank continuity of forest where each tree seemed of a different family and none known to him except the mahogany, parent of English furniture. You were a wandering ant here, nothing guided you when the path died at the edge of a cliff or swamp, you followed the compass and on either hand life continued stealthily while you passed. Proby felt the first mosquito bites torment his forearm under the shirt. Thank god for quinine in his saddlebag. Later, in the hammock slung between mahogany trees when all was sleeping save the night watch, tapping, calling, scratching on forest floor and roof, he drank his ration of whisky. Tomorrow or next day they might reach those ruins called Tikal, photographed forty years ago by Colonel Joe Maudslay; and from there, perhaps, to forest secrets where Colonel Proby would leave his own good name behind him.

'BOPPE HAS INVITED himself to supper again, he doesn't leave us alone,' Harris said.

'We need to be more alone?'

'It's what I've always wanted.'

'Let Monsieur Boppe come, we won't notice him while he's here or miss him when he goes away again.'

Her voice sounded neutral, in abeyance like the voice of a hooded hostage. He knew, and she knew, and he believed Milan knew and wished that their triangle must be dismembered. At what cost? as Von Storck had cried repeatedly in the August night.

THE ASSAULT in the dark did Proby's painful duty for him. Both horses, attacked first, went down with throats cut; then Milan, stooping over his fallen mare, was struck by a dart which hung on and dangled from his neck like a thorn on spines. Proby removed it, causing a deep wound for the flow of blood to wash life and mischief away.

The colonel reached Flores on the third day, delirious although making perfect sense to himself, and as he was armed and had some money he was carried back to the railhead slung between two mules. The seniors of the village, not anxious for a visit by the authorities, decided he'd had a lucky recovery from snake bite but would suffer for years to come from long term effects. Whisky relieves pain but is the worst possible treatment for venom, they reported.

THE VICE-CONSUL came over from Guatemala City to drive the King's Messenger down to the Pacific in the Legation motor car. There were no farewells. Colonel Proby, whose state was far from coherent, said only that he he would carry away in the bag Oliver's bulky personal papers and take care of them.

'What could Oliver have left?' Theo asked as they sat on the balcony in the evening, overlooking the voided dome of San José.

'Oliver noticed everything.'

'Yes, he was a very intelligent man. But when death reaches the brain intelligence is lost.'

'Unless someone writes it all down.'

'I believe Oliver was seldom sober long enough to do that.'

'I think Oliver wrote. I think he wrote because he was not happy.'

Xenia was still saying strange things, though she seemed calm again. Sacrifice had been taken, or offered and taken, in the forest of sacrifices so that those who were left could live and grow old. Would they? She was young, perhaps she couldn't even ask herself that question.

'Milan . . .' she hesitated; 'I think Milan was very tired. He lost all that he needed to live.'

'What was that, Xenia?'

She didn't answer this question directly. 'Perhaps he didn't love his life any more,' she said.

'He could have died years ago with Princip.'

'Rotting to death in a cell under ground?'

'They expected death on the Sarajevo bridge.'

'Yes.' For the first time in days Xenia smiled. 'I thought you would never be free from us. Now I see I am the one not free.'

Theo believed he knew better than to argue with that. 'I'll leave the Service,' he said once more.

She smiled again. 'Then we will go and live on an English farm, and Monsieur Boppe will be an ambassador.' Tentatively, she reached out a hand which had been still by her side for days, and Theo, tentatively also but greatly relieved, took it in both of his.

'And keep our names out of the history books,' he said, well aware that this hung on Colonel Proby's good will, and that old soldiers may tell tales, once the guns are silenced, at last.

THE END.

By the same author

David Crackanthorpe is author of the award-winning *Stolen Marches* and other novels

"Stolen Marches is a serious novel that tackles the inner life and moral relativities of people caught between the moment and the scramble to find a foothold in the new order…a relish for the colourful, telling detail . . . a refusal to prettify or simplify events and their effects and, at the same time, a respect for a good story and a well-orchestrated plot…a thoughtful, ambiguous and unshowy reprise about the way humans behave after a great water-shed in history."
Elizabeth Buchan: *The Times*.

"Two superb period thrillers by last year's Sagittarius winner, David Crackanthorpe – I would back these two gripping accounts of resistance and collaboration in occupied France against Sebastian Faulks or Robert Harris any day."
Boyd Tonkin: *The Independent*.

"Ingenious and fresh plotting is matched by a fastidious and striking craftsmanship in the use of language. The author's at times discursive style always fastens the reader in an ineluctable grip, and the result is a highly unusual novel."
Barry Forshaw: *Good Book Guide*.

"Crackanthorpe's writing style, economical but beautiful, effortlessly evokes the baking expanses of Africa and the festering racial and international tension of the late 1930s. The novel…succeeds in being both unsentimental and moving, historically convincing yet unlaborious."
Helen Salzman: *The Observer*.

"A tremendously powerful, complex and accomplished novel…I felt the presence of Africa on almost every page, the heat, the harsh beautiful landscape, the lurking predators."
Selina Hastings.